SO-AIA-561

Mangroves and Monsters

Mangroves and Monsters

Sharon Cupp Pennington

Draumr Publishing, LLC
Maryland

Mangroves and Monsters

Copyright © 2009 by Sharon Cupp Pennington.
All rights reserved. No part of this book may be
reproduced, stored in a retrieval system, or transmitted in any
form or by any means without the prior written permission
of the publishers, except by a reviewer who may quote brief
passages in a review to be printed in a newspaper, magazine,
or journal.

Any resemblance to actual people and events is purely
coincidental. This is a work of fiction.

Book jacket design by Rida Allen.
Artwork from iStockphoto.

ISBN: 978-1-933157-31-3
PUBLISHED BY DRAUMR PUBLISHING, LLC
www.draumrpublishing.com
Columbia, Maryland

Printed in the United States of America

Dedication

To Dorothy Swanson. What can I say, dear Dorothy? You're a smart, clever, funny woman, and a voracious reader without whom this novel wouldn't have been nearly as much fun to write.

To my beloved Wayne, who is and always will be my Brent St. Cyr.

Acknowledgements

As always, I pay homage to my fellow members of the good ship Writing Well, past and present, who read these chapters until their eyes blurred and brains muddled. In particular, I owe tremendous debts of gratitude to Benjamin Hall, Jake Steele, Hope Clark, and Barrie Kibble. I couldn't have accomplished the writing of *Mangroves* without you.

And, again, it is my privilege to thank Dorothy Swanson for her endless hours spent reading, researching, and offering valuable insights...and for her unwavering support of this project. Every author should be so lucky. I've got the next plot thickening inside my brain, Dorothy. You ready for another go?

The creative recipes mentioned in this novel, and many others, can be found at http://www.campbellkitchen.com/. Or, as Charlie Cooper would be quick to point out, on the backs of Campbell's Soup can labels.

Mark Thomas Beck's musical mentoring muppet, Oscar the Grouch, can be seen on the award-winning PBS program *Sesame Street*.

Chapter One

*W*ounds heal in stages. Numb one day, ants crawling under your skin the next. Itchy in the sweltering heat; achy in the cold.

Weird.

Charlie Cooper scratched the three-inch scar on his shoulder where he took a knife's blade during the botched kidnapping of a student nine years ago. Despite a Herculean effort by police, the poor boy died anyway—a few months shy of his eighth birthday.

"Sorry, kid." Cooper yanked off his New Orleans Zephyrs cap and tossed it on the bistro chair next to him. Sorry for what? *Christ.* That he survived three days in an abandoned well, and his student didn't? That he carried this damn scar as a constant reminder he failed to save the boy?

That only a few years after the abduction, still blinded by revenge, he couldn't see the jewel he'd found in Angeline St. Cyr? Almost five years had passed since the auto-pedestrian accident that reportedly killed the supermodel—*reportedly* being the operative word. Which brought him to the only reason he had journeyed to Jacqueme Dominique, an island the size of Vermont, located east of the Lesser Antilles.

Call him fanatical or foolish, delusional even, but he had never bought into the hype regarding Angeline's sudden death and subsequent cremation her boss had fed to the press.

If Cooper saw her again, he knew he would recognize Angeline no matter how horrendous her scars. Hell, they'd lingered in his bed the entire weekend before the accident, and he had memorized every delectable inch of her.

Charmed by Angeline's quirks, Cooper had both cursed her annoying habits and admired her tenacity. He had loved the supermodel, and loathed her. Now he only wanted the truth, even if it left him twice devastated.

Thunder rumbled in the distance. Sea breezes popped the restaurant's green- and white-striped awnings but offered little respite from the heat and humidity that accompanied incessant June showers.

Cooper mopped his face with a navy bandana, then tied the damp kerchief around his neck and slumped back in his chair at the sidewalk table that allowed a pigeon's-eye view of the small souvenir shop he had left forty-five minutes ago. While awaiting the shop proprietor's return, he refueled on the Cross-Eyed Pelican's legendary conch chowder, cassava bread, and steamed vegetables with mango chutney. Rumor had it tourists flocked to Jacqueme Dominique to sample the Pelican's peppery fare.

He took a long draw of water, squeezed his eyes shut, and chased it with a couple aspirin, chewing slowly until the tablets dissolved to grit. Garlic and ginger assailed his senses, and he opened his eyes to a smiling waitress.

She placed a second bowl of steamy chowder in front of him, her drawl as far a cry from this exquisite paradise as Cooper's home in Louisiana. "You stayin' long, sugar?"

He stared at the shop across the street. "Don't know yet."

The waitress refilled his water glass and moved to the next table where an attractive woman, raven hair braided to her waist, told a joke involving a naked spinster, red knee-high socks, and a ping-pong table with one short leg. Deeply tanned, she was dressed for the bush in an olive shirt with wide flap pockets, belted khaki shorts, and suede half boots with thick, cuffed socks. The fedora on the table in front of her could have been a prop from an Indiana Jones movie.

A burley construction hand laughed so hard at her joke he almost knocked her off his lap, while his co-workers slurred drink orders for a concoction called a Bloated Bag of Monkey Spunk. Barely noon, and the rained-out hardhats already felt no pain.

The raven-haired woman winked, and Cooper noticed what the men apparently hadn't: she wasn't drinking. He figured one—maybe all four—of the hardhats would get rolled for their recently-cashed paychecks before midnight.

And they say women are the weaker sex.

Cooper slugged more water and patted his shorts pocket, feeling for the aspirin bottle again.

A bell jingled across the street as the shop's door opened. The man crossing the threshold tipped the scales at two-eighty easy. Dressed in baggy cargo shorts and a shirt sporting yellow hibiscus blossoms, he backed the door open and a skinny woman in oversized sunglasses exited. She stopped long enough to add another bag to the four he already balanced, this one red to match his ruddy complexion.

The man waddled after the woman, hitching up bags every other step. The door fell closed.

No Angeline St. Cyr.

Cooper shoved his meal away with a shaky hand when the shop's bell jangled again. The brunette clerk he'd spoken with earlier held the door so a tall, slender woman could enter. She wrestled an armload of packages wrapped in brown paper, a wooden cane hooked over her arm. A wide-brimmed straw hat obscured her face, but Cooper's gut screamed "Angeline!" so loud he thought he'd called her name.

No one around him stirred.

The woman disappeared inside the store.

He stood and dug in his pockets, scattering bills and change amongst the plates and cutlery. A nickel dropped to the sidewalk; he let it spin. He raced into the street and collided with a teenager on a rusty blue bicycle.

"Watch it, mister!" the boy said as he jammed his foot down to keep his balance.

Cooper shouted over his shoulder, "Sorry." He skirted rain-filled dips in the cobblestone avenue and stopped short of reaching for the door's brass handle. His stomach churned. Never too late to turn and run. He considered the option—for about half a second. He'd come too far, followed too many dead-end leads to retreat because of nerves or the prospect of disappointment.

Cooper needed answers, and he'd be damned if he left this island without them. Hell, he had been damned to sleepless nights and all-consuming misery for the last five years.

Yep, he needed answers—and answers he'd get.

His reflection in the glass made Cooper wish he'd showered and shaved, and at least ran a brush through his hair. Though he was visibly fit, his thick brown mop now kissed the top of his collar. "You look like a bum," he said, tugging off the cap and finger-combing his hair.

He yanked open the door, and the blessed cool of air-conditioning washed over him. A pair of creaky ceiling fans with blades shaped like palm leaves rotated lazily. The shop smelled of ink and plastic, cocoa butter and suntan lotion. Behind the counter, the brunette assisted a customer selecting earrings.

The tall woman had disappeared.

A young couple entered, four laughing children in tow, and further distracted the clerk.

Cooper made his way undetected through a rainbow collage of t-shirts and postcard racks to a narrow door in the back marked PERSONNEL ONLY. He knocked on the door and eased it open. Inside, he spotted another door to the right. From behind it came the sound of water splashing; a feminine voice hummed a soft, familiar tune.

Funny, he didn't recall ever hearing Angeline hum.

A battered wooden desk faced the office entrance; its left side butted the wall below a partially opened window. A light shower pebbled the glass pane, and the smell of fresh rain wafted in through a two-inch gap.

To the left stood an upright tan file cabinet. He tugged on the handle. Locked. Dumped on the terracotta tile floor beside the cabinet were the string-tied parcels, along with her silver-handled cane and wide-brimmed straw hat.

Cooper reached through the mini-blind and slid the window shut. Turning back to the desk, he thumbed through the rain-spattered mail, most of it addressed to A.C. Dubois.

The name cinched it.

His mind leaped back to New Orleans five years ago, to the old St. Louis Cemetery and a cursed nickel lifted from the grave of a hoodoo woman named Simone Dubois. Lord, the lousy-ass luck that had followed: a mugging, and then the horrific accident. How fitting Angeline should adopt Dubois' name. Guess she figured the old gypsy owed her.

An envelope slipped from Cooper's fingers and parachuted under the desk. He crouched to get it, and rising up, struck his head on an open drawer. His elbow slammed the wall when he fell against the chair behind the desk.

"Can I help you?"

He shook his head to silence exploding bottle-rockets, then stared at the woman standing over him. He wanted to laugh, cry, swear, shout; he couldn't breathe. "It *is* you." Cooper scrambled to his knees, latching onto the chair's arms for leverage.

She placed her hands on the back of the chair as he heaved himself up. "You don't belong here," she said, but the desire in her pale green eyes spoke differently.

For someone who went to great lengths for anonymity, Angeline St. Cyr didn't seem surprised to see him. He straightened and wiped his palms on his denim shorts. She looked different—but the same. Same slender nose, tip turned up ever so slightly, same almond-shaped eyes, and same full, pouting lips; her sultry voice as much Texas as any long-horned steer.

In his fatigued brain, it made a kind of bizarre sense.

She wore her blonde hair cropped short, boyish. He swallowed hard. A discolored scar snaked from under her left eye, down her cheek to the delicate curve of her chin. His gaze moved to her gold starfish earring, and then back to the scar.

"There's a magnifying glass on my desk if you need a better look," she snapped as she closed her eyes, her spiked lashes like spiders against pale skin. "When you're done, you can tell me how you found me, Cooper...and how soon you'll leave."

Angeline stiffened as Cooper came around the desk to stand in front of her. She couldn't read his expression, not that she'd ever been able to decipher his moods. That, oddly enough, had been part of his appeal.

A wave of nausea slid through her like ink blackening every nerve and cell.

"I can't do this." Her stomach heaved, and she covered her mouth with her hand. *Oh, God.* She pivoted, then rounded the desk and stumbled into the bathroom. Slamming the door, she flipped the lock, lurched for the toilet, and threw up until there was nothing left inside but confusion and overwhelming fear.

Their reunion wasn't supposed to happen like this.

She almost laughed. What reunion? These past few years, she'd run from Cooper, as far and fast as she could.

Angeline grabbed a rolled washcloth from the basket over the toilet and soaked it under the faucet. Who was she kidding? Even at her darkest point in rehab, when every step, every stretched muscle meant blinding pain, she'd held onto the dream of this moment. It was only a matter of time before a man with Cooper's money, resources, and confounded stubbornness figured out the truth about her death.

Secretly, she'd counted on it.

Three and a half years ago her former boss and mentor, cosmetics mogul Mathieu Fournier, had warned her Cooper had been asking around, doling out cash for clues from as far away as Paris and Milan. It was Mathieu who convinced her in the wisdom of closing her shop on the Bahamian island of Mayaguana and moving to the lesser known Jacqueme Dominique.

Still she went about her life with the renewed hope that Cooper would continue his pursuit. Her heart stalled every time the bell rang on her shop's door. She searched the faces of men in the crowded town square and in restaurants during peak tourist seasons. Throughout every season.

Well, he had found her. Now what?

Angeline held the damp cloth over her face and drank in the coolness. Her thumb brushed the indented scar. She straightened, dropping the cloth in the sink, and forced herself to look in the mirror. Her flushed face heightened the scar's blanched skin, forming a hideous river of white in the face of a woman the world had deemed perfect.

Cooper knocked on the door. "You okay in there?"

Hell, no, she wasn't okay. She was falling apart.

"You might as well come out, Angeline. I'm not going anywhere." The man wore stubbornness like a tailored jacket. He always had.

"Give me a minute," she said.

"Take as long as you need."

The cushions on her chair whooshed. Casters creaked. It sounded as though he'd sat behind her desk.

Angeline lowered the lid to the toilet and sat, folding her arms across her stomach. Rocking forward, she drew deep, steadying breaths. Silence magnified the tick of the small clock on the wicker étagère. Two minutes passed, then five. Finally, she stood, filled a glass with water and rinsed her mouth. She straightened her blouse and skirt, then unlocked the door.

Cooper had stood by the time the door opened. He came around the desk and stopped no more than a foot in front of her. The heat from his body, mixed with the smell of his sweat, rolled toward her like an invitation. The look in his widened eyes spoke of concern.

She would've preferred the wise-cracking arrogance she remembered, anger and shouting. Then she could shout back and release this stifling emotion.

His gaze traveled from her head to her toes. She shifted her slight weight from one leg to the other as he circled her.

The broad-shouldered V of Cooper's six-foot frame narrowed to a lean waist. His perpetual tan came from his French-Acadian heritage, but he wore his dark hair too long now. The length added to an unkempt, almost rough, appearance. His wrinkled shirt hung loose, his piercing hawk-brown eyes bloodshot, beard more than a couple days old. Not at all the *Neat Nancy* she remembered from their time together at Raison-Bell Amandine, the mansion outside New Orleans he'd inherited from his bastard of a grandfather.

This Cooper struck Angeline as dangerous.

His hand touched the nape of her neck, and his fingers' unsettling warmth tumbled a shiver down her spine. He leaned in and whispered next to her ear, "You've got some explaining to do, Slick."

She cringed at the old nickname that no longer fit. "Not here." She faced him, squared her shoulders. Her gaze met his and held steady, though her insides quivered. "My shop gets busy in the afternoon."

He touched a finger to her chin, lifted in defiance. "You name the place, and I'm there."

"You're staying at the Hotel LeNoir."

He raised a questioning brow.

"There are only two hotels in Port Noel," she explained. "The LeNoir's on the water. I remember how much you loved the sound of the... I'll meet you in the lobby at six-thirty."

The corner of his mouth lifted in a crooked half-smile, at odds with the glare that bore into her. He raised his hand, held it inches from her scarred cheek, then let it drop to his side. "Don't even think about running," he said. With a curt nod, he turned, yanked open the office door, and left.

She followed as far as the first round of t-shirts when the cell phone in her skirt pocket chirped "Anchors Aweigh."

Brent.

Her hands shook, and she had trouble freeing the phone from her pocket. She flipped it open. "Hello."

"Hey there, sis."

"Your timing is perfect."

She pictured her brother's laughter deepening the lines around his hazel eyes when he said, "One of my better qualities. What's up, kid? You sound stressed."

Even though she was three years older than him, Brent always called her kid. "Cooper found me," she said.

Her brother's laughter died on a muted swear. "I can be there tomorrow morning. Just say the word."

She smiled. "Thanks, Brent. You don't know how much it helps me knowing that. But I can handle Cooper." At least, she prayed she could.

"How did he react to seeing you?"

Reaching into the garment round, Angeline straightened several yellow t-shirts with the shop's name, Pearls, and a tropical mermaid motif imprinted on the backs. "Hard to say. Surprised, I guess. But not really. You know he's been searching for me for a while. We're meeting later."

"He gives you any grief...like I said, Angie, say the word and I'm on a plane tonight. Right now I've got a union meeting. It should last until four, then I'm in for the evening. ESPN's encoring the Johnson-Norwood bout. I'll keep the phone handy."

She knew he would. "Okay. Thanks." She also knew he'd watch the boxing match with their ailing father. "Don't come unless I call, Brent. Mom and Dad need you."

"You got it, sis." He disconnected.

Angeline returned the phone to her pocket. Of course Cooper was surprised at seeing her. She remained but a glimmer of the woman who'd left him after their heated argument over her obsession with success and his need for vengeance against a Dutch kidnapper named Willem Voorhees.

They'd argued in his bedroom on a rainy afternoon much like today.

"You were going to leave, just like that?" he said.

"You didn't think I'd stay, did you?" She raised a fist to her throat and played her best improv hand. "My God, you did. You actually thought I'd be content with quilting bees and bake sales, crying babies and coupons the grocer triples on Thursdays."

His eyes darkened with pain.

She summoned another miserable wave of courage and forced a laugh. "My face is known all over the world, Cooper. I'm on magazine covers and billboards. I walk into restaurants without a reservation and get the best table. At the theater, people trample each other for a glimpse of me, and I love it. All of it. It's who I am. It's what I am." She pretended to struggle with zipping her overnight bag. "Don't look so wounded."

He simply stood there, stunned, disbelieving.

"Many men want to bed me and never get the chance," she said. "You got the carousel ride, and the brass ring. Consider yourself a winner. I do. Now I've really got to go. Meetings, you know." Tears didn't flow until she was seated safely in her cab.

The next day, the world had learned of her death.

Chapter Two

Brent St. Cyr pulled into his parents' driveway at a quarter of six. The safety meeting at his union hall ran long which further fueled his temper. He turned off the engine of his blue stepside Chevy Silverado and scrubbed a hand over his face.

So, Cooper thought he'd pop back into Angeline's life?

Like hell.

Charlie Cooper meant trouble, and Brent's sister had suffered enough. Brent didn't trust people with too much money or time on their hands, especially money they hadn't earned with a lick of honest work and sweat. Cooper had ample time and an inheritance stout enough to capitalize a third-world nation.

Brent stared out his windshield at nothing while his anger simmered. He would be damned if he allowed the bastard to bring an ounce more misery to Angeline.

The porch light went on. His mom must have seen him drive up.

He hated being late and feared his dad would change his mind about the trip to his condo to watch the heavyweight fight. It seemed much harder nowadays to convince him to leave the house.

Brent lived in Galveston. Nevertheless, he stopped by his childhood home in Hamlin's Grove once a week, twice if work allowed.

His siblings thought he worked too much, which left no time for women. Maybe they were right. His job mooring ships along the Houston channel anchored him—he grinned at the pun—and his woodworking hobby centered him, but his social life equaled a zero.

Hell, he was only thirty-one. He kept fit, and worked out a couple times a week. Women still took second glances. He had time.

The front door opened, showing his mother standing a yard or so inside the house.

Brent eased out of the truck, slipped his keys in the pocket of his faded jeans, and trotted up to the porch. Stooping, he kissed her cheek. "Hey there, pretty lady."

She reached up and shoved a lock of coffee-colored hair off his forehead. "Your dad's been watching for you from our bedroom window for the last hour," she said. "Something about another book?"

No boxing tonight. "Sorry, Mom." Brent circumvented the stairs on their left, behind the door, and headed down the short hall to the master bedroom. He called back to her, "Union meeting ran long. I'll explain to Dad."

An hour later, he leaned against the doorjamb to his parents' cozy yellow kitchen and watched his mother set a plate of homemade spaghetti she'd heated in the microwave on the table. "Don't you ever get tired of being a mom?" he said.

"As long as you don't start bringing your laundry home." She dragged a dining chair out and gestured him to sit. "I hate doing laundry." She sat in the adjacent chair at the maple breakfast table they'd bought at a going-out-of-business sale when he was nine. "Did you read to your father?"

"Zane Grey." Brent sat and reached for his iced tea. "*Wild Horse Mesa.*"

His mother moved the shaker of parmesan cheese closer. "Didn't you already read that one?"

He laughed over the rim of his glass. "Twice."

His father had suffered a heart attack, then a stroke, after learning of Angeline's death.

Frankly, Brent didn't care how many times they read Grey's *Mesa*. He was thankful his dad was still around so he could read to him. "Dad's asleep." He tore a hunk of French bread off the remnant of a seasoned loaf. "By the way, I spoke with Angie today."

His mother's eyes lit at the mention of her only daughter. "How is she?" They had gone a year believing Angeline was dead before learning the truth from his older brother, Nick. It had been the best of days, and the worst.

The fact that Nick kept such a jarring secret seemed unforgivable at the time. Brent had bloodied his brother's lip and blackened his eye, even after Nick had explained he'd been called in as a consulting orthopedic surgeon for Angeline. By then, their father was in the intensive care unit of a Houston hospital, prognosis uncertain, and their mother exhausted.

Brent frowned as he thought of Nick's deceit. Family shouldn't keep secrets. He turned to his mother. "Didn't you and Dad visit her in February?"

"The first week in March," she said. "We stayed four days. Not nearly long enough. Did you have a reason for calling her?"

"Nope. Had a few minutes between jobs and thought I'd check in. Good thing, too." He dashed cheese over his pasta. "She says Cooper's found her. And I'm telling you, Mom, if that man causes her any trouble, I'll kill him."

Coming to Cooper's hotel was a colossal mistake. The front desk clerk rang his room, but he didn't answer.

Of course he didn't.

"He's making you wait," Angeline muttered out loud. Like he waited for the last five years. She approached the bank of elevators, where she stopped to adjust her gauzy peasant blouse and smooth the pale floral skirt that hung to her ankles. Why was she even here? She ought to tell Cooper to go straight to hell and get on with her life.

That's what she ought to do.

"He's dragging this out, taking his sweet time of it," she grumbled. "Hoping you'll suffer." Checking room numbers as she walked down the softly lit hall, Angeline stopped in front of B-246 and knocked.

Nothing.

Angeline tugged a few strands of close-cropped hair tickling the nape of her neck as she surveyed the corridor. She wouldn't give Cooper the satisfaction of learning from the desk clerk she'd been here and then run like a scared girl—or a guilty one.

She knocked again, louder, more insistent.

A beefy man wrapped in a white towel stepped out of his room four doors down and deposited a Room Service tray in the hall. "Sugar," said the female voice from inside. "Get your sweet ass back in here. Mama's still hungry." Grinning, the man nodded at Angeline, patted his belly, and retreated to his room.

Sex. Angeline pounded on the door. She hadn't thought of what sex was like with Cooper in about...ten seconds? Not that she intentionally kept herself *virginal*, she was simply too busy to allow another man in her life.

Besides, seclusion made for a safer haven.

After a few more agonizing seconds, the door opened. Cooper smiled, stepping aside only far enough so they brushed against each other in the narrow entry. His shirt hung open, the top snap of his jeans unfastened, and his bare feet pale against the lush green carpet. Weariness hung in his eyes, but he'd gotten a haircut and shaved. He smelled of soap and shampoo, something lemony.

Oh, God.

His breath warmed her cheek when he leaned in and whispered, "I wasn't sure you'd keep our date."

She practically threw herself into the spacious room. "You would have been back in my shop tomorrow," she said, a little too rushed, too breathless. "And again the next day, and...this isn't a date."

Cooper circled her. "Meeting, reunion. Get-together. Call today whatever makes you comfortable, Slick."

Humph! If her comfort was his priority, he would have stayed away. Or searched for her sooner.

He stopped in front of her, eased his hand up, and slid the

lightweight shawl from her shoulders.

Her swallow seemed the only sound in the room. Confusion muddled her thinking.

When he reached for her open-topped straw purse, she tightened her grip on the tortoise shell handles. He pulled; she yanked. The back and forth motion threw her balance off, and she placed her hand on a nearby dresser. "Don't call me that idiotic name," she said. "I'm not—"

"The woman I fell in love with?" The purse stilled. Cooper used it to draw her close again. Mere inches from her shoulder, he inhaled a noisy, exaggerated breath. "You smell like her." He took the purse from her trembling fingers and tossed it on the overstuffed chair behind them. "Remember that first day at Raison-Belle Amandine, the drenching downpour?"

He backed her to the wall near the open French doors where a warm evening breeze washed over them. Along with nerves, the stir of air prickled her skin.

Hands braced against the wall on either side of her shoulders, Cooper leaned into her, not quite touching foreheads. "You smelled like wildflowers then," he said, "and rain."

She licked her dry lips, unable to summon the snappy comeback she so desperately needed.

"I used to hate the rain." His breath feathered her bangs as he spoke. "And wildflowers gave me an itchy rash. *All over.*"

Need bordered desperation.

Coming here was crazy.

"There were times," he whispered, "when I closed my eyes and thought back to that day, I swear I smelled you."

This meeting bordered on lunacy. "Don't do this, Cooper." Sweat beaded on her forehead. Her palms grew clammy as she clenched her hands at her sides.

"Ask me to stop, I'll stop." His lips touched her damp forehead, the tiniest spark of a connection. "It's that easy."

No, not the least bit easy. She didn't want him to stop. There, she dared think it. "There are things we need to talk about, things you don't understand. Things you don't know about me. You haven't seen—"

"I understand *need*, Slick. Trust me. I've lived and breathed and drank need for five hellish years." He kissed the tip of her nose. "Most nights, I swore I'd go crazy from needing you. Maybe I did go crazy. Maybe all of this is a lovely illusion." His warm lips brushed hers. "Nope," he whispered inches from her mouth. "Not an illusion." She blinked. Another jolt of electricity filtered down to her toes when he said again, "Ask me to stop. It's just... that...easy."

"No," was all she managed.

He stepped back, buttoning his shirt as if they hadn't been a hairsbreadth away from one another. "You hungry?" He tucked in the shirt's tail, then snapped his jeans. "I could eat a stretch Hummer."

She staggered away from the wall, shrugging off the wave of absurd heat burning through every cell. "There's a restaurant on Fonteneau." She couldn't keep the quiver from her voice, and the weakness fueled her annoyance. "It's run by a couple of transplanted Floridians." Babbling irked her. "They serve American cuisine. Steak, baked potatoes, sautéed mushrooms. It's within walking distance, quiet, dress is casual." She inhaled a deep breath that did nothing to steady her. Her stomach had remained queasy all afternoon, and she could hardly work in her little shop knowing he was so near.

"Perfect." Cooper grabbed a pair of sneakers from atop the worn, black carry-all perched on a spindly luggage rack. He sat on the foot of the unmade bed and patted the space next to him.

She sat in a chair near the louvered doors overlooking the avenue where sounds of early evening drifted up: a woman's high-pitched laughter, the upbeat rhythm of a steel drum band, tires grinding wet cobblestone, and a policeman's whistle. A man's sing-song voice hawked exotic bouquets. Anthuriums—heart-shaped for lovers. Bird of Paradise and heliconia, orchids and Proteas. Island orchids could last a month or more with proper care.

She blinked again.

"Aren't you going to ask about Braeden?" he said, lacing his shoe.

"Brag hasn't wasted any time," she whispered. *Not like me. Like us.* "One little girl, Maggie, almost four, and Elizabeth Anne, twenty months. Her second pregnancy was easier than the first. I do keep up."

He stared at her a full-blown minute before tugging on his other shoe. "You mind explaining that?"

"I couldn't let my family, my parents, continue believing I died." She had thought of Braeden often during the past five years, and picked up the phone so many times, only to disconnect when someone answered. She had thought of Cooper, too.

Dear Lord, there were nights, miserable and alone in her bed, when she thought of nothing but Cooper.

Gathering her purse and shawl, Angeline shook off her guilt.

He stood. "Ready?"

Their walk down the empty corridor and endless elevator ride remained mortuary quiet. His hand braced against the frame, Cooper blocked the elevator doors from prematurely closing on Angeline when she exited into the hotel's lobby. It irked him that she'd cared about her parents' suffering but didn't give a blip to his.

"You don't have your cane," he said, securing a firm hold on her elbow when they left the hotel. He was mad as hell, yet this insatiable hunger snowballed inside him whenever he put his hands on her. How did a guy deal with that kind of flip-flopping emotion?

"Don't need it." She listed to the right a degree with every step and amended the obvious before he could. "Guess I do, sometimes. If I'm tired. I have fallen, and it's embarrassing. People don't know what to do."

"And you don't want to draw attention to yourself." Cooper shook off the image of her falling, helpless. His grip on her elbow tightened. "Can I ask you something?"

"Could I stop you?"

"The facial scar, why haven't you had it—"

"Fixed?" She let go a barely audible laugh. "You can say the words, Cooper. I'm not sensitive."

They stopped on the uneven sidewalk. "Yeah," he said after a long pause. "Guess you're not." Anger bubbled below the surface; he thumped it aside.

"Your question?"

"It's not like you don't have the money, or Mathieu Fournier's connections in the world of cosmetics and…cosmetic surgery. Hell, your oldest brother's a doctor. Why do you still have the scar?" They resumed walking.

"Watch this." She steered them into the path of an elderly couple dressed for fancy dining, wing-tipped shoes and pearls. "Beautiful night, isn't it?" She addressed the pair in a voice that oozed southern charm. "Perfect for dinner and a nice walk afterwards, don't you agree?"

The couple stopped mid-conversation, glanced at her, and then quickly away. The woman fumbled with the shoulder strap on her glitzy purse; the man mumbled something about too much rain and insufferable humidity, the salty air. He studied his polished shoes and the cruise ship anchored in the harbor. His gaze never came back to Angeline.

She leaned into Cooper as they continued down the walk. Her heady, seductive scent of jasmine enveloped him; chased by the damnable hunger.

"The scar makes me invisible," she said. "Another block, and it's all that couple will remember. Not my hair color or my smile, what I'm wearing or what I said, not even the handsome gentleman on my arm."

She laughed again, and the sound of her laughter pleased him, stirring the hornets in his gut. He let go of her arm. "No one recognizes you," he said.

She reached for his hand. "Exactly."

Her fingers wrapped around his, warm and inviting. Invisible snakes slithered up his spine and sifted the sand clogging his brain.

"Don't get me wrong," she added. "It's not like there weren't a dozen eager models ready to replace me, to replace *Angeline*. More power to them. But the paparazzi are merciless." She stopped in front of a stucco and brick building on the corner. The green and black neon sign overhead flashed Galloway's Grill. "Here's the restaurant."

The waiter ushered them to a table in front of a window where the full red moon hovered inches above a horizon of glistening black sea. Cooper pulled out Angeline's chair, draped her shawl over the back, then ordered water and white wine. The wine was for her. He needed a clear head.

When the waiter moved on, Cooper spoke. "The scar makes you invisible. I get it. The paparazzi are like swarming insects. I get that, too. But you turned your back on the people who care about you. Your best friend. Do you know the depth of grief Braeden suffered? What it's been like watching her?"

She buried her face in a menu. "Do you know this is the first time we've sat down to a meal you didn't concoct from the back of a Campbell's soup label?" she said, her voice forcibly light.

The waiter returned with their drinks, but before Angeline could order, Cooper lurched out of his seat. He caught his chair as it tilted sideways and heaved it under the table.

Heads all around them turned.

He snatched the menu from her and shoved it at the waiter so hard the twenty-something man gasped and took a giant step backwards. His colorless lips formed a small, comical O. Diners at the adjacent table stared, forks halted midway to their gaping mouths.

"I thought I could do this." Cooper's hands twisted on the carved back of the wooden chair. "Act casual, make fucking nice, talk about shit that doesn't matter. *Soup.* What I really want to know is how in hell this happened? You let me think you were dead. Damn it, Slick. A cremation and bogus memorial service?" The chair shuddered when he let it go and raked a hand through his hair. "My gut told me the ashes in that jade box Fournier guarded so closely weren't yours. I should've listened. But I didn't know which way was up then. I've never felt so desperate. I imagined you. Dreamt you. Now that I've found you," he shook his head, "I don't know what to do with you." He wrenched a twenty from his jeans pocket and tossed it on the table. "I don't know what to fucking do with all this anger."

He stormed out of the restaurant.

Angeline gulped her wine in three choking swallows, set the rocking glass on the table, then grabbed her purse and wrap. She couldn't leave things the way they were.

The waiter called after her, "You ought to give him some space, miss."

Space? They'd had too much space already.

Caribbean winds chased a chill around the huge mangrove tree in the center of the town square, stirring the odors of rotting fish and vegetation in dead-end alleys and narrow side streets as she hurried after Cooper.

He barreled through the crowd half a block ahead, hands shoved in his pockets, shoulders hunched.

No sense calling out.

She caught up to him waiting for the hotel elevator.

He jerked her inside and slammed his fist into the fourth floor button as a suited man approached. "Catch the next one," Cooper barked.

Angeline reached for his shoulder and steadied herself. "I'm so sorry. If you'll give me a chance, I can explain." Her wrist burned where he grabbed her and turned them both as his mouth devoured hers. Heat crept in through her toes, slithered upward, and nestled in her belly. She unfastened his belt buckle, never disconnecting mouths.

He yanked her blouse out of the skirt, reached under with one hand, nudged her bra aside, and roughly kneaded her breast. They surfaced for air, dove back under. A bell dinged, and he pummeled the button that kept the elevator doors from opening with his free hand.

Her breath became his; his tongue hers as flames engulfed them. The bell dinged a fourth time, the elevator doors opened, and he backed them out, an awkward waltz toward his hotel room as he fumbled in his pocket for the key card.

She whispered into his mouth, "Hurry. Please."

The streetlamp shining through the French doors he'd left open three or four inches cast a shadowy light in his room. He dropped the key card, and kicking the door to the hall shut, whipped the blouse over her head. He shoved her floral skirt down, and she stepped out of it by bracing herself again on his shoulders.

She'd been forever off balance with the man.

Angeline wedged her hand between them and popped the snaps on Cooper's jeans. He wriggled out of them as the back of her knees brushed against the huge mahogany bed. They both fumbled with his shirt buttons.

"You okay with this?" he huffed, as they freed the last button.

She gave a quick nod, peeled off his shirt, and tossed it aside.

He lifted her, placed her on the bed. The mattress waffled as he straddled her.

Angeline blew out a quick breath while every glorious second of making love to Cooper rushed back to her in this bright light of need—then it came to a crashing halt. Her hand shot to the middle of his chest. "Wait."

He froze on the verge of penetration. "What is it?"

"Are you teaching?" she asked, breathless.

"Huh?"

"Answer me, Cooper." A bead of his sweat dropped between her breasts and trickled down to her naval. God, she wanted him. "Teaching," she whispered. "Please tell me you've gone back to teaching."

A strangled silence ensued while he digested her question. Cool air stirred when he rolled off her.

"You're not. I suspected as much." She scooted to the edge of the bed, stood, and gathered her clothes. Anger and disappointment battled desire. "Nothing has changed then, has it? You're still so blinded by revenge against Griffie MacDonald's kidnapper that nothing else fits in your life. Not teaching, or friends, or family or...*love*. You're so embedded in the past, Cooper, you can't see the future."

Oh, God. Giving in would be so easy. So satisfying. So...

She itched with need and chastened herself. Why did she have to analyze their situation to the nth degree? She'd wanted him here; he was here. Why couldn't she just surrender to the mind-numbing sex? She had dreamt of this moment with Cooper; she'd wished and prayed for it.

And she knew exactly why sex with him was impossible.

"I've been searching for you, damn it." He raised up, braced himself on his elbows, his eyes shadowed by the semi-darkness.

"Along with hunting Voorhees, no doubt." She slipped her blouse over her head. The thin fabric caught on her earring, and she peered at him through the neck opening. "Tell me I'm wrong, Cooper."

His gaze shot to her breasts, then to the lacy bra crumpled on the floor behind her. "I haven't sought Voorhees in well over two years," he said.

She righted the blouse, reached down, and snatched her bra. "Then you had someone else do it for you."

His silence spoke volumes.

"This is pointless, don't you see?" She stepped into her skirt and tugged it over her hips. "I wish our lives were different. You can't fathom how badly I wish that. But our situation hasn't changed." She backed toward the door, tucked the bra in her purse, then scooped up her shoes.

He leaped from the bed and grabbed his jeans, tripping as he fumbled to get his legs in them. "Everything's changed."

She shook her head. "Not what matters."

"You bailed when we were getting good, Angeline. You're bailing again now. You owe me."

If he only knew. She stood there, wanting to go to him, needing to run. "You're a danger I can't afford, Cooper, especially if you're still playing tag with a monster like Voorhees." She reached for the door, opened it. He moved toward her, but she held up her hands. "Don't follow me. Please. Just leave Jacqueme Dominique, and forget you ever saw me here."

Chapter Three

*F*orget he ever saw her?

Cooper might as well fill the gaping hole Angeline had left in his heart with Silly Putty. He snapped his jeans, stumbled onto the balcony. There he watched her climb into the rear seat of one of several green van's used to taxi tourists around the city, the Chrysler Grand Voyager with the pizza-sized Bondo patch on its damaged rear fender.

Don't follow her? Not bloody likely. Not after five long years of searching.

He reached the street in time to see the same van return. She couldn't have traveled far.

Cooper flagged the driver and spoke to him through the open window. "I'm supposed to meet the fare you just dropped off at her place for dinner." He lifted his watch into the lamplight. "Wouldn't you know, she forgot to write down the address, and I'm running late. Can you get me there?"

"For sure, sir." The cabbie tapped his barrel chest with a wide finger. "Bernard can do it."

Cooper opened the passenger door. "I'd like to buy some

flowers on the way."

A grin split the man's brown face, exposing pristine rows of white teeth. "Ah, yes, Bernard knows the perfect place."

"Mind if I sit up here?" Cooper slid in the passenger's seat before the guy could answer.

Buying flowers took half an hour longer than he expected. Bernard stopped at a small flower shop two streets over and interrupted his brother-in-law's dinner, spouting poetic notions of love and romance. Apparently the island of Jacqueme Dominique was legendary for kindling amorous affairs of the heart.

The way their reunion had progressed, he and Angeline needed a bonfire of bouquets. Hell, he might as well burn down the entire building that housed the shop.

Bernard's brother-in-law wiped his bearded chin and grumbled obscenities behind a beige linen napkin. Accompanied by his beaming wife, as round as she was short, the still-petulant man opened his fragrant store. In a matter of minutes, he produced an exquisite bouquet of heart-shaped flowers, and Cooper was soon on his way again.

They drove another half mile and turned a corner. Bernard stopped his van in front of a two-story white house with a sprawling yard, its tapered columns and lengthy galleries lit in flickers of red and blue from a pair of tan police cars parked at miscued angles on the road. A black coroner's vehicle sat with its rear doors open.

Cooper swallowed hard. The sight of squad cars jerked him back to the night of the auto-pedestrian accident in New Orleans, to those slow motion-moments in the emergency room when he didn't know the extent of Angeline's injuries.

To the instant he was told she had died.

He exploded from the Voyager, sprinted across the yard, bounded up the brick walkway, and shoved past the baby-faced policeman manning the open entrance doors.

"Wait," the officer called out. "You can't go in there."

Like hell. Cooper shrugged out of the young man's grasp and entered a large central hall. Massive pocket doors stood open on his left, and he quickly surveyed the expanse of modern and antique furnishings in search of Angeline.

She sat in one of two upholstered easy chairs flanking a

dormant fireplace with an elaborate carved mantle. A giant of a suited man stood next to her, his hand poised on the edge of the mantle's ornate whitewashed wood.

Angeline shot out of her chair.

"Mrs. Dubois!" The suited man grabbed for her arm and caught nothing but air.

Cooper barely registered the *Mrs.* before she was across the room and all over him, screaming, crying, arms flailing.

"Bastard!" Her palm connected with his cheek, and a volley of stars burst in front of his eyes. The bouquet of red flowers flew from his hand as he attempted to ward off her attack. "You did this!" she shouted.

A second blow glanced off his chin. He bobbed, and the next swipe hit his shoulder. What in the hell was she talking about? What had he done, except find her?

Two uniformed policemen raced forward and wedged them apart, forcing Cooper back several steps.

"We had a good, safe life." Angeline shouted over the short officer's khaki shoulder. "I made sure of it. I made sure of—"

"Stop, Mrs. Dubois." The giant wrapped his mammoth arms around her, pinning her arms to her sides. She seemed to melt into him. "This will get us nowhere," he said, as he ushered her back to her chair. "Sit. Please."

Her eyes held a look of utter despair. She slumped into the chair, her pale skin appearing almost translucent against the royal-blue damask upholstery.

In spite of his confusion, a resurgent need to protect Angeline overwhelmed Cooper. Two officers held his arms. He pitched, trying to free himself. Stacked books fell from a bumped table. A blue and white lamp toppled, shattered. Cooper dragged the cops with him as he struggled to reach her, and their scuffling feet ground porcelain shards into the hardwood floor.

"This is a crime scene," roared the suited man, apparently in charge. "Get him outside. Now."

Cooper heaved one way, the other. He had no intention of leaving.

Bernard's thick accent sounded behind him. "What is going on, man?"

No one answered.

A latch clicked, and floor-to-ceiling pocket doors opened on Cooper's right; the coppery stench of blood wafted in on the swirling air. He recognized the smell of death and twisted his body toward the brightly-lit room. The interior held a blend of wicker furniture and bamboo accents, fabric in vibrant yellows and blues and greens.

A happy room.

Stark contrast to the bloodied white sheet spread on the floor in the forefront.

Sandaled feet, toenails painted soft pink, protruded from the sheet's edge, and farther up, a small mangled hand, missing its ring finger. Inches from the woman's corpse lay a machete, its black leather handle, knuckle guard, and sickle hook barely visible in a pool of coagulating claret.

Cooper's mind raced. USA made, military issue, with a cold-rolled steel blade, capable of slicing two inches of wood in a single stroke. Barely an inkling as to what a blade like that could do to a human.

He couldn't swallow past the lump pushing against his Adam's apple. The machete he used to clear brush from the banks of the Mississippi River behind Raison Belle-Amandine came with a black nylon sheath and honing stone.

He hadn't seen any of it in—

Angeline's gasp jerked him back to the present.

"Who?" was all he managed to ask.

She pointed a trembling finger at Cooper, then gazed at the suited man, a mix of fear and astonishment in her glassy eyes. "He let them kill poor Rose. You saw what they did to her, Chief Zeller. You saw it." She covered her face with her hands and sobbed. "Oh, God. They've taken my baby."

The Chief motioned a female officer to bring a fringed throw from the nearby sofa's edge. He draped the pale green wrap over Angeline. "I can help you, Mrs. Dubois." He pulled a silk handkerchief from his coat pocket and folded it in her hands. "Let me do my job, eh?"

She nodded, even as her chest convulsed with heart-wrenching sobs.

The man lifted several plastic bags from atop a painted chest next to her chair and carried them to where Cooper still struggled to free himself.

"Outside," he ordered.

The larger officer wrenched a billy club from his belt and thrust it at Cooper's midsection when he didn't move fast enough. He backed Cooper out the front doors to a row of four white, arrow-back armchair rockers. The guy threw a wicked jab, and the smoldering contempt in his piercing eyes said he intended to inflict considerable more damage.

Cooper raised his hands. "Take it easy, man. I'm going."

He sat in the third rocker and turned the chair slightly. Through the window, he kept watch over Angeline.

Baby? His mind numbly repeated the word.

"I am Daniel Zeller, Mr. Cooper, Chief of Police." The adjacent rocker creaked under the weight of the giant's six-foot-four, one hundred ninety-plus frame. Zeller's square-jawed face held a broad nose with flared nostrils, and lips that seemed set in permanent disapproval. His cocoa-colored skin offset dark eyes and black, bristly hair cropped so close it appeared painted on. He gave Cooper a cool, appraising once-over as he gestured the hostile officer away.

The policeman returned the billy club to his belt. He joined the short cop at the far end of the gallery.

Cooper turned to Zeller. "You know who I am?"

"I make it my business to learn as much about the strangers visiting my city as possible. As difficult and time-consuming as this is, you were easier than most," the Chief said. "I know what you've done, where you've been, who you associate with."

A pear-shaped man carrying a black doctor's bag scurried onto the porch. He stopped long enough to whisper something to the Chief before disappearing inside the house.

Zeller drew Cooper's attention back to his evidence. "What can you tell me about these?"

The larger plastic bag contained a copy of *Vogue* magazine. Dressed in a silver gown, her hair in a sweeping up-do and laughing eyes flirting with the camera as only she could, Angeline graced the vintage cover.

Cooper leaned forward. He tightened his wrist to keep his unsteady hand from betraying a volatile mix of concern and alarm. "The man who left this knows of Angeline's past, as you surely must." His statement didn't appear to faze Zeller. "May I?" The Chief nodded, and allowed him to handle the smaller bag. Cooper turned it over and studied the photograph inside. "Like you, they also know of my past." His stomach roiled. "The boy in the picture is Griffie MacDonald. He was my student, and I guarantee you, the man who killed him is on this island and probably in your city."

Zeller rocked forward. He clasped his hands between his legs, rested his elbows on his thighs. "You were also with the boy when he was murdered, yes?"

"What does it matter where I was then?" Cooper said. "I already told you there's a monster loose on your island. His name is Willem Voorhees, and you'd better damn well make it your business to find him."

"No!" Angeline screamed, and both men lurched from their rockers.

Zeller ordered Cooper back into his chair. The Chief went inside, and after a hushed exchange with the doctor, returned. "We will continue our conversation in my office," he said. "I've asked someone to stay with Mrs. Dubois. The doctor will remain until they arrive. He's given her something to calm her."

Cooper straightened. "You're arresting me?" Obvious from her scream, the idea of being *calmed* went over with Angeline about as well as the threat of his being locked in a cell the size of a broom closet. No windows, no air. Restrictions heightened by the absurd fear he'd fought almost ten years to control.

The Chief summoned the two officers lingering at the opposite end of the veranda. "You are, how is it your U.S. authorities say, Mr. Cooper, a person of interest? Now, you will come with me of your own accord, or one of my officers will handcuff you and drag you along."

Some choice. Cooper stood. He glanced through the tall window at Angeline, still seated in front of the fireplace. "You sure she won't be alone?"

Zeller's quiet laughter unsettled him. "As sure as I am that you have information regarding this crime."

The angry officer placed his hand on Cooper's forearm, but Cooper shrugged it off and started down the brick path toward the first cruiser. After three or four steps, he glared back at Zeller. "In the States, the accused also gets one phone call."

"Ah, yes," answered the Chief. "You will get such a call once we are done with our talk."

His *talk* with Zeller turned into a grueling Q&A that ended after midnight. Amidst recounting every lousy second that lapsed before, during, and after Griffie MacDonald's kidnapping and murder, Cooper learned the dead woman in Angeline's home was her nineteen-year old housekeeper, Rose Cassell. The photographs of the girl's naked body, her throat slit ear to ear like a grossly exaggerated grin, would stay with him forever.

He shuddered at the *what-ifs* reverberating around his weary brain. What if Angeline hadn't followed him back to his hotel when he left her at the restaurant, what if they hadn't engaged in...almost-sex? Hell, he was hard as a railroad spike and a breath away from *Hallelujah!* when she asked if he had gone back to teaching.

His obsession with tracking Voorhees, the Dutchman, had stood as a bone of contention between them five years ago. Apparently, it still was and with good reason, given tonight's events. The cryptic clues and horrific murder were Voorhees' trademarks.

Cooper leaned forward in his chair at the utilitarian table in the sparsely-furnished room apparently reserved for grilling *persons of interest*. "I'd like to make my phone call now."

A jacketless Zeller, white shirt sleeves rolled to his elbows, shuffled a handful of papers and stacked them in his open briefcase. He stood, grabbed the black telephone at the far end of the table, and slid it across to Cooper.

What if Angeline had walked in on her intruder? What if she'd tried to stop him from taking her child? Would she have been raped and butchered like Rose Cassell?

Cooper shuddered at the image.

Her child? His exhaustion burrowed bone-deep. "The call's long distance," he told Zeller.

Minutes into his questioning, the Chief had produced a photograph of Angeline's boy. The small-framed kid had brown hair—bowl cut—dark eyes, and a devilish grin that clearly warned trouble would find him if you turned your back for five seconds.

And trouble had done exactly that.

Cooper rubbed the nape of his neck and rolled his shoulders, a useless effort to ease the building tension. Was he looking for characteristics unique to Angeline in the child's features, or glimpses of himself?

God, where was the boy?

"I'm sure your call will be brief, Mr. Cooper." Zeller unrolled his shirtsleeves, buttoned the cuffs, then adjusted the knot in his paisley tie. "Please tell your Detective Montgomery that you will be my guest for the night. For you own safety, of course. Until we know for certain this Voorhees you speak of is indeed involved in tonight's mayhem, and what it is he intends."

"You know about Montgomery?"

Zeller stopped in the doorway, straightened his shoulders, and lifted his chin in a posture of superiority. "As I said, Mr. Cooper, I make it my business to learn as much as I can about strangers to my city."

Yeah, well, how in hell did he miss Voorhees?

The Chief left him to his phone call, but Cooper suspected Zeller listened from behind the one-way mirrored wall running parallel to the conference table where he sat. Cooper dialed the bayside cottage in Hamlin's Grove, Texas. The line rang once, then twice. He heard fumbling, swearing.

"Montgomery here."

He turned his back to the glass and spoke low. "It's me. Coop. I'm in trouble."

"So what the hell's new?"

"I mean big trouble, Sandman." Using the boyhood nickname he'd given Sanderson Montgomery shrank the distance between them. "I've found Angeline."

"Who is it?" Braeden's voice sounded far away and drowsy.

"Go back to sleep," Montgomery told his wife. "I'll take the call in the kitchen."

A door clicked shut. Cooper envisioned the former New Orleans detective padding barefoot down the short hall to their informal kitchen with the tomato soup walls, stopping for a quick peek in a room where two little girls slept under the watchful guardianship of fairies, dough-eyed dragons, and winged unicorns.

Godchildren. They were a responsibility he should have shared with Angeline.

"Have you been drinking, Coop?" Montgomery sounded fully awake now.

"Not a drop." Cooper switched the phone to his other ear. "I told you she was alive, Sandman, my gut said so. And I found her. I found Angeline."

"For God's sake where? How?"

"On the Caribbean island of Jacqueme Dominique, not far from the Antilles, near Pavlatos. I'm in the capitol city of Port Noel."

Montgomery swore softly. "You okay?"

"Hell no, I'm not okay. But it's too complicated to get into over the phone," Cooper said. "I'm in jail, and Angeline's on her own. No telling what she'll do. I need you to come here. Guess it wouldn't hurt for you to talk to this joker Zeller either, and convince him my mug's not plastered in post offices from the Florida Keys to San Francisco."

"You can put him on before we hang up. First, you need to tell me how to find you."

Cooper forced his focus to details and relayed as much information as he could. Montgomery's silence said he took it all in.

"Thanks." Cooper scrubbed a hand over his face when they were done, then exhaled long and hard. Relief eased some of the strain in his shoulders. "Oh...and, Sandman?"

"Yes?"

He lowered his voice and cupped his hand around the receiver. "Bring your gun. Voorhees is here."

Zeller's cells encompassed the ground floor of the stationhouse, lit sparingly by a bare, low-wattage bulb in a stairwell. Cooper couldn't see the size of the cages, but he felt the suffocating closeness the second the steel-barred door shut him in. The place reeked of mildew and metal, with undercurrents of vomit and human excrement.

The stench was scrubbed and faded but still endured. Like old memories—like scars.

The officer exited, slamming the solid door to the stairwell and smothering the light like a water-doused fire.

Damn Zeller.

Cooper's mind snapped from Angeline, distraught over her missing child, to a shot of the well where Griffie MacDonald died. He and the boy had spent three days trapped in that putrid hole in Louisiana, water rising from a torrential downpour. The last few hours of the final day, he had held a dead boy in his arms. If Cooper lived to a hundred, he would never forget the moment the kid's warmth waned from his thin torso, and death's iciness seeped in.

Cooper sat on the floor at the front of the cell, in the corner nearest the door, and drew a deep breath. Sweat glued his sticky shirt to his back as he leaned against the cold bars. There would be no room in his lungs for air once the claustrophobia took hold. He couldn't let that happen. Not here, certainly not now, when he needed to hold things together for Angeline and...her child.

When it was imperative he locate Voorhees.

A female voice came from behind Cooper, making him jump. "Helps to relax if you breathe slowly."

He twisted his neck and saw nothing but shadow in the blackness. "Are you real?"

Her laughter rang light, almost musical. Out of place in this dungeon. "As real as your obvious dread of cold, dark holes. Relax," she said again. "Breathe slow and deep. How long have you lived with your fear?"

Too long. He rested the back of his head against the bars and willed his constricted lungs to expand. "It's not working."

"Close your eyes and envision light," she whispered. "A huge, white light. Almost blinding, it's so bright."

Again, he tried to see her. "Who the hell are you? What are you doing here?"

Traces of Ireland laced her voice. "That's not what's important. Got your eyes closed, lad?"

"Yes."

"See the light?"

"No."

"It'll come. Now, picture yourself atop the tallest, grandest mountain you can imagine."

That part was easy. He'd visited the Grand Tetons with Montgomery's family when he was twelve.

"It's really cold on your mountaintop," she said. "Nothin' but that ol' devil wind surroundin' you. He licks at your clothes and tussles your hair, fills your lungs with his glory." After a few minutes of silence, but for his labored breathing, Cooper heard her say, "Keep it slow, that's the trick my da taught me. You're doin' good, lad. If you like, I'll tell you this joke I know about a naked postmistress, orange knee-high socks, and a ping-pong table with one short leg."

Chapter Four

The jangle of keys and clank of a steel door unlocking roused Cooper. He didn't intend to fall asleep; he hadn't thought he could sleep in a space so confining.

Still huddled in the corner near the door, he turned and searched the adjoining cell for the mysterious woman. Vacant.

The young officer who unlocked the door moved aside, and Detective Sanderson Montgomery stepped forward. "Well, if you aren't a sorry-ass looking sight." Montgomery dressed in creased jeans, a white western shirt, sleeves rolled to his elbows, and the standard cowboy boots; his flattened blond "hat hair" a testament to the straw Stetson in his hand.

"It's about time you got here." Cooper gripped the bars and heaved himself up. "What time is it anyway, noon?"

"Try five after. Hell, it took me an hour to process you out of here," Montgomery said. "How 'bout a little gratitude."

Cooper glimpsed from one man to the other. "There was a woman in the adjacent cell last night. Where is she?"

The young cop said nothing.

The detective laughed. "You're delusional."

"I'm serious." Cooper rubbed sleepy grit from his eyes with his palms. "She sat on the floor behind me. She talked me through—"

"I'm game," Montgomery said. "What'd she look like?"

"I couldn't see her. It was too damn dark. But she told me this stupid joke." Cooper's gaze shot to the brown fedora with the leather hatband on the bunk in the bordering cell.

Montgomery flung the steel door open wide, making it clatter against the bars. He gave Cooper a fleeting chest-hug and patted his back several times with the hand holding his cowboy hat. "Come on, man. Don't know about you, but I could use a meal."

Cooper inhaled a steadying breath and peered over his friend's shoulder. "No Braeden?"

"I'm not gonna tell her yet. Not until I've seen Angeline, not until I've talked with her about what happened in New Orleans. I won't have Braeden hurt, Coop, not by anyone."

Cooper nodded. It seemed an epidemic of hurt had already overrun this island.

The two men left the cells, climbed the stairs, and started down the narrow corridor of black linoleum floors and whitewashed walls. They passed a barred window, and glancing outside, Cooper noted the green taxi parked at the curb across the cobblestone avenue. The flower-hunting driver, Bernard, sat in the square under the shade of a sixty-foot mangrove tree, his infinite legs stretched and crossed at the ankles, a newspaper folded beside him on the bench.

Bernard caught sight of him and straightened. He snapped a two-fingered salute and welcoming grin.

Cooper returned the greeting. At least he'd made one friend on this damned island.

A door clicked open at the end of the hall. Cooper recognized the lean officer toting the billy club from the day before by his pencil-thin mustache and clench-jawed sneer.

Chief Zeller stepped into the hall, dressed in what looked like the same tan, lightweight wool suit he sported yesterday, only this time he wore a powder-blue dress shirt, his tie wide gold and blue stripes. The man definitely dressed for success.

But success at what?

"Detective Montgomery!" Zeller's brown cap-toed oxfords devoured the hall as he rushed to shake Montgomery's hand like they were buddies. "My secretary announced your arrival." He led the detective back to his office. "Come, she's made a fresh pot of coffee, a special island blend that will surely compare to any in your beautiful city of New Orleans." His smile turned upside down when he spotted Cooper. "You need to stop by the front desk and collect your belongings," he said. "Be sure to sign for them."

Cooper would've spat the sour taste the man left in his mouth on his speckled 50's linoleum, but he figured someone other than the Chief would have to clean it up—probably another jailed tourist, guilty of trying to pay for a lavish island dinner with his maxed-out platinum card.

He called after Montgomery. "I'll meet you outside."

The detective nodded, then disappeared inside Zeller's office. The door latched with a definitive click.

Cooper stopped at the front desk. Just his luck. *Billy-club Cop* dumped a brown clasp envelope on the desk, then shoved a pen and clipboard at him. "Sign the form," was all the man said, but it was enough that Cooper caught his thick accent. He wasn't island born.

Determined to make the officer wait, he counted every bill in his wallet and the change scattered across the desk. "Thanks." Cooper stuffed his wallet, keys, a hotel matchbook, and loose change in his pockets. He exited the stationhouse, bounded down the front steps, and crossed the street.

Bernard waited under the gargantuan mangrove tree.

"No fares today?" Cooper said.

The driver jumped up. Pages from his newspaper separated and drifted to the ground. "Bernard was worried about you." He waggled a broad finger. "Jail is not a good place. No, sir, not a good place at all."

Cooper smiled. He would never get used to the man referring to himself in third person.

Bernard gathered the wayward pages and stuffed them in a nearby trash receptacle. "You need a ride to your hotel, yes?"

Cooper wadded a newspaper page the driver missed and vaulted it into the can. "Definitely yes." His skin crawled from spending the night on the floor in Zeller's jail, and he craved a hot shower in the worst way. "But we need to wait for my friend." He sat on the vacated bench. "May I ask how long you've lived on Jacqueme Dominique, Bernard?"

The black man resumed his watch from the adjacent seat. "Ah." He clapped his big hands. "Lucky Bernard. He is thirty-eight years old his last birthday, and all his life he has lived in paradise. Mother and father, grandfather and grandmother. Many generations past, and with such a fertile sister, many generations to come."

Cooper sighed. He had a history in New Orleans, too, but little of it revolved around family. Not like he imagined it was with Bernard, or with Braeden and Montgomery and their little girls.

Not like he imagined it could be with...

"No wife?" he asked the dark man.

"Alas, no." The cabbie picked a piece of lint from his khaki trouser leg, flicked it away, and grinned. "No pretty wife for Bernard, but he is never without hope."

"You're a sad looking pair." Montgomery injected his observation into Cooper's misery.

Cooper rose from the bench. "Just waiting on you. What did you and Dapper Dan have to talk about?"

"You." Although the Stetson already shaded his eyes, Montgomery slipped on his signature aviator sunglasses.

They walked toward Bernard's van, the driver a couple of long-legged strides ahead of them. Cooper went around the front of the Voyager, swung the passenger door open, and climbed in. "Figured you'd forget to bring me coffee. To the hotel, Bernard," he said as soon as the driver settled behind the wheel. "You and I still need our morning caffeine."

In his room, Cooper showered and changed while Montgomery called home. He listened through the open bathroom door as his friend fed Braeden a tidy song and dance about spending a few days in New Orleans with his mother. From the gist of the one-sided conversation, it seemed Elizabeth Montgomery's wedding to Bull Scully—Montgomery's late father's partner, another cop—would finally take place in the winter after a lengthy on again-off again engagement.

About damn time.

Cooper stepped out of the bathroom, toweling his hair.

The light tone of Montgomery's voice indicated Braeden bought every delicious detail. "Okay then," he said, as he shot Cooper a thumb's up. "Give the girls kisses and hugs for me, and tell Maggie to stop crying. She can talk this evening. Yeah. Eight o'clock, I know. I'll call early enough." Another pause. "You bet. Yeah. Me, too. Always." He hung up with a silly grin plastered across his lips, but his expression quickly turned serious when he placed the phone in its niche. "I stall Braeden much longer, and she's liable to divorce me when she finds out what all this is really about."

They didn't keep secrets. Cooper envied them. "We won't let that happen, Sandman."

They both turned at a knock on the door.

"Bernard here," came the sing-song voice from the hall.

Montgomery opened the door, while Cooper poured the remaining coffee he'd ordered from Room Service in a third cup. He promised Montgomery a stop by the Rusty Pelican before returning to Angeline's. They needed sustenance for the long evening ahead, and time to discuss Rose Cassell's murder and the missing child.

Bernard dropped them off in front of Angeline's house, then headed to an anniversary party at his sister's, promising to return by eleven. Cooper glanced at his watch. Five past six.

Before following Montgomery to the door, he stood a moment and reconnoitered the area, taking in more than he had a chance to the night before. The island's ever-present mangrove trees flanked the yard in clusters, their spaghetti bowl-roots snaking out of the earth like loosed serpents. Heady fragrances perfumed the salty air. Velvety red and hot pink Bougainvillea bordered the herring-bone walkway and bled into flourishing beds of Hibiscus, red Torch Ginger and banana trees, not yet mature.

The house, fashioned in typical West Indies style architecture, appeared cool and comfortable. Iron-enclosed galleries surrounded the structure on three sides. Six massive Doric columns on the brick ground floor sustained the second story—most likely constructed of cypress—and the slender colonettes above spanned the second-floor gallery, supporting a hipped roof broken by dormer windows and four chimneys. It seemed a lot of house for one woman.

Cooper noted the cop car parked a quarter mile down the road. Conspicuous. He lifted the brass knocker. It clacked three times before the brunette clerk from Angeline's shop opened the door.

"Can I help you?" she said.

"We're here to speak with Mrs. Dubois." Cooper already filled Montgomery in on Angeline's phony name, but he'd be damned if he would use it much longer.

The woman peered through a two-foot gap she allowed in the door. "Are you with the police?"

"Yes, ma'am." Montgomery opened his worn brown wallet, displayed his badge, then flipped the wallet shut before she realized the Hamlin's Grove Police Department was several bodies of water away with zero jurisdiction on the island.

She waved to the policeman down the road who had exited his car. He waved back, and she opened the door wide enough the two men could enter.

Conspicuous—and easy.

Cooper recognized the baby-faced officer from the day before and figured he radioed Zeller as soon as they drove up. Worse case scenario: they could all be dead by the time the Chief arrived, including the rookie. Some protection.

"Where is she?" He followed the brunette into the twenty-by-forty-foot central hall. The doors remained closed to the room where Rose Cassell had so brutally died.

The girl must have noticed him staring. "I've arranged for a crew to come and clean that room day after tomorrow," she offered. "Chief Zeller said it would be okay."

Montgomery nodded. Cooper crossed the space and stood at the bottom of the stairs. He studied the detective, and figured it was only a matter of time before his friend slipped inside the sunroom to poke around Zeller's processed crime scene. His gaze drifted up the delicately carved staircase with its white spindles and rich, dark wood balustrade, then back to the brunette.

"I hope she's sleeping," she said, as if warning him not to disturb Angeline.

"I hope she's not." Cooper ascended the stairs, calling to Montgomery, "A pot of coffee would be nice." He and Angeline needed to sort what had transpired between them, and they would start with the paternity of her missing child.

"Coop?"

He turned and stared down at Montgomery. "What?"

"Go easy on her. I mean it."

"Yeah, okay."

"I'll be there in a few minutes."

Cooper bounded up the stairs and down the hall, knocking and simultaneously opening doors. He didn't expect a child's room when he opened the third door to his right. The décor was all boy. Wooden trains and miniature cars traffic-jammed one corner, while painted bookcases filled with colored storage boxes and children's books lined the two sidewalls.

Running his hand across the colorful hardback open on the dresser, Cooper closed the book and stared at Braeden's photograph on the dust jacket. He turned it over and fingered an invisible line under the title, *Platypus Pearl and the Case of the Trembling Trumpeter*. He thumbed through the first few pages of bold print and recalled standing in line three hours at W. H. Smith in Paris last November to get his hands on a copy, although Braeden insisted she'd give him one if he would fly home in time for Christmas.

He'd settled for an Easter autograph, and spent the holidays searching for Angeline.

Cooper needed a moment. His mind traveled back to the photograph Zeller had shown him during his interrogation. How old was her child? He massaged his temple where a tiny brass band struck up a chorus, his mind too muddled to do the math.

He frowned. Surely, if the boy was his, Angeline would've found a way to let him know.

The alternative didn't conjure pleasant thoughts either. He tried to shake off the image of her with another man—perhaps the Frenchman, Mathieu Fournier. He blinked away mind-snapshots of Angeline and her former boss making love, her belly swelling as she carried the old man's child, laughing and planning their future, decorating this room.

Cooper sat on the edge of the bed and nudged aside the red corded spread. He lifted a mechanical robot from atop the vintage seaman's trunk that served as a bedside table. *Optimus Prime.* Montgomery's little Maggie was all about the Transformers, too.

Ironman guarded the boy's domain as he glared down through his metallic mask from a poster tacked to the wall opposite the foot of the bed; Batman glowered from over a navy headboard stamped with red, white, and blue stars, as if the Caped Crusader might descend at any moment and clear the room of all evil-doers.

Where were the super heroes when the monster stole Angeline's boy? Where was his dad?

A Louisville Slugger leaned against the closet frame. Cooper rose, crossed the space, and picked up a leather mitt from the floor beside the bat. Against his outstretched fingers, the glove seemed so small. He closed his eyes, raised it to his face, and breathed in the scent of leather and a boy's sweat.

Voorhees hadn't contacted him yet, but he would. Children were trouble, and keeping the boy in one place an extended amount of time wasn't smart. If the Dutchman was anything, he was smart. But he wouldn't hurt the kid. Cooper would bet his life on it. Gladly.

He returned the glove to its spot below the bat. Studying the rest of the room, he tried to get a feel for the boy. He ran his hand along the edge of the four-drawer chest positioned diagonally in the corner, its surface crowded with a child's treasures. A jar of multicolored marbles caught his attention: cat's eyes and maggies and cold, hard steelies. He had a similar collection when he was a kid. A sailboat lamp joined the marbles, along with a glob of modeling clay and a couple crayons. He would lay odds the boy's favorite color was blue.

A full-length mirror leaned against the wall beside the dresser and next to it, painted letters affixed above the window proclaimed that JACK lived here.

JACK. It was a good, solid name.

Not French.

You could count on a guy named Jack to be strong and reliable, friendly.

No, Voorhees wouldn't harm Angeline's Jack. Not like Griffie, the boy taken by mistake, whose truck-driving dad couldn't afford a ransom. The Dutchman carried another agenda, with an old score to settle. This time, *this boy*, was the snare that would at long-last get him Cooper.

His head jerked toward movement in the doorway.

Chapter Five

Angeline braced herself against the bedroom door's frame. "How dare you come in here," she said. "Get out."

Cooper noted her sagging shoulders. *Too early for defeat.* He wouldn't allow either of them the luxury of giving into it. "Not until we talk." He needed to whip up the emotion in Angeline, bring her anger back to the surface. Get some answers.

"I have nothing to say to you." She wrapped her violet kimono robe tighter and stepped aside, pressing her back flat against the open door like she feared having to touch any part of him when he exited.

Which he had no intention of doing. "I have a right to know if the boy is mine."

It was clearly rage sending the splotches of red to her cheeks. "You show up, my housekeeper is murdered, and my child stolen. We both know who did this, Cooper, and we know why. And you want to talk to me about rights? Get out."

"Montgomery's downstairs."

For a long moment, she stood there, clinging to her robe as if it were constructed of steel supports instead of luxurious silk.

"Bastard."

"Zeller locked me in his jail. I needed help," he said. "Unlike you, I rely on the people who care about me."

She crossed the room, her limp more pronounced, and began methodically making the boy's bed, smoothing the blue- and white-striped sheets, straightening the corded comforter. Stacking pillows. The silver and red robot returned to his place of honor in the center of the topmost pillow.

"Did you tell Braeden?" she asked without looking at him.

"That's Montgomery's call."

Her back straightened, and she moved toward him, determination in every wobbly step. "You know what, Cooper?"

Her cheeks were swollen from crying, and her eyes glassy and red-rimmed, haunted by despair he'd inadvertently caused. The sight of her so distraught tore at his heart, and guilt burdened his shoulders. He mentally kicked himself.

"I don't care who you tell." Angeline's voice rose to a shout. She stirred the air with her hands. "Tell everyone. Tell the whole damn world, if that's what it takes to get my son back." The flailing motion of her hands threw her balance off. Her knees bumped the square activity table at the room's center, and she crashed to the floor scattering Lego blocks and kid-size chairs.

Montgomery dashed in, the brunette on his heels. The girl pointed an accusing finger at Cooper. "What did you do to her?"

Angeline struggled to her knees. She righted the blue table, lifted a yellow chair and set it straight, then a green one. The red chair came apart in her hands. Sobbing, she latched onto the small saddle seat and brought it to her breasts. "You saw what Voorhees did to Griffie MacDonald, Cooper. You were there." Her ashen complexion blended with the scar, but heightened the dark circles beneath her eyes. Both spoke of enormous fear. "Don't let him do that to Jack. *Please.*"

Guilt or anger, maybe both, glued him to his spot by the window. The paternity discussion was delayed, not over. "I'll get him back, Slick."

It was a promise he would damn well keep—or die trying.

Montgomery coaxed Angeline up, and with an arm around her waist, turned to the brunette. "Where's her room?"

Standing wide-eyed near the bed, the girl sprang to action, her relief palpable at having a job to do. She pointed to the hall. "That way. Left. Two doors down. I'll stay with her."

Montgomery regarded Cooper with cool speculation. "There's coffee in the kitchen." He scooped up Angeline and started after the young woman. "Don't argue, Coop. You look like you could use a cup and a few minutes to pull it together. Take them. I'll be down as quick as I can."

Cooper had been in the spacious kitchen an hour and fifteen minutes when Montgomery entered. The room had been recently updated, as noted by the placement of a large central island and ultra-modern stainless steel appliances.

Montgomery carried a silver and black cordless phone.

Cooper slid his mug of lukewarm coffee aside. "Who you calling?"

"It's fifteen 'til eight. I almost forgot to call Maggie." The detective raked a hand through his sandy hair, then pinched the bridge of his nose. "Damn, Coop, Angeline wants Braeden here. She all but begged me." He punched a few buttons and held the receiver to his ear. "I mean, I understand it, and I'll make it happen if I can. But this isn't exactly somethin' I can tell Braeden over the telephone." He held up a dismissive hand before Cooper could respond. "Hey there, Mags. What you doin' answering the phone?"

"Daddy!" was said with such exuberance that Cooper heard it from the other side of the table. Realization hit him like a loaded cement truck: the Sandman was living the life he wanted.

"Popsicles in the bathtub? No way." Montgomery laughed. "Mommy ate a green one? And Tulip spit hers in the water? Yeah, gross. I like the red ones best, too. Listen, Mags, put Mommy on for a minute."

Cooper stood. He skirted the table. "You going to tell her?"

Montgomery shook his head. "Gonna catch the red-eye into Bush Intercontinental-Houston." His raised finger silenced Cooper. "Braeden, honey? Yeah, you heard right, the red-eye. I know. I planned to stay longer, but somethin's come up. Don't worry, I'll catch a cab. Be there in time to fix you guys hotcakes for breakfast. Okay. Me, too. Get some sleep now. We'll talk in the morning." He disconnected.

"Tulip?" Cooper carried his mug to the sink and dumped the bitter coffee.

"Yeah. Braeden bought Maggie a pair of wooden shoes at a festival at her preschool and ever since Annie started walking, she can't keep her little feet out of them. They stuck her with the nickname. It'll grow on you." Montgomery punched another number into the phone.

"Now who are you calling?"

"Clarice Ambrose."

Cooper nodded. The retired math teacher lived a quarter mile from their bayside home in Hamlin's Grove. She and Braeden were tight, a surrogate mother-daughter kind of thing. Who better to watch the girls while Braeden and Montgomery flew back to the island?

"How do you plan on telling Braeden about Angeline?" He didn't envy his friend the delivery of such startling news. Hell, Cooper had hardly digested the revelation himself, and he'd set out to find her.

"Damned if I know." Montgomery completed his call, and then poured himself a cup of coffee. He held up the near-empty pot. "You want some of this?"

Cooper shook his head. He'd reached the "strung-out on caffeine" phase thirty minutes ago.

The detective emptied the carafe. Glass clinked against stainless steel as he set it in the sink. He opened the adjacent cabinet's door, and then the door on the opposite side. "Know where Angeline keeps her cream and sugar?"

Cooper opened the cabinet closest to the stainless range, shut it. He reached for the brushed nickel handle on a narrow pantry door. "Never knew you to girlie-up your cof—"

When he halted mid-sentence, Montgomery crossed to where he stood. "I'll be damned," he said. "Would you look at that?"

Cooper was looking. He reached in the cabinet and turned a can of Campbell's soup, and then another. Like resolute soldiers, they sat, row after row, each can with the "how to" of a one-disher on the back label, each waiting to weave culinary genius in

Angeline's gourmet kitchen.

She'd taken a page out of his own neurotic cookbook by alphabetizing the cans, lining them up straight and tidy, only hers didn't face the front of the cupboard. How like her to put her own spin on things, turning the backs of the labels face-forward so she could group them by recipe.

Both men laughed as if they'd been desperate for a moment of lightness since their arrival. Montgomery inhaled a deep breath; laughter left tears in his eyes. "Looks like you taught the lady a trick or two about cooking," he said.

Cooper bit his lower lip; he sure had. Starting with that first tuna casserole he had created for Angeline at Raison Belle-Amandine, the recipe straight off the back of Campbell's Cream of Mushroom soup. It had been a day of firsts for them: first time she trusted him enough to fall asleep in his car; first time he shared his childhood home with her—a generosity he didn't wear well.

First time he kissed her, and damn if she hadn't kissed him back.

Hurt and anger welled in him as he moved to the window to peer outside where a restless wind shook the mangrove trees, and light from the fullest moon he'd ever seen danced across the sea. His emotions were all over the place. Up, down...sideways.

He spoke to Montgomery's reflection in the glass pane. "Why did she run from me, Sandman? Why'd she feel the need to hide?"

The detective placed a comforting hand on his shoulder. "Those are questions you'll have to ask the lady, Coop. Hell, that's the understatement to beat all understatements. Did you talk about the boy while you were upstairs?"

"I know we need to talk about him, but how? When? Her child is missing. Given the way her housekeeper was butchered, the fact there have been no ransom calls, no calls period, the boy could be..." He wasn't ready to go there. "This is my fault."

Montgomery left him to retrieve the sugar bowl from a nearby cabinet. "That's ridiculous."

"Is it? By searching for Angeline, by finding her, I led Voorhees straight to her door. She's right, I let the Dutchman steal her boy. How do we get past that?"

The detective removed a spoon from a drawer. He added two heaps of sugar to his cup and stirred. "Voorhees isn't responsible for the angst of the world, Coop. You got any proof it was him?"

"I told you about the magazine cover and the photo of the MacDonald kid. He had to have planted them."

Montgomery eyed him over the cup's rim. "Circumstantial," he said.

Cooper shifted a can of soup from one hand to the other. "My gut says it's him."

"Not enough."

"Then help me find proof, Sandman. Help me end this. I can't make my feelings the focus when Angeline stands to lose everything...and I need my feelings out there. I want to clear the air about the boy, but I can't. Did she say anything to you?"

Montgomery shook his head. "She wanted to talk about Braeden, and make me understand why she let her best friend think she was dead."

"I'll never understand."

"S'pose I do. Some of it anyway. But it's not me she's got to convince. Braeden's feelings will be jumbled, if I can even get her here. Mostly, she'll be pissed."

Cooper skimmed the recipe on the soup can's label: *Two-step Garlic Pork Chops*. It sounded easy. If only life could be. "I should go up and try to talk to Angeline again." He returned the soup to the cupboard.

"Like I said, the two of you will have to sort it out." Montgomery finished his coffee. His mug joined the carafe in the sink. "It might be wise to wait until after the boy's found. If he's—"

"Jack," Cooper said without preamble. He closed the cupboard door and turned.

"Huh?"

"Her boy's name is Jack," he added. "And I will find him. When I do, Voorhees is a dead man."

Voorhees appointed him the Onlooker. The dark-clothed man crushed his cigarette in the damp sand. He crouched in the sanctuary of the mangrove cluster three or four yards from the weathered picket fence separating the house's rear yard from actual beach. Through a bank of windows, he studied the two men as they stood in the kitchen.

The two outsiders.

Americans.

A cup of their expensive coffee would taste good after his cigarette. Strong and hot. Desire called from his groins, and the Onlooker touched himself as he grinned into the night. Hot and tight, like the young housekeeper he'd had in the sunroom the day before.

She was a fighter that one. She'd jerked and clawed and kicked. Voorhees had smacked her good when she bit him.

The big Dutchman took her first like he always did. The boss turning the little virgin into a whore. Voorhees liked the others to watch. Afterward, he went upstairs to talk to the boy, to relieve the one who'd stayed up there while the others had their way with...

Ah, yes. She'd said her name was Rose as she stripped off her clothes, slow like Voorhees instructed, delusional that cooperation would spare her life. She had believed the Dutchman's promises, foolish girl. She had even offered to fetch the hiding boy for him.

Voorhees had plucked that lovely flower. Plucked her good. Then they'd all had a petal or two.

The Onlooker laughed quietly, caressing the tiny ring on a gold chain around his neck. He'd severed her finger and taken the ring while someone else held his hand over her mouth to muffle her screams.

Spitting in the sand, he kneaded himself, threw back his head and sucked in the dank night air. He had been the last one to have the housekeeper. Most of the fight was gone out of her then, but he had kept it interesting by placing the machete between her breasts and watching her eyes grow round as the cold steel touched her sweat-slicked skin. Fear perfumed her, and he'd found it a cloying aphrodisiac.

He had thought about the blonde woman from the magazine covers as he thrust deep inside the girl, envisioning her beneath him. Pity about her face. But scars marking a woman turned him on. Especially if he could add another to her collection.

Voorhees expected a call. The Onlooker tugged a cell phone

from his pocket, punched in the number, and let his boss know he completed today's charge. With the device tucked neatly into a potted Allamanda, he'd return home and on the way, stop at one of the seedy waterfront bars to harvest himself another rose.

As promised, Bernard and his cab arrived promptly at eleven. He did an immediate turn-around and delivered Montgomery to the airport. After giving Cooper a blistering lecture on protocol and plain old good manners, the young clerk from Angeline's store headed home.

The rookie cop still held vigil down the road.

Cooper inspected the locks on every door and window on the ground floor, then headed up to check on Angeline before crashing on her sofa. Halfway up the stairs, the telephone in the kitchen rang.

He froze, then checked his watch. Twelve-thirty. Only bad news called this late.

As he raced down the stairs, he missed the bottom step and slipped. He scrambled up, sprinted down the hall, flipped the light switch in the kitchen, and dove for the unit on the counter. He answered on the fourth ring, his heart in his throat. "Hello?"

"Mr. Cooper?"

Chief Zeller.

Pain twisted in his gut. "Yes?"

"My officer should be at your door any moment now."

The rookie.

"Okay." The brass knocker sounded; Cooper turned. "I'll let him in."

"Wait."

He'd almost reached the front doors. "What?"

"You need to get Mrs. Dubois to the station right away," Zeller said. "My officer will drive you."

Cooper was afraid to ask, yet he had to. "Are you calling about the boy?" He unlocked the doors and threw them open. The rookie stood there, grinning, as if he'd single-handedly solved a crime of intergalactic proportion.

Cooper dropped the phone before the Chief could get his words out. "Tell Mrs. Dubois we have found her—"

Angeline sat in the rear of the tan Ford Crown Victoria, shoulders hunched, elbows resting on her knees, and hands clasped beneath her chin. The young officer turned the heater on at her request, but an iciness crawled through her. She'd changed into faded jeans and a black cowl-neck sweater. As she stared at her feet, she realized she still wore her zebra slippers. They were a gift from Jack last Christmas, chosen from her shop's inventory. He had selected lions for himself.

Sweet, handsome, funny Jack. Her boy. Her world.

She whispered yet another prayer of thanksgiving that he was safe, and oddly, that Cooper was here and she hadn't endured the horror of the kidnapping alone. She laughed inwardly. How ironic. If it weren't for Cooper and his blind vengeance against Voorhees, the Dutchman wouldn't have bothered with her and Jack in the first place.

She sighed. Her mind wrestled with her heart, neither winning.

Were Cooper's sins any worse than hers?

Lowering her hands, she grasped the seat on either side of her hips as the cruiser made a sharp right. She brought her attention back to Cooper, seated beside her. "That's all Zeller told you? Not whether Jack was okay or hurt or—"

"I'm sorry," he said. "Letting you know seemed the only thing that mattered. I didn't ask questions, just threw the phone down and ran upstairs."

"Okay. That's okay." She rocked. Nerves. Her knees stung from the spill she took earlier when she ran into Jack's play table. The arthritis in them—fallout from the New Orleans' accident— would flare up big-time tomorrow. "Jack wouldn't be at a police station if he was hurt, right?" She gave neither man the chance to answer. "He'd be at a hospital. Of course, he would." Leaning forward, she placed her hands on the mesh screen barricade separating the cruiser's rear seat from the front. "Can't this thing go any faster?"

The young officer met her gaze in the rearview mirror. "Getting you there as quick as I can, ma'am," he said. "As quick as I can."

He barely got the cruiser parked in a space behind the

stationhouse when she threw open the door and bolted from the car.

Cooper grasped her elbow as they hurried around the side of the building and up the steps. Shoving open the door, they rushed into the reception area.

Angeline's eyes scanned the room, almost void of people so late at night. "Where's Zeller?" she shouted, tapping the dispatcher's window. "Where is my son?"

A buzzer sounded, and a narrow door opened to her right. A flash of blue and green shot out. "Mommy!"

Chapter Six

The boy burst through the door and Angeline scooped him in her arms, both of them waffling from the impact of their embrace.

Cooper placed a hand on her back to steady them. He nodded to the police chief. "Zeller."

"Mr. Cooper." The Chief snapped his fingers and gained the attention of the dispatcher. "Bring Mrs. Dubois and her son hot chocolate, please." He turned to Angeline, still hugging Jack and asking a million questions of the boy. "I've arranged a room where the two of you can talk," he told her. "I will fill Mr. Cooper in on what I know."

She nodded. Jack laid his head on her shoulder, his gangly arms tight around her neck. The notion of family gnawed at Cooper.

He ached to be this boy's dad.

"There are no words." Angeline visibly struggled with her emotions as she reached for Zeller's big hand. "Thank you."

Cooper took Jack from her before she collapsed. His heart stumbled when the boy rested his head against Cooper's chest. A buzzer sounded again, and they followed Zeller down the narrow whitewashed corridor that eventually led—as Cooper so well knew—to the Chief's office at one end and the stairwell to the basement cells at the other. It seemed eons since the long hours he had spent there with the mysterious owner of the brown fedora.

By the time Zeller settled Angeline and Jack in one of the interrogation rooms, the rookie arrived with two cups of hot chocolate and a paper plate of flaky coconut pastries. Cooper followed the Chief to the adjacent room outfitted with a one-way mirrored window.

"I thought you would want to keep an eye on them," Zeller said.

"You thought right." This new, nicer Daniel Zeller presented a puzzle. Cooper suspected the Chief wanted more from him.

Zeller pulled out a chair at a table much smaller than the one they sat at the other night. "Sit. Please." He took the chair on the opposite side of the table, his back to the glass.

"Did the boy tell you anything?" Cooper watched as Jack wolfed down several pastries, and Angeline hovered. Unable to keep her hands off him, she occasionally brushed crumbs from the boy's green t-shirt.

Cooper imagined her stomach tied in fist-sized knots, as his was.

"Only that a nice man took him to the beach under the guise of meeting his mother," Zeller said. "The man gave him a ride on a fast boat. It was dark, he can't remember the boat's color for certain, but he thinks it was white with red stripes or letters. The man had yellow hair. They played..." he checked his notes, "*Chutes and Ladders* in the boat's cabin while they waited." Zeller offered Cooper a rare smile. "The boy won many times," he added. "The man only once. When Jack's mother didn't meet them, he slept in a big bed where the yellow-haired man let him eat breakfast. Apparently, breakfast in bed is something his mother doesn't allow."

"They didn't hurt him?" The need for action grated on Cooper. He stood, walked to the mirrored window, and placed his hand flat against the cool glass. "I mean, he looks okay."

"Physically, it appears Jack is in good shape. For that we should be most grateful," Zeller said. "I have arranged for the doctor to meet us at the hospital. The boy must stay there tonight and be examined. Protocol. I haven't told Mrs. Dubois yet."

"It's Miss St. Cyr. You saw her photo on the cover of *Vogue*, you know who she is. What's the point in keeping up this pretense?" Cooper moved behind his chair. "Where did you find Jack, how?"

"The boy was walking in the square just after midnight," the Chief said. "He told us he was going to his mother's store."

Bright kid. Cooper sat. "Who found him?"

"The taxi driver, Bernard Dumelle."

He had never asked the driver's surname. "Surely you don't think Bernard's involved?"

"Jack did not recognize Dumelle." Zeller took a small plastic bag from the back of a manila folder. He slid the bag across the table's scarred surface. "This was pinned to his shirt, and the driver kept the presence of mind to leave it attached to preserve evidence. Quite commendable."

The Chief never said he exonerated Bernard.

Cooper lifted the bag, turned it over, and inspected a glossy red and white bulls-eye, perhaps three inches in diameter. A closed safety pin was attached to a punched hole at the top of the target, the way kids' name tags are pinned on in preschool. He set the bag on the table. "This was on Jack's shirt?"

"If you will note the reverse side." Zeller turned the bulls-eye over and tapped its center. "It's from an archery catalog." He returned the evidence to the back of his folder. "Do you have any idea what it means?"

The implication seemed as clear as Cooper's certainty the Dutchman's game was far from finished. "I told you about Voorhees last night, before you locked me in your jail. The Dutchman is sending a message," he said. "He wants me to know he can put his hands on Jack or Angeline, both of them, whenever he wants. Voorhees never intended to hurt the boy. I'm his target."

Zeller closed the folder. "Why you?"

"I'm probably a fool telling you this, you being the law in Port Noel, but until a couple years ago, the single-minded purpose in my life was to find Voorhees and kill him for what he did to that boy in the photograph you showed me at Angeline's. Obviously,

I didn't succeed. But I helped fund an organization that thwarted a number of kidnap attempts Voorhees orchestrated. I cost him a lot of time and money." Cooper stood and shoved the metal folding chair under the table. He turned toward the exit. "When I discovered Angeline might still be alive, I stopped bothering with the Dutchman. I've been searching for her ever since."

Zeller's eyebrows shot up in surprise. "You were a mercenary?"

Cooper almost laughed. The man boasted he knew everything about everyone coming to Port Noel. "That's not what I said, Chief. I'm a teacher. No more, no less. I subsidized a lion's share of the group's missions, but I never worked for them. Hell, Zeller, I don't even own a gun. Eventually, they disbanded."

"I understand, then, how this Voorhees might seek retribution against you." Zeller also rose from his chair. "But I do not understand how his returning Jack moves him any closer to that goal. I've watched the way you look at the woman and the boy, Mr. Cooper. Killing the child would have devastated you."

"Yeah." Cooper's gut clenched yet again. "I haven't figured out Voorhees' motive either."

"He hasn't contacted you?"

"No."

Zeller regarded him quizzically. "When he does, you will tell me, yes?"

Not likely. Cooper opened the door and stepped into the hall. "I won't interfere with your investigation, Zeller, if that's what you're asking." *So long as you don't interfere with mine.*

The ice cream Angeline promised Jack in the hospital wasn't nearly as enticing as the ride in a real live police car. The rookie gave an award-winning performance: a toot of the horn, siren blip, speaking exaggerated police jargon into a dead microphone, and shining the spotlight on Angeline's store when they drove past.

Jack didn't stop laughing the entire fifteen minutes it took to reach their destination.

Seemed Zeller's clout filtered into all aspects of his city. It didn't take long to get the boy examined, admitted to the hospital and in a room, private only because there was no other patient his age.

Jack was asleep by four in the morning.

Angeline slept on a short sofa nearby, her endless legs bent slightly at the knees, feet hanging over the edge. She'd lost a slipper. Cooper brushed a blonde tendril from her forehead. He placed the slipper on the sofa next to her. She stirred, moaning softly. Their talk about Jack's paternity loomed like a cordon between them, a wall he intended to bring down as soon as possible. He wanted more from her—hell, he wanted everything—and clearing the air seemed the only way to get there.

Zeller appeared in the doorway. "May I speak with you a moment?"

There was no getting away from the man.

As he ushered the police chief deeper into the hall, Cooper inhaled the cloying scent of disinfectant...a mix of pine cleaner and ammonia, laced with something antiseptic. He hated hospitals. "Have you learned anything else of Voorhees' whereabouts?" he asked Zeller.

"Sorry, no."

Standing where he could see anyone entering or leaving the room, Cooper said, "What did the doctor say about Jack?"

"The boy seems no worse for the experience. It appears his abductors treated him well, and fortunately, he did not see or hear the housekeeper murdered." The Chief straightened a framed watercolor print on the wall. Titled *Amalfi Sunrise,* according to the small brass plaque beneath it, the artist captured a serene setting of pastel boats under a blue, cloudless sky. "In a few days," Zeller added, "this will all be forgotten."

No way. The lithograph still hung crooked; Cooper gently tapped the corner. Better. "When can I take them home?"

"The doctor will see the boy again this morning. After that, you may take them home anytime you wish."

He faced Zeller. "Will you post extra security at Angeline's?"

"My force is small, Mr. Cooper. I can spare a few officers tonight, to keep watch over her and the boy at the hospital, and I will post a man when they go home. Other than that, unfortunately, I must turn my attention to more pressing matters. There is, as you recall, a murder to solve. If problems arise, additional officers can be at the residence within minutes."

"Yeah." Cooper considered how easily Rose Cassell was murdered and Jack taken. With Montgomery's help, he'd find a better solution.

Zeller stared down the hall toward the elevators. "I must leave now, and you should go home to rest. I'll have someone call when the doctor releases the boy."

To friggin' hell with rest. Cooper needed to get back to Angeline's sprawling house and secure things. Locks needed changing, floodlights on the beach, and a security system installed.

He'd even buy a big dog, several if need be.

Jack would like that.

Four hours later, Cooper walked toward sunlight streaming through the small squared windows on either side, and in the transom, of the single-paneled rear door inside Angeline's house. Exhaustion plagued him, and sleeping downstairs on her sofa left him stiff and sore.

The clock on the mantle in the great room chimed ten. Earlier, when he returned from the hospital, he woke the only locksmith in the city, and the man promised to stop by that evening and stay until locks were sufficiently changed. They'd have a security system installed by the weekend.

Cooper detoured by the kitchen. While the high-end coffeemaker gurgled politely, he punched Montgomery's number in the portable phone.

A woman's voice answered. "Hello?"

Phone wedged between his ear and shoulder, he poured coffee into a mug. "Morning, Braeden. This is Coop."

"I know who it is." Anger added an uncharacteristic sharpness to her Texas drawl. "And I know you're calling about Angeline."

"I'm calling because the police found Jack." He forgot she'd never met Angeline's son.

Sounds of jostling, then muffled conversation filled the line. Montgomery came on. "The police found the boy, where?"

"Voorhees let the kid go, just like that. Bernard found him wandering in the square last night on his way back from dropping you at the airport."

"Was Jack hurt?"

"He's in the hospital but, no, he doesn't appear to be hurt."

"Thank God." More muted conversation, as if Montgomery placed his hand partially over the receiver. He came back on the line. "Braeden wants to know how Angeline's coping?"

"She's elated, of course, and exhausted. I haven't seen her this morning, but I'm sure she's still a bundle of nerves."

He sure as hell was.

Cooper left the kitchen, opened the rear door, and stepped outside while Montgomery continued talking. The eighty-degree weather had already warmed the bricks beneath his feet. It amazed him what a difference a day made—or a night. The sun shone brighter, the sky bluer.

Yeah, but this brilliant sun and clear sky also shined on Voorhees. Wherever he hid.

Cooper carried his coffee across the yard's dew-dampened grass to the wrought iron table in the gazebo situated not far from the picket fence and private beach. The air smelled of the sea and invigorated him. Gulls cried overhead, arcing, occasionally diving for breakfast on the fly. He was starved.

"Braeden doesn't sound like she took the news well," he said to Montgomery.

"Hold on a minute, Coop. Maggie's headed off to school. Pucker up, Pumpkin." The phone went silent for a few seconds. "Okay. I'm back. Braeden's dealin' with her anger in that quiet way of hers. You know, too busy in the kitchen to talk, work to wrap up in her studio, meetings. Anything to keep from blowin' up at me. S'pose I should be grateful, but her silence drives me nuts, and she knows it." He laughed then. "I'm hopin' she'll calm down by the time we get there, especially now that Jack's been found. By the way, our girls are coming with us."

Cooper's breath stilled. "Bring the girls here? That's insane."

"We don't have any choice. Clarice Ambrose fell steppin' out of the bathtub and broke her ankle. She's gonna be laid up a while. Braeden's granddad is out of the country, another European tour, and Mother and Bull are in the midst of wedding plans."

"But—"

"It'll be all right, Coop. My girls already have passports so that's not an issue, and I'll see to their safety. You know there's no way Braeden will stay home now that she knows Angeline is alive. She's pissed, but that doesn't stop her from caring."

"Okay. I'll call Bernard as soon as we hang up, and go get Jack and Angeline. When are you flying back?"

"We've got a few things to see to first, for sure tonight. I'll leave you a message as soon as I know."

"Bernard'll drive me to the airport."

"Don't bother him. We'll need a rental car while we're there anyway."

"See you when you get here then." They disconnected, and Cooper left his bottle of aspirin next to his full mug of coffee cooling on the table. He headed down the steps and crossed the yard to the beach.

Four additional targets, and two of them children. Damn it to infernal hell. How would he keep them safe?

White sand sifted between his toes as he walked the shoreline and reconnoitered the immediate area. The rear of Angeline's home fronted the ocean which afforded no security. Nothing prevented a boat from dropping anchor in the shallow waters, allowing Voorhees' henchmen to row ashore, gain entry to the house, rape and murder the young housekeeper, snatch the boy, and be on their way. It probably happened in a matter of minutes.

Not for Rose Cassell.

Wind rustled the trees, and flowering shrubs painted the shoreline in Technicolor greens and reds, purples and yellows, as far as the eye could see. A wave rippled over his feet. Orange and black fiddler crabs scrabbled in and out of the infinite network of spindly mangrove roots.

Life as usual on the island of Jacqueme Dominique.

Angeline and Jack were easy prey amidst all this splendor— and he had allowed Voorhees to find them by forgetting about the Dutchman's need to even an old score.

But this wasn't a time for guilt. He checked his watch again and dialed Bernard.

Half an hour later, the green Voyager pulled up in front of the hospital.

The driver waved his big hand in front of Cooper's face when he pulled out his wallet. "Bernard cannot take your money this time. This is a day of celebration for the young mister and his mother. My fare is his welcome home gift."

"Okay." Cooper nodded. "But only this once."

"Bernard should wait here while you go in and get them, yes?"

"That'd be great., and Bernard..." Cooper touched the big man's arm through the open driver's window. "Thanks. You know, for bringing Jack home."

"I have told you before, Mr. Cooper, Bernard is a lucky man. Finding the boy proves this, yes?"

Cooper smiled. Hell, yes. He turned and sprinted up the hospital steps two at a time.

Angeline and Jack waited in the lobby. She hurried toward him. "We didn't think you'd ever get here." Her face showed more color, but the dark half moons beneath her eyes spoke of worry and fatigue. She tugged the boy from behind her. "Jack, you remember Mr. Cooper from last night, don't you?"

Calling him Mr. Cooper rubbed a raw spot.

The kid nodded. "You rode with me in the police car," he said.

"I sure did. But today, we're riding in Bernard's green taxi." He hoped some day soon, the boy would associate him with something other than a ride in a cool cruiser. "Come on, buddy." He took one of Jack's hands, Angeline took the other. "Let's get you home."

Chapter Seven

They had been home less than an hour when Angeline joined Cooper on the ground-floor gallery. "I wanted to thank you for hanging around last night," she said. "I appreciate it."

He didn't need thanks, he needed the truth. "You look tired."

"I am. But it's a good tired, you know." She plucked a brown leaf from amidst the blue, funnel-shaped blossoms and waxy foliage in a huge terracotta pot, then dropped the leaf off the gallery's edge. "I should plant more of these," she said, and faced him. "Did you know Europeans believed periwinkles possess the ability to ward off evil? The French called them violets of the sorcerers, magic plants." Her voice held a trace of melancholy. "We could use some magic." After plucking several more leaves, she dusted her hands. "How 'bout you, Cooper?" she said. "Get any sleep last night?"

Just like that, she reverted to their previous conversation. He foolishly hoped for a little of that magic—and the one answer that kept him from enfolding her in his arms. "I'll stretch out this afternoon. Where's Jack?"

"In his room, and none too happy I broke the chair at his

play table. The red one *would* be his favorite. Right now, he's inventorying his other toys, since I'm so careless." Apprehension sharpened her laughter. "Maybe he'll allow me in his room again when he's...oh, I don't know...thirty? By the way, I'm supposed to tell you that you can come up anytime. He says he's got something to show you."

He hated the awkwardness between them, but there wasn't much he could do about it. Magic or no magic, she was the one keeping secrets. "Yeah?"

"I think Jack's talking about his ant farm," she said. "It's his pride and joy, so make a big deal."

A cell phone emitted its muffled tune, interrupting their conversation.

"Is that your phone?" he said.

She walked toward him. "Mine's upstairs. I thought it was yours."

He shook his head and began searching the array of colorful pots that crowded the narrow gallery where the sound seemed to come from, while trying to place the familiar melody.

She assisted in the hunt. "Don't stop ringing."

"This is nuts." He recognized the song as he snatched the phone from the base of a potted Allamanda, its yellow trumpet-like blooms spilling over one edge of the gazebo.

Vintage Phil Collins. "Another Day in Paradise." *Voorhees.*

Cooper almost dropped the phone trying to get it open. He turned his back on Angeline. "Your beef is with me, you sick son of a bitch."

The Dutchman clicked his tongue. "An emotional man is a careless man, Teacher. You should know this."

"I'll give you emotion, Voorhees. Name the place. Or do you only go after small boys and defenseless women?"

Angeline came around the front of him. The color she'd regained in her complexion all but disappeared.

"Ah, yes. Little Rose," Voorhees said. "She was an unexpected treat, that one. Did you know she offered me the boy while I was inside her? Begged me to take him." He laughed again. "I believe she would have dragged young Jack down the stairs herself if I told her she could live."

Angeline moved closer. "What does he want?"

Cooper motioned her to be quiet, then watched her eyes blaze as anger erupted inside her.

"Is that Angeline?" Voorhees said. "I'll bet she's twice the fuck the little whore was, eh?"

Bile rose in Cooper's throat. "Shut the hell up."

The Dutchman's wicked laughter filled the line. "Perhaps we can share the woman. I'll play gracious host and let you have her first. You haven't said, Teacher, is the boy yours? Or did someone else sire a son from your woman while you were...estranged?" He snorted. "Oh my. I suppose that makes her someone else's woman, doesn't it?"

Angeline snatched the phone from his hand. She marched across the yard and gallery, jerked the door open, and stormed inside.

Cooper followed.

"You listen to me, you perverted freak." Her words spewed contempt. "If you even think of getting near my child again, I'll kill you myself. Do you understand? I'll kill you with my own—"

By the time Cooper wrestled the phone from her icy fingers, Voorhees had disconnected.

"He's messing with the wrong woman." Angeline grabbed a checkered cookbook from the kitchen counter and hurled it across the room. The book clonked against the fireplace, then dropped like a leaden bird to the hearth. It's metal ring binder popped open, spilling pages. "I'll kill him." She fisted her hands. "I swear I will."

It dizzied Cooper trying to keep up with the conversation while she tromped from one room to another. A geometric-print pillow from the sofa in the great room suffered the same fate as the cookbook, another and another, until he caught Angeline's arm. "He won't get near Jack again, Slick. I promise."

"Why should I believe you?" She wrestled free, grabbed a pillow from the floor and tossed it back on the sofa, retracing her steps. "Because Voorhees spared Griffie MacDonald? You showed me the photographs at Raison Belle-Amandine, remember? If I was naïve before, I'm not now. Or maybe I am. I stupidly thought

I could make a new life for us here, a safe life." She picked up the last pillow. "Until you showed up."

Cooper took the pillow from her, wishing like crazy for some of that magic she spoke of outside. "Look, I know you're scared." He dropped the pillow on the couch. "Hell, I'm scared, too. But I need an answer from you before this goes any further, and it has nothing to do with this damn phone call or Voorhees. I held off asking as long as Jack was missing." The Dutchman had pissed him off, and Cooper was trying not to take it out on her. But enough was enough. There were issues they needed to deal with, and the boy's paternity topped the list.

Angeline went to the kitchen.

Cooper followed, watching as she gathered the pages of the cookbook, then jammed them inside the red and white cover.

"What did you hold off asking as long as Jack was missing?" She wouldn't look at him.

"Is Jack my son?"

Her hands stilled. Anger punctuated her next statement with resentment. "I wish you'd never come here."

"You have a right to your feelings. So do I." Nausea burned a hole in his gut; he repeated his question. "Is the boy my son, Angeline? I have a right to know."

"Jack is my son, Cooper." She crossed the kitchen and slammed the disheveled cookbook on the granite countertop. "*My son*." Salt and pepper shakers rattled. A beige candle on a carved wooden holder toppled over. "He belongs to me."

"You're not answering the question." By not answering his question, she did answer it.

Hands still grasping the cookbook, Angeline began to cry. The strain of the last few days, the not knowing, and then the unexpected relief, poured out of her in breathless sobs that rattled Cooper to his core.

"Okay, it's okay." He moved toward her but held back actually wrapping his arms around her. "We'll find time to sort through the Jack stuff later." The Jack stuff? What else could he call it? The boy's paternity was no longer in question. Cooper reached out and thumbed a tear from her cheek. "Right now, I've got to figure a way to flush out Voorhees and end this nightmare."

"Wait." She grabbed his arm when he turned to leave. "The cell phone, we should give it to the police."

He gazed down at her hand, then into her eyes. "This phone is Voorhees' way of keeping in touch without being traced. It stays with me."

"The phone's untraceable, how?"

He studied the make and model. "The phone is most likely stolen, or purchased black market. Every time Voorhees replaces the SIM card, also stolen, this particular model automatically changes its IMEI number."

She wiped her face with the heel of her hand. "I'm supposed to know what that means?"

"International Mobile Equipment Identity, a code unique to each device. Once the SIM card changes, the unit randomly generates a new and unique IMEI number."

She sniffed. "I hate cell phones."

He understood her sentiment, especially now. "It only sounds complicated. The IMEI number identifies the unit, not the unit's user."

"I don't understand."

"If the phone's bought legit, the subscriber is identified by the transmission of an identity number stored on the SIM card. The illegitimate user changes phones by removing the card from one unit and putting it in another. Thus the phone becomes untraceable, in theory anyway."

She raised her hands in front of her. "Stop. I'll never understand all that tech talk. I'm not sure I want to. Voorhees planted the phone. We know that. What we need to figure out is why. I mean, he's already returned Jack. What is his motive for staying in touch? What more does he want from us?"

"I don't know yet." Cooper had his suspicions. "But, until we do know, I keep the phone."

Angeline's straightened posture told him that she accepted the status quo. For now. "What happens next?"

"You let someone else run your shop while you stay here with Jack. That way I'll know where both of you are, and that you're safe."

She nodded. He knew mentioning the boy's safety would do

the trick.

Angeline left the kitchen, entered the great hall, and headed for the stairs. Hesitating on the bottom step, she kept her back to him. "The name on our son's birth certificate," she said, "is Charles Jackson Cooper."

Angeline sat near the head of her burled walnut four-poster bed. She leaned back and rubbed her temple. A headache inched toward the indented scar in her right eyebrow where she had stitches after the New Orleans' accident. Cooper's reaction to her telling him Jack was his son puzzled her. She had expected anger, accusations, and name-calling. He'd done none of that.

She dumped a shoebox on the bed beside her and tossed its carcass on the floor with the other six empty boxes. Anger she could deal with.

Anger might expunge some of her guilt—and oh, how she needed it erased.

She didn't see how Cooper stayed on his feet and made phone call after phone call. He took endless notes, and poured over island maps and charts. Watching him added to her angst.

Maybe this rabid use of energy was his way of dealing with the stress and uncertainty. He was, after all, a man who reveled in life's minutiae, in numbers and lists. Attention to detail kept Charlie Cooper's head on straight.

More power to him.

Angeline sorted the box's contents and separated them into piles: postcards and letters, photographs, ticket stubs, and construction paper greeting cards. Normally she hated busy work. But normal was now a word foreign in their lives.

At least Jack slept in his room, seemingly unaffected by the events of the last few days.

She stacked a pink Mother's Day card, a red and green one from the Christmas when Jack turned three, and then a folded white Valentine, its blue heart cut and pasted by small, clumsy fingers.

There was never a Father's Day card. She shoved aside festering remorse and separated a photograph from the others. Protecting Jack was the right thing to do. It was her job, and it had always been the right thing. The events since Cooper found them proved that beyond any guilt-produced doubt.

She set another photo aside and tried to keep her mind off the phone call from Voorhees, and the fact that no other calls followed. Cooper said he wouldn't let the Dutchman near their boy, and she desperately wanted to believe him, to have faith. But she'd sensed someone watching the house all evening. She glanced beyond the tufted window seat where dusk settled lethargically as if this nightmare somehow evaporated into the humid Caribbean air. She saw nothing beyond the gazebo and weathered fence but sea and sand, and the eco-friendly mangroves that flourished on the island.

Nerves were getting the better of her.

A short while ago, Cooper deposited one of Zeller's officers downstairs and left without explanation, leaving her feelings jumbled. Not that he owed her an explanation. Turn-about was fair play, after all.

A sharp rap sounded at the door. She assumed it was the young cop and called, "Come in."

The door eased open.

Angeline stood. Letters and ticket stubs rained over the empty shoeboxes. "Brag?" She crossed the room and embraced her childhood friend.

Braeden's shoulders stiffened at her touch. "The policeman let us in."

Angeline stepped back and tried to gauge her expression. "I wasn't sure you'd come."

A myriad of emotions passed over the petite redhead's ashen face: hurt, anger, relief, confusion. "I came because Montgomery convinced me it was the right thing to do," Braeden said. "I don't know if I'll stay. I'm seriously mad at you." She skirted Angeline, stopped in front of the window, and stared out at the sea. "He said I should give you a chance to explain. Everybody deserves a second chance." She sat on the window seat, her back board-stiff, hands fisted in her lap. "So, I'm listening. Explain."

"Oh, Brag. I'm exhausted. I can't do this now. Please don't ask me to."

"Come on, Angie. Give it a shot." Braeden's words remained

clipped and cool. "You were always good at improvisation. I'm a captive audience because I gave Montgomery my word, and my word is worth something."

In all the years they'd known each other, Angeline never recalled her friend spewing sarcasm. Certainly, she'd never been the object of it. She returned to her spot on the bed and picked up the crude white Valentine, needing something of Jack's to hold onto; something as solid as her love for him—and her fear of loving Cooper.

God, it seemed she'd run on fear for an eternity. Braeden was right; it was time to set things straight.

"I don't know where to begin," she whispered.

"Let me help." Braeden stood again, her eyes narrowed with soul-deep hurt. "There were these two friends, you see. They grew up together, and endured the best and worst of times. Pimples, braces, freckles, and bad haircuts. Boyfriends who were worse than the haircuts. They clung to each other when one of them cried herself to sleep every night after her parents died." She crossed the room, plucked a book from the bookcase, and studied the title before thrusting it back in its niche. "Together forever..."

When her voice broke, guilt gnawed at Angeline. How could she have been so blind to the hurt she caused Braeden, so callous in letting it endure for years?

"They wrote that sentiment in their yearbooks so even when they became rich and famous," Braeden said, "they wouldn't forget. I still have my yearbook, Angie." She faced Angeline and waved her hand toward the crowded shelves. "Where's yours?"

"I didn't forget, Brag. Not like that. Not on purpose. I never, *ever* set out to hurt you." They were suddenly sixteen again; the year Braeden tutored her to a *C-* in Algebra, and Angeline gave her the nickname. Not because Braeden bragged about her academic proficiency, but because she didn't.

Then they were twenty. One of them taking her first assignment as a fledgling reporter, creating fictional characters in the dead of night and dreaming of best sellers' lists; the other scoring her first international magazine cover and a big paycheck.

Braeden returned to the window seat, and Angeline mustered her courage. "I died, but the doctors were able to get me back.

At least, part of me." The words poured out. "I didn't remember the accident, or the time in emergency, or hospitals, or flights. Nothing, and no one. Transient Global Amnesia, the doctors called it. Obscure glimpses came to me now and then, nonsensical snippets, but nothing concrete. Mathieu Fournier filled in the gaps...his version of the gaps anyway."

She dragged an upholstered slipper chair close to the window and sat a few feet in front of Braeden. "At some point, I remembered shopping with you in the French Quarter the morning of the accident, trying on absurd hats, and buying that silly designer purse. Clearly a knock-off that I paid too much for. I remembered eating sugary pralines from a white paper sack. We licked the stickiness from our fingers."

She leaned forward and propped her elbows on her knees. "The months before the accident were blank. Then more snippets, like I dreamt someone else's life. Then months of pain, followed by grueling hours in rehab and re-learning the simplest tasks. I couldn't even tie my shoes, Brag, or recite the alphabet. There were times I swore dying would have been easier." She straightened. "Don't get me wrong, I'm not asking you to feel sorry for me. I wouldn't. I don't deserve it."

Angeline reached for Braeden's hand and inwardly sighed relief when she didn't withdraw. "I didn't remember Cooper for most of my pregnancy," she continued. "I assumed the baby I carried was Mathieu's, and he let me believe it. That we'd been a couple. He wanted me to believe it."

"But why?"

"I suppose he wanted it to be true. Mathieu was in love with me. Maybe he still is, in his way."

"But you and he never..."

Angeline laughed, albeit nervously. "Had sex, Mathieu and me? No, never. He's older than my dad, Brag."

"I still don't understand how he thought he could get away with the lies."

"Because I didn't remember, Mathieu figured he would create memories for me, for us. And I bought into it. Then I went into labor with Jack, and bam, there was Cooper's face stuck in my brain. Followed by a flood of memories and heartache. Don't ask me how a baby survived that horrible accident. I hadn't a clue. I still don't. But Jack was my miracle. In a strange way, he kept Cooper close to me. He gave me purpose."

"You must hate Mathieu Fournier."

"That's the oddest part, I don't hate him. When I fully recovered my memory I knew Cooper was Jack's father. I hadn't been with another man for months before you and I came to New Orleans. You know that. But I couldn't be sure how Cooper would react to the news. He believed I was dead. The whole world believed it. And frankly, I was in no shape to deal with the media circus that would accompany the revelation that I survived...and had a child. I mean, how bizarre is that? It's every grocery store rag's fantasy headline. So I plunged into rehab, and worked as hard as I could to make a life for Jack and me. Before I knew it, a year passed, and another. Then Mathieu told me Cooper was looking for me, and I still didn't know what to do."

"You could've told Cooper."

"It's so easy to say that now, to see it. But not then. I didn't know how he'd react, what he would do. So I took the coward's way out and ran."

"Do you still see Mathieu?"

"I told you, we had no relationship, nothing intimate. He calls, and stays in touch. He sees that Jack and I want for nothing. But I believe guilt drives Mathieu, not love." Guilt was emotional baggage Angeline knew all too well. She'd carried it long enough., and now that Cooper was here, that biting guilt manifested itself in anger.

Anger at Mathieu Fournier—and herself. But, most especially, anger at Cooper.

"Why didn't he look for me sooner, Brag? Why did Cooper wait so long?"

Braeden rose from the window seat and walked to the bed. She picked up a Christmas card, then turned. "This has all been such a mess," she said. "Like a snowball that never stopped rolling. Cooper got caught in the drama of our lives. He helped us pick up the pieces after Thomas Seaborn's death. Through Montgomery's recovery, my difficult pregnancy, and Maggie's birth. Why didn't you get in touch with him, Angie? You could've. Why didn't you call me? You let us all believe you were dead."

"I did, and I realize that's hard to digest. Certainly, hard to forgive. But you have to see the situation from my perspective, Brag. I needed to think of Jack. The world considered me dead which, in this weird way, created a safe haven for the two of us, a kind of normalcy. If so much as a whisper got out that I was alive, well, you know what the paparazzi are like. My body needed mending. My feelings needed sorting. Memories of Cooper's revenge for Voorhees hung over me like a blade. A foreboding I couldn't shake. Before my accident, all he could see or talk or think about was finding the man and killing him." She hesitated. "If only he had."

Angeline stood. She set the chair aside and paced a strip of hardwood floor illuminated by slivers of moonlight from the window. "There were so many variables out of my control. In the beginning, Mathieu took it upon himself to protect me from cameras, publicity, and prying eyes. How could I fault him for that? He eventually enlisted Nick's help, but only because of Nick's orthopedic skill. He's the best in his field, and I needed him. No one knew, or could even say how I would come out of all this, how much damage was permanent. My dad had his heart attack right after the accident, then the stroke, the additional shock of finding me alive might've killed him then. Mom was beyond exhaustion. Everyone needed protecting." She pulled the open drapes further aside. "As soon as my parents and brothers were strong enough to learn the truth, Nick told them. He and Brent fought over it."

The moonlit sea glistened. Unable to shake the sensation that someone watched from beyond the gazebo, Angeline shut the drapes. "My brothers were so close before," she said. "But this situation left a wedge between them. They don't talk about it, but I'm not sure Brent will ever truly forgive Nick, and I hate that."

"Nick should have told me, too."

"He gave his word, Brag." She sat next to Braeden on the window seat. "I forced him, medical ethics. I was Nick's patient. By then, you and Montgomery were married. You'd been through so much. The stalking, then the shooting. He almost died. Knowing about Jack and me meant you keeping our secret from Montgomery, or Montgomery lying to Cooper. I couldn't ask that of you, either of you. You had your girls and this perfect life. Secrets didn't belong there." Her gaze met Braeden's. "And frankly, I wasn't ready. Not for Jack's confusion, and Cooper's wrath, for dealing with my own mixed-up emotions. I screwed up, and I can't begin to tell you how sorry I am."

For the longest moment, they simply stared at each other. Finally, Angeline reached over and brushed a tear from Braeden's freckled cheek. "Please don't hate me, Brag."

"I came here ready to be so angry with you," Braeden said. "Now I feel like life cheated all of us. Mathieu Fournier cheated us, but so did you. We have so much time to make up, and I want that. Really I do."

"So do I."

"We'll start with baby steps then. I'll get to know Jack, and you do the same with my girls. They're down the hall, and we'd better go check on them. I think I heard Jack say something about an ant farm?"

"Your girls are here? Are you sure it's safe? I mean, I'd love to see them. It's a dream come true, the perfect homecoming for Jack. Oh, Brag. Thank you."

Someone knocked softly at the door.

"Braeden, honey? You guys need to eat something."

Montgomery.

Both women laughed, albeit tension-filled.

"He's trying to make up for not telling me about you as soon as he found out," Braeden said.

The door opened; Angeline stood.

"Can we come in?" The detective crossed the threshold. A red-haired, freckle-faced little girl held his hand.

She glimpsed from mother to child, then back. "Maggie?"

Braeden nodded. "The one and only Magnificent Mags."

Angeline breathed deeply to keep the moment from overwhelming her. "Come on, Maggie." She walked past a smiling Montgomery, slipped the child's hand out of his and into hers. "Let's go see Jack's ant farm."

Night vision binoculars suspended from a thin strap around

his neck, the Onlooker observed the two women from the deserted beach below. When they had closed the curtains, it was his signal to leave. He was tired of these dark clothes that made him one with the night. They were heavy and hot, itchy from the sand. Even the breeze drifting in from the sea offered minimal relief.

Crouching behind his favorite cluster of mangroves, he lit a cigarette, dragged the cell phone from his pocket, inhaled deep, and then punched in Voorhees' number. "Not much happening here," he whispered. "The women are still upstairs. American cop's in the kitchen. I see him through the windows." He sat back on his haunches and blew a wispy plume of smoke toward the sea. "There are more children," he said, and grinned. "Little girls."

Voorhees sounded pleased. He constantly went on about how long he'd waited for this opportunity, the right moment, the perfect set of circumstances to even his score with Cooper.

"You can count on me, boss." The Onlooker stood, crushed his cigarette in the wet sand, then ground a young fiddler crab into a protruding root, laughing at the crunching sound. "Another half-hour, yes. I'll do it."

Damn crabs were a nuisance and overran the island. But he'd tolerate them again tomorrow night, and the next if need be, because of his assignment. Now that Voorhees discovered Cooper's Achilles heel, the game would heat up, and the rewards promised the Onlooker were incalculable.

Chapter Eight

Cooper stood on Angeline's front gallery at noon the next day. Gulls cried overhead, gray silhouettes against another brilliant sun. Temperatures reached mid-eighties.

Before he could knock, Montgomery opened the door. "Braeden wondered when you'd come around."

"Where is everyone?" Cooper spent a restless night in his hotel room, thinking about all that had happened, what might still happen, and how much he wanted Angeline despite his residual anger regarding her deceit.

He didn't fall asleep until dawn.

The detective opened the door wider and waved at the taxi driver. "Bernard's not coming in?"

"He's on the clock. We'll use your rental to get around."

They closed the door and walked shoulder to shoulder down the wide hall.

"Braeden's in the kitchen," Montgomery said. "The girls are out back with Angeline and Jack. Good looking kid, by the way. Lucky he takes after his mother."

Cooper smiled in spite of the uncertainty about his relationship

with Angeline. Charles Jackson Cooper. Today he had a son. *Wow.*
"You know?"

"Angeline told Braeden, Braeden told me." Mongomery folded his arms across his chest. "Better get used to it. By the way, Chief Zeller wants to see us about that passport you failed to surrender. I promised we'd stop by around four. It's important to mind your *P's* and *Q's* with a guy like Zeller, Coop. He's territorial, almost has to be, and you never know when you'll need his department's help again."

Cooper stopped next to the stairs and faced his friend. "I don't need lectures on police protocol, Sandman."

The detective offered a wry smile. "Wouldn't dream of it." He turned toward the kitchen. "You hungry? We ordered takeout. Did you know there's a KFC that delivers right around the corner from your hotel? Hope you like thighs and biscuits. That's about all the kids left."

It was Montgomery's not so subtle change of subject.

"Did Angeline eat?"

The detective's laughter echoed in the sparsely decorated hall. "Like a horse."

Braeden rushed out of the kitchen, wiping her hands on a blue dishtowel. "Charlie!" She raised on her tiptoes, hugged him, then kissed his cheek. "Food's on the table. I'll get you some iced tea. Sweetened or unsweetened?"

Cooper moved to the nearest window overlooking the backyard and peered out. "Unsweetened for me. Sweetened for her. She needs the sugar." Angeline wore a pink shirt with white slacks cuffed at the bottom, her endless legs tapering to bare feet. She waded in shallow water with two little redheads. "She and I need to talk." He turned to Braeden. "Maybe you should call her in?"

"Maybe you should go out and get her," she replied. "I'm still mad. Oh, and take this." She snatched a pink cardigan sweater from the back of the deep brown sofa and shoved it at him. "Angie keeps rubbing her arms like she's cold." She latched onto Montgomery's elbow when he started to follow Cooper to the back door. "We'll bring the tea out," she said. "Tell Angie we're taking the kids downtown in forty-five minutes. Souvenir shopping and dessert. And no, the two of you can't come."

Cooper breathed a sigh of relief. He and Angeline needed the chance to talk and figure out where things stood between them. He watched her from the gallery for a few seconds before heading down to the beach. She seemed blissfully happy, and he longed to share in her euphoria.

And he could allow himself to—once he permanently removed Voorhees from the picture.

On the beach, Angeline took the sweater from him, slipped her arms in the sleeves, and fastened a couple buttons. "I wasn't sure you'd come back," she said. "Not that I blame you. This is so much more than you bargained for when you came looking for me." She shifted her gaze to the laughing children. "Brag brought her girls, Maggie and little Tulip. Aren't they the sweetest things?"

Cooper surprised himself with a genuine smile. "She and Montgomery are planning to take the kids souvenir shopping in forty-five minutes."

Angeline turned toward the fence. "I should change then."

He caught her hand. "Uh-uh. We don't get to go."

She frowned. "Letting Jack out of my sight won't be easy."

"He's safe with Montgomery, and they won't go far. Braeden wants to check out your shop."

Angeline shoved the sweater's sleeves to her elbows. Prerequisite to digging in the sand, he supposed. "I hope she likes it," she said. "You know the shop's name, *Pearls*, comes from the lead character in her children's books."

She picked up Annie, and several feet away, Maggie greeted them with a conch shell she'd found. The girls stood with Angeline, laughing and inspecting the perfectly formed shell, listening for sea sounds in its pinkish hollow.

Cooper walked across the beach, ten feet or so, to where Jack squatted, scooping sand and shoveling it into a green pail. Being a dad scared the hell out of him, but he was anxious to get started. He sat in the packed sand. "How you doing, sport?"

"Good." The boy poured water in the pail from a smaller yellow bucket. He wore denim shorts and a red t-shirt with a row of surfboards across the front.

Cooper steadied the larger pail with one hand. "I like your shirt."

"Mommy picked it," Jack said. "I like my orange one with the dolphins." He stirred the mixture of water and sand with a stick.

"Why don't you change into the orange shirt then? You have time, and I can help. You can wear it shopping with the girls. Bet they like dolphins, too."

"Nah." Jack dumped the concoction and started again. "Don't got it no more," he said. "The man took it."

Cooper released the pail and rose to his knees. "What man?"

"You know." The boy drew a letter in the sand with the stick, *J* for Jack. His next words were barely audible. "The man on the boat."

Angeline never said Jack wasn't wearing the same clothes when they found him. But she'd been with Cooper at his hotel, and busy in her shop earlier in the day. If she didn't come home in between, she wouldn't know what her child wore when Voorhees stole him. His heart stilled. Why did Voorhees find it necessary to change Jack's clothes?

Jack drew another letter. "The other boy got it," he said, not looking up from his task.

Cooper placed his hand on the stick and stopped the *A* before he could finish. "There was another boy on the boat with you, Jack? You sure about that?"

Jack's eyes grew wide; his face sobered. "Yes."

"What did the other boy look like, do you remember?"

His small shoulders rose and fell in an ambiguous half-sigh. "Like me."

"And this other boy, do you remember his name?"

"He didn't say nothin' to me." He finished the *A* and started on *C*. "Mostly he cried for his mommy, and I covered my ears."

Braeden called from the open back door, and after a minute or two, disappeared inside with Maggie and Anne in tow.

Cooper stood. He brushed off the seat of his jeans, and then Jack's shorts. "Let me help you with that." He and the boy gathered the buckets and sticks.

Angeline met them at the edge of the mangrove cluster.

"I'll see him off," Cooper said, unwilling to relinquish Jack's hand.

She opened her mouth to protest, closed it, then nodded. "Have a good time, sweetie." She kissed Jack's forehead. "Listen to Braeden and Montgomery, okay? Stay close to them."

Cooper led the boy through the rickety gate and around the side of the house. Angeline was right. It was damn hard seeing Jack leave the safety he could best provide.

After a few minutes, he returned to the beach to find Angeline and debated whether he should tell her about the other boy. She sat on the steps of the gazebo, staring out at the sea. He climbed the steps and eased in behind her.

She angled her head slightly and gazed up at him. "I can't help thinking about Rose," she said.

"I'm sorry that happened." He decided not to tell her about the missing boy until he knew more.

"There's a crew coming tomorrow to clean the sunroom," she continued. "I almost forgot what happened in there until Jack questioned why I locked the doors. I didn't know what to tell him. We've been too busy for him to miss Rose." She leaned into the juncture of Cooper's thighs. The back of her head rested against his abdomen, her elbow on his knee. "I don't want to be here when the cleaners come." She absentmindedly brushed sand from his ankle. "I don't want Brag or the children here either."

He was quite certain she didn't realize how the intimate gesture awakened the need in him. "I'll see to it," he offered. Need snowballed to hunger, and he was a starving man. "Where will you and Braeden take the kids?" He intended to know where they were every second of every day, from here on out.

"I don't know." Angeline seemed to mull possible itineraries. "The island doesn't have a mall. Jack loves to look at the fishing boats, and sometimes the workers let him climb aboard. But after what's happened, I don't want him near the docks."

He didn't either. "I think that's wise."

She dusted sand from his fingers.

He turned his palm up and closed his hand around hers. She appeared thinner, more frail than the woman he remembered from New Orleans. But, having watched her these last few days, he knew exactly the opposite was true. She remained one of the strongest women he knew, and his admiration for her had increased tenfold.

"There's a quaint fire station," she said. "And a small museum with a saltwater aquarium. Fish and seashells and," she shuddered, "snakes. Lots of yucky stuff. Both get high marks from Jack. I'm sure he'd love showing the girls around."

They sat for a few minutes, hands clasped, looking out over the ocean dotted with sailboats and the occasional tanker or fishing trawler. Until today, this very moment, he hadn't realized how much he had missed her. Not only the sexual intimacy, but knowing she was within easy reach.

"What happened to us, Slick?" he said finally.

"I don't know." She released his hand and pulled herself up using the railing, slow, awkward; the fluid motion from when he'd first met her, when she reigned at the top of the modeling game, now gone. He feared she'd go inside, perhaps run again, but she sat on the step next to him so they could see each other while they talked. "Guess I got scared," she said.

"Of me?"

She placed her hand on his cheek. "Of loving you."

He turned his head and kissed her palm.

"Of *not* loving you," she added. "If that makes any sense."

Her hand remained on his cheek, as did the scent of Jasmine he'd dreamt of during all those lonely nights. The want in him grew.

"I'd been modeling since my teens," she continued. "In this business, you get a reputation for showing emotion, heaven forbid you give your heart away, and someone crushes you. You were different than the men I'd been with. You didn't want to stop at sex, Cooper, you wanted me. A relationship. The whole package, blemishes and all. It scared me to death. It still does, I suppose. We only knew each other a short while. You hadn't seen me in my world, not really. What if you didn't like the other me, the woman who played to the cameras? What if you found her shallow and self-indulgent and—"

"No." His hand speared the air. He didn't want to hear her say it, even though that was how he saw her, at first, before that final weekend. Before he told her about Griffie's kidnapping and saw how she reacted to the boy's death and his parents' grief. "We could've worked on that," he said. "You told me the gig with Fournier was your last."

"It would've been." She laughed then, and raised a hand to the scar on her face. "I guess it was."

"Don't." He brushed her hand away from her cheek. "I don't give a damn about your looks. Hell, I carry my own scars."

"Yes, you do, and that was another part of our problem. As long as Voorhees lives, you can't commit to anyone. I understand it now. Believe me. I hate Voorhees for what he did to Rose, and what he could have done to Jack. What he did to you."

"I hate that I brought him into your lives."

"I know you do." She folded her hands under her chin and rocked a little.

"But the truth is, if I could change it, Slick, I don't know that I would. If Voorhees hadn't followed me here, would you have told me about Jack?"

She chewed on her lower lip for an extended moment. "I'd like to think, yes. But I honestly don't know."

"God, we're a mess."

"We've certainly made our share of mistakes."

"Yeah, well." He draped his arm around her shoulders and pulled her close. "I won't make another one by leaving you and Jack."

"And I won't run again."

"So, where do we go from here?" he said.

She stood and brushed off the seat of her slacks. "I'm going up to straighten Jack's room while he's gone. He's still got me exiled."

"Want help?"

"Sure." Still clinging to the rail, she offered her hand and pulled him up. "Did you eat?"

"Not hungry." Actually, starved was a better word. But food wouldn't satisfy the yearning Cooper suffered.

"I ate enough for both of us."

He noticed her pink sweater on the lounge chair, next to her untouched glass of tea. "Want me to get those?"

She shook her head. "I'll bring them in later. I need to finish

Jack's room before he gets home."

"Wait a second." He took her hand at the back door. "Just so you know..."

Her right eyebrow raised in a questioning slant that highlighted the small, puckered scar above her eye. "What?"

He opened the door. "I went back to teaching two years ago, part-time, undergraduates. No tenure track this time. I didn't want the hassle."

"I'm glad for you, Cooper. Really." She stepped inside. "Going back in the classroom is huge. Was it as hard as you expected?"

He thought about it. "Tough question. I don't do the summer camps for kids anymore. Maybe someday I will, but not yet." He pulled the door shut, flipped the lock, and took one last glimpse at the shoreline before following her into the great hall and up the stairs.

"Goodness," Angeline said when she opened the door to Jack's room. "Someone's already cleaned. Either that, or my Untidy Thomas has turned into a neatnik." She laughed. "My money's on Braeden."

She turned too fast; they collided, and she grasped Cooper's forearms for balance. Time froze for a fraction of a second, a heartbeat. A blink. Her hands eased to the nape of his neck. She coaxed his head forward. "I'm so lucky," she whispered, her lips inches from his. "I have Jack. We have Braeden and Montgomery and their two precious girls in our lives, and we have...you. We do have you, don't we, Cooper?"

"I'm not going anywhere."

They kissed, and the world around them faded. Angeline backed him into the hall, unfastening the buttons on his shirt. He sucked in a deep breath and damn near choked on it when her fingernails grazed his chest.

He slipped the pale pink polo shirt over her head and stared at the lacy bra beneath. Scooping her in his arms, he dipped to open her bedroom door. He kicked it shut once they were inside, and set her down before he flipped the lock.

The drapes were drawn. They left the room cool and shadowed, and blocked out the heat. Blocked out the world and its miserable predicaments: good guys, bad guys, missing children, and evil

Dutchmen. For a moment, at least, the lousy lot of them held no place here.

Angeline's gaze fixed on his. She unfastened her bra, let it drop. Cooper tugged the zipper on her slacks, she the one on his jeans. Clothing pooled around their ankles. He nibbled her ear lobe, fed his insatiable hunger on the erogenous zones on her neck and in her shoulder's hollow, and reveled in her shivered response.

"I want to forget these past few days," she whispered. "If only for a little while."

He stood and bent her back on the bed, devouring one breast, kneading the other. Straddling her hips, he eased into her. She arched her back, her hands on his buttocks, the greed in her eyes declaring she intended to have it all this time. He thrust deep, hard, again. The fire burned hotter, the all-consuming flames higher.

Need, hunger, time, and space.

Only one thing remained relevant: *consummation.*

An hour later, she rested her head on his shoulder, her hand on his chest, leg draped over his thigh. "Wow," she whispered.

He promised himself the next time their love-making would be slow and languorous, each second savored. "Yeah," he said. "Wow pretty much sums it up." He ran a finger along her collarbone, and then the creamy curve of her shoulder. His fingers stopped at the small welt six or so inches above her elbow as a memory surfaced. Braeden carried a similar scar from the day of the auto-pedestrian accident, and Joan Baines, a friend and emergency room nurse in New Orleans, had speculated both scars resulted from a bullet— perhaps the same bullet.

Weeks after the accident, Joan expressed her suspicions to Montgomery, and then to Cooper. Off the record, of course.

He nuzzled Angeline's earlobe. "Tell me about the accident, Slick."

She straightened, drew up her knees, and wrapped her arms around them. "My memory's like a crossword puzzle, Cooper, with only two-thirds of the words filled in."

"Then tell me the parts you remember." The urgency to push her nagged him. "It's important." He hated taking her to a place in their past that was so painful.

She sighed. "Okay." She seemed to collect her thoughts. "My work for Fournier wrapped up. Brag and I shopped on Canal Street. Nothing unusual about either of those. We started back to the hotel for lunch, and to pick up our luggage. Emotionally, I was all over the place. Giddy the photo shoot went well and the ad campaign launched successfully, sad because I was leaving..." She glanced at him. "Because I was leaving you."

He smiled.

"Don't let it go to your head," she added. "I never would've admitted my feelings for you then. Brag and I were meeting Mathieu at the airport but not for a few hours, so there was no need to rush. I stepped into the street and...*and*...that's where my old life ends." Worry lines formed in her brow. "Why are we rehashing this now?"

If Cooper couldn't jar Angeline's memory, he'd be forced to tell her about Joan's bullet theory. He eased up, rested his back against the high headboard, and pulled her to him. She settled in the juncture of his thighs, and he grew hard again.

He linked his hands beneath her breasts, nuzzling the nape of her neck. "Tell me about your injuries," he whispered next to her ear. "I know your legs were badly broken. What else?"

She recited a quick inventory. "Fractured hip, wrist. Lacerations. Head trauma, which caused the amnesia, internal injuries., and of course, my face."

"What about the scar above your right elbow?" He touched her arm. "This one."

Frustration edged her voice. "I was in a coma, Cooper. I can't tell you about every nick and scrape. What's one more scar anyway?" She raised up again and leaned forward, reaching for her robe.

"Where are you going?"

She stood, shrugged into the kimono, and tied the belt in a loose knot. "We need to get dressed. Jack will be home soon, and finding us in here will confuse him. I don't like talking about the accident." She retreated into the closet and called out. "You can shower first."

Without so much as a sneeze, she'd dismissed him. Was the gunman one of her fuzzy memories, a half-filled blank? Was the shooter Voorhees?

He scooted to the edge of the bed. "Someone shot at you or Braeden the day of the accident, Angeline. Joan Baines worked emergency that night. She said you both had identical wounds, as if the same bullet grazed you." He attempted to reign in the urgency raising his voice. "Hell, the Sandman and I went back to the accident scene. We found the damn bullet."

She came to the closet door, jeans and a white shirt in hand, her face flushed and pinched with resentment. "Why are you doing this? Who is Joan Baines? What bullet?"

Jack called out, and a multitude of footsteps sounded on the stairs.

Cooper snatched up his clothes and swore under his breath at the lost moment.

Chapter Nine

Cooper exited the house with Montgomery at three-thirty in the afternoon, leaving the women in the kitchen with their coffee and a few moments of peace and quiet—to discuss, he was fairly certain, Joan's bullet theory.

The children drew dinosaurs in Jack's room. Kids and crayons, he couldn't help questioning the wisdom in that.

More to get used to. But he was up to the challenge.

"Okay," Montgomery said once they settled in the blue Ford Taurus he had rented at the small island airport. "Spill it."

Cooper took his sweet time fastening his seatbelt. "I don't know what you're talking about."

"Sure you do. We take the kids shopping, leave you two on the beach, looking all sad and lost, *so confused*. We come back a couple hours later, you've got a stupid grin on your face and Angeline's humming. By the way, your shirttail's stickin' out of your zipper, and you did your buttons up all lopsided the way Maggie dresses herself. You might want to fix that before we meet with Zeller."

Cooper quickly righted the buttons. "Braeden didn't notice,

did she?"

Montgomery laughed. "For Jonah's sake, Coop, she's a writer. They love detail. Who do you think pointed the shirttail out to me?"

"Great."

Montgomery eased the rental to a stop at the corner. "I gather you and Angeline have resolved the amnesia issue."

"What's to resolve, Sandman? It is what it is. Neither of us can change that."

"And what of Mathieu Fournier's part in keeping her and Jack away from you?"

Cooper scrubbed a hand over his face, feeling stubble. He'd forgotten to shave. "I'd like to put Fournier in a wheelchair, but what good would it do? He stole from us, but he didn't win. Now he has to watch me make a life for the three of us. Wherever we end up, here or in the States, I'll see it's a damn good life."

They parked the Taurus between two cruisers in the lot behind the stationhouse. It irked Cooper being summoned to Zeller's office like a kid in trouble at school, especially when he left his conversation with Angeline unfinished. The issue of a shooter needed to be addressed.

He stopped on the steps and stared across at the square bustling with tourists and vendors. "I told Angeline about Joan's bullet theory," he said.

"Bet she reacted to that revelation about like Braeden did when I first arrived in Hamlin's Grove after the murder of the Delacroix brothers."

"Yeah." A vendor passed them, wheeling his flower-cart along the cobblestone walkway. The ocean breeze carried the scent of pink and fire opal heliconias, orchids and birds of paradise, and blended the floral fragrances with drifts of garlic and ginger from the crowded sidewalk eateries. "She's confused, and skeptical. Angry because she doesn't remember the actual accident. Afraid because she can't say if Joan's conjecture holds an ounce of truth."

Montgomery headed up the steps. "You told her you have the bullet, right?"

Cooper hurried after him. He reached around the detective

and grasped the door handle. "Her knowing I have the bullet made things worse, made her more afraid."

The detective stepped inside. "So what's next?"

"I'm hoping, in time, Angeline will remember being shot. You know I've always believed Voorhees was involved. With all that's happened here, I'm more convinced of that than ever."

They stopped in the reception area outside the dispatch window. "That's another vague issue," Montgomery said. "Braeden told me about the dreams she suffered after Thomas Seaborn's death, and her conviction that Voorhees saved our lives because of you. But it doesn't make sense, Coop. You caused the guy nothin' but grief. Why would he bother saving us?"

"We can't analyze a man like Voorhees because we don't think like he does. My opinion?"

Montgomery nodded.

"The Dutchman spared you and Braeden because he could. It's that simple. He's the one in control, playing God. Your lives were meant as a reminder of that, and the fact it could've easily gone the other way if he'd wanted it to. Don't you see, it's all about him calling the shots. That, and the fact Voorhees revels in the chase. He's not done with me yet."

Inside his office, Chief Zeller poured himself a cup of coffee and one for Montgomery, then he carried his mug to his desk, sat in his creaky chair, and steepled his hands in front of him. His gaze hammered Cooper. "You have a passport for me, yes?"

Cooper tossed the blue booklet on the desk. He walked over to the Mr. Coffee gurgling atop the black half-file in the corner. It seemed he and the Chief had reverted back to that first day's animosity, which left him unsure what to do with the information Jack had revealed on the beach. He poured himself a cup of coffee, carried it to the window, balanced a hip on the wide ledge next to a potted gray-green aloe plant, and stared out.

Killer view.

Beyond the wild tamarinds and willowy dagger trees with large, yellow inflorescences, spread a sumptuous blanket of green, eclipsed by an imposing charcoal-gray mountain range. He wondered where, in all this grandeur, Voorhees had stashed a boat with Jack onboard.

Was the other boy still with him?

Zeller's stentorian voice intruded. "Don't you agree, Mr. Cooper?"

Was the other boy even alive?

"Agree to what?"

"Detective Montgomery informed me that he and his wife brought their girls to the island, and I suggested the Dubois residence might require alternate safety measures."

"It's the St. Cyr residence." He'd grown tired of reminding the man. "And additional protection couldn't hurt."

"I think, between you and me, we've covered security." Montgomery took a drawn-out sip from his mug and studied Cooper over the rim. "Besides, we don't want to spook the women or the kids, and...Nicholas and Brent St. Cyr are on their way here. The two brothers double our manpower."

"What?" Cooper rose. He caught the aloe plant as it slid forward. Coffee sloshed over the floor and his tennis shoes.

"They caught a flight this morning." The detective tugged on the bob dangling from the front pocket of his jeans and retrieved a gold watch Cooper recognized as belonging to Montgomery's grandfather. "Let's see, guess it's been about three hours ago."

"Why didn't anyone ask—"

"Wasn't up to you. "Montgomery shot him his *we'll discuss this later* look.

Cooper closed his eyes and inhaled deeply. Too many people and too many things happening too damn fast.

Zeller leaned back in his chair, the look on his face demonstrative of how displeased he was at the undermining of his authority. Yet again. "I must insist these brothers stop by my office and introduce themselves. I would also require copies of their American driver's licenses and their passports. It would be a pity if my men mistook them for perpetrators and shot one, or both. We wouldn't want that to happen on top of a small boy's kidnapping, now would we?"

Cooper didn't like the implication. Nor did he like the idea of two additional people underfoot while he dealt with a man as volatile as Willem Voorhees.

Montgomery tried his hand at damage control. "I'll make sure they know to come here first," he said.

Zeller seemed appeased. He scooted his chair around, opened the safe behind his desk, and deposited the passport inside.

Cooper didn't give a flying flip. "We need to get back to the house then. There are arrangements to set in place."

While the Chief and Montgomery exchanged parting pleasantries on the stationhouse steps, Cooper marched over to the square and sat in his customary spot under the giant mangrove. He turned on Montgomery as soon as the detective stepped into the tree's shade. "Why in hell didn't anyone see fit to discuss the arrival of Angeline's brothers with me?"

"You were out all day yesterday, Coop. When was there time?" Montgomery paced in front of the bench, occasionally scouting the crowded square. "Besides, this isn't about your damn comfort. It's about Braeden, Angeline, and the children. The perpetrator who took—"

"Voorhees."

"Huh?"

"Voorhees stole Jack."

"Show me the proof, Coop, and don't talk to me about gut instinct or that damn bulls-eye again. This could be anyone's idea of a sick joke. Jack likes the waterfront and hangs out there every chance he gets. He said the kidnappers kept him on a boat. Lots of boats come in and out of the harbor. All kinds of boats and lowlife—"

"I spoke with Voorhees."

Hours later, the Onlooker stepped onto the gazebo behind the darkened house. He crept over to the lounge chair, balanced his cigarette on the chrome edge, and stared at the pink sweater. Lifting it, he rubbed the luxurious cashmere against the side of his face and reveled in her intoxicating scent. He was hard in an instant.

Voorhees assigned him no deliveries tonight. In fact, the boss would be furious if he knew of the Onlooker's insubordination. He'd seen the Dutchman shoot underlings for less. Hack off hands and feet. A shudder rippled down his back. Slice off ears.

But he learned as a child to crave that certain danger in doing the forbidden.

His cigarette fell like a dive-bombing firefly. He ground it into the wide-planked floor with his boot as soon as it hit. With his gloved hand, he picked up the glass she'd left by her chair. He took a languid sip, swished the amber liquid in his mouth, over his tongue and under it. Returning to the water's edge, he swallowed slow and savored the tea's warmth and lingering sweetness. Much like he imagined the woman would taste in all her forbidden places. Pouring the remaining tea over the mangrove roots, he laughed at the scurrying fiddler crabs. He scooped a young crab in the glass and carried it to the gallery.

A light went on inside the house at the top of the stairs. He hurriedly set the empty glass upside down on the narrow ledge in front of the back door, the small crab trapped inside. He stuffed the pink sweater inside his zippered jacket, took one last look around, and turned toward the sea.

Laughing, amused at his cunning with the house now so full of people, he took the expanse of yard in a few effortless strides. He went through the gate, leaving it open, and jogged down the deserted beach.

Chapter Ten

Brent St. Cyr tugged on his Astros ball cap, then collected his lone carry-on from the plane's overhead luggage bin. He fished out another bag and handed it to Nick, then gestured his brother toward the exit where other passengers already filed out. Getting to Angeline and Jack was taking too long. "I can't believe they waited to call us," he said for the umpteenth time since they boarded a plane in Houston. "We're talkin' kidnapping, for Christ's sake. And murder, damn it. I just spoke with Angie the other day and her only concern was that Cooper had found her. I knew the guy would bring trouble with him." He had only met his sister's housekeeper once, but Brent had liked Rose Cassell. "What if the bastards had killed Jack, too?"

Always the gentleman, Nick smiled and thanked the flight attendant before descending the portable steps to the tarmac. "Losing your temper doesn't help, little brother. I still don't understand how you hold Cooper responsible for all of Angie's problems. Seems to me the man's only fault is in loving her."

Brent followed Nick down the steps. He blew out a frustrated breath. Ninety degrees and humid as all get out. For a minute, he swore he was back in Texas. But setting down at this peewee airfield didn't compare to landing at Houston's bustling Bush Intercontinental Airport. His brother's unflappable diplomacy made him want to spit nails. "If Cooper hadn't dragged Angie off to that relic he calls home in Louisiana after Braeden's mugging," he told Nick, "she would have left New Orleans the same day Fournier's photo shoot wrapped up in the cemetery."

"You don't know that."

"Sure I do. She made plans to take Mom and Dad out for an anniversary dinner. Reservations at Landry's on the Kemah Boardwalk. She told me so. Heck, I thought about meeting them there."

Nick stopped walking; his face blanked, and the corners of his mouth turned down. "No one invited me."

Brent clapped him on the back. "You were at the Philadelphia conference. La-de-da keynote address, remember? You took that pretty physical therapist with you, Lissa what's-her-name."

"Chambers," his brother said. "Melissa."

"Yeah. That's the one. You still seein' her?"

"What does Melissa Chambers have to do with your grudge against Cooper?"

"No grudge, bro. Nothin' but pure, unadulterated fact." Brent hoisted his canvas bag over his shoulder with purpose. "If that son of a bitch Cooper didn't sweep Angie off her feet with his good ol' boy charm, money, and mansion on River Road, she never would've gotten hit by that car. Hell, she lost her career, lost her way for a few years, and almost lost her life. Now Cooper shows up here, Jack gets stolen, and Angie's housekeeper butchered. In my book, he lays claim to the blame. If the man's got any sense at all, he'll damn well stay out of my way."

By eight o'clock that evening, the children dreamed in bed and the adults sat around the table in Angeline's formal dining room. Braeden, Montgomery, Angeline, Brent, Nick, and finally Cooper, who was not at all happy with the congregating crowd. Forever the cop, Montgomery insisted they include Zeller. Cooper sat at the head of the table; Montgomery at the opposite end, with the Chief seated on his right.

Montgomery opened the meeting. "Coop has something to tell us. Most of you already know Voorhees called, but there's a new development. Coop?"

Cooper scrubbed his hands over his face. This idea of Montgomery's was either the best he ever had—telling everyone about Voorhees and what Jack said about the other boy—or a real stinker because it involved too many people. "I talked with Jack this morning on the beach," he began. "He told me there was another boy on Voorhees' boat. Later Angeline and I found a cell phone hidden near the gazebo out back."

Brent spoke up, his sarcasm close to the surface. "Hidden cell phone's a little cloak and dagger, isn't it?"

The guy had brushed up against Cooper an hour earlier, practically rolled over him, with nary an apology. He understood a brother's love and the inherent protectiveness that accompanied it, but Brent St. Cyr didn't corner anybody's market on concern for Angeline and Jack.

"Voorhees called," Angeline directed her explanation to her brother. "That's how we found the telephone." She turned to Cooper. "Do you believe Voorhees kidnapped the other child from somewhere on the island?"

The last thing he wanted was to heap more worry on her. "We have no way of knowing that for certain, but we're assuming so."

Nick, apparently the less imperturbable of the two St. Cyr males, addressed the Chief. "Have there been any other boys reported missing?"

Cooper wished both brothers would high-tail it home.

Zeller stood to address the group, empowered by the opportunity to flex his bureaucratic muscle. "None on Jacqueme Dominique," he said. "Not that I've learned of. We have three major cities on the island, two of them ports, but countless villages and farms are scattered throughout the land. Shacks and lean-tos on river junctures and tributaries. Mountain dwellings. There are many dangers here. Children go missing in forests and mangrove swamps every other day. As you know, there are also many islands occupying the Caribbean and Atlantic, even as far away as your Gulf of Mexico. The boy could have come from any of these, or none of them."

"So what do we do?" Braeden pressed Montgomery. "We can't ignore that we know the boy's out there."

He straightened. "Unfortunately, for now Voorhees calls the shots. We only have Jack's word about another boy, and he's only four. That isn't enough proof to take to a higher authority." He glanced at Zeller. "No offense intended, Chief."

Zeller's reply was a curt nod.

"What about the phone?" Brent said.

"The phone is hard, if not impossible, to trace," the Chief added.

"Who has it now?"

Cooper spoke up. "I do."

"Coop's holding onto the phone makes perfect sense," Montgomery interjected. "He's the only one here who has a history with Voorhees. If there's any hope at all of finding out if and where this other boy is, we wait—"

"Maybe it's his *history* that bothers me." Brent came up out of his chair, his glare and annoyance thrown at Cooper in lieu of Montgomery or Zeller. "Voorhees steals Jack the same day Cooper shows up on the island." He waved his arms ape-like. "He returns Jack once Cooper's ingratiated himself in Angie's life. *Again.* You ask me, that's a tad too convenient."

"Son of a bitch." Cooper sprang from his chair.

Brent drew back his fist.

Nick caught his brother's arm. "Sit down, Brent."

Cooper charged around the table.

Montgomery cut him off, almost knocking Braeden from her chair in his haste. "These kinds of accusations get us nowhere."

Brent shrugged free of Nick's grasp. Anger reddened his complexion as he faced the others. "Cooper's actions don't make you the least bit suspicious?" he yelled.

Angeline joined the fray. Inches from Brent's face, she said, "Sit...down."

Her brother sputtered a second, then threw up his hands and dropped onto his chair.

She turned to Cooper, still restrained by Montgomery, and pointed her finger at him. "You sit, too."

Cooper blew out an aggravated breath and warned Brent over

Montgomery's shoulder, "You better stay as far away from me as you can." He sat and addressed the others at the table as if Angeline's brother were invisible. "I hold onto the phone. When Voorhees calls, we deal with it. And he will call. I know how to play the man. I'll get him to boast about the boy, tip his hand."

Zeller said, "You must keep me informed, Mr. Cooper. You should have called when you first discovered the telephone. Certainly when you learned of this other boy." His gaze inventoried those around the table, before coming back to Cooper. "If you do not keep me informed, you will be talking to this Dutchman from a cell in the basement of my stationhouse."

"Finally," Brent mumbled. "Somebody with a lick of sense."

Angeline shot Cooper a warning look.

He let Brent's comment go, more concerned with Zeller. He'd quickly soured on the Chief's threats. If the focus hadn't switched to this other boy, she and Jack would be aboard a plane bound for the States, to the safety of Raison-Bell Amandine and the undeniable protection he could provide there. "I understand."

"That's it, then." Zeller closed the meeting. He turned to Angeline. "Now, I need a few minutes to talk with young Jack."

The game of "Musical Guests" inside the beachfront house unsettled Cooper. But he had to admit Angeline's disposition had improved an astounding one-eighty since her brothers' arrival.

"Haven't you caused my sister enough misery?" Brother Brent scowled from the other side of the gate leading to the beach.

In the shade of the mangroves, Cooper turned. "Meeting's over, St. Cyr," he said. "Don't start with me."

Brent St. Cyr stood taller than Cooper, six-two or maybe three. He knew from past conversations with Angeline that her brother was around thirty, and next to the youngest of four St. Cyr brothers.

Four, jeez. At least they'd left the other two at home.

Brent's ruggedness and broad-shouldered frame stood a testament to his livelihood. He wore jeans and a plaid shirt with a gray cotton shaker crew under it, sleeves shoved to his elbows, a sport's watch on his left wrist, and black Squall boots. A small scar parted his dark brown hair with the slightest peppering of premature gray at the temples.

Cooper noted a hint of Angeline in her brother's eyes, minus the crow's feet from working outdoors. Good looks ran in the family.

Brent crossed the sand, stopping where the tide rushed ashore. "You need to go home, Cooper, and I sincerely hope this Dutchman follows you. Whatever happens here, we'll take care of Angie and her boy. That's what family does."

"Did Angeline say this is what she wants?" Brent folded his arms across his chest, and the man's silence further incensed Cooper. "I thought as much. Did she remind you that Jack is my son?"

More silence.

"I didn't think so." Cooper shrank the distance between them. "That makes me Jack's family, pal, and I'm not going anywhere. Deal with it."

Brent chewed on his lower lip. He uncrossed him arms and planted his blunt-tipped finger in Cooper's chest. "You cause my sister any grief, *pal*, and you deal with me."

Cooper poked back. "I'll be damned if I'll have some ship-chasing, channel jockey telling me what to—"

"Break it up, jerks." Nick wedged himself between them, shoving Brent back a step. "Angie's watching from the window," he said. "She just got her boy back, remember? I'd say that's more important than either of your inflated egos."

Cooper turned toward the house in time to see the upstairs drapes close.

Red-faced, Brent sputtered a second like he couldn't find his voice. Then he turned, stomped through the gate, and crossed the yard. He yanked open the door and disappeared in the house.

"Sorry about Brent." Nick stood beside Cooper. "He can be a hothead, especially where family's concerned. You either love him for it or..." He shrugged.

The opposite of his brother, the doctor carried the dubious honor of being the eldest St. Cyr sibling, older than the channel jockey by at least seven years, and closer to Angeline's five-ten height; thin build, fair complexion, sandy hair. More the GQ type, with his dark v-neck sweater, white shirt, tie, and penny loafers.

It also appeared he liked a little more flash than his blue-collar brother, given the silver TAG Heuer chronograph strapped on his wrist.

Nick gestured down the beach. "Let's walk."

There go the expensive loafers. Cooper cast one last glimpse at the upstairs bedroom, light seeping around the closed curtains.

"Did Angie tell you her theory about someone being in the gazebo last night after everyone went to bed?" Nick said.

News of an intruder stopped Cooper cold. "What makes Angeline suspect someone was here?"

"Couple of things." Nick scooped up a shell and tossed it into the sea, then brushed his fingers on his pants to rid them of sand. "Her sweater's missing," he added. "She's sure she left it on her chair yesterday."

Cooper remembered the sweater. Not exactly earth shattering evidence. Still an uneasy niggle rooted at the base of his spine. "Did she ask Braeden about it?"

"They say they've checked everywhere."

"You said a couple of things. What else?"

"Tea. Angie says she never touched hers yesterday. You were with her. She left a full glass next to her chair. This morning the glass sat empty on the gallery, turned upside down. Someone trapped a tiny fiddler crab underneath. Come on, I've got one other thing to show you."

They headed to the gazebo. The ornate structure appeared new, and Cooper wondered if it had been replaced since the last hurricane.

Nick walked to the lounge chair Angeline had occupied the day before. Metal scraped wood as he shoved it aside to reveal a black smudge the size of a mini-Frisbee. "Looks like somebody put his cigarette out here. I know Montgomery doesn't smoke, how about you?"

Cooper didn't need to think about it. "I haven't smoked in seven hundred and twenty-six days, four hours, and..." He pushed the button at the top of his watch. "Twelve minutes."

Nick raised a brow.

Cooper grimaced. "Sorry. I've always been weird about numbers."

"This smudge, along with the sweater and glass, has Angie spooked," Nick said. "Rose's murder, Jack's kidnapping, now the mysterious cell phone and another missing boy. It's too much for her."

"Okay." Cooper knelt for a closer look. He rubbed his hand over the smudge and sniffed his fingertips. "So we keep watch from now on," he said, standing. "Assign shifts." He gestured toward the house. "Covert activity ought to be right up Brent's alley."

Nick laughed. "Got bro's number, have you? Let's go talk to him about it. He's a control freak, and it drives him crazy when he doesn't have a handle on things. That's why Angie told me her suspicions first. Family's what matters to Brent, which amazes me that he's never married. You're Jack's family, Cooper, that makes you ours."

Terrific. Cooper followed the doctor inside and reached for his elbow. "Hold on a second."

"Yes?"

They stopped in the hall, near the kitchen. "You lay the situation out for Brent and decide which shift you want me to take. I'll talk to Montgomery in the morning. He can take first shift tomorrow night. Right now, I'm going up to check on Angeline."

"Sure she wants to see you?"

"We're working on it."

Nick locked the door. "Don't upset her."

Cooper headed for the stairs. He called over his shoulder, "Don't worry about it."

Angeline turned at the knock on her bedroom door. She slipped Jack's picture under her pillow. "Come in."

The door opened, and Cooper stuck his head in. "Hey there."

He had held his own with Brent out on the beach, but she suspected he would.

"I wanted to apologize for what you saw earlier between your brother and me," he said as he crossed the room. "I'll watch it from here on out."

"Brent won't make it easy for you," she said. "He's always been my protector, even when we were kids. It's worse since the accident. He didn't hurt you, did he?"

Cooper tossed her a pained look that said, "get real." She laughed and scooted over so he could sit on the edge of the bed.

"Nick told me about the things you found in the gazebo, and about the fiddler crab and glass on the gallery." He sat. "Sorry I wasn't here."

"You can't be everywhere."

He took her hand, turned it over, and kissed her palm.

She laughed and eased her hand away. "That's not happening tonight, Cooper. We have a house full of guests and children." It was hard to be serious with him nibbling on her fingers. "Besides, there's something more I didn't tell Nick."

He released her hand and straightened. "What's that?"

"The other evening, when Brag and I were in here talking, I couldn't shake the feeling someone was watching us." She moved past him and padded barefoot to the window, then eased back the drapes. "Down there on the beach."

"You saw someone?"

She turned back. "I said it was a feeling. You know, like intuition or something."

He moved beside her at the window. "Those mangroves offer an intruder the perfect cover. Your brothers and I could clear them tomorrow."

"Absolutely not." She spoke without hesitation. "Mangrove trees are eco-friendly. They protect the coastline from erosion and storm surges, they provide nesting areas for pelicans and spoonbills and...Jack loves them. He hides there, builds forts, and plays pirate." She took a much-needed breath.

He raised his hands in mock surrender. "I get it. Don't touch the trees."

She took hold of the lapels of his shirt. "That's one the of things I like about you, Cooper, you're a quick study." She coaxed him closer, smiling. "Why don't you study this."

"Aw, jeez."

Angeline closed her eyes and savored the feel of his mouth on hers. Warm and possessive, hungry. It was the kind of kiss that curled a girl's toes, hot and wet and endless.

Or maybe she only wished it endless.

They came up for air, faces equally flushed. He nudged the pillow on the bed over, and Jack's photograph fell out.

She grabbed the picture before he could. "I wanted to give this to you earlier," she said. "But there wasn't a time when people weren't around." She handed him the photo. "I took it at the start of the summer and had duplicates made." She lifted one shoulder slightly. "Family. It's not right that you don't have Jack's picture." There were so many things she hadn't done right.

"Where is Jack?" Cooper turned the photo over and stared at the back where she'd written the date and the boy's age. In a few months, Jack would celebrate his fifth birthday. He'd damn well be there.

"Asleep," she said. "So are the girls."

"Yeah. Playing is hard work."

"You missed so much," she said, as though reading his thoughts. "If I could take back the way I did things, I—"

"You never asked for that car to hit you, Angeline." He lifted the comforter and motioned her to climb in bed. "When I think that I could've lost you, it scares the hell out of me. But we've got a second chance. Not many people can say that. I'm not going to waste it with regret. Neither should you."

She slid under the covers, then reached for his arm when he started to turn away. "You can stay with me awhile...if you're good."

"That's expecting a lot after today," he said.

"We don't have to talk, unless you need to. I don't want to be alone."

Cooper took his wallet from the rear pocket of his jeans, opened it, and slipped the photo inside. He returned the wallet to his pocket, then reached for the armless chair beside the window seat.

"Not there." Angeline patted the bed next her. "Like you said, after today..."

Cooper closed the drapes, then sprawled atop the covers on the side of the bed nearest the window. He folded his arms behind his head on the pillow, crossed his legs at the ankles, and stared at the ceiling. "That was nice this afternoon," he said. "Unexpected, but nice. Real nice."

"Yes." She slid further under the comforter, with its autumn hues of gold and burnt sienna and brown, and closed her eyes.

"You warm enough?" he said after a few moments of easy quiet.

"Uh-huh. Do you have Voorhees' phone?" She raised on her elbows. "Do you think it was him on the patio before?"

"Not likely." He turned on his side, fished the cell phone from his jeans pocket, and set it on the comforter between them. "Voorhees sends someone else to do his dirty work."

She picked up the phone and turned it over. "Let's say it was him," she said. "As frightening as the idea is of him being dangerously near Jack again, wouldn't it also mean the other boy is close? Don't you think that's a reasonable assumption?"

"It's a possibility, Slick."

"I was wondering, I guess, if Jack said anything else about the boy? What he looks like, hair color, nationality. Is he tall or short? You see on television all the time how sketch artists draw people using witness descriptions. Maybe—"

"They might as well take of photograph of Jack," he said. "He told me the boy he saw looks like him. But that might've been because he wore Jack's t-shirt. You know, the orange one with the dolphins on it?"

"Voorhees dressed the other child in Jack's clothes?" She shuddered. "That's sick, Cooper. I don't want to think about it."

"Then don't."

Angeline drifted to sleep, nestled in his protective arms, Cooper's soft snore gently sweeping the top of her head. For that brief moment in time, she couldn't imagine wanting anything more.

They'd been such fools.

Chapter Eleven

Someone grabbed Cooper by the shoulder, shook the devil out of him, and whispered, "Wake up, you son of a bitch."

Cooper slit an eye, bringing the darkened bedroom and its intruder into focus.

Brother Brent.

Slipping off the bed, Cooper placed his hand square in the middle of the channel jockey's bare chest, and guided them both to the foot of Angline's bed. "We'll talk in the hall," he said. Walking around the bed, he switched off the fancy lamp with the bead-trimmed shade. He picked up Voorhees' cell phone and jammed it in his pocket.

Brent waited in the open doorway. His dark hair stuck out in all directions, making him appear every bit the wild man he was turning out to be. "What do you think you're doing?" he said once they stood in the hall.

Cooper eased the bedroom door closed. "What in the hell are you doing asking me what I'm doing, St. Cyr?" He poked Brent's broad chest with his fingertip. "Can't you see your sister finally fell asleep?"

"I saw you—"

Cooper gave another jab for good measure. "Do you realize how hard it's been for her to get any rest?"

It was like stabbing a frozen side of beef. The only movement from Brother Brent was the twitch in his jaw.

"I know that," he ground out between clenched teeth. "But I'll be damned if I let you take advantage of Angie, and it looks like that's exactly what you're—"

"What it looks like is none of your business. For the record, I was sleeping on *top* of the covers, and your sister's not sixteen. She's a grown woman. A bright, intelligent woman. She doesn't need some jock of a brother making her choices." He dropped his hands to his sides, then turned full circle. "Jeez. Did they have a ban on brains in Texas the year you were born, Brent? You're unbelievable. Un*fucking*believable."

"It's your watch."

Cooper's tirade screeched to a halt. "What?"

"Outside," Brent said. "Nick told me you were up next. Montgomery takes first watch tomorrow night. Did he get it wrong?"

The sap seemed almost hopeful. "Why didn't you say so?"

"I went to wake you, but you weren't in your room."

Oh, yeah. That was another stick-in-your-craw annoyance. Dr. Nick had assigned them rooms, like frigging scout camp. Once he moved his gear from the Hotel LeNoir, Cooper would bunk in Jack's room.

"What time is it?" He started down the stairs, the channel jockey on his heels like a steroidal shadow.

"Half past twelve."

Cooper faced him. "Don't suppose you made coffee?"

"Brewed a pot before I went looking for you."

At least the big lug did one thing right. Cooper scrubbed his hands over his face and up into his hair. "What time should I wake your brother?"

"Three. It starts getting light around six."

Each man turned, one going up, the other down.

Ten minutes later, light from the moon's reflection off the sea illuminated the kitchen enough that Cooper didn't need to switch on a light. Steaming cup of coffee in hand, he eased open the rear door, crossed the cool veranda floor barefooted, and then the damp grass. He settled on the steps of the gazebo. Wind wrestled the surrounding shrubs and flowers. The only other sounds were waves breaking against the shore.

He set the cup beside him and leaned back on his elbows. His mind revisited the afternoon, echoing Angeline's sentiment after they'd made love. *Wow.* He smiled. They still had it.

Although the day's warmth and humidity lingered, wind stirred the scent of ginger and sweet odors of cinnamon trees and oleander. This island paradise seemed a great place to raise a kid, unencumbered by cloying smog and traffic snarls, schools overrun with drugs and gang activity and crowded with so many students an instructor could hardly think let alone teach.

Angeline had fashioned a good life for herself and Jack here. Cooper stood on the third step and arched his back, working out the kinks the last few stress-filled days had dealt, still trying to figure out what to do about it all. If he stayed on the island, he gave up Raison-Belle Amandine, his family home. That, in itself, was life altering.

But, hell, he'd do it in a heartbeat if given the opportunity for a future with her and Jack.

A camera flashed on the beach next to the mangrove trees.

"Hey!" He bounded down the remaining steps, then hurdled the white-washed fence's short pickets.

Like falling dominoes, lights flickered on in the house room by room, flooding the shoreline and encapsulating the intruder at the water's edge in a yellow-white glow. The man snapped one last photo before he kicked up sand running.

Cooper huffed after him. He never heard the rear door open, or the clamber of footsteps on brick. Next thing he knew, Brent ran beside him. The big man dove for the intruder's legs, his tackle sending a camera and backpack flying.

A sharp edge connected with Cooper's temple, then bounced off his shoulder. He scrambled forward and latched onto the man's sleeve as Brent wrestled to keep the guy down. The three rolled. Wet sand coated them.

"I've got him!" Brent yelled. "Call the police."

Cooper let go of the man's sleeve, grabbed the backpack, and stumbled toward the house.

Nick stood on the veranda in horn-rimmed glasses and striped pajamas, a cordless phone pressed to his ear.

Angeline peered around Nick, her hands clinging to either side of her brother's waist.

Brent yanked the intruder up by the yoke of his dark jacket. "Who the hell are you?"

"Press," the man wheezed. "*Global Times.*"

"That rag ain't the press," Brent said. He called to the others, "Looks like we've got ourselves a genuine *paparazzo.*"

Cooper swiped the blood trickling down his cheek with the back of his hand. He unzipped the reporter's navy backpack and shook the contents on the sand. Kneeling, he rifled through it and searched for ID.

Bingo. He waved the guy's wallet over his head.

"Hey!" the man gasped. "I know my rights."

Using his grip on the man's jacket to bring the shutterbug within inches of his nose, Brent said, "How much they payin' you to scare the hell out of my sister and her kid?" He jerked the jacket several times so the man appeared boneless.

Cooper heard a rip.

"Whatever is it," Brent sputtered, "it ain't nearly enough." His punch dropped the guy face-down in the sand and receding tide. He dragged the reporter toward the house.

When Chief Zeller arrived a few minutes after two, Cooper waited at the breakfast table with Angeline. Nick had swabbed some nasty-smelling stuff on his temple, then applied a butterfly bandage. Now he poked around on his shoulder, which Cooper insisted wasn't injured.

It hurt like hell.

The intruder was laid-out on the floor, a foot or so inside the rear door, where Brent had dragged and dropped him. He'd tied his hands and feet with clothesline rope and a knot he called *The Constrictor.* The big guy squatted on his haunches next to the reporter, arms crossed, his back against the wall. Sand dusted him from head to toe. He resembled an albino gorilla but appeared pretty damned pleased with himself.

"Name on his driver's license is Wallace," Brent said as Zeller thumbed through the guy's wallet. "First name's Walter, if you can believe that." He laughed. "Walter Wallace. Who sticks a handle like that on their kid?"

Zeller didn't seem amused.

Neither was Cooper. He studied Angeline's pallor and quiet demeanor, the tremble in her hands as she poured coffee into mugs from a tray on the table.

Calamity only took one reporter learning her true identity—and he'd arrived. By noon, the island would be crawling with the likes of Walter Wallace.

No, Cooper didn't find one speck of humor in it.

Their hands touched when Angeline passed him a mug, but she didn't look at him. He couldn't blame her. His search had led Voorhees straight to her island sanctuary, albeit unknowingly, and then the Dutchman stole Jack, the press learned of the boy's kidnapping, and now...

Guess he could add blowing Angeline's cover to his catalog of sins.

The reporter moaned.

"Bring him to the sofa," Zeller ordered.

"Get your hands off me." Wallace jerked his shoulder. He tried to sit. "I'll sue you for every dime you've ever made," he told Brent. "Hell, every dime you'll make in your whole sorry life."

Brent stood over him, fisted his hands on his hips, and issued the dare. "Do it."

The bruising around Wallace's cheekbone and swollen slit of an eye forecast a substantial shiner. His focus hit on Angeline. "I can't believe I came here to investigate a child's kidnapping and stumbled onto the scoop of a lifetime. Angeline resurrected!" His chin raised toward the ceiling as if he thanked the Almighty. "This is every reporter's dream story."

"And you will sit on this story." Zeller crossed the room to stand in front of him. "Or you will sit in my jail until you rot." He turned to Brent. "Untie him."

Brent yanked the knots loose. He hauled the reporter stumbling down the central hall to the great room. Cooper and Angeline followed, along with the Chief and Nick.

"Too late." Wallace practically sang his response. He rubbed his wrists, then unzipped his jacket pocket and produced a compact black and red gadget. "Secure, wireless. Sharp as a staple," he boasted. "Twenty gigabytes of image storage, capable of transferring state of the art photos to any remote server. Namely, my editor." He sounded like a bad infomercial. "Don't you love technology?" He turned to Angeline, all smiles. "You're tomorrow's headline, doll. Hell, you're a month of headlines, and a fat paycheck. I'll be a legend by noon tomorrow."

Cooper lurched for Wallace, but Angeline stepped in front of him. She placed her hand against his chest. "I was a fool to think I could stay hidden," she said. "It's weird, but I almost feel relieved."

Nick approached Zeller, and the two men huddled in the hall outside the partially closed pocket doors. The Chief motioned for the young officer he'd stationed by the front entrance. "Arrest him," he said.

Wallace lost his bluster when the policeman approached, handcuffs drawn. "For what?" His already sallow complexion blanched bloodless. He sprang from the seven-foot sofa and barricaded himself behind it.

Zeller took his time answering. "We'll start with trespassing. This beach is posted private. Then we'll add interfering with a police investigation, resisting arrest, and assault on an officer. My dear Mr. Wallace, I can make your stay in Port Noel a long and extremely unpleasant one."

Cooper didn't think the Chief had it in him.

So, what if he did. Jailing Walter Wallace didn't solve their immediate problem.

Cooper turned from his spot at the dining room window, his hands shoved in the pockets of his faded jeans. A hammered-copper shelf clock sat on the far mantle. Six-fifteen. His attention returned to the window. The sun fought for exposure in an overcast sky. A few small fishing boats dotted the horizon, and he couldn't help wondering if one of those boats carried an extra passenger.

Zeller had left for the stationhouse around four o'clock in

the morning, a handcuffed Walter Wallace in tow, though Cooper figured the Chief wouldn't hold him long. Most of the charges he rattled off were bogus.

Everyone else had dressed and now sat, engrossed in animated conversation, around the carved mahogany dining table.

Cooper turned from the window. "You're what?"

Angeline repeated her announcement, "I'm going to talk to the press. Chief Zeller is arranging it."

Brent lurched out of his chair and began pacing. The half-eaten pastry in his left hand stirred the air. "It'll be a media circus." He stopped next to his sister. "You sure you're ready to live in that fishbowl again, kid? And what about Jack?"

She sighed. "I understand your concerns, Brent, but I should've done this a long time ago. By hiding, I hurt the people I love," she said. "I won't do that anymore. Jack has this huge extended family now, and he should be able to enjoy them like other children do." She reached for Braeden's hand. "Do you realize, Brag, that Jack's never experienced a birthday party attended by lots of kids?"

"Okay," Braeden said. "We need a plan."

Montgomery sat beside her. "Spoken like a true writer," he said. "Always wanting every *t* crossed."

Nick scooted back his chair, stood, and walked to the kitchen. "I'm surprised Zeller agreed to a press conference," he called out. "This island isn't that large. Most of the countryside is wilderness. Jungle, mangrove swamps, and rainforests. Mountains that drop into the sea." From the sound of water running and metal clinking against glass, he was making another pot of coffee. "The police will have zero control."

Cooper couldn't stomach more caffeine. "You need to think about this carefully, Slick. Going public changes everything."

"I'm counting on that." Angeline followed Nick to the kitchen. Seconds later, she came back with a full cup of black coffee. Not her usual fare. Her gaze lit on each face around her table. "My mind's made up, and I don't want any of you trying to change it."

She couldn't afford what little weight she'd lost these last few days, and Cooper wondered if she ate any of the pastries Nick had bought at a nearby market.

"There's more." She scanned the table's occupants again, ending with him. "You probably won't like this either, but I believe it's worth talking about."

Nick called out from the kitchen, "What's that?"

"I want to tell the press about Jack's kidnapping."

"Why," Brent said, "when we already have him back?"

Cooper passed Brent as the two paced a narrow strip of sunlit hardwood floor. Their gazes met briefly; neither flinched. "It won't flush Voohees out," Cooper said to Angeline, "if that's what you're thinking."

"Maybe, maybe not. But nothing else is happening, and time is passing quickly. If you can get me a photograph of Voorhees by the press conference, Mathieu Fournier will guarantee a million-dollar bounty on his head."

Cooper narrowed his eyes. "You called Fournier?"

"He's the only one I know with that kind of readily-available money. How many of Voorhees' men will stay loyal with such a prize dangling in front of their collective noses?" She spoke with a conviction he hadn't heard in a while. "I want Voorhees." She pointed a steady finger at him. "And I mean to have him."

Nick brought the carafe to the table. "What time is your press conference?"

"Four o'clock."

Brent frowned, his brow furrowed. "That's a little sudden, isn't it?"

"The announcement's already gone out," she said. "Quick action is the Chief's idea of crowd control when the reporters swarm. Thanks to Mathieu, the conference will go live via satellite all over the world. Voorhees will have no place to hide."

She'd have no refuge either. Cooper studied Angeline's face, the determined set of her jaw. He reverted his attention to the window and churning sea. A storm brewed, in more ways than he cared to think about. "You'll set yourself up as a target, and possibly Jack."

"I've considered that." She turned to Montgomery.

He picked up where Angeline left off, directing his explanation to Cooper. "Braeden and I are taking our girls home this morning. Jack is coming with us."

Braeden nodded her agreement.

Cooper opened his mouth to object, but Montgomery stopped him with his raised hand. "Jack will be safer in the States. I know my job, Coop. I'll see he's protected."

"It's the only way," Angeline added. "I realize we don't know who this other boy is, where he comes from, or who his parents are. But I feel an obligation to get him back, at least to try. You should, too."

Cooper thought about what she said. He still didn't like it.

Brent slammed his fist on the table, sloshing coffee from everyone's cup. "I vote no."

The guy possessed a flair for the dramatic.

"You don't get a vote." Cooper placed his hands on Angeline's shoulders. She leaned into him. "This is your sister's call, and mine."

"Thanks," she said. "You're right, Brent. It will be a media free for all, for a while. But you watch television, Entertainment Tonight, TMZ, Access Hollywood; the paparazzi latch onto a story, flood the market with photographs, and next week it's old news. I'm not even a celebrity anymore, just a former model with a few scars. They'll tire of me fast. But Voorhees won't."

"We'll come with you," Nick said. "Present a united front. We should also look into hiring additional security for the house."

Angeline reached up and placed her hand on Cooper's, still resting on her shoulder. "That settles it then."

Brent exhaled a noisy breath. "There's Mom and Dad to consider. If you insist on going through with this...this *plan*, I need to make sure they aren't in the line of any paparazzo's fire. You don't give me much time." He headed toward the hall and stairs. "But I've got a couple of buddies I can call. They'll see Mom and Dad are out of the city before your press conference, somewhere safe from the cameras and newshounds. That way, maybe Mom won't have to tell Dad about Jack's kidnapping." He paused on the bottom step and turned, a look of incredulity on his face. "Damn it to infernal hell, Angie, this'll be a mess."

Chapter Twelve

rent's room faced the front yard, and through his window he could see a light rain falling. With so many people staying at Angeline's house, he and Nick shared quarters.

Whoopee.

Two cop cars sat outside, one across from the house, the other farther down, their occupants hunkered inside, out of the inclement weather. Before the reporter's unexpected arrival, Chief Zeller said he could spare one officer, and only for another day or two. Angeline's press conference had upped the ante.

Brent unfastened his watch and placed it on the dresser. By the time he called his mother and then changed into street clothes, it would be eight o'clock Central Standard Time.

He punched his parents' number into the telephone, thankful his mom was an early riser. "Hi, Mom. It's Brent."

She laughed. "I know my boys' voices. Where are you, son? I've been calling since yesterday evening."

"Calling, why?"

"Sunday," she said. "You usually come to dinner. I thought it would be nice if we took your father to a movie afterward. We go so seldom now, and the new James Bond film is showing at the Cineplex."

"Sunday dinner, right. I won't be there." If he worked things right, neither would they. "Something's going on. I need you to listen and stay calm, okay?"

"Now you're scaring me."

"I don't mean to." Damn, he wished he could tell her in person. There was simply no better way to say it. "Jack's okay now, but he was kidnapped, Mom."

"Kidnapped, how? Who?"

He gave her a partial truth. "The police are working on that."

"Oh, God."

A chair scraped the floor. She'd sat. Good.

"He isn't hurt," Brent told her.

"Did they want money?" His mother's voice rose a squeaky octave, a signal she strained for control. "Are you telling me, Brent St. Cyr, that your sister and her child were in danger and no one bothered to call me—"

"There wasn't time. It happened over a couple of days. The kidnappers stole Jack, then they returned him. It's complicated, and I don't want to go into details over the phone."

"You're on the island, aren't you?" Her toned sharpened as control turned to anger. "Is Nick with you? I've been trying to reach him, too. Why didn't you tell me? I'm not some fragile old woman you've got to protect, you know. Angeline needs me, and Jack is my only grandchild. I should be there."

"Nick's here. Listen, Mom. I'm calling because we need your help."

"I'll do anything."

He debated how much to tell her. "There's this creep, a paparazzo."

"A who?"

"A paparazzo. You know, a celebrity photographer."

"A photographer took Jack? That doesn't make any sense, dear."

He blew out a frustrated breath. "No. The photographer didn't take Jack. But he found out about Angie and her accident, that she's still alive. He's threatened to blow the whole story wide open this morning. Angie's holding a press conference this afternoon. She's trying to cut him off, steal his thunder, I don't know. There'll be a live broadcast at four o'clock island time. Afterwards, the media will swarm your place. We can't let Dad find out about Jack. We can't let him know about any of this."

A momentary silence lapsed. "You're right," she said. "We should go somewhere."

"I've got a buddy coming to your house. You remember Craig Drummond, don't you? He owns a lake cabin up near Trinity. It's quiet, secluded, safe, and the kitchen's fully stocked. You only need to pack clothes and toiletries. Craig will help you, and I'm calling David and Adam when we hang up." He'd almost forgotten his brothers. *Damn.*

"Adam is in school," his mother said.

Brent rubbed the back of his neck. *Right. Sam Houston State. Not far from Trinity. Perfect.* "Adam will meet you at the cabin. Dad will think it's prearranged, like a school break or something. David should come up later. The point is getting the two of you out of the house as soon as possible."

"Okay. We can do this," she said in the take charge Mom voice he'd hated when he was thirteen. "You take care of Angeline and Jack, and we'll take care of your father. Don't worry about us."

"I love you, pretty lady. Don't forget Dad's fishing gear, and those audio Zane Grey novels I gave him for his birthday. Okay?"

"Call me the second the press conference is over, do you hear? And don't hold anything back."

"I promise. As soon as it's over." He disconnected, then dug in his wallet for David's cell number. Working for Texas Parks and Wildlife, brother number two would be in the field. He punched in the number.

Ten minutes of a condensed version of what went down, and David was onboard.

Brent called baby brother Adam next, and gave him the abbreviated scenario he gave David, along with directions to Craig Drummond's cabin. Neither sounded happy about being kept in the dark, but his brothers both agreed protecting their father from bad news was paramount.

Once upon a time, they wouldn't have kept any kind of news from their dad.

Next Brent arranged for a friend from Hamlin's Grove Police Department to keep an eye on the family home. That done, he retrieved a phone book from the top shelf in the closet and thumbed to the page he'd dog-eared last night. After a few minutes of good ol' boy cajoling, the manager of the small island airport relinquished the name of a freelance bush pilot. It was time he surveyed the lay of the land.

The bush pilot's phone rang four times before a woman answered. She sounded half soused.

"Is O'Leary there?" he said.

She laughed, a glorious robust rumble probably induced by booze. "Speaking," she said.

"I'm sorry." Brent sat behind the kidney-shaped mahogany desk. "I meant Mr. O'Leary." He ran his hand over the leather-lined surface. It was a fine example of Victorian Revival, worth five or six grand easy. "Is *he* there?"

"Sorry, dude." Her laughter turned to annoyance. "No mister here. You looking to hire a bush, you get me. The name's Kat."

He spent the next ten minutes trying to assess Kat O'Leary's piloting know-how, while a husky male voice in the background gave an inspiring testimonial to her other skills, the kind of proficiency women usually left off their resumes.

They haggled over the price for flights over the island, extended across a two-day period. Warmth crept into his face when she finally said, "You bring the cash, I can get you off by eleven."

An hour later, leather knapsack in hand, he took a taxi to the car rental office at Port Noel's airport, procuring—to his amazement—a late model Ford Escape. He asked for and received directions to O'Leary's place, meaning the car rental attendant walked to a large window in the terminal and pointed outside.

The hangar stationed at the far end of the tarmac stood about the size of a high school gymnasium. A forlorn Cessna sat in the middle of a dirt runway.

After parking the rental in front of the hangar's open doors, Brent exited the Escape and approached the plane. "Hello," he called out. "Anybody here?"

A female voice answered from the plane's other side. "Depends on who sent you to collect," she said. "And how much I owe them."

He stooped to peer under the aircraft's belly, beyond the oversized tundra tires. A pair of suede hiking boots, planted in the mud and muck, sprouted a pair of shapely legs from cuffed white socks. He followed them around to the other side of the Cessna, where the legs disappeared into a pair of butt-hugging khaki shorts. The woman straightened, turned—and stole the air from his lungs.

"Kat O'Leary?" He could only hope.

"In the flesh." She tossed a long, raven braid over her shoulder and extended her hand. "Well, not exactly in the flesh. But I am Kat. You my fly-over?"

He nodded. She stood about five-foot-seven or so, medium build, tan. If she wore makeup, it didn't show.

"Bring the cash?"

Brent gave another nod.

Her widening grin magnified the tiny gold flecks in her greenish-blue eyes. She held out her hand, palm up.

"Oh." He dug in his pocket and produced a thick roll of bills secured by a red rubber band. Nick complained that he carried too much cash and ought to use plastic like normal people. Wasn't going to happen. "By the way, my name's Brent St. Cyr."

Her appraisal slid from his toes to his face in a nanosecond. She took the money and gestured toward the plane. "Stow your gear inside. I'll be right there. Pre-flight inspection."

Brent peered under the raised clamshell cargo door of the dusty, single-engine Cessna with its faded red and white paint job. He shoved his knapsack behind the passenger's seat and noted a spring poking through the torn red cushion.

The inspection part sounded promising.

A chorus of clucks, squawks, and quacks sounded from the darkened recesses of the plane's interior. He leaned in for a closer assessment, then glanced over his shoulder at his pilot. "Did you know there are chicken coops in the rear of the..."

Apparently Kat O'Leary's idea of pre-flight inspection

included counting every single bill in the wad he gave her. She even held several hundreds up to the sun to check for watermarks. "Humanitarian flight," she said, never taking her eyes off old Ben Franklin.

"Huh?"

"Billy Boudreau doesn't get his chickens, his kids eat beans and rice. They hate beans and rice. You a humanitarian, Saint Brent?"

While she continued unrolling bills and counting them, he walked around the Cessna looking for—heaven only knew what. Cracks in the propeller maybe, holes where rivets should be? Pools of leaky fuel seeping into the dirt, broken struts, or roosters nesting under the cowling?

Seeming satisfied, Kat rolled the bills, replaced the rubber band, and stuffed the wad in a quickly zipped shorts' pocket. She folded three segregated fifties, tucking one of them in her bra while the others went into one of the deep flap-pockets of her olive shirt.

"Well?" She turned to Brent, hands raised. "What you waiting for, Flyover? Climb in."

Ready or not, by five o'clock, five-thirty at the latest, elements of Angeline's peaceful island existence would change. Hands braced on the porcelain bathroom sink at the local high school where Zeller had arranged the press conference, she stared in the mirror. The snaking scar never seemed more pronounced, yet she refused Braeden's suggestion to disguise it with makeup. She must be crazy.

And her life had already changed.

Cooper had integrated himself into her daily routine so fully Angeline didn't know what she'd do if he left. She almost thought *normal routine*, but nothing about any of the past few days' occurrences registered in the normal range.

Jack—who had never been away from home, let alone his mom—was well on his way to this great stateside adventure with Braeden and Montgomery, giddy with anticipation about his first plane ride. New places, new people, new friends.

Brent had stashed her parents in some loaner cabin in the

woods, her father oblivious to the exposure they faced. And somewhere, on this exquisite island she loved, there existed a frightened little boy in the hands of a monster.

Today she took the first step toward ending that. No more hiding. No more fearing a paparazzo would jump out of the mangroves, snap a photo, and the next day her picture would show up on the cover of some grocery store rag.

Nope. No worry about that. Tomorrow her photograph would appear on every news venue she could imagine, and then some.

Voorhees no longer controlled their lives.

Nick guarded the bathroom door. He had taken her picture with his digital camera after their meeting around the dining table, and a local photo shop printed copies for distribution to the press. They also included a fact sheet and brief history of what had happened to her, including as little detail as possible while still keeping it honest.

As promised, Cooper produced a photo of Voorhees, and Mathieu Fournier arranged the bounty. Luckily, he and Cooper didn't have to see each other.

Nick knocked. "It's time," he said.

She dragged open the heavy door. "Have you seen Cooper?"

Stress tinged her brother's voice. "Not yet, but I'm sure he's here."

"Okay." She smoothed the front of her linen jacket. "Maybe I should've worn the blue dress. You know, the one with the white buttons?"

"You look fine." Nick smiled too much. His tired eyes and the fret lines in his brow gave away his concern. "You look great," he said. "Really."

Angeline touched the side of his face. "Liar."

"You know you love me anyway."

"Speaking of brothers I love," she said, "do you have any idea where Brent's gone?"

"He's not keen on you doing this, so he's probably off somewhere sulking. He'll show when the press conference winds down and offer whatever help he can."

Chief Zeller stuck his head out the door at the end of the hall which lead to the backstage area of the auditorium. He motioned them to hurry.

Angeline straightened her skirt. She walked in her safest flats, refusing to use her cane in front of a crowd of scoop-mongering reporters. Under strong protest from both Nick and Cooper, she had decided the auditorium's heavy curtains, standard burgundy velvet, should be open when she took the stage. The press might as well get used to her limp. She had.

Inside the back-lit room, using the metal rail for support, she climbed the short flight of stairs and positioned herself to walk on with Zeller. She spotted Cooper across the way, where he stood with his arms crossed and legs widespread, talking with a deputy.

Their gazes met and she mouthed, "Thank you."

He nodded, unfolded his arms, and gave her two thumbs up offering support she knew wasn't heartfelt. He had spent the morning throwing every objection her way he could think of. She appreciated his effort to protect her, but no argument would change her mind.

Zeller stepped up and offered his arm. "You can do this," he said. "Keep your mind focused on your boy and getting your life back."

Odd. Angeline never thought of the man as tender. Yet he'd gone out of his way these last few days to offer solace, and she wouldn't forget his kindness.

She glanced once more at Cooper, nodded, then inhaled deeply before stepping into the light…and opening Pandora's Not-So-Lovely Box.

Brent and Kat toured the island's north side by air for several hours, with his gaze glued to the landscape. His hands gripped the seat on either side of his hips, and for the time being he'd managed to avoid getting poked in the butt by the maverick spring.

Brent wasn't sure what he hunted. A remote compound of some sort, or a cabin where Voorhees could come and go undetected? Steal a boy and hide him out? A boat dock maybe?

So far, he noted nothing suspicious.

The island was surrounded by white sandy beaches, with most of its inhabitants populating the south side where cities and townships were strung like lanterns along the coast. The interior consisted of horizon-to-horizon swamp and rain forest, interrupted by the occasional river or indiscriminate tributary, and as they approached the mountains, breath-stealing waterfalls. The Cessna was but a mosquito's buzz in the air, an insignificant noise above all the splendor.

"Landing strip," Kat said out of the blue.

"Landing?" He all but squeaked the word as a rectangular clearing materialized on one end of a mesa, sandwiched between a raging river and a dark carpet of green.

"Used to be an old sugar cane plantation," she explained. "We've got a few of them scattered over the island. Abandoned decades ago. Not much left of this one. House and mill are gone, but the road's still passable."

Brent frowned. "Road?"

Cinching her seatbelt, Kat guided the Cessna into a series of approach loops so sharp the horizon went parallel with the side windows.

His head spun. He closed his eyes and swallowed bile.

"Hey, hey." Her voice became a remote echo amidst the buzzing mosquitoes.

Nausea punched him in the gut.

"Take this." The plane lurched as she shoved a gallon-size plastic bag in his hand. "Barf bag," she said. "The cleaning crew on this airline is me. You redecorate my cabin, and it's you."

Brent's eyes shot open. "You're kidding, right?"

"Breathe deep," Kat instructed.

He emitted an obscene sucking noise.

She laughed. "Again. There you go. I've got a great joke for you about a naked school teacher, purple knee-hi socks, and a ping-pong table with one short—"

"Already heard it," he grumbled. In fact, he'd retold variations on the same joke for years. "Just get us on solid ground. Preferably in one piece."

"I noticed the cap you're wearing back at the hangar." She still tried to distract him; it wasn't working. "International Longshoreman's Association. You a longshoreman?"

"Boatman," he stuttered. "L-Linehandler."

He assumed she grinned at the color leeching from his face.

"Never had me one of those," she said. "But I've heard that longshoreman do it in the water. You do it in the water, Saint Brent?" The Cessna leveled off. She focused on the upcoming cliff face where the landing field began.

He couldn't take his eyes off her. Drop-dead gorgeous popped in his head. Not in that prissy, debutante ball kind of way, but sassy and tough, independent. A combination of iron and Irish lace.

Clearing the cliff by a hiccup, she set the plane down. The Cessna rolled to a smooth stop, its propeller cutting a neat swath in the tall overgrowth.

"Whoooohoo!" escaped before Brent could bury it. He pumped his fist, shrugged out of his seatbelt, and slapped the instrument panel in front of him with both hands. Then he stopped, swallowed hard, and simply stared at her.

Biting her lower lip, smiling, Kat O'Leary looked like she knew he wanted to kiss her—and she liked what she knew.

Chapter Thirteen

The hands barely crept across the white face of the oversized, black-framed clock opposite the school's stage. Reporters filled every seat at the chrome and red cafeteria tables. They stood along the back wall and congregated in front of doorways. A buzz of unintelligible conversation hung in the air, interrupted by the occasional cough or sneeze.

Zeller ordered no cameras or cell phones be used during the press conference, under threat of confiscation. But Angeline knew better than to believe in a fairytale of total compliance.

Fifty minutes into her announcement, she had covered her accident, coma, and rehabilitation, briefly discussed Jack, and opened the forum to questions lasting another twenty minutes. She was spent.

A reporter shouted above the din. "So what's it like to be reincarnated without actually dying?"

She couldn't see him, but his question threw her.

When she didn't immediately answer, Chief Zeller leaned into the microphone. "Please stand to ask your questions." He'd stationed his men throughout the crowd.

Midway back from the stage, a man rose. He wore his sandalwood hair slicked straight back. Glasses rimmed in chunky black frames bridged his boxer's misshapen nose, and the thick lenses magnified obsidian eyes, so dark there appeared no iris at all. Sandalwood echoed in the tuft under his bottom lip.

Angeline blinked away dizziness and steadied herself with both hands on the podium. "Do I know you?"

Another reporter shouted, "Answer his question, or move on to the next one. We got deadlines, doll."

Walter Wallace? She searched the crowd for the reporter's face—and found him slouched in a chair at the end of the front row. There he sat, center stage on the second row, and again on the third. He stood at the back of the room.

Walter Wallace appeared everywhere, and when Angeline blinked, nowhere. Wallace was gone.

She licked her dry lips, then squeezed her eyes shut as a wave of dizziness overcame her. When she opened her eyes to address the room again, the reporter in the dark glasses was gone, too. She swayed. Had the men been there at all? She glanced to Zeller, who moved quickly to the podium

The Chief bent over and spoke into the microphone. "This," he pointed to the enlarged photo of Willem Voorhees on a black easel beside him, "is the alleged perpetrator of Charles Jackson Cooper's abduction, as well as a number of other kidnappings on an international scale." He answered the volley of questions that followed with brevity and patience. After another twenty minutes, he said, "That concludes this press conference, ladies and gentlemen."

Nick escorted Angeline from the stage as the Chief added, "You will find the answers to any other questions in the packet you received when you entered the auditorium. Now I insist you return Miss St. Cyr's graciousness by remaining seated until she exits the building."

A buzz of conversation erupted.

Cooper met her at the bottom of the short flight of stairs. "What happened up there?"

"I-I guess I froze."

"Let's get you out of here," he said. "Bernard's watching for us behind the school." With his arm around Angeline's waist, they made their way to the exit.

She couldn't stop the quiver in her voice and tried disguising it with laughter. "I think I'm going to be sick."

Cooper stopped in the corridor. He took her face in his warm hands and studied her. "Need to stop by a bathroom?"

She placed her palm flat against the mint green tile. "Give me a minute. It should pass." He didn't say so, but Angeline knew a minute was all they chanced before the hall swarmed with hungry reporters. "Okay," she said after a handful of deep breaths.

"You sure? We can detour by the teacher's lounge, get a Coke, and rest a while on the couch."

She shook her head. Home was what she needed. "The sooner we get to the house, the sooner I can call Jack. Do you think they're home yet?"

"The flight left at eight, they layover in Miami. Why don't we wait until morning to call? Big day today, they'll be tired. Braeden will want to get Jack situated, get them all bathed and in bed. Let's cut her a break. Okay?"

"I hate it when you're so reasonable," she said. "Okay, tomorrow. But first thing."

Bernard held the rear passenger door of the Voyager open as they hurried outside.

Brent gripped the Cessna's door handle, ready to disembark, when he realized landing wasn't part of his prepaid parcel. "Why did we set down?" he said. Out the plane's windshield he noted a gaggle of leering vultures convened at the edge of the landing field—such as it was.

"I told you before, Flyover, this is a humanitarian mission." Kat unfastened her seatbelt. "Come on." She stood, and back hunched, made her way to the gutted rear of the Cessna where she preceded to unlatch and lift the cargo door. "You gonna sit there or what?"

The thought had occurred to him. Brent eased out of his seat and climbed in the back, no small feat. Together they lugged eight clucking, squawking wire coops forward. He counted twenty-two hens, two lucky roosters, and two unhappy ducks, one of which tried to take off his thumb. Two blue and white Igloo coolers followed, plus a canvas tote brimming with mail and several brown paper-wrapped packages postmarked in the States.

"Damn, woman, what do you have in these?" he said, as he dropped the cooler he lugged in front of the cargo door.

"Jump down," she yelled. "I'll hand them off to you." Once he was on the ground, she pointed beyond his shoulder. "Our helpers have arrived."

Brent set his cooler down and turned at a creaking sound. A wagon drawn by two gray nags, both sadly looking one wheeze away from the glue factory, pulled alongside the plane. Plum-sized flies buzzed their ears and swishing tails.

He batted several insects away from his sweat-slicked forehead. The wagon resembled a movie prop, or a holdover from another century.

A lanky man climbed down from the seat. He went to the wagon's rear and lowered the tailgate. Five laughing children spilled from the back. He grinned sheepishly at Kat, and then swiped his straw hat from his head as she approached. Tan and rail-thin, the man wore light-colored trousers, belted low, and a white t-shirt. He appeared clean-shaven, his attire immaculate, and dark bristly hair cropped military close.

They hugged briefly, did the cheek-kissing bit Brent recalled from countless foreign films, then launched into an animated, hand-gesturing tête-à-tête in what sounded like Pigeon French.

Kat made the introductions. "Brent St. Cyr," she said. "This is Billy Boudreau, a good friend. Billy...Brent. He's my flyover."

How good a friend was Billy Boudreau? Brent nodded and extended his hand. "Nice to meet you."

Billy cleared his throat. "The pleasure, she is mine." His accent sounded more Cajun than French; his grip firm and strong, hand calloused. It seemed they both belonged to the blue-collar brotherhood.

The children stood in a uniform row as if they were the reception line charged with greeting the queen. They looked to range in ages from four years to ten or eleven: four boys, and one dark-haired, rosy-cheeked munchkin. No fancy dress or patent leather shoes for this little lady, but she appeared as crisp as her father in denim shorts and a yellow cotton shirt.

She shoved a wild mane of dark curls out of her face, bestowed a gap-toothed grin on Brent, and he fell in love.

It took twenty minutes to load the wagon with everybody pitching in. Billy secured the coops and coolers by threading rope through the wire cages and attaching the knotted ends to the wagon's sides. He deposited four of the children next, the two older boys in the back behind the coops and the two younger ones up front on the seat.

Brent caught Kat grinning and watching him over the man's thin shoulder as he retrieved a bottle of water from his knapsack and handed it to his exotic little shadow. The girl ran to the other children, chattering in a squeakier version of the Pigeon French. Brent chug-a-lugged the second bottle, letting the cool liquid spill down his shirt front.

Why did Kat's stare make him feel all cranberry-jellied inside? He never reacted that way to women, not even remotely.

After a brief exchange with Billy, she walked back to where Brent stood beside the vintage Cessna. "Billy's invited us to dinner."

"But—"

"You paid for two days of my time." Kat gazed at the sky. "We've seen all we can today, and I'm working on some ideas for tomorrow."

"Still—"

"Other than the clients he meets for his guide business, Billy's family is isolated. The children are home-schooled, and guests are an occasion." Frustration at having to explain lowered her voice a degree. "They see me all the time, but you're a big deal, Flyover. Santa and the Easter Bunny and a big old Jack-O-Lantern all rolled into one. We're actually going to eat at the table." She swiped at a loose strand of raven hair, but it stuck to her grimy forehead. "I accepted Billy's invitation for both of us." Her unflinching gaze dared him to argue. "Come on. You have the time." She looped her arm through his and steered Brent toward the wagon. "And you might just learn something."

He'd already learned one interesting fact: tough-as-drought Kat O'Leary was a marshmallow. "How far is it?" he said.

She laughed as she hoisted herself onto the back of the wagon with the giggling children. "Too far to walk." She extended him her hand.

He was barely settled when Billy Boudreau jerked the reins and clicked his tongue. "*Allons!*" he shouted to the nags. "Let's go."

Brent wouldn't soon forget the trek on the jostling cart. Kat O'Leary sat so close he could feel her heat through the damp layers of denim and cotton. He smelled her sweet female sweat. Hens clucked, and ducks quacked. Five giggling children jabbered in French behind them, pointing out this and that.

Not that he understood one garbled word.

Occasionally his pixie shadow smiled shyly, opened her treasured bottle, and shared its liquid gold with the other children. It shamed Brent how they acted like fizzy water was the greatest invention ever. He hadn't even paid a buck for it, and he'd left more than one bottle unfinished on a job site.

It took them an hour down a dirt road cut in the overgrowth to reach their destination. To Brent's astonishment, time seemed fleeting.

As the children helped unload Kat's bounty, a robust dark-haired woman came out of a simple frame and stone house. She carried a shallow pan of water and a bar of soap. Within minutes, hands were washed and children seated at one end of a long, rough-hewn table under a canopy of mosquito netting.

The woman disappeared inside the house and returned with a clean pan, a new bar of soap, and a thick towel. She presented the lot to Brent with a broad smile.

His head jerked in Kat's direction.

"Hey." She raised her hands in front of her. "Don't look to me for help, Flyover. Nobody sits down to Mia's table dirty. I'm next."

Mmmm. He'd hang around for that show.

Brent searched the surrounding area and spotted a cluster of thick trees. On the side away from the children's peering eyes, he peeled off his damp shirt, hung it on a branch, and began dousing himself with water.

Heaven couldn't possibly feel this great.

"Not bad." Kat leaned against the closest tree, arms folded across her full breasts. She took the towel from the branch Brent draped it over and offered it to him. For the briefest moment, it dangled between them.

Then his mind flashed to the husky male voice he had heard in the background when he first called her, to the intimacies the man relayed about her anatomy in vivid detail.

As if she could read his thoughts, Kat tossed the towel at him. "Would you hurry it up," she said. "The children are hungry, and they can't eat until everyone sits."

Twenty minutes later they gathered at the rough-hewn table. The simple meal, cooked on an open fire, consisted of black bean soup over yellow rice, served with cassava bread, sliced mango, and star-shaped carambola. The mosquito-netting tent kept a few dozen flies at bay.

Brent grinned. *Beans and rice.* He'd lay odds tomorrow Mia served chicken. He found the food delicious and filling. After thanking his hostess, he hoisted himself onto the wagon's bed. He leaned back, hands clasped behind his head, and watched Kat go through the ice chests with Mia. She'd called it "women's work" and shooed him away when he offered to help.

It was hard to fathom she packed so much in such a small space. Toothpaste, soap and shampoo, combs and brushes. Dry staples for cooking, books and chewable vitamins for the children, first-aid and school supplies. There were even a number of floor puzzles, which the giggling horde quickly made off with.

Billy Boudreau stopped near the wagon. He tugged a pouch of Redman Select from his back pocket, opened it, and inserted a generous wad of tobacco in his mouth. Brent declined the offer. Billy sighed his contentment. "Mia don't allow chew near the little ones," he said after a minute or two of obvious bliss. "Come. Let's walk off dinner."

"Sure." Brent slid from the wagon and joined him on a narrow trail leading to another building considerably smaller than the house. A tall radio tower rose among the trees and wilderness, a cue that civilization stood at the ready.

Billy stopped beside the building and gestured toward a parked Jeep, partially covered with a faded green tarp. "Waitin' on a part," he said.

Brent walked around the Jeep. The all-terrain vehicle appeared vintage; military surplus kept in prime condition. He lifted a corner of canvas and peered under. "I see that."

Billy whipped the tarp off and cast it to the ground. "Funny," he said, as his thick Cajun accent rolled past the tobacco bulging his cheek. "When I soldiered for Uncle Sam, if a man wanted to make sure no one took his Jeep, he removed the distributor cap, pulled the rotor, and then put the cap back on. Everyone had a key, you know."

Brent didn't know. He'd never served.

"Another gent hops in..." Billy spat over his shoulder before continuing, "He tries to start the Jeep and thinks it's broke down. Ain't no soldiers out here. No one drives this Jeep but me. I pull the damn distributor cap and rotor off to work on it, lay 'em on the ground, turn my back for a second and *trop tard*, too late! Damn monkey done run off with both. *Pas de bêtises.*" He laughed then. "No joking. Now I'm out here waiting on a part that's probably sitting in a tree within spitting distance, and the owl-eyed bandit is having himself a fine laugh at Billy Boudreau's expense. Lord, don't it beat all?" He spat again. "So, *quoi tu veux?*" His gaze slid toward Brent. "What y'all want with our Kat?"

Brent almost swallowed his tongue.

Billy laughed again. He moved a step closer. "I like you, man, did from the minute we shook hands. You seem to have a lick of sense and Mia, she appreciates that in a man. But mind your manners around Kat. I won't take kindly to her heart getting broke like this Jeep here."

So, there was a point to their walking off dinner. Brent wanted to get pissed but couldn't. Kat took care of the Boudreau clan; they took care of her. *Family.* Inwardly, he chuckled. He hadn't been on the receiving end of the *no sex with my daughter* talk since prom night, circa 1992.

"We ought to get back." Billy picked up the tarp, and Brent helped him cover the Jeep. "Be dark soon, and I need to see you and Kat back to her plane." He waited until Brent caught up, then trudged down the path.

Brent noted Kat's curious stare when they returned. With all the items sorted and put away, he and Billy stowed the empty coolers back in the wagon.

The man turned to Kat and gestured toward the seat. She shook her head, came around to the back, and hoisted herself up next to Brent for the return trek to the Cessna.

They traveled a few potholed yards down the dirt trail with the children running after them, giggling and waving good-bye.

Kat waved back. "They have no refrigerator," she told Brent. "Billy lives life simple and likes it that way. But tonight, his children will have chocolate milk."

And puzzles, he thought. A giant fire truck, the solar system, a fairy tale castle. Milk and puzzles, such small and inexpensive gifts, yet these kids seemed so pleased. As pleased as the woman who delivered their treasures.

She was also a puzzle, this one; and he aimed to put the pieces together.

Several hours later, Kat hugged Billy Boudreau and saw him on his way.

"Do you do this often?" Brent asked as he watched her climb inside the Cessna via the raised cargo door.

"When I can. Every couple weeks or so, I guess, when Billy needs supplies or has mail or I drop off a client. He runs a wilderness guide business." Kat smiled at him, something she hadn't done since the washing incident behind the trees. "Whenever I have a rich tourist onboard footing the bill for gas." She flipped the long braid over her shoulder. "Today that was you, Saint Brent." She disappeared into the shadows of the Cessna's cargo hold, and after a minute of jostling and grunting, returned with an armload of canvas, mosquito netting, and rope. She dumped the lot in his arms.

Brent eyed the knotted rope with suspicion. "What's this?"

"Hammocks," she said before retreating into the plane's shadowy depths.

He dropped the bundle on the ground beside him. "As in...you tie them to the trunks of trees, hammocks?"

She laughed, again that glorious robust sound he remembered from their first conversation. Only this time, no booze. Maybe there never was any booze. "Unless you want to sleep on the grass,

Flyover." Kat came to the door. "I wouldn't advise it."

He reached up, gripped her waist, and lifted her down. He enjoyed watching her eyes widen with surprise. "Why can't we sleep inside the plane?" he said.

Her look was quickly replaced by annoyance. "You can, if you're scared. I prefer my hammock." She sorted the bundle into two piles, picked up half, and handed it back to him. Then she lifted the other half and carried it to a cluster of giant trees at the clearing's edge. She knotted one end of rope around a tree, then the other around a larger tree.

His gaze flitted from her magnificent trees to the Cessna, several times. Okay, he'd give it a shot. Dragging one end of rope in the dirt, he hoisted his bundle and went in search of the perfect tree. It didn't take long to find it.

Brent's tree stood maybe twenty feet. Its thick trunk split into a Y over his head, like an inverted divining rod, and dispersed amongst its shiny green leaves—pointing down as if to say *Tie your hammock here, boy*—hung small, sweet-smelling green fruit. Like baby Granny Smith apples. A smaller tree grew within close enough proximity he could tie off the hammock's other end.

Perfect. Whistling, he began constructing his bed. This wilderness bit wasn't so hard.

They'd been home little more than an hour and already Cooper felt a release in his pent-up nerves. Now, if he could only accomplish the same for Angeline, who seemed strung tighter than piano wire.

In her bedroom, she spoke to him through the open bathroom door. "I don't remember talking to reporters being so exhausting."

Steam filtered through the narrow doorway. He'd thrown together soup, sandwiches, and tea while she showered. Placing the tray on a gate-leg table, he noticed the stack of board games under it. He leaned against the door's frame to watch her rub her short-cropped hair with a thick towel. It was a sight he'd never grow tired of. "I thought Zeller did a good job handling the crowd."

Angeline dropped the towel on the granite countertop and

picked up a brush with a curved tortoise shell handle. "Yeah," she said. "The Chief still surprises me." Easing past Cooper, she crossed the room, opened an ornate wardrobe housing a small television, and switched on the set. Her *faces* appeared side by side on the screen. She waved toward the headshots. "Yesterday's me, and today's me. Not exactly new and improved."

Cooper turned up the volume. They listened as a long-jawed anchor relayed the day's breaking story he called "The Resurrection of a Supermodel." The man went on to mention Jack's kidnapping, then ended his segment with the photograph of Voorhees. The Dutchman's sinister eyes watched them as if he knew they watched him.

Angeline stood there long after the news went to commercial.

Finally, Cooper reached around her and switched off the set. They needed a diversion in the worst way. "You should eat."

"I'm sick of people telling me that." She faced him. "Do you think Voorhees has seen the broadcast?"

"It's a possibility."

"How soon do you suppose we'll hear from him? Do you have his cell phone with you?"

He patted his pocket, sat in a chair at the table, and picked up his sandwich. He'd left the phone on vibrate during the entire press conference. "He'll call when he calls. By the way, in case I didn't already say it, you pulled off a gutsy move today."

She sighed and slid into the other chair. "I almost blew it, I was so scared. I mean, it was nothing like before, when I used to—"

"Didn't show." He took a huge bite from his sandwich. *Diversion.* His mind cranked into overdrive. "I was proud of you. I am proud."

She smiled. "Really?"

"You kept your cool, answered their questions. Didn't you see how they watched you? Didn't you hear how quiet they got?"

"Guess I was too nervous."

"Well, I saw and heard it." He popped the last bite of sandwich in his mouth and said, "Eat your soup."

She fished a dumpling from her bowl and slurped from the

spoon until it disappeared in her mouth.

Cooper wiped his hands on a paper napkin and tugged a game out from under the table, turning the box over. *Battleship*. He returned it to the haphazard stack and inventoried the remaining games: *Connect Four*, *Operation*, *Mousetrap*, and something called *Hi Ho Cherry-O*. He'd never heard of most of them.

Angeline finished her soup, then leaned back in her chair. "That was good."

Cooper piled their dishes, bowls, and glasses on the tray and set it on the floor by his chair. He lifted the *Connect Four* game, placed it on the table, and opened the box. He dropped the lid beside the crowded tray.

"What are you doing?" Angeline said.

There were all sorts of diversions, all types of R and R: working a sweat, chilling, solitude, and a good book. Taking her away from today's press conference, from reporters and kidnappings and lost boys, called for the extreme kind. "Do you happen to know where your brothers are?"

"It's weird, but Nick is having dinner with Chief Zeller. Heaven only knows where Brent's gone. What are you doing, Cooper?"

"Setting up our game." He herded small red discs on the table in front her and yellow discs in front of him. Then he positioned the blue plastic grid between them.

"I see that much," she said. "I've played *Connect Four* a hundred times with Jack."

"Not like this, you haven't." He dropped the first colored disc, and it clattered to the bottom row of the grid. He stared at her. His gaze moved to the juncture of her robe's overlapping lapels.

Laughing, she pulled the robe tighter.

"Won't do you any good," he said.

She laughed again. "Why not?"

"I'm adding a new twist to the game. We'll call it *Cooper's Strip Connect Four*."

"But I'm only wearing a robe. You're fully clothed."

He grinned. "I know."

Angeline deposited her first red disc in the center slot of the blue grid. It fell to the bottom. Cooper dropped his yellow disc to the left of the center, blocking her on both the left and top. Her next disc went right of the center and his disc above hers.

He rubbed his hands together and grinned while she frowned. At a diagonal, he was one move away from her surrendering the robe.

She went to the right and low; he followed, blocking her fourth disc—and her win. She huffed a breath, stirring her bangs, then chewed on her bottom lip, and rubbed her chin. Next move, she played right; he went left, no gain for either. She moved right again, and the fourth yellow disc fell into place.

He had her.

She stood and loosened the knot of the robe's belt ever so slowly. Whipping the belt from its loops, she let her robe fall open as she draped the belt around Cooper's neck, her breasts inches from his face. "There you go," she said, sitting, not bothering to pull the robe together this time. "One item of clothing discarded. Want a rematch?"

Hell, yes. He emptied the grid on the table; red and yellow discs scattered.

This time, she started in the left corner, her red disc cascading noisily to the bottom. He went to the center of the grid. She followed, as did he. Now there were three discs in the center row. Yellow, red, yellow.

"It's your move," he said, after an extended pause.

"I'm thinking." She played the center again.

So did he.

Yellow, red. Yellow, red. Yellow.

He grew hungry and hard.

A red disc fell to the bottom, left of the center. He deposited his yellow disc above it. Both went left again.

He sucked in a deep breath. They each needed discs on the left to reach the winning four; it was her move.

She smiled as she held her red disc above the left-sided slot, then veered right. The disc clattered to the bottom.

Cooper dropped his disc in a slot. "You're killing me," he whispered.

"Not yet," she said. This time she moved left.

He blinked, scratched his head. His win went out the window. She was pretty damn good. At this rate, he might get the robe off her by midnight. "Tired of playing?" He hoped.

"Oh, I don't know." She ran her long fingers down her throat, rubbing a tiny circle between her breasts. "Jack and I could play this game for hours."

Well, hell. He studied the half-filled grid. Diversion *was* his brainstorm. He went to the right; she followed, and he almost jumped out of his chair when the fourth yellow disc eased into place.

He had her.

She peeled off one shoulder of the robe.

Or did he?

She shed the other shoulder and let both slip to her elbows, revealing mounds of creamy white and taut nipples.

"Come on," he said. Maybe this wasn't such a great idea.

A little shimmy followed, and the silken fabric slithered to Angeline's waist.

"Enough." He stood, whipped off his shirt, wriggled out of his jeans. Lifting her, he cleared the game with one arm, sending the grid and discs flying. He sat her on the table. The robe cascaded over the edge as his mouth traveled down her long torso. He stopped at her scarred legs and drew a quiet breath.

Her hand went to his shoulder. "Don't look at them," she whispered.

"Your scars are as much a part of our future as Jack is." Cooper kissed the six-inch blemish bisecting her right knee, then the hollowed pockmark next to it the size of his thumb. He moved to her left leg and kissed the series of puckers and indentions road-mapping the pale skin below her misshapen knee. Nick had already told him how the bones in Angeline's shattered leg resembled a box of Chiclets chewing gum when he got to her, and how he had puzzled the pieces back together using a series of graduated metal rings, pins, and gauges. He called the contraption "the lizard," although its technical name was the Ilizarov.

It didn't take Cooper but fifteen minutes of research on his laptop to learn that, in orthopedic circles, the esteemed Dr. Nick reigned as "King of the Lizards." That's why Fournier brought him in on Angeline's recovery.

Thank God.

He retraced his path, easing his hands along the backs of her legs, rejoicing in her quiver as he nibbled his way to her belly button then feasted on her breasts.

Cradling her bottom, he pulled Angeline to the table's edge. She clung to his shoulders and cried out as he thrust into her.

Chapter Fourteen

Cooper waited until Nick returned home before leaving a sated and thoroughly distracted Angeline sleeping contentedly in her bed. Returning one last time to the Hotel LeNoir, he dug the key card from his jeans pocket, along with a yellow Connect Four disc. He grinned as he pictured her silky robe crumpled on the floor next to the game table. It wouldn't hurt her brothers to speculate about their relationship; especially Brent, the control freak.

He unlocked the door, set the key card on the double dresser, and flipped the tiny disc in the air before placing it next to the card. He'd return the key to the concierge on his way out. Until this conflict with Voorhees was over, longer if his luck held, he would stay at Angeline's place.

Cooper took the cell phone from the pocket of his light jacket and tossed it on the bed, puzzled Voorhees hadn't called yet. Surely he'd seen the news coverage.

As if on cue, the phone emitted its "Paradise" melody, startling him. He answered on the second ring. "Tell me about the boy," he said. "Why release Jack, only to take another child? Or did you already have him in place when you took Jack?"

"You need a lesson in gratitude, Teacher."

The Dutchman's clipped words sent a chill up Cooper's spine. He opened the French doors and stepped onto the veranda, pressing the phone tighter to his ear. "Tell me about the boy."

"You think you can force my hand by holding a press conference?" Voorhees sputtered, his accent thickening. "What a fool you are. Or perhaps you thought this would gain you favor in the woman's eyes?"

The boulevard brimmed with music, vendors, and tourists. "If you're looking for another bout of verbal sparring over Angeline, you'd best peddle your gouda on another street corner, Dutchman. I'm not buying. Talk to me about the boy or stop wasting my time."

Voorhees spoke with brutal detachment. "I chose him carefully."

Cooper walked back inside. "From where?"

"He's the mirror image of your Jack."

That wasn't an answer. "Putting Jack's clothes on the boy doesn't make him Jack. He's nothing to me. You taking him is nothing to me."

"Then perhaps you should have a listen."

It took Cooper little more than a second to recognize the sound of water. Rushing, pouring, rising. *Lethal.* "Don't do this, you sick freak."

The phone went silent; the dial tone buzzed in his ear. He fought to calm his racing heart, but all Cooper saw was Griffie MacDonald's sheet-draped body loaded in a coroner's wagon. Suffocating anguish closed in. Crossing his arms, he yanked his sweat-drenched shirt over his head and threw it toward a chair. He paced in widening circles, unfastened his jeans, shimmied out of the damp denim, then stopped, bracing his arms on the low dresser.

This wasn't the time to fall apart. Not when Angeline needed him. Not when he needed to put the bastard Dutchman out of business for good.

A wave of nausea hit him, and he doubled over in dry heaves. His chest tightened. He flipped open his suitcase, tossing clothes aside until he fished out a folded paper sack. He clamped it over his mouth and nose, sucked in, then blew out. The paper crackled as it contracted with each desperate draw of air.

After two or three minutes, the dizziness left him. His heartbeat returned to normal, and Cooper surfaced calmer. But far from composed. He turned the shower on as hot as he could stand, curtain open, and let the water pummel his body until the tension ebbed and he regained control.

Control was what he needed if he was to save this boy.

Brent dumped the canvas on the ground, almost had the snarled hammock untangled when the sky opened. Gray clouds snuffed the sun's rays; rain peppered the landscape.

Great. More humidity.

His inherent St. Cyr stubbornness took over. After several tree-hugging tries, he slapped the end of the rope around the tree's giant trunk and began tying off his hammock.

"What are you doing?"

He whirled at the sound of Kat's raised voice.

Her face appeared ashen, her eyes round with something akin to panic in them.

He dropped the rope like a hot poker. "Hanging my hammock?"

She grabbed his arm, dragging him after her as she broke into a run.

His foot caught in a twisted vine, and he tripped over tree roots protruding from the ground.

Kat hauled him up. "There's a river ahead."

They stumbled toward the overgrowth.

"What'd I do?" He ducked, and a low-hung branch grazed his cheek. As he raised his hand, he felt the ooze of blood.

She knocked his hand away. "Don't touch your eyes."

"Why are you so pissed?" He heard the sound of rushing water. They plunged forward.

"Manchioneel tree," was all she said before shoving him into the icy river.

He came up sputtering and coughing. "Are you crazy?"

She dove in after him, shoving him under, massaging water into his hair, splashing it in his face and eyes. "I must be," she shouted. "Taking someone as green as you into the bush."

He swiped water from his face. "Tell me what I did."

"Show me your hands." When he held them out, she turned them over, checking his palms and wrists, knuckles and fingertips. "You scared me, Flyover."

"What is this?" he croaked. "Some backwoods initiation? Next thing I know a tribe of howling pygmies will jump out of the trees, yell 'Gotcha!' before they toss me in a cauldron of bubbling gunk."

She extended her hand. "Give me your shirt."

"I'm not takin' my damn clothes off."

"*Now* you get shy." She pointed her finger at him and said, "Don't move from this river. I'll be right back." She sloshed out of the water and tromped up the bank, slipping, sliding, shoes squishing. Sopping fabric clung to all the right places. "Shit!" was the last word he heard her say before she disappeared into the brush. When she returned, his skin had pimpled blue with goose bumps, and his chattering teeth sounded like Morse code. But he still stood in the waist-deep water.

She dumped a towel and blanket on dry ground. Gesturing to an outcrop of flat rock at the river's edge, she popped the oversized towel in her hands. "Take your shirt off and sit there."

He sat, unbuttoned his shirt, and shrugged out of it.

"The manchioneel tree is poisonous. *Deadly poisonous.*" She yanked the shirt from his hands and tossed it on the bank nearer the rushing water. "You don't climb the manchioneel. You don't touch it, sniff it, or go within a mile of it." Squatting, she scrubbed his shirt on a large rock, and then beat the drenched fabric with a small branch. "You don't pluck its leaves or eat its devilish apples." She eyed him over her damp shoulder, still pounding. Anger heightened the Irish in her brogue. "Ya ever seen Snow White?" She didn't give him the chance to answer. "That old wart-nosed crone doesn't hold a candle to the wickedness in this tree. My da always said it's the devil himself that's rooted in the manchioneel."

His shirt got dunked in the river. She lifted it and dunked again. "You don't use the manchioneel's branches for firewood, *ever*, and you sure as blazes don't stand under it when it's raining.

Jesus, Joseph, and Mary, Flyover! The manchioneel can blind you. It'll blister the skin right off you. Give me your pants."

Blistering skin, blindness? Brent kicked off his shoes. He hopped on one foot, then the other, tugged off his socks, and shimmied out of his jeans. He handed them over, flinching when Kat beat them on the rock the way she did his shirt. The woman had anger issues.

"What am I going to do with you?" She averted her eyes and extended her arm behind her.

Brent took the towel from her outstretched fingers, then a green army blanket. He sniffed. It smelled like hay...and chickens. He didn't see any point in telling her the rain had stopped. She was river-drenched. Besides, the view of her bouncing breasts draped in thin, wet fabric wasn't half bad.

She kept his socks but handed back his shoes. "Put these on so you don't step on a snake on the way back to the plane. I'm going to lay our clothes in the sun. While we still have sun."

Our clothes? He wrapped the blanket tighter around him. "What will you wear?"

"I've got an old shirt and pants in the plane. They'll do for tonight." With the clothes bundled in her arms, she started toward the Cessna, calling over her shoulder, "Give me twenty minutes."

He gave her twelve.

On his way to the cargo hold, Brent passed his shirt, pants, and socks spread out on the Cessna's wings like the human prey in a sci-fi movie that had had the life force sucked right out of it. Her clothes were there, too.

A smaller humanoid—with boobs.

He fingered the black bra she'd attempted to hide under her drying shirt.

"I made you a bed in the plane."

He jerked his hand away at the sound of her voice.

"Your clothes should be dry by morning," she said. "Mia packed a thermos of hot coffee in one of the coolers. You should drink some."

"So should you." He spread his towel on the plane's wing, next to the female humanoid. "You were in the river like me. You got chilled like me."

Kat sighed. "There's only one cup."

"So?" He raised his hands, then grabbed for his blanket toga before it dropped. "I grew up with three brothers and a sister. I know how to share."

She stomped toward her hammock, shouting back to him, "I was an only child."

Was that a hitch in her voice?

"Don't ever do that to me again, Flyover."

Brent frowned as he crawled inside the plane. She'd spread a sleeping bag on the floor of the cargo hold and tied mosquito netting to the passenger seat. He surveyed the landscape. Wisps of fog hovered over the terrain.

She had settled in her hammock, several yards of mosquito netting and the brown fedora hiding her face.

The woman was definitely a puzzle.

After digging the thermos out of the cooler, Brent slipped off his shoes and placed them by the open door. Then he unzipped the sleeping bag and burrowed in. He rested his shoulders against the back of the passenger's seat, poured coffee in the plastic thermos lid, and sipped slowly. The filtering warmth thawed his frozen insides.

Once finished, Brent screwed the cap on the thermos and set it on the floor. Easing further into the sleeping bag, he shoved his knapsack under his head and turned on his side. As he tugged the quilted camouflage over his shoulders, he studied Kat's gently swaying hammock across the way. The tip of her half-boot peeked over the edge, below the draped netting.

He never met a puzzle he didn't like, or couldn't solve.

Finally warm after his river baptism, Brent settled in. Night fused with the cosmos in this smidgeon of paradise, and a gazillion dazzling stars swept the treetops as if seeded by God's own hands. Melancholy howls broke the silence, the chorus of the concealed. A nocturnal croon. Something flew out of the treetops nearby, and he yanked the sleeping bag up to his nose.

Nothing wrong with Tarzan sleeping inside the plane, and Jane sleeping in a hammock.

Nope, not one damn thing.

Cooper returned to Angeline's house a few minutes after ten with Voorhees' call weighing on his mind. Tomorrow all hell would break loose. Tonight she needed quiet, another diversion.

They both did.

He found Nick stretched out on the sofa and wondered where in the hell her brother found a copy of the *New York Times* on Jacqueme Dominique.

The aroma of sautéing onions drew him to the kitchen and Angeline. An opened Campbell's soup can sat on the granite counter—Cream of Mushroom, the old standard, and one of his all-time favorites.

"I know," she said when he peered over her shoulder at the skillet. "As if I didn't have enough bad habits, I adopted one of yours."

"What are we making?"

"*We* are making Beef and Mushroom Dijon. Here." She passed him a colander of small, white mushrooms. "Slice these. They go in the skillet with the onions." She moved beside him at the counter and began slicing sirloin into strips. "I talked to Jack."

He removed a knife from the drawer near the sink. "I thought you decided to wait until morning to call."

"Brag knew I'd miss him. They went out for pizza, and she let him call when they got home."

He sliced the first mushroom and popped half in his mouth. "How's Jack doing?" There was comfort in the two of them working side by side. He wanted more. Hell, he craved an endless supply.

"Having the time of his life. The airplane ride was awesome. The attendant gave him those miniature wings to wear, and he sat by the window. He adores the girls, of course, but still thinks Tulip's a funny name. Tomorrow he and Montgomery are catching fish for dinner."

"Yeah, right." He chuckled, envisioning a trip to the seafood market in Kemah. The Sandman loathed the water as much as Cooper hated closets, and as he recalled, the way Angeline detested snakes. He returned the sliced mushrooms to the colander. "What next?"

She picked up the red and white can. "Um...I add the

mushrooms to the onions. You pour the wine and see if Nick wants anything?"

Right.

Nick called from the living room, "Glass of wine sounds good." He came around the corner. "Zeller's put a couple extra men outside."

Cooper poured the wine in two glasses. "Saw them when I drove up. Any visitors since the press conference?"

"It's creepy how quiet it's been," Nick said. "Guess all those reporters are working on tomorrow morning's headlines. Things will probably pick up then."

Angeline scooped the vegetables in a glass bowl, rinsed the skillet, added olive oil to the sizzling pan, and then the steak. "I hope so."

The two men turned and stared at her, mouths agape.

"Well," she said, "wasn't that the point of holding a press conference?"

Cooper handed Nick a glass of wine; he passed Angeline the Dijon-style mustard and a wooden spoon. "I gather Zeller has no new leads?"

Nick set his folded newspaper on the edge of the table. "Nothing."

Cooper realized he hadn't seen the channel jockey since this morning's meeting around the dining table. "Has anyone heard from Brent?"

They answered in unison, "No."

"I don't suppose he carries a cell phone either?"

Angeline continued mixing parsley with white rice. She spooned the meat mixture over it. "Why do you say that?"

"I don't know," he said. "I guess Brother Brent doesn't seem to me like the sociable type."

Nick snorted, almost choking on his wine.

"Stop picking on Brent." Angeline set two extra plates on the counter. "It's not fair when he isn't here to defend himself."

"He's not here for his watch either." Nick placed his glass on the table next to the newspaper. "Reminds me of when we were kids and shared chores."

She filled the plates and handed them to him. "Take these out to the officers across the road. When they're done, they can send the other two policemen in with the empties."

Her brother headed outside, and Angeline turned to Cooper. "Watch?"

"We're taking shifts on the beach." He pulled out a chair and motioned her to sit. "Guess we double up tonight. Wherever Brother Brent is, I hope he gets lucky and comes back in a better mood." He grabbed two oven mitts and retrieved the loaf of French bread from the oven.

"How did you know I made bread?"

He laughed. "Smelled the garlic." They made a good team.

Nick returned, and they finished their meal with cordial conversation about the weather, island flora and fauna, and the upcoming holidays. There was no mention of the boy on everyone's mind—or the monster holding him.

Cooper kept the phone in his pocket on vibrate again. A wave of nausea rolled through him as his mind replayed the call received in his hotel room. Telling Angeline would only cause her more suffering, and he'd tried hard to keep her mind on other topics. He thought about their game of *Connect Four*, and his nausea settled some. "Think I'll go up and rest a few minutes," he said, standing. "I'll take the first watch."

Nick pushed away from the table. "Since you two cooked, I'll clean up."

Cooper smiled. Doc's offer didn't sound heartfelt.

Angeline laughed. "All this help would be easy to get used to."

"Don't bother." Her brother stacked the plates on the table and added the cutlery. He held up his hands. "These are the tools of my trade, and it costs me the devil to insure them. If there wasn't a dishwasher in your state of the art kitchen, sis, I wouldn't be offering."

"Oh, I'll help." Angeline picked up the empty glasses. "You've always been such a whiner."

Cooper left them to their banter and headed upstairs to think.

No one had turned on the outside lights.

Fate.

The Onlooker rowed his small boat into the shallow water. He stopped a safe distance from shore. Tonight the boss had entrusted him with another delivery, equally as important as the one he had made before.

He squatted in the boat, feet widespread to steady himself, and grabbed hold of the orange t-shirt by its yoke and denim shorts by their backside. He lifted his charge and laid him face down in the water with hardly a ripple. One hand on the damp mop of sandy-brown hair, he shoved it toward shore.

Chapter Fifteen

An hour had lapsed since dinner. When Angeline didn't join Cooper for his nap, he phoned Chief Zeller and filled him in on Voorhees' call at the hotel.

"You're certain he won't harm the boy?" Zeller asked the same question twice.

"Wouldn't serve Voorhees' purpose." Cooper hoped he injected more confidence than he felt. "If he kills the boy, I have no reason to hang around. I told you before, Chief, the Dutchman wants me. The boy is only a means to that goal."

"You will tell me if he calls again, yes?"

Impatience rippled up Cooper's spine. "I called you this time, didn't I?" He cooled his temper at Zeller's prolonged silence. "Yes, I'll call."

After adding a few more cautionary words, the Chief disconnected. Cooper slid his feet into worn deck shoes and left the bedroom. Angeline's laughter struck him as he neared the bottom of the stairs, and he smiled.

Yep, having her brothers around had made a definite difference. And that knowledge still pissed the hell out of him.

"What's going on?" he said as he entered the kitchen.

"The officers sent their plates back for seconds." Angeline wiped her hands on a floral apron. "Nick says it's only because they're starving." She handed Cooper the two refills. "If you'll help him carry these plates, we can feed all four men at once." She lifted a bottle from the sleek granite countertop. "While you're outside, I'll pour the wine."

"None for me," he said. "I took first watch, remember?"

The men were gone less than five minutes. As they opened the front doors, they heard Angeline's scream.

Cooper beat Nick to the rear door by a heartbeat.

Angeline stood on the brick gallery, hands raised in front of her face. A glass of wine had shattered at her feet, spattering droplets of red on her white tennis shoes and beige slacks.

He mistook the splotches for blood and rushed to her aid.

"In the water," she said, shoving him away. "I was going to sit in the gazebo and wait for you, then I saw it."

Cooper searched the water. Air froze in his lungs when he caught sight of the orange t-shirt, blue shorts, and tennis shoes. A Jack-size torso wore them.

Nick grabbed his arm as he broke into a run toward the beach. "Don't touch anything."

Caught in a combative push and tug, neither man relinquishing, it took them several more minutes to reach the sand.

"Let go of me, you son of a bitch," Cooper yelled. "You don't understand. He might still be alive. A kid can last a long time in the—"

"Body's bloated. Looks like he's been in the water a while." Nick ducked when Cooper swung at him. He wrenched his cell phone from his pocket. "I'm calling Chief Zeller." They scuffled toward Jack's mangrove hideout. Nick shoved harder, and used his shoulder to impede Cooper's forward motion. He lowered his voice. "Get a grip, man! Angie's coming. You don't want her seeing this."

Cooper's thrashing ceased. Growing up in New Orleans, on the banks of countless bayous and the Mississippi River, he'd seen his share of bloated, decaying bodies pulled from the water. Nick was right. It was a memory he didn't want Angeline to know.

Two officers tore around the side of the house, weapons drawn.

"In the water," Nick yelled.

The policemen ran to the shoreline, one of them shouting into a two-way radio.

Light from a newly installed flood-lamp faded into sifting shadows at the water's edge, and the incoming tide beat a steady rhythm against the shore. It seemed as though the wind held its breath.

Angeline reached the mangrove cluster a minute or two behind them. "Dear Lord."

Cooper turned, blocking her view. "Let's go back," he said. "We don't want to get in anyone's way." His throat tightened, chest ached, palms itched from wanting to touch the floating boy. He swiped them against his jeans before he grasped Angeline's hand and pulled her through the gate and toward the gazebo. A ton of guilt pressed in on him. He'd read the Dutchman wrong, damn it, and somebody's kid paid for it.

The taller cop hurried back. He stopped in the sand on the other side of the white pickets, his colorless face encapsulated in the house's moody light. His grim expression matched the disbelief in his eyes.

"You *are* going to get him out of the water, aren't you?" Angeline said.

"No, ma'am. Not yet." He shifted and re-shifted from one leg to the other. Change jangled when he shoved his hands in his pockets. "I'm sorry. We can't move him until the Chief gets here with the crime scene techs and the coroner. We can't do anything but protect the integrity of the scene." He looked back to the water, where waves rocked the child, and he blew out an audible breath. "I have a boy of my own," he whispered.

It seemed an eternity as they stood there, no one speaking, their stares fixed on the sea.

Finally, Nick placed a hand on his sister's shoulder. "You should go inside."

Angeline shrugged off the gesture and shook her head. "Do what you want, but I'm not going in." She stepped away from him, as if he might try forcing her. "His mother isn't here," she said. "We don't even know who she is. If this was Jack, I would want—"

"We all stay," Cooper added. "But let's sit here." He led her up the gazebo steps to the lounge chairs. Her movements were clumsy, shakier than usual.

Nick called out to the officer before following them. "I'm a doctor. If there's anything I can do to help, please tell me."

Angeline sat in the nearest chair, her entire body quaking. Her gaze never left the small corpse.

Nick rubbed her shoulders. "Be right back." He sprinted across the yard and hurried into the house. The door slammed. Several minutes later, he returned with the pale green throw from the sofa, two glasses, and a bottle.

She stared up at him.

"Brandy." Nick poured amber liquid into one glass. "Drink it." He draped the throw over her shoulders, then poured liquor into the second glass.

Cooper waved the glass away and continued pacing an area behind the chairs.

Nick gulped the brandy in a couple swallows.

"Where is Zeller?" Angeline wrapped the throw more snugly around her. "I want that baby out of the water. *Now.*"

Nick wiped his mouth with the back of his hand. "Hold on," he said. "Here's the Chief."

Daniel Zeller marched around the side of the house, the way his officers had come. He went directly to the waterline, followed by three additional policemen. The tide had beached the body.

The techs quickly set up mobile lights and photographed the scene.

Angeline cringed with every flash.

It killed Cooper seeing her so distressed, and knowing he carried the blame.

Kneeling next to the body, the coroner grasped the boy's clothes and turned him over. The sea emitted a perverse sucking sound as if unwilling to surrender the child.

The nearest officer staggered to his feet, one hand folded across his waist. "Sweet Jesus," he said. The half circle of men blocking the view from the gazebo closed in. "It's a hoax," the officer called out. "A goddamn hoax."

Cooper bounded down the steps, followed by Nick and Angeline.

She took hold of his elbow and peered around Cooper at the cops. "What do you mean?"

"A doll," Zeller said. "Get it out of the water."

Cooper heard Angeline whisper behind him. "Thank God."

Relief palpable, he whispered a thanks of his own. Better the monster to have the boy, than the sea.

Two officers dragged the limp torso further inland and dumped it on the sand. Its round, mocking eyes stared at the night sky.

The Chief rested a hand on his belt. "Miss St. Cyr?"

Angeline stepped from behind Cooper. "Yes?"

He pointed to the corpse. "Do these clothes belong to your son?"

She stared at the doll; everyone stared at the doll. Then she nodded.

The painted face appeared grotesque under the artificial light. The body was perfectly proportioned, the hands, arms, and legs so eerily human-like. Cooper shuddered. The fine rooted hair was so similar to Jack's.

"How could anyone be so cruel?" Angeline's eyes widened with disbelief as she searched the face of each man surrounding the doll. "Why would he make us believe this was a dead child?" She turned and stumbled toward the house, her limp so pronounced Cooper thought she'd fall.

Nick blocked him when he hustled to follow. "I'll stay with her," he said. "You should talk with Zeller."

As Nick led his sister through the rear door, the two men sat at the iron table in the gazebo approximately six yards from the beach. Zeller spread his notebook under the light. "I assume Voorhees hasn't called since this afternoon?"

"No." Cooper batted away an insect, his gaze fixed on the doll as three of Zeller's men zipped it into a body bag for transport, although he seriously doubted they would find additional evidence. "Voorhees will call," he said after a few seconds. "He'll need to boast about how clever he is. How much he's able to slip by us. How he fooled me, goddamn it."

"Call me the second you hear from him." Zeller closed his notebook and returned his pen to the inside pocket of his suit coat. "I won't speak with Miss St. Cyr before I go, but assure her that she did the right thing this afternoon by holding the press conference." The Chief stood. He frowned toward the sea as one of his men extinguished the last mobile light and packed it away. "You've got yourself a cunning enemy, Mr. Cooper. You must remain vigilant."

The morning sun couldn't break through the clearing's thin layer of ground fog soon enough for Brent. He'd tossed and turned, then tossed some more. Dive-bombing intruders lusted after his ears and nostrils, even when he stretched the sleeping bag over his head. He swore Kat gave him the mosquito netting with a hole in it on purpose to get back at him for scaring her. A moth flew in Brent's mouth and stuck in his throat, despite his hacking fit. He washed it down with cold coffee and shuddered.

Kat's half-boot still peered over the hammock's side; her fedora hadn't moved.

Exiting the sleeping bag, he swung his legs out the door and stood, arching his back, then reaching down to touch his toes. He tucked the green blanket around his hips and padded barefoot to the Cessna's wing to retrieve his clothes. He shrugged into his shirt, dropped the blanket, and yanked up his boxers. When he reached for his board-stiff jeans, a brutal stab of pain shot up his right ankle. He cried out. His butt hit the ground hard, and he bent his knee to inspect his foot.

A reflexive kick catapulted the culprit from its perch on his big toe, and the unmistakable shape of a spider scurried toward the brush. Brent rolled to get out of its path.

His scream brought Kat to the plane. "What is it now?"

"There!" He pointed to the spider, which appeared one hairy leg away from changing its mind about the brush and coming back for seconds. "Step on it!" he yelled. "Step on—"

"Don't be such a girl." Kat walked over, squatted, and picked up the offender. She brought the spider within inches of her face. "It's only a little pink-toe," she said.

Brent gingerly touched his foot. "I know. Hurts like the devil, too."

She laughed. "I meant the spider, Flyover. It's a juvenile pink-toed tarantula." Kat walked over to him and extended her hand. The culprit leered at Brent from its roost on her palm. "You can tell it's a juvenile by the iridescence. See this greenish color?"

"Yeah, well. Baby or not, it bit me."

"You got bit?" He could've sworn she stifled a laugh behind her look of concern. "Let me see." She helped him over to the cargo hold where they sat side-by-side in the doorway, his bare legs brushing against her khaki trousers. With his foot rested on her knee, Kat poked the wicked-looking welt on Brent's toe.

He jerked. "Ouch! Damn it. That hurts."

"I know it hurts." She probed and prodded. "But it won't kill you. Let's get your jeans on, then your socks and shoes."

"You're kidding, right?"

Kat laughed and retrieved his jeans. She held them open so he could insert his feet. "Are you aware how many times a day you ask that same question? It's got to be a million, at least."

Brent grinned. "You're kidding, right?" He shoved his feet in the jeans and stood, wobbling.

Kat eased the jeans up his legs.

To describe the motion as erotic struck Brent as ludicrous. For Pete's sake, she was dressing him—not undressing him. Sweat trickled down his back. He forced his concentration to the trees behind Kat, the sunlit sky, the damn humidity; and for the first time in his life, Brent St. Cyr prayed for a limp penis.

Finally, Kat buttoned and zipped his jeans. "Come on." She handed him his socks and shoes. "Your foot's already swelling. The shoe will help you walk on it until I can get you in your car and to the doctor. Now, put them on. We won't lace the shoe, okay?" She stood, walked to the Cessna's wing, and gathered her clothes. She tossed him the lot, and he caught the pitch one-handed. Her lacy bra dangled down his arm.

Great.

"I'll get the hammocks," she said.

Twenty minutes later, the Cessna lifted into the air. After another half-hour of flight, Kat stared over at Brent, and his insides went all gooey. Was it possible to love the way a woman smiled at him—and hate it at the same time?

"What?" he said, straightening. He loved her smile because it lit up her face and accented those flecks of gold in her eyes. Hell, because it just plain made him feel good and took his mind off the bad situation unfolding around him with Angeline and the missing boy. He hated her smile because it usually meant she was laughing at him.

"How's the foot?" she said.

"Hurts like my feelings every time you poke fun at me."

"Sorry, but I left the first aid kit with Mia and Billy. *For the children*." She laughed.

"Ha, ha." He sank low in his seat, and the wayward spring poked his backside. Moving his leg, hoping for more comfort, he winced as pain spiraled from the injured toe. The damn shoe couldn't get much tighter. "S'pose you're calling me a baby now. Earlier, when the damn spider bit me, I was a girl."

"Uh-uh." She led the plane into another series of sharp approach loops. "You're anything but a girl, Flyover."

Out the side window, he spotted the small island airport. "What in the hell's that supposed to mean?"

Kat appeared to concentrate on the runway and beyond it, the dirt landing strip she staked claim to, but Brent caught her chuckle. She tapped her chin with a long finger. "Let me see now..."

Piano fingers, his granny would've called them.

Long and soft and warm and—

Whoa!

"I pegged you for boxers right away," she said. "Nice to know my instincts were right."

He coughed, as heat flooded his face. "How long were you awake while I was dressing?"

"Long enough to know there's not an ounce of fat on you, and you're definitely not a girl."

He leaned back in his seat, tugged the bill of his cap to his brow, and crossed his arms over his chest. "I'm ending this conversation," he said. "Now."

She snickered. "I still owe you a day's worth of air time."

He slit an eye under the cap. "You mean I don't get a refund?"

"Not unless you're willing to fight my creditors for it." She cinched her seatbelt, and on the next loop, the horizon slid parallel with the side windows.

He'd almost adjusted to the lurch it caused in his stomach.

"Besides," she said, "it gives you the chance to ask me to dinner."

Angeline hadn't slept more than an hour the entire night, in part because Cooper never came to bed. She stood in the kitchen making toast, though nausea roiled through her each time her mind flashed an image of the grotesque doll. Eating seemed an impossibility.

Nick stood at the window, a cup of coffee raised to his lips. He gestured outdoors, where Cooper stood at the water's edge, barefooted, his jeans cuffed around his ankles.

Cooper stood statue-still, and Angeline couldn't help wondering what he was thinking. Their lives had traveled a non-stop obstacle course of emotion since he found her. Another man would've run by now.

But Charlie Cooper was no ordinary man.

"He's been out there since sun-up," her brother said.

Which meant Nick suffered a sleepless night, too.

"I'll take him some toast and coffee in a minute." She placed the coffee beans back in the freezer, removed two mugs from hooks under the cabinet, and set them near the black and chrome Cuisinart Grind and Brew. "With all that's happened, it makes me nervous Brent hasn't called."

"Yeah. I'm starting to worry, too." He didn't look at her but added, "Found a phonebook on the desk in our room last night. Brent circled the airport's number."

"Surely he wouldn't leave without telling us."

"He circled a car rental place, too."

"You know Brent," she said. "No telling what kind of plan he's concocting."

"Or who he's concocting it with," Nick said

Angeline poured coffee in the mugs, her gaze fixed on the window as Cooper reached in his pocket. Her hands froze when he brought out Voorhees' cell phone. She returned the pot to the heating plate and left the kitchen. Standing beside the dining table, she watched Cooper waving his arms and pointing at the ocean. She sidestepped.

Face drawn, flushed with anger, he raised a hand to his temple and began shouting.

She set down the breakfast tray and moved quickly to the back door, calling over her shoulder to her brother, "Something's going on."

They reached the water in time to see Cooper draw back his raised arm. Angeline ran; she grabbed for the cell phone in his hand. Too late. He jerked away and let go. The device sailed through the air and plummeted into the sea.

He spoke with bitter resentment, "I'm through playing Voorhees' game. Jumping through his damn hoops. No more."

The phone disappeared beneath the water's surface.

"What about the boy?" Angeline's stomach knotted. Her gaze darted from the water to Cooper's implacable expression. "How will Voorhees get in touch with you?"

"He knows how to reach us, Slick, and me carrying this phone isn't keeping that boy alive." He shoved past her and tromped across the beach. "After last night's stunt," he called back, "I'm done."

Angeline followed. "What did he say that's made you so angry?"

"More of the same. Nothing."

"No clue where he might've stashed the boy?" Nick said.

"None." Cooper headed toward the house, covering yards of grass in a few strides. He went inside.

Angeline hurried after him. "Where are you going?"

Nick entered last and pulled the door closed, the lock clicking behind him.

"Soon as I change clothes," Cooper said, "I'm meeting with Zeller."

She and Nick spoke at once. "I'm coming, too."

He turned. "No." He jabbed a finger at Nick and said, "Find your crazy brother. We may need him."

Angeline flinched when he pointed to her.

"You call Montgomery. Fill him in on the doll, and while

you're at it, talk to Jack. It'll make you feel better."

Chapter Sixteen

ooper came downstairs twenty minutes later, thankful Angeline hadn't followed and listened in on his telephone conversation with Bernard. He and the taxi driver needed a quiet place to formulate their plan.

Nick was calling the airport from his cell when Cooper passed on his way to the front of the house. Searching for Brother Brent, no doubt. Angeline sat at the dining table speaking to Jack on the phone.

He stooped and kissed her forehead. "Give him my love," he whispered.

Bernard pulled up outside as Cooper closed the double doors. He poked his head back in and shouted to Nick, "Slip this dead bolt."

"Where to today?" Bernard said as Cooper climbed in the passenger's seat and slammed the door.

"Somewhere quiet, where we can have a drink and talk."

"Ah, yes," the driver said. "Bernard knows a great place."

Cooper figured as much.

Neither man spoke as they drove down Port Noel's main

boulevard. Souvenir shops and restaurants, the police station, town square, and small hospital where they'd taken Jack slid by in a kaleidoscope of sun-kissed normalcy.

They reached the outskirts of the city. Bernard turned into a narrow alley flanked on the left by an empty storefront, and on the right, a white stucco dive called Brizzy's Sandbar. The driver parked his van in a small, empty lot behind the joint.

Inside, they sat at a rear table, near the unisex bathroom and a vintage pinball machine: *Bally's Hocus Pocus*. Cooper hadn't seen one since his twenties. An OUT OF ORDER sign, taped across the machine's colorful backbox, obscured the magician's hat and shapely assistant. Duct tape blocked the ball shooter knob.

Brizzy's smelled of booze, old grease, and stale cigarette smoke. An undercurrent of bleach washed through on a cross-breeze from open windows. The beefy man waiting their table was a walking cliché: dingy Ocean Pacific t-shirt stretched across his bulging midsection, cigarette pack rolled in one sleeve, pencil-thin black mustache, tattoos on his gargantuan biceps—a red heart on his left arm, with the name "Lola" inscribed in its banner; an eagle and an American flag on the right.

The man clapped Bernard on the back. "Bernie, my man. What'll it be?"

"Coke," Cooper interjected. "Two." He took another look around the bar, caught sight of a cockroach crawling on a corner wall and added, "In cans, with straws, if you have them."

"Living dangerously, eh?" The man slapped the table's edge with a damp red- and white-checkered towel, which sent another roach tumbling. He threw back his head and released a belly laugh that ran deeper than the gut protruding over the grease-splattered tablecloth tied around his waist. "Two cokes straight up." He went behind the bar, still chuckling. "The straws'll cost ya extra."

"Tell me you don't come here often, Bernard." Cooper rubbed his hands together. He eyed the bathroom door with no intention of going in.

The cabbie propped his elbows on the table. "You said somewhere quiet and private. Brizzy's is perfect, yes?"

Perfect, sure. If you wanted to catch something penicillin wouldn't chase.

He leaned conspiratorially close. "What favor did you wish to ask of Bernard?"

Brizzy brought their drinks and placed two paper-wrapped straws on the table.

Cooper waited until he'd gone back behind the bar, then drew forward. "I need your help, my friend. And I won't lie to you, it involves a great deal of risk."

Bernard popped the tab on his drink. "I will gladly help," he said.

"I talked to Voorhees this morning. He's the man who kidnapped Jack and now holds another boy. He's willing to trade."

"Trade?" The taxi driver unwrapped his straw and shoved it in the can. He took a sip, then set his drink aside. "This does not sound good."

Off the top of his head, Cooper could summon a few superlatives for how it sounded: dangerous, insane, suicidal. "It's the only way I'm guaranteed the boy, Bernard. Voorhees wants me. We make the exchange, and he gets what he wants. But, without you, my plan isn't worth spit. I need you to wait near the square. I'll walk the boy to your van, you drive like the devil's gaining on you. Take the boy to Zeller. The Chief will see he gets home."

"But, what of you?"

Cooper shifted in his chair. "I got lucky before, outside New Orleans. Maybe I'll get lucky again. With the boy safe, you see, I can afford to take chances. Make a run for it. The swamps on the island aren't all that different from the swamps I grew up in. Like I said, you get the boy the hell away from there. Get him safe, and don't hesitate. I'll handle whatever happens next."

The front door thumped. Angeline glanced at the clock on the digital panel on her stainless steel range. Cooper had been gone two and a half hours. Thinking it might be him, she walked out of the kitchen, then froze at the sound of someone fumbling with the lock.

Cooper kept a key.

Pounding commenced. "Open the damn door!"

Brent.

She released the deadbolt.

Her brother hobbled in. He kept his left knee bent so the toe of his tennis shoe skimmed the floor. Beads of sweat dotted his ashen face, and his arm draped the shoulders of a shapely woman, her expression equally grim.

Angeline hurried after him, drying her hands on the dishtowel sewn into the waistband of her apron. "What happened, where have you been?" She ducked under Brent's other arm and helped them down the hall and into the great room. "We were worried, and it appears, with good reason."

The young woman reached across Brent's chest and extended her free hand. "Name's Kat O'Leary," she huffed. "Sorry we have to meet under these circumstances."

Nick rushed down the stairs. "I thought I heard the door. Here, let me help." He relieved Angeline and eased his brother down on the sofa. "What circumstances are we meeting under?"

"Spider bite," the woman said, breathless. "Pink-toed tarantula."

Angeline dragged the ottoman closer. She lifted Brent's leg onto the cushion. "How bad is it?" As a child, she recalled spider bites turning into painful infections.

"The pink-toe's bite isn't usually this bad," Kat said.

"How on earth did you manage a run in with a tarantula?" Angeline grabbed Nick's bag from under a nearby table and handed it to him.

"Thanks." Nick turned to Brent. "Don't suppose you told her you're allergic to spider venom." He frowned, withdrew a syringe from his bag, and set it beside his brother on the sofa. "I didn't think so."

Kat stepped forward, her faced pinched with worry. "I usually carry an extractor kit in my plane for emergencies like this," she said. "But I left everything with—"

"Let's get his shoe off," Nick said.

Brent leaned against the sofa. He squeezed his eyes shut. "Don't make such a big deal, Doc. Just do it. By the way, Kat's a bush pilot."

Their heads jerked in Kat's direction.

"Bush pilot?" Angeline glanced back to appraise her younger brother.

"Kat...ouch, damn it!" Brent grimaced, his lips forming a thin, pain-laced white line. "This heavy-handed quack is my brother Nick. Mom always wanted a doctor in the family. You ask me, his calling leans more toward meat packing."

Nick tossed the woman a quick nod, then grinned at Brent. "Wait until you get my bill."

Angeline held Brent's ankle, while Nick tugged the untied laces out of the shoe's eyelets. He spread the opening as wide as he could and eased his brother's injured foot out.

Brent latched onto the cushion's back. He released a ragged breath.

Nick discarded the shoe, peeled off the sock, and emitted a low whistle. "Nice job, Brent. I'm surprised you could walk on this."

Angeline turned to Kat, wondering where her brother and his lovely bush pilot spent last night. She extended her hand. "I'm Angeline, by the way, sister to the spider victim."

Apparently, Nick wondered the same thing. "Where were you that you needed your shoes off, little brother?" He tore the plastic off the syringe with his teeth, spit the wrapping on the floor, squirted a few drops of liquid in the air, and inserted the needle near the bite. "You'll probably need a couple more of these." He stood, disappeared for a moment in the kitchen, then returned with a glass of water and two small white pills. "Better take these."

Brent and Kat exchanged glances, but Angeline noticed only Brent's complexion burned a deeper red. Normally, her thick-headed brother turned into a big baby when it came to needles—but not a whimper this time.

Impressive.

She gave total credit to the mysterious Pilot O'Leary.

Cooper unlocked the double doors and slipped inside Angeline's house at a quarter of eight in the evening, Voorhees a constant on his mind. But he'd formulated a plan, and it was doable. At least the part about getting the lost boy home.

Thanks to Bernard.

He walked down the hall to the back door and peered out. Brent slept deep in one of the lounge chairs on the gazebo. A dark-haired woman sat cross-legged on the wide-planked floor next to him, her back propped against the chair's side. She appeared upset—and eerily familiar.

"Hey, there." Angeline came out of the kitchen. "I wondered when you'd get home."

Home. He could easily get used to hearing that. "Hey yourself." But he wouldn't dream about domestic issues tonight. "Who's the woman on the patio?"

"A friend of Brent's."

"The attachment's obvious by the way she brushes his hair from his forehead. A little too friendly-like." Cooper moved to the window for a closer look. "Where does he know her from?"

She hooked her arm through his, stirring additional thoughts of home and a promising future.

He nudged them aside.

"She's a bush pilot," Angeline said. "If you can imagine that. Her name is Kat O'Leary, and she's got this wonderfully Irish accent. Baby Brother doesn't realize it yet, but she's got him hooked, filleted, and ready to fry. Isn't it great?"

Yeah. Great. Cooper's mind drifted back to his first day in the Rusty Pelican and the soused hardhats at the adjacent table. *Her wink.* He considered the night he spent in Daniel Zeller's jail, and the soft-spoken woman in the next cell, with a hint of the Emerald Isle in her voice. He'd bet his genuine Margaritaville parrot flip-flops both encounters were with the same woman. *This woman.*

Now, what to do about it?

He considered his previous run-ins with Brother Brent, and the way the guy charged in when he and Angeline slept. Nothing, that's what he'd do. Absolutely nothing.

Brent St. Cyr was on his own, and Cooper would love to strike a match to the fireworks.

Angeline interrupted his reverie. "Where'd you go today?"

"Here, there. Spent most of my time with Bernard." It wasn't exactly a lie. "He needed to discuss something personal. Family troubles. Confidential, you know."

Angeline looked like she didn't know but would love an explanation.

They needed a change of subject. "You cook anything this

afternoon? I'm starved."

"Nope, sorry." She dragged him toward the kitchen. "Galloway's delivered steaks, baked potatoes, and a disgustingly fresh salad I'm sure you won't appreciate. The dressing's to die for. We ordered for you."

He didn't want to let her go. "Sit with me while I eat?"

She gave him a quizzical look, then nodded. "I'll pour us some tea. Your dinner's in the oven."

Cooper reached for a couple of quilted green mitts with Texas blue bonnets stenciled on them, then opened the oven door. "You can fill me in on what Jack's been up to," he told her while she removed a pitcher of tea from the refrigerator.

The patio doors swung open, and Brent limped across the threshold with help from his bush pilot.

"Let me get that for you." Cooper got to the door before it slammed into Brent's hunched shoulder.

The woman's jaw dropped when she saw Cooper, recognition seared into her wide eyes and blanched complexion. "Thank you." She averted her gaze.

"No problem." Cooper studied Brent. "What happened to you?"

"Spider bite," Angeline said.

"Wouldn't happen be a black widow, would it?" Cooper couldn't resist the gibe.

Kat O'Leary's head jerked in his direction. "T-Tarantula," she quickly explained. "Pink-toe. Normally, it wouldn't be any worse than a wasp sting, but he's allergic."

An hour later, the setting sun ebbed into a crystal-black sea. Brent complained of a headache and retreated to bed. Nick followed a short time later, with a couple more of the small white tablets for his brother, saying he'd take the midnight watch.

Angeline talked on the phone upstairs. Jack again, then Braeden. It appeared the two women were mending fences, and the prospect provided Cooper a modicum of comfort. He'd grown close to Braeden during the last five years; she was good for Angeline. They were good for each other. If, after tomorrow, he didn't come back...

No. He wasn't ready to go there.

Cooper carried a cup of strong coffee to the gazebo and sat on the steps leading down to the beach. The door opened behind him. He shot a glance over his shoulder as the bush pilot stepped out.

She crossed the yard and stopped at the border of yellow Allamanda framing the architectural structure. Not too close, yet close enough anyone coming from the house wouldn't hear their conversation.

"Allergic, huh?" he said. "Isn't that something."

"It's not what you think."

"And what do I think...*Kat*?" Cooper twisted his body to face her. "I can call you Kat, can't I?"

She ran her hand along the lattice of white-washed wood. "You think I'm some kind of whore who picks up tourists for whatever I can fuck them for," she said. "I see it in your eyes, Mr. Cooper. But that's not who I am. It's not what I do."

"I've always believed there's only one kind of whore." Cooper cringed at his own abruptness; he sounded like his grandfather. "Let's see if I can put this in perspective." He set his cup on the plank floor behind him. "First time we meet, you're at the Rusty Pelican sitting in some jerk hardhat's lap, rubbing your...rubbing all over him like an alley *cat*. Next time you're sitting in jail, cozying up to me."

Her eyes narrowed with anger. "That's not how it happened, and you know it."

"I know your type, O'Leary." He should. Frances Jean Cooper had been cut from the same cloth. His mother thought she'd hit the lottery when she got pregnant by Charles Raison. She never imagined he'd ship out to Viet Nam before marrying her, and get himself blown up by a grenade.

But, hell, Frannie always made the best of her less than stellar circumstances. *Life gives you lemons, you bake a pie.* She lived by the creed, and didn't even wait for the bits and pieces of Charles to chill in a grave before selling his bastard child to dear old Granddad for fifty thousand dollars and a one-way bus ticket to Monroe, Louisiana.

Yeah. He knew Kat O'Leary's type all too well. His grandfather had beat it into him with sickening pleasure at every opportunity.

Frannie played; Cooper paid—and such was his childhood.

Kat took several steps toward him. "You didn't mind my type when you were cowering in a tiny cell, kneeling on the floor, afraid to move, praying to breathe."

He checked his watch. "Any port in the storm," he told her.

"Men. You're such hypocrites. Here." She opened her hand. "These are the keys to Brent's rental. I didn't want to just leave them."

"How will you get back to town?" *Like he cared.*

When he didn't take them from her hand, she dropped the keys beside Cooper on the step. They clattered down two more. "Not that it's any of your business, but I called for a cab. I'll wait out front for it. Tell Brent he can get in touch with me for his refund."

"Refund?"

Kat crossed the yard, anger showing in her stiff stride. She reached for the door, jerked it open. "Yeah. He paid for two days with me," she called out before stepping inside. "He only got one."

Barely seven the next morning, Angeline dressed in a floral skirt and crisp white blouse. "I'm going to my shop today." She sat on the bed and slipped her feet into white, open-toed shoes with her customary flat heels.

Cooper ran his finger down the middle of her back and delighted in her responsive shiver. Last night was the second time they'd gone to bed together and actually slept. *Nice.* "I honestly don't see why you have to go in at all," he said. "It isn't safe." They'd rehashed the same argument over breakfast. And again, while she brushed her teeth. He hadn't scored any points then either. "I have errands to run this morning," he added. "Maybe I'll stop in."

"Nick used the same ploy last night when he asked my plans for today." She stood, crossed the room to an open mother-of-pearl-inlaid jewelry box on the chest of drawers in the corner, and selected a pair of small, gold hoop earrings "I'm a big girl, Cooper. I don't need the men in my life checking up on me. Anyway, Zeller's nice young deputy will be with me."

The rookie. Great. "Your brother told me there were a few reporters hanging around the house while I was gone."

"There were. But Jack isn't here, so I don't care." Angeline fastened one earring, then the other. "Let them take their pictures, inundate television and cyberspace with them. Their ambition makes me old news all the faster." She took a quick peek in the mirror. "I can handle it." She retrieved her purse and a light sweater from the closet. "Besides, every time my photograph shows up in a news broadcast or on the front page of a grocery store rag, so does the one you provided of Voorhees." She gave him a thumb's up and followed it with, "Power to the paparazzi. Now, give me a kiss and tell me to have a good day."

An hour later, Cooper met Brent at the top of the stairs. Angeline's brother had managed to get his shoes on, but he still walked with a grimace. "Jeez." Cooper lent him a shoulder. "Maybe you should stay downstairs until you're mobile."

Brent laughed. "Maybe you're right. Hey," he stopped midway and sucked in a deep breath, "have you seen a spare set of car keys?"

"On the table in the hall. Your pilot gave them to me last night before she left." They reached the bottom step. "She said I should tell you to call for your refund. Something about you paying for two days with her and only getting one."

"Don't make it sound sordid, Cooper." Brent limped to the small, round table next to a wooden bench in the hall and snatched the keys. He jammed them in the pocket of his khaki Dockers. "She's a bush pilot, for Christ's sake. I wanted to check out the island from the air, see if I couldn't figure out where this Dutchman had stashed Jack. Then I got bit. She owes me a flight."

"Guess you need to take that up with her. I'm only telling you what she told me." Cooper crossed the hall and entered the kitchen. He needed coffee in the worst way, even old coffee. He lifted the carafe and poked his head out the door. "You want some of this?"

"Nah. I'm headed for the Office of Records. Zeller's arranged for me to study aerial maps of the island. Kat told me what to look for. You're welcome to come if you want."

The coffee settled like lead in Cooper's stomach. "Got chores to do around here this morning." He lied. "A few calls to make." Well, the latter wasn't a lie. He needed to check in with Bernard one last time before translating their plan into action.

"I'm game." They turned as Nick descended the stairs, dressed in pleat-front tan chinos and a ribbed navy sweater vest with a pale blue shirt under it, sleeves rolled to his elbows. He could've stepped out of a Land's End catalog. "Aerials sound like a good idea, little brother," he added. "Never ceases to amaze me how your mind works."

Cooper saw them to the door, then watched as Brent's rented Ford tore out of the driveway with Nick at the wheel.

The rest of the day flew by in a series of missteps. He missed Bernard by one fare around ten o'clock, Angeline in her shop at noon by fifteen minutes, and her brothers at the Office of Records by half an hour.

No matter. He'd done what he needed to.

Finally he and Bernard connected under the giant mangrove in the square at four o'clock.

"I don't think this is a good idea, Mr. Cooper." The driver sat on the bench next to him, crunching on a bag of banana chips.

"Voorhees jumped on the idea of a trade, like I knew he would, and I don't see any other way of getting the boy." Cooper leaned back, resting his outstretched arms on the rear slats of the wooden bench. "Once you have the kid safely in your cab, Bernard, get the hell out of here. I need to know he's safe."

Chapter Seventeen

Cooper had been to the house and back. Luckily, Angeline and the rookie were still at her shop. He took a couple quick, deep breaths before stepping onto the red cobblestone square. Trusting Bernard with the boy was a leap of faith, but faith was all he had. No one else knew what would occur over the next few hours.

Beyond keeping this appointment with Voorhees, Cooper didn't know either.

He would be in the devil's hands by nightfall. That much was fact. He ran a hand through his hair and forbade his fatigued brain to consider the consequences of his actions. The missing boy would no longer be missing, and for the moment, his safety was the priority. Cooper removed his sunglasses. He hooked the earpiece through a buttonhole in the lapel of his knit shirt. Voorhees dictated what he should wear: short-sleeved red shirt, khaki shorts, and oversized sandals. No watch.

The Dutchman had clearly mastered the art of abduction. The red shirt? Easy to spot in the thick, green overgrowth—if Cooper managed to escape. The shorts and the shirt's lack of sleeves left him vulnerable to insects, razor-edged leaves, and prickly vines. Oversized shoes made running impossible. None of the clothes suited a trek through a virgin rain forest or the deadly mangrove swamps inhabiting the island's interior. But, he'd been in a worst fix.

Once.

And he survived—just.

The green Voyager chugged around a corner at the far end of the crowded square. It stopped in front of the magazine stand across the street. Bernard got out, chose a newspaper from the rack, and after a few minutes of loud and over-friendly cajoling with the clerk and several patrons, dropped his handful of change on the counter. He carried the paper back to his van, spread the pages on the hood, and pretended to read. Occasionally, the cabbie glanced up or spoke to a passerby, always facing the square. The screaming-orange hibiscus blossom, courtesy of his brother-in-law, stood out like a beacon pinned to his white cotton shirt.

Easy for a kid to spot.

Per Voorhees' instructions, Cooper sat on the bench under the enormous mangrove tree. The boy should join him there in about...out of habit, he lifted his wrist.

Groups of passengers, now laden with souvenirs and multi-colored shopping bags, were tendered in small boats to the cruise ship anchored in the harbor, eager to rest and ready themselves for the evening's meal and festivities. The Cross-eyed Pelican's lunch crowd came and went, and now dinner patrons chatted with wait-staff under the patio's striped awning.

Flower venders, ready for home and shade, lowered green umbrellas on red three-wheeled carts. A steel-drum band drew a boisterous throng to one corner of the square where couples spooned scantily-clad bodies against each other, laughing and swaying to a sensual reggae beat. Cameras flashed intermittently.

Cooper licked his dry lips and leaned forward, hands clasped between his thighs, his stomach a mass of knots. Part of him desperately wanted to walk away.

A lone boy entered the square and started down the path flanking its perimeter. In one hand, the kid grasped an orange hibiscus blossom. Cooper eyed a similar flower on the bench next to him, wilted by the sun's heat after too long a wait.

"Don't get up," he cautioned himself. "Keep it casual. Let him find you."

The boy continued walking, turning his head side to side, left to right, searching. The moment he spotted Cooper, his demeanor changed. His back straightened, pace increased, arms swung at his sides. *A little soldier.* He stopped six feet away and withdrew a handful of papers from his pocket.

Baseball cards?

The kid sorted a card from the pack and stuffed the others back in the zippered compartment of his blue cargo shorts. He looked small and dirty, unsure what he should do next. He walked a few steps closer, within three feet of the bench now. Lifting the card, he studied it. His head tilted back as his gaze took in the giant mangrove, sliding up its massive trunk, then moving to the wilted orange blossom on the bench. He stared at Cooper.

Come on, kid. Get over here.

He fought an urge to go to the boy—so eerily a facsimile of Jack that the sight of him stole Cooper's breath. He wanted to snatch the kid and break for Bernard's van, but an unexpected kink in the bargain would prolong the inevitable. Angeline and Jack were only free of Voorhees if he surrendered himself.

That was the deal.

One man would die. If it proved to be the Dutchman, the world became a saner, safer place. If fate chose him—not that Cooper wanted to die, not when he was within reach of the life he'd only dreamed of—Voorhees would have no reason to give another thought to this island paradise, to Angeline and Jack, or Braeden and Montgomery in far away Hamlin's Grove.

They were but small fish in the business of murder, abduction, and million-dollar ransoms. This meeting was personal.

Cooper squared his shoulders so the kid got a clear view of his face. *That's it, kid. A few more steps.*

The boy eased up on the bench, swinging his grungy feet. Back, forth. Dried muck powdered his hands, dotted his clothes, and caked beneath his fingernails. He studied the photograph clenched in his small fist. "You're supposed to take me to my mom."

"Yeah," Cooper managed, once his breathing resumed. "And you're a brave boy. Can I see the picture?"

The kid hesitated, his eyes narrowed, like he wasn't sure he'd get it back. He placed the photograph on the bench between them. Cooper knew better than to pick it up. The kid had lost so much these last few days; trust became everything at this juncture.

No borders indicated the picture belonged to a larger photograph. He knew the *where* but not the *when*. It was clearly taken outside Tujaque's, across from the French Market on Decatur Street in New Orleans. The restaurant's specialty was beef brisket, dress casual. He'd dined there too many times to remember one specific occasion.

"It got wrinkled in my pocket," the boy said. "But I didn't lose it."

"That's okay. No one cares about a few wrinkles." Cooper wondered how Voorhees had obtained the photograph. Or rather, when. The image was old; he was thinner, not so tan. Montgomery, grinning like a fool beside him, wore a beat cop's uniform.

"The mean man gave it to me." The boy's legs swung faster, harder, and bumped the underside of the bench. "He called me a baby cause I cried." He lowered his voice. "But I ain't no baby. I'm five." His frown slow-motioned into a melon-slice grin, as if he had discovered a secret, or a ploy he might use again. "The big man gave me a chocolate bar. I didn't cry no more. 'Cept when I got hungry."

Mean man, big man? There had been at least two creeps on the boat with him.

Cooper forced a smile. He spoke slow and deliberate. "I like chocolate, too, kid. By the way, I'm Cooper. But my friends call me Coop. What's your name?"

The boy's kicking legs stopped. "Tommy."

"Tommy. I like that. Bet your friends call you Tom."

The kid nodded.

"Okay, Tom. Why don't you tell me your whole name so I can get you to your mom and dad faster."

Tommy's chin quivered. His eyes glassed over. Cooper suspected the mention of his mom did him in. The kid had dark eyes, brownish-gray. They reminded him of a dusty road after a drenching rain. "Mark Thomas Beck," the boy said. The kid grew quiet and drew back. His face sobered. He stared off into the distance.

Cooper inched closer. "What is it, Tom?"

"That man's giving me a mean look."

He searched the immediate area. "What man, where? Don't point. Tell me what he looks like."

"Across the street. By the big blue car."

The man stood near the passenger door of a navy Lincoln with tinted windows, legs spread, hands on his hips, his jacket shoved back enough to reveal a shoulder holster beneath a suit too dark for island comfort. The Lincoln stood out like a pink flamingo in a drab yard. One of those temporary magnetic signs stuck to the front door. Advertisement for a local realtor.

Cooper slipped his arm around the boy's shoulders. "He's not giving you a mean look, son. He's giving me one. I needed to meet him, and I'm late."

"I don't like him," the boy said.

"Well, you know what? I like talking to you, Tom. But I do have to leave."

The boy's voice hitched; he grabbed Cooper's hand. "I don't want you to go."

"It means a lot to me for you to say that." Surprisingly, Cooper meant it. "I need you to do something for me first. Okay?" The boy's face lit. Cooper pointed to Bernard's Voyager. "See that green van over there?"

Tommy nodded.

"See the man standing next to it, the one with the orange flower on his shirt? He's my friend. His name is Bernard, but I bet he'll let you call him Bernie. He's going to drive you to the police station."

The boy's back straightened. "Will my mom be there?"

"You bet. As soon as you give the nice policeman your name, he'll call her. Your dad, too." Angeline's image flashed in Cooper's head, her elation at learning the police had found Jack.

"Will they be mad?" The boy scooted forward and stuffed the photograph back in his pocket. "Sometimes my dad gets mad when I don't listen or leave my toys out."

"Nah. They've missed you," Cooper said. "Today you're going to make them real happy."

"Okay."

"All right then. I'm going to walk you halfway to the green van." They stood, and the suited man slipped his right hand inside his jacket, casual-like, his stare cemented to Cooper. "I want you to be careful crossing the street." He gave the kid a nudge.

"You'll watch me 'til I get there?"

"Yes."

The stiffness left Tommy's shoulders. "Will you come see me at my house when I get home? I got neat stuff in my room. I'll show you."

He stepped forward, ruffled the boy's hair. "If I can come, Tom, I will. That's a promise. And you know how important promises are, right?"

Another nod. The boy exaggerated his look both ways before stepping into the street.

Bernard's gaze locked on Cooper, and for a second or two, they stared at each other. He went around the van and opened the passenger side door. Tommy climbed in. Bernard fastened the boy's seatbelt and slammed the door.

"His name is Mark Thomas Beck," Cooper told him. "Tell Zeller."

Reggae music fused into a backdrop of white noise. The suited man approached in Cooper's peripheral vision. Two more thugs joined him. The Lincoln crossed the street and eased along the curb ahead of them.

Cooper was ready. Time to pay the piper—or, if he had any luck left at all—to filet the piper.

The closest goon, his hand tucked in his jacket, stood no more than two feet from Cooper when the Voyager sped by. Tommy waved. Cooper gave him a two-fingered salute as the three men herded him toward the Lincoln. He couldn't see inside the sedan, but the rear door gaped open like a black hole ready to swallow him.

He prayed to hell not.

The larger thug bear-hugged him as if they were old buddies, all the while patting down Cooper's pockets and any other place he might conceal a weapon. Satisfied, he said, "Get in."

The Lincoln's interior reeked of the fake new car smell administered by detail shops. *A rental?* He got in. The hugger followed, sandwiching Cooper between himself and another no-neck goon.

The car traveled an hour and forty-three minutes according to the clock in the dash. They'd left the city after ten.

They pulled over to the side of a dirt road. The thug opened the door and unfolded his wrestler's frame from the rear seat. He stooped and peered in the back. "Get out."

Cooper obliged.

"Search him," the suited man said. "Empty his pockets."

Cooper turned, placed his hands on top of the Lincoln, and spread his legs. The dark roof burned his palms.

One of the men frisked him, took his money and wallet, book of matches. "Shoes," he ordered.

Cooper slipped off the sandals, not that he could've done much in them anyway.

The man tossed the shoes over the car and into the brush.

Intense pain exploded at the back of Cooper's head. The sensation of falling and the ground coming up too fast enveloped him. Blackness consumed him.

When Cooper came to, night had fallen. At least he thought the darkness surrounding him indicated night. He squeezed his eyes shut, tried easing them open again. The excruciating pain felt like someone drove a spike into the back of his head. Rope burned his wrists, which were tied behind his back. His ankles, lifted toward his shoulders, were numb. He wriggled. Couldn't roll over, couldn't sit. The rope around his neck tightened with each motion. He let his eyes adjust to the lack of light. The side of his face rested against cool concrete. The place stank of decay and motor oil. Insects buzzed around his head.

Garage?

Too empty. No mechanic's tools.

Boathouse?

Possible. Lots of rope. Couple of life jackets.

He couldn't see behind him, but he thought he heard rustling water.

A door creaked open. The yellow-white sphere of a flashlight bounced on the walls and ceiling, and ended in his face. He slammed his eyes shut.

"So, you're awake." A man's laughter erupted, raspy and tobacco roughened.

Not Voorhees.

"I was beginning to think I hit you too hard."

The suited goon.

Grabbing the rope at his back, he turned Cooper face down on the floor and poked at the back of his head. "Nah," he said. "You don't look so bad." Another croaky laugh. "For a dead man." He yanked on the rope.

Cooper slid to his side, and the noose around his neck tightened. Choking, wheezing, he sucked air through flared nostrils. He caught the flicker of shiny metal in the flashlight's beam, scrunched his shoulders, and prepared for a different kind of pain. The noose slackened; his legs dropped. He sucked deep, although his hands remained tied behind him.

The man dragged him to his feet and hauled Cooper out of the building, weaving, stumbling. He tried to stay focused, but thinking hurt too much. Using what little light the crescent moon allowed, he surveyed the area through a haze.

The ramshackle boathouse stood in a small clearing at the juncture between two waterways. Jack's boat rose and fell with the waves at the end of a rickety pier. White, with red stripes. The kid had pegged it right.

The boat bustled with floodlight-silhouetted activity. He counted three hulking shadows, maybe four. Better odds than he had hoped for.

No Dutchman, but Voorhees didn't do grunt work.

The goon hauled him up by the rope around his wrists. Cooper went down on one knee, then his butt, sliding on the muddy bank. Muck coated him, oozed between his toes, and burned his ankles where the rope had rubbed them raw. Time eluded him.

Dragged toward the pier, Cooper couldn't control his footing, like walking backwards at a squat. The only thing holding him up was the rope in the man's beefy hand.

At the edge of the low pier, the thug dropped him. Cooper's

temple smacked the side of the boat, and the starless sky burst with a million shards of light. The guy grabbed him by the shorts and dumped him onto the deck. Within seconds, the engine sputtered, vibrating the wood beneath his ear as they moved to God knows where.

He squeezed his eyes shut, pictured Angeline, and wondered dully if he'd ever see her again—and Jack.

Oh, God. Jack.

He'd yet to learn that Cooper was his dad.

Chapter Eighteen

Cooper stayed away all day. He hadn't called, or stopped by Angeline's shop at lunchtime with scrumptious coconut shrimp and thick island onion rings, accompanied by the disarming smile that easily stirred the want in her these days. Not that he said he would show up. Rekindling their relationship was still so new. Maybe she just expected it.

Angeline opened the cupboard and ran her finger along the row of soup can labels. She reached beyond her little soldiers to the cans of Swanson broth at the back of the cupboard, and she wondered if Cooper had discovered Campbell made more than soup. If not, then she finally one-upped him. At least in the kitchen.

Ah, yes. She smiled. Pork Tenderloin Cubano with Mango Mojo. She eyed the clock on the range. Twenty minutes of prep. Thirty minutes to cook. Surely he'd be home by then, and she hoped, with news of Voorhees or the missing boy.

If she hadn't impressed Cooper with her gastronomic wizardry the other evening, she would tonight. She organized her ingredients: chunky salsa, bread crumbs, chorizo sausage, orange juice, brown sugar, cilantro leaves, and butter-flied pork tenderloin. "Oh," she reached into the fruit bowl, "and one fat mango for the mojo."

It never hurt to throw in some good mojo.

"What are you doing?" Nick leaned against the doorframe, arms folded across his chest.

She had no idea how long he had watched her. "Cooking dinner."

"Takes me less prep getting ready for surgery." He walked to the sink, turned on the tap, and washed his hands. "Since Cooper's not back yet, I guess I'm your sub. How can I help?"

The offer was her brother's not-so-subtle way of seeing she stayed busy. She passed Nick the box of croutons, a small baggie, and a wooden rolling pin. "Have you seen Cooper today?"

He stared at the objects and chuckled. "This looks technical."

"Oh, here." She opened the box, dumped a handful of croutons in the baggie, pressed the seal strip, slapped the bag on the countertop, and ran the rolling pin over it. "Voila, bread crumbs." She handed him the rolling pin. "I need a cup and a half."

Laughing, he went to work. "To answer your question, no, I haven't seen Cooper since this morning. Did you ask Brent?"

"Ask me what?" Her younger brother took Nick's spot in the doorway.

"Both my guardians home at the same time?" she said. "How convenient." Her brothers smiled with clenched jaws. The fret lines around their eyes spoke of concern and frustration.

"Careful, little brother." Nick held up the rolling pin. "You hang around Angie's kitchen long, and you'll get a chore. She's turning into Mom. How's the foot?"

"Hurts like a spider bit me." Brent crossed the kitchen, lifted the box of croutons, poured a few in his palm, then popped them in his mouth. He chewed noisily.

Nick set the rolling pin aside and lifted the baggie. He shook the crumbs to the bottom, then handed the bag to his sister. "See you got your shoe on."

"Yeah, the foot's better." Brent turned to Angeline. "What did you need to ask me?"

"Have you seen Cooper?"

"Not since this morning. I asked if he wanted to go with us

to look at aerial photos of the island. He turned me down." He glanced at Nick. "Didn't Cooper say something about hanging out with that taxi driver? You know, the guy who drives the green van with the patched bumper."

"Bernard," his brother said. He turned to Angeline. "Did you call him?"

"Well, no." She combined the salsa, orange juice, cilantro, brown sugar, and mango in a blender. "Here." She slid the blender over to Nick. "You do this while I make the call."

He made sure the Oster's lid was secure. "How long?"

"I don't know," she said. "Until it's smooth." With the blender whirring in the background, she dug out the phone book, fingered through the business pages, and dialed the cab company. There was only one on the island. "Hello, yes," she said. "May I speak with Bernard?"

"He's a driver," Brent said to no one in particular. "He won't be there."

Nick checked his watch. "It's a little after seven. Dispatch can get him on the radio."

His brother laughed. "You've lived in the city too long, Doc. This isn't Yellow Cab. What do they have, all of three vehicles?"

Angeline moved into the central hall. She turned away from their chatter and concentrated on the voice at the other end of the line. "He didn't come in at all today? Is that unusual?" The blender stopped. She peered over her shoulder. "Do you happen to know where Bernard lives?"

Her brothers came out of the kitchen.

"I wouldn't ask you to break a rule, but it's important," she told the dispatcher. "Okay. I understand. No, I don't need a cab. But thank you." Angeline disconnected and turned to her brothers. "The man on the phone said Bernard hasn't been around all day." She chewed on her bottom lip, shoving worry to the back of her mind. There was no room for it; anxiety and fear already resided there. "The man also said something else disconcerting. Bernard's only lived on the island a few months. I would've sworn Cooper said he grew up here. Do you think they went somewhere together?"

"Look," Nick said. "Like I told you before, it's early. I'm sure

Cooper will show. Meanwhile, let's get this meal cooked. I'm starved."

Angeline caught the look of concern he shot Brent. Who did her brothers think they were fooling? Wherever Cooper had disappeared to, her gnawing gut screamed trouble had followed him.

Cooper drifted in and out of consciousness, aware only of the moan of the boat's engine and the hypnotic rocking motion as it crept through the water. If he kept his eyes shut, the pain in his head remained a dull throb.

Then the engine stopped, replaced by shuffling feet and clanking metal, thuds and scrapes. A heavy object rolled across the deck. It slammed against the boat's side and sent agonizing vibrations through his skull.

"Up you go." The same goon that had dumped him grabbed Cooper's arms and hoisted him over his shoulder like a sack of feed. Huffing, the thug stepped off the boat and carried him a short distance down a pier.

About ten feet, Cooper figured, as he forced his eyes open. Wooden planks passed beneath his face in a blur, adding to his nausea. He swallowed bile. Only his hands remained tied.

A light rain fell, pelting a rat-a-tat rhythm on the tin roof of the building they entered.

The thug dropped him on a stone floor, and Cooper's head bounced. More pain. Grasping the rope that bound his hands, the man dragged him to the back and looped the knot over a hook high on a post, suspending Cooper's arms above his head.

"Where?" was all he managed to ask.

The man grabbed him by the hair, yanked his head back, and leaned into him, their faces inches apart. "Where there ain't nobody gonna find you, son." He stank of tobacco. An unidentifiable smell lingered when he backed away, oddly sweet.

Cooper's head spun; his stomach lurched. He clamped his eyes shut.

"Hey, you." The guy slapped his cheeks hard enough that Cooper flinched. "I need you awake when the boss gets here."

Hours passed. At least, it seemed that long with his hands going numb above him. Activity in and around the arched doorways of the building ceased. Somehow Cooper managed to fall asleep.

He awoke to the sound of wood scraping across brick. Huge arched doors opened on one side of the building, and he squinted as daylight flooded the interior.

Tobacco Man approached, a knife in his hand.

Cooper blinked. Today the guy's thick neck supported two heads. He stuck the blade between Cooper's wrists and sliced the rope clean. His arms thumped to his sides.

"Get up," the man said.

Cooper tried to stand. Nothing doing. His swollen hands were as useless as anchors tied to a horse's tail, but he managed to get to his knees.

"Bring him." The thug said. Two men grabbed Cooper under his arms, raising him on rubbery legs.

They left the building and dragged him down wide brick steps, maybe fifteen yards, to a coppice of macaw palms dispersed with tree ferns and woody vines. They let go, and Cooper hit the ground face first in decaying leaves and moist soil.

A booted foot rolled him over on his back. "Teacher."

Cooper's squinted his watery eyes. The sun's halo prevented him from seeing the man's face, but he recognized the thick Dutch accent. He spit, trying to clear his mouth of debris, and struggled to his knees again. "Voorhees."

The Dutchman squatted, bringing their faces level. "You don't look happy to see me, Teacher...and you led me to believe you wanted this meeting so badly."

"I wanted the boy." Cooper slid to a seated position. "I got the boy." He braced his back against a gommier's thick trunk and got a clear view of his captor—as if he'd ever washed Voorhees' face from his memory.

In this case, as with other infamous deviates, evil wore the face of an ordinary man: lean, pale, high cheekbones tinged pink as if in perpetual blush, nose slightly hooked. Cooper might've described Willem Voorhees' looks as pleasant, until his gaze reached the Dutchman's ice-blue eyes, flat and emotionless as a shark's.

A thousand needles pricked Cooper's hands from the inside

as fresh blood circulated through them. He flexed his swollen fingers, willing away numbness the tight rope had caused. "I don't like cowards who pick on women and defenseless children," he said. "If you were a man, you'd send your henchmen packing, and we'd settle this. Just you and me."

"You cannot goad me." Voorhees dug a red and gold box from the inside pocket of his light-colored jacket. He flicked open a gold lighter, lit a brown cigarette, and exhaled a plume of smoke that smelled distinctively of cloves. "I have waited too long to end this game of cat and mouse we've played, Teacher, and I have much in store for you."

The Onlooker parked his green Voyager between a thick stand of mangrove trees and the river. He glanced over his shoulder at the boy, sleeping soundly in the back seat. Exhaustion simplified getting the child to their destination.

He smiled. The boy's trust in Cooper made him a willing participant in the final stage of the Dutchman's game. Of course, Cooper's reliance in the Onlooker had also been most vital to a triumphant conclusion.

Caribbean zouk poured from the radio, a blend of compás, reggae, and salsa rhythms. Bernard imagined himself swaying with the beautiful Angeline. Holding her close, their entwined bodies knowing the familiarity of lovers.

He grew hard in an instant.

Perhaps he would take her on the floor of the sunroom, naked and terrified, as the little Rose had been. His machete would rest between Angeline's full breasts, his manhood pumping inside her as she screamed and kicked and clawed, which would only serve to excite him more.

Too bad Cooper couldn't be there to see Bernard possess his woman. By then, the American and the now sleeping boy would be dead.

He intended to secure Angeline in his hideaway deep in the mangrove swamp, where he would feast on her again and again until she begged death's mercy. Her possession belonged to him, as long as he desired, to do whatever he wished. And, all these weeks watching her, *watching them*, he had wished plenty.

There would be money to burn, and time to burn—the flesh of Cooper's woman to burn.

All part of his bargain with Voorhees. Compensation, the Dutchman called it. For the Onlooker had played his part of humble taxi driver magnificently, so eager to listen and serve and please.

Bernard snapped his fingers and moved his broad shoulders to the zouk's sensual grind, mindful to keep watch out the window for his signal to bring the boy.

Voorhees sliced the air with his hand.

Tobacco Man jerked the rope he used to bind Cooper's wrists again and secured the knot. He shoved Cooper aside, then vanished into the overgrowth at the clearing's edge.

The Dutchman pointed to Cooper and said, "I want him standing."

Two men hauled Cooper to his feet. He shook his head to clear the ringing and spit again, trying to rid his mouth of grit. "That's all you've got?" he croaked.

"You know me too well, Teacher." Voorhees turned his head toward rustling sounds coming from the brush.

Tobacco Man charged through thigh-high ferns and ground-hugging vegetation dragging Tommy by the scruff of his shirt.

"Bastard!" Cooper shouted.

Tommy spotted Cooper, and the boy's thrashing stopped cold. Terror in the kid's wide eyes morphed into betrayal and disbelief.

"You sick son of a bitch." Cooper lurched toward Voorhees, struggling against his ropes. "We had a deal. You get me, the boy goes home." He froze at the sight of Bernard. Guilt riddled Cooper. Not only did he allow the boy to be set up, he'd set up the cabbie. Unless he could come up with something—hell, anything—they would all die at the hands of this monster. Cooper squinted through the pain in his head for a sign from the driver. "I'm sorry, Bernard."

Bernard's hands remained untied, and he was a big man. Both might work to their advantage. His gaze moved to the driver's face, and what he saw turned his blood to ice water.

The cabbie offered a wide, satisfied smile. "Bernard is a clever man, yes?"

Angeline drew back the drapes so the morning sun burst in, washing over her room like a diamond-bright gossamer sea.

Still no word from Cooper.

It wasn't like him to disappear. She frowned and gripped the curtains tighter; she was the one who ran.

They had made great strides these last few days, gained eons of lost ground. And it was more than good sex. She enjoyed having Cooper around. His humor and wit, the way he so easily kept her on her toes.

She wanted him to play a significant role in Jack's life, even if he chose not to remain in hers. Surely, by now, he knew that.

A knock at the door startled her. She hurried across the room and yanked it open. "It's about time you got home—"

Brent stepped back, two cups in his hands. "Sorry, kid, it's just me. Saw the light under your door. I wanted you to know I was up and made coffee."

She opened the door so he could enter and gratefully accepted the teeming brew. It smelled strong. Perfect for her mood. She gulped a couple stout swallows. The coffee scorched her tongue but fired her system.

"Nick's on the beach," Brent said. "He's restless. Says he's already been all over town with a photo of Cooper. He stopped by the police station on his way back."

Angeline blew across the coffee's rippling surface. "And?"

"The Chief made a few phone calls to neighboring jurisdictions, hotels, and restaurants. The guy knows everyone."

"Anything?"

"Nope. Cooper's vanished. Got any other ideas?"

She took another sip and shuddered. "We could try to find Bernard again, but we don't even know where he lives. What if he's left the island?"

"You talking about Bernard or Cooper?"

"Both I guess. They're supposed to be together. He said the driver was dealing with personal issues, a family problem, and he was trying to help."

"If they left the island by plane," Brent said, "their names should be on a roster. But I can't imagine Cooper up and leaving without letting you know. Tell you what, as soon as they open, I'll call the airport, maybe even drive over there. Only a few flights come and go. It shouldn't be hard to learn if either man was on one. Maybe Kat can help."

"That would be wonderful." Angeline spotted a small red *Connect Four* disc under the game table. She picked it up, rubbed it between her thumb and forefinger for luck, then slipped it in the pocket of her jeans. "I'll stay by the phone," she said. "In case Cooper calls."

"You'll hear from him, kid. Wait and see." Brent scratched the back of his neck. "Guess I'll head downstairs then. Want some toast with your coffee?"

"Give me a few minutes, and I'll make us breakfast." She shrugged when he studied her. "I need the work. Besides, I missed the chance to grill you about this mysterious Kat O'Leary of yours." She smiled. "And I want to know everything."

It was the truth, though it pained Angeline to hear of Brent's newfound love when the man she cared about had simply vanished.

What in the hell did a man say to the lowest form of treachery?

Cooper watched, dumbfounded, as Voorhees draped his arm across the taxi driver's shoulders. "Bernard works for me," the Dutchman said.

Bernard's toothy grin widened.

"What'd he promise you?" Cooper lurched to break free of the thugs holding him. "Money, power, a new van? I hope whatever it is, it's worth it, knowing you're responsible for what happens to this boy. You could've let him go, man, dropped him anywhere."

Tommy started to cry.

Cooper couldn't look at him, or breathe. Fury rose from deep inside his gut. "So what now, Dutchman? You going to throw me in some hole with the kid like last time?"

Voorhees extracted a handkerchief from his pocket and walked over to Tommy. Lifting the boy's chin, he wiped tears from his eyes. "That's exactly what I'm going to do with you, Teacher." He turned to Bernard and said, "Bring them."

Huge sobs wracked Tommy's thin shoulders as he tried to worm free of the man's grasp.

"No!" Cooper shouted. "He doesn't go in until I do."

"As you wish." Voorhees turned back to him. Sunlight glanced off the gun in his hand. He fired once. The bullet penetrated Cooper's thigh; his legs gave way. "Again." The men hoisted him, sending a funnel of pain up his legs and back. "Last time you survived three days clinging to the other boy as if he were your own. Let's see how many days you hold onto this one, knowing he replaced your Jack."

Cooper didn't hear the report from the second shot, but he felt the bullet's heat pierce his shoulder, jerking him back.

Voorhees moved no more than two feet from him. "Pity I won't be here to see," he said. "I prefer to vacation in a more civilized place. But, not to worry, I'll send someone back to see you don't suffer *too* long."

Two men dragged Cooper to a pit, maybe ten feet deep and three feet wide. A trickle of river water bled into the hole from a trench they dug. It would fill slowly—unless it rained.

Cooper almost laughed through the blinding pain. This *was* a rainforest.

Bernard lifted Tommy and held him over the opening.

His back hunched, Cooper jerked his head up. "Don't, Bernard!"

The driver froze. He dangled the wriggling boy in midair as he shot a glance to Voorhees for direction.

"First me," Cooper yelled. "Untie my hands, Dutchman. Untie me."

Voorhees raised his open hand toward Bernard. "And what would be the sport in in cutting you loose?"

"I can't hold the boy if my arms aren't free." Cooper's mind ran amok. He latched onto any plausible gambit. "Come on. You're a clever man. You've stacked the deck against me; I never saw it coming. And you're right. I probably won't make it this time. But there's more sport in me trying to stay on my feet with the weight of the boy than without. You don't untie me, and he drowns first. I have nothing to lose. My struggle's over."

Voorhees rubbed his chin as though considering the argument's validity. He nodded to one of his men. The thug slid a knife from the scabbard on his belt, turned Cooper, and sliced through the rope binding his wrists.

On a second nod from Voorhees, the man shoved Cooper into the hole. His bare feet hit mud. He bounced off the wall and cried out from the tearing pain in his thigh as his body buckled. Fighting to stay alert, he positioned himself to cushion the boy's fall.

He didn't think he'd ever erase the bastard's laughter from his memory—or Tommy begging Bernard not to drop him. After a few seconds of grunting and scuffling, the cabbie tossed in the boy.

Chapter Nineteen

Brent parked his rented Ford in front of the open hangar doors. He hadn't heard from Kat since she drove him back to Angeline's after the spider bite incident. The attractive bush pilot's absence shouldn't bother him.

Then why'd he feel so damn hollow?

He walked around the front of the Escape. The Cessna sat inside the hangar, its cargo door open. He surveyed the plane's interior. No chicken coops, no hammocks, no pilot.

"Kat?"

A small office occupied the hangar's rear corner. The sign on the door read CLOSED, but he saw through the small window she sat behind a beat-up wooden desk, cluttered with paperwork, and stared off into space as if she'd lost her favorite socks. He knocked and opened the door at the same time.

"If you've come for your refund," she snapped, "you'll have to get in line."

He tugged off his ball cap before entering, folded it, and stuffed it in the rear pocket of his jeans. "A 'hey, how are ya' would be nice."

She huffed a breath, which stirred her coal black bangs. "You're walking, so you must be okay."

He heaved two thick, green binders onto the floor and sat in the only other chair. "Would've still been nice if you called and checked."

Bolting from her seat, she sent papers flying. A Styrofoam cup bounced off the heaped trashcan and rolled on the concrete floor. "You want me to ask," she all but shouted, "I'll ask. How you feeling, Saint Brent? How's your foot, your spider bite, your sister and brother...your damn, happy-go-lucky life?"

"Ouch." He lifted his injured leg and rested the ankle on his other knee. The chrome and plastic chair squeaked as it rocked. "Guess somebody's havin' a bad day."

She grabbed a stack of papers off the desk, stomped across the small space, jerked open a file drawer, stuffed the papers inside, and slammed the drawer shut with such force the windows rattled. Returning to the desk, she slumped in her chair.

"Whoa, hold on now." He came around the desk and squatted in front her, placing his hands on her knees. Her skin was warm, soft in a tough-girl way. "I didn't come here to pick a fight. If I wanted to pound someone, I'd go back to Angie's house and beat on Nick."

Kat stared at him, opened her mouth, then closed it.

"Nick deserves it," he added. "And, if he doesn't, I can come up with an occasion worthy of a beating from when we were kids." He straightened his legs, leaned forward. "Once Nick flattened the tires on my bicycle and made me late delivering my paper route. Almost cost me my first summer job. For sure, he deserves a pounding for that. Another time, he threw my new sneakers over the telephone wire. Tied the laces so they dangled real pretty. I still owe him for that one, and—"

She pressed a finger to his lips, shushing him. "Thank you," she whispered.

"For what?" He couldn't wipe the silly grin off his face if some fool paid him a year's worth of double-stacked cheeseburgers and seasoned curly fries.

Damn, she smelled good. Like vanilla or fresh-baked chocolate chip cookies. Something edible. She looked even better, with her sleek hair cascading around her shoulders, instead of pulled back in the usual braid.

"I don't know," she said. "Picking up the pieces of my lousy day, I guess."

A woman as stunning as Kat O'Leary shouldn't have lousy days. "Now you're gonna need to help me up," he said, wincing. "Bad foot's got a cramp in it. Don't think I can stand."

She laughed and took hold of one of his arms; his other arm went to her desk for leverage.

He stood and braced himself on the edge of her chair. Leaning into her, he smothered her lips with his mouth.

She uttered a cute little sound of surprise, then something more carnal as the kiss deepened and tongues turned up the heat.

Changing directions, Brent dove in for seconds. Kat's chair rocked against the wall as his mouth chased the pulse down one side of her neck, then up the other.

"Holy moly," he gasped when he surfaced. "You taste terrific."

She raised her hand to her throat, then two fingers to her lower lip. "Must be the chocolate bar I ate for lunch," she said.

He smacked his lips and forced himself back to his seat. "Didn't taste like any chocolate bar I ever ate."

She flung her dark hair over her shoulder, then straightened her shirt concealing her cleavage.

Damn it.

"Why are you here, Flyover?"

"Oh, yeah, business." He raked a hand through his hair. She had this twitchy way of emptying his head. "I need to hire you again."

"I still owe you air time." She pulled the open desk calendar closer. "Where do you want to go?"

"That's the kicker, you see. I'm not exactly sure. The same area we searched the other day, I guess, or close to it. My sister's friend, Cooper, has come up missing. I think you met him the other night."

The look in her eyes flattened, and the flush in her cheeks deepened. "I did."

Curious. He gestured out the window. "I came from the

terminal. Cooper hasn't left the island, as near as any of us can tell. Unless, of course, he left by boat. But I think he would've told Angie. We've searched everywhere else we can think of and came up with zip. My gut says something's wrong, Kat, the worst kind of wrong."

She stood, returned to her file cabinet, and opened the drawer. With her back to him, she said, "Your Mr. Cooper doesn't like me. I say good riddance."

Brent blew out a sigh. "He and I have had our issues, too. But my sister loves the guy. He's the father of my nephew, Jack. If he's in trouble, I gotta help him. That's what family does."

She kept her back turned. "Not everyone's family."

Since when did he start thinking of Cooper as kin? "What's that?"

"Nothing." Kat glanced at her watch. "It's eleven o'clock. Can you come back at two?"

"Sure. Great." He stood, still reeling from the kiss, tugged the baseball cap from his pocket and slipped it on backwards. "See you at two then. Angie and Nick will be with me. Is that a problem?"

They convened around the Cessna at a minute past two. It surprised Brent to find the plane's rear seats installed.

Kat shrugged at his quizzical look. "I don't always need them," she said. "I've packed supplies, too."

"Humanitarian mission?"

"Something like that." She climbed in and pointed behind him. "Hand those up to me."

The four of them formed a bucket brigade, and in fifteen minutes, packed and loaded the two blue coolers, sleeping bags, blankets, towels, extra water, and clothes.

"Wait a second." Nick sprinted back to the rented Ford Escape and retrieved his doctor's bag. "You know," he stopped in front of Angeline, "just in case."

"What about fuel?" Brent touched Kat's arm, and heat shot to the soles of his feet, ricocheted, then settled like molten lead in his aching groin. He longed to lie barefoot, naked, somewhere cool and dark. Buried so deep inside this woman, he'd chase release for a hundred years.

Damn Cooper.

"Already took care of the fuel." Kat surveyed the group, hands balled on her hips. "Guess we're ready."

Conversation fell into forced casual as they boarded the plane and settled in. Angeline sat behind Kat, who twisted in her seat and unfolded a map. The others leaned in.

"This is where I think we should start our search." Kat drew an imaginary circle on the map with her finger. "It's actually an extension of the area Brent and I checked the other day. Farther in, and closer to the mountains. There are a few abandoned sugar plantations and millwalls on the island. I know, off hand, of several, and can easily find what's left of them. One's in this area." She tapped a section of map. "And another here."

"Wait a minute," Nick said. "Wouldn't Zeller know of these plantations, too? You'd think he would've already checked them."

"It's not that simple," Kat explained. "Once humans abandon a place, the forest claims it at a speed you can't begin to imagine. Maps drawn when the plantations were fully operational are vague. Unless a mill and plantation house survived together, as an identifiable unit, it's hard to spot them from the air, even if you know they're there. And there are no longer roads to speak of. Not that cars can't make it out there, but most travel by boat."

Angeline jerked a corner of the map and pulled it closer. "How can you be so sure this is the area to search?"

"I pass over the island all the time," Kat said. "That's why Brent and I started with this area. It's easier to travel and a more likely hiding place. But not so easy that just anyone would stumble upon it." She poked the map again. "Here, see?"

Angeline studied the area. She nodded.

Kat folded the map, with the quadrant she'd designated to investigate on the outside. She handed it to Brent.

For the next two hours the Cessna swept rivers and emaciated tributaries resembling bony fingers, lush valleys, and gray-topped mountains that wore cloud cover like a shroud. She'd set up a complex crisscrossing grid so they wouldn't miss anything.

Brent kept his binoculars focused on the terrain. The rainforest canopies stretched for miles, seemingly unbroken. It amazed him that even an ounce of sunlight burrowed through.

"Eighty percent of rainforest life exists in those trees." Kat tapped her narrow side window. "The canopy leaves, billions of them, act like solar panels," she said. "Changing light to energy. Animals take to the tree tops because of the high yield of fruits, seeds, and flowers there."

"It's awe-inspiring." Nick adjusted the magnification on his binoculars. "And big corporations wonder why you islanders fight so hard against deforestation—"

"Saving the forest is all well and good," Angeline interrupted. "But how are we supposed to find Cooper in all this?"

"If he's out here," Kat reassured her, "we'll find him. I promise."

Brent scanned the horizon and mumbled, "Ditto."

"Hold on." Nick lifted the binocular strap over his head and pressed the glasses to his window. He pointed. "I see smoke. Over there, near the river."

Brent tossed Kat a perplexed look. "Billy and Mia?"

She steered the plane in a wide loop and veered low. "They live along the river, yes, but a ways from there. It'd take us a day, maybe two, depending on weather and stamina, to reach their house from that area."

"There it is," Brent said. "I see it, too. Looks like a fire, or what's left of one. Smoke's thinning in places. I think it's a car."

Angeline grabbed Nick's binoculars. "It's a van, Brent. Bernard drives a van. Can you get us down there, Kat?"

Kat cinched her seatbelt. "I'll land in the valley. We'll go into the forest on foot. It's the only way. I need to radio the airport first and let them know we're investigating a fire. They'll call the police and tell them we'll report what we find."

Brent admired her professionalism as she spoke into her handset. Brisk, businesslike. Impressive. Then she maneuvered the Cessna into a series of sharp landing loops.

Voorhees' men covered the pit's opening with branches so only a glimmer of sunlight stole through, having sieved beyond the thinning canopy at the river's edge.

Within a few minutes, Cooper heard a boat's motor crank, then gradually fade as it headed downriver—the Dutchman had fled. He sat with his back against the earthen wall. The humid pit reeked of decaying vegetation and brackish water, and his body wore the pain from his wounds like a second skin. He wouldn't get on his feet until he needed to.

Tommy stood next to his shoulder; a mewling sound coming from deep in his throat. He'd wet his pants, but Cooper pretended not to notice. In a few hours, they'd both be drenched, and it wouldn't matter anyway.

"You okay, Tom?"

The boy quaked from head to toe. "Uh-huh."

"Good. We need a plan." Boy, did they ever. "My leg is bleeding, and we have to make it stop. Okay?"

Tommy nodded.

"There's a hole in your t-shirt, probably from when you fought Bernard."

The kid stared down at his clothes. A look of wide-eyed astonishment ambushed his dirt-smeared face.

"I'm sorry I sent you with Bernard, Tom. I thought he was my friend."

Tommy said nothing but continued to rock back and forth.

Silence was okay. They'd have time enough later to talk through the taxi driver's betrayal. God willing. "I need you to give me your shirt," Cooper told him. "Then we need something like a stick."

Tommy pulled his soiled t-shirt over his head and surrendered it.

Cooper took off his red knit shirt and slipped it over the boy's head.

The shirt fell to Tommy's ankles, making him let go a nervous laugh and say, "Looks like a dress."

"Yeah, well." Cooper tussled the kid's sweat-slicked hair. "Big shirt for a big man. And you were a big man up there, Tom. I was real proud of you. Now I'm going to make a tourniquet to stop the bleeding from my leg. I'll buy you a new shirt when we get out of here, okay?"

Another nod.

Using the hole as a start, Cooper ripped the t-shirt in half. He tore the lower half again and looped the shirt's hem around his thigh. "When we were in the park, you took my picture out of your pocket, so I'm thinking the bad men didn't search you. You got anything else in there, Tom? Something we can use?"

Tommy unzipped the deepest pocket on the right side of his shorts. He fished out a laminated baseball card—LaRoche of the Pirates—a couple of marbles, and a black comb.

Maybe the kid was from Pittsburgh?

But now wasn't the time to ask. Talk of family would only get him crying again.

Cooper shook his head when the boy held up the comb. Tommy carefully slid the photo in a smaller pocket fastened with Velcro. He unzipped the deep compartment on his left side and produced a small rubber ball, a ruler, and a pair of Spiderman sunglasses with the right lens missing. Cooper eyed the ruler. It was short, six inches, metal with a cork backing. It wouldn't easily slip.

He pointed to the ruler. "Hold onto that."

Tommy separated the ruler from his other treasures.

Cooper twisted the shirt's hem and formed a loop. "Slip it in here," he instructed the boy.

Tommy slid the ruler inside the loop.

Cooper turned the metal strip until the binding was as tight as he could stand. The bleeding slowed quite a bit. "Now we have to keep it tight," he said. "But that's my job—"

A guttural scream erupted, splitting the silence of the last half-hour. Their heads jerked upward.

Cooper touched the side of the boy's face. "I don't know what's happening up there, Tom, but we're not going to think about it. Okay?"

Another, more vigorous, nod—followed by another scream, less human, like a wounded animal.

The water in the pit drenched his shorts but was rising slowly. Cooper folded the top portion of the t-shirt into a thick pad and tied it around his wounded arm with the torn middle strip of fabric. The bullet had exited, leaving two wounds. The front puncture was bullet-sized, but he knew from discussions with Montgomery, exit wounds were larger and caused significant damage to muscle and tissue.

Another scream erupted, not quite as loud as the others. Cooper pulled the boy onto his lap, tucked his head against his chest, and covered his ears.

Tommy's thin shoulders rose and fell with a disheartening sigh, followed by a shudder that traveled the length of his spine.

He stroked the boy's temple. "Let's rest a minute, Tom."

Next thing he knew, Cooper woke with a start. He glanced up. Sunlight riddled the latticework camouflaging the pit's opening but not nearly as brightly as before.

Dusk.

The walls closed in on him, and his old nemesis surfaced on a tidal wave of nausea-laced dizziness. He squeezed his eyes shut and counted backwards as panic set in.

Thirty, twenty-nine, twenty-eight...

He opened his eyes, glanced up. The water pouring in from the river cut a groove in the bank of the opening, gurgling like a partially blocked faucet as it dribbled down the wall. The level rose another foot while they slept. He didn't know how the difference measured in real time, but they couldn't be in this pit when night fell.

Twenty-seven, twenty-six...

Shifting the boy to his good leg, he loosened the tourniquet. If, and when, they got out of this stinking hole, he didn't intend to lose a leg.

Twenty-three...

Tommy stirred.

Good. They needed to stand. He wet his hand and washed grime from the boy's cheeks. "Hey there, Tom."

The kid's eyelids fluttered open, and the emotion in his brown eyes flattened with the memory of where he was. His lower lip quivered, his voice a scratchy whisper. "How're we gonna get out?"

Cooper studied a possible escape route up the wall. "I'm working on it."

Eighteen, seventeen...

If he stood Tommy on his shoulders, the boy might reach the opening. What then? What if the kid couldn't maintain his balance? Hell, he was weak as a pup himself. What if he couldn't stand long enough to lift the boy? "Let's get up for a minute, Tom. Okay?"

The boy stood.

It took Cooper longer. Clinging to the wall for support, he managed to keep his footing. "I have an idea," he said. "You ever been to the circus, Tom? Seen those acrobats standing on top of each other? Pretty cool, huh?"

The usual nod.

"That's what we're going to do. I'll crouch down, low as I can with my bad leg, and you're going to climb on my shoulders."

The boy's face blanked. "I'll fall."

Cooper licked his parched lips. All this water and he couldn't drink. "I won't let you fall. You'll hold onto the wall. Like this, see?" He tightened his jaw against the pain and placed his hands flat against the wall, moving one up, then the other. "Like walking, but on the wall. You can do that, Tom, can't you?"

Another nod.

"I knew you could. I'll stand real slow." Like he had another choice. "And you move your hands like I did. The higher you get, the easier it'll be. See those tree roots at the top there?" The boy raised his head. "When you get high enough, you grab those and pull yourself out."

Scared or not, the determination in Tommy's eyes said he was committed to the plan. "What about you?" he said. "Who's gonna pick you up?"

Cooper almost laughed. Mark Thomas Beck was a kid wise beyond his years. He hadn't thought that far ahead. One fact he was sure of, there'd been no more screams from above. Not since they woke. No sounds other than the barks, howls, and screeches indigenous to the surrounding forest.

Better for Tommy to take his chances up there, than down here where death awaited opportunity.

"We have to take it one step at a time, Tom. First we get you out. Then we worry about me. You ready to try?"

Kat stood in the Cessna's shadowed interior. She pitched Brent a brown and green plaid shirt, then tossed a similar shirt to Nick. "Your jeans and high-topped tennis shoes are fine, but you both need long sleeves." She tossed another shirt to Angeline. "For protection," she added. "And you'll need these."

Angeline looked down at her blue peasant-style crop top, khaki Capri pants, and studded flats, then she stared at the faded jeans and scuffed ankle-high boots Kat offered her. She pointed to the boots. "I don't think I can walk in those."

"My feet are bigger than yours. Put them on." Kat's voice didn't invite debate. "I don't want Doc here to have to treat you for snakebite."

"Snakebite?" That was the only word she needed to hear. Angeline snatched the clothing from Kat, then turned to her brothers, who stood gawking. "Do you mind?"

They answered in unison. "Uh, sure." Then they jumped to the ground.

"I'm glad we have a few minutes to talk." Kat sat on one of the coolers. "I don't know how long it'll take us to get to whatever's burning," she said. "But I wish you would stay here."

Angeline sat on the other cooler and kicked off her stone-colored shoes. "No way."

"We can move faster without—"

"*No.*" She inserted the tone she'd sharpened on four overprotective brothers. The accident left her damaged, but she was no cripple. "I don't give a damn how long it takes me to get there." She shrugged into the sleeveless green tank Kat had handed her with the shirt, pulled it down, and tucked it into the jeans. "I'm going."

"Okay." Kat knelt in front of Angeline and inched thick, cuffed socks up her feet and ankles. The suede boots followed. She double-knotted the laces, while Angeline threaded a leather belt through the loops in the baggy jeans.

Angeline stood, and for a few seconds, stomped around in the boots.

"How do they feel?"

"I'll probably get blisters." She couldn't keep the nerves from her laugh. "But I've had blisters before. You should've seen the stilettos we wore on the catwalk. These?" She pointed at her feet. "Piece of cake."

Kat handed her the cane. "Socks'll help with the blisters." She slung the straps of her backpack over one shoulder and lifted a mean-looking carbine rifle. "Ready?"

Angeline abhorred guns. She reached for Kat's hand when she turned toward the door. "Thank you for helping me look for Cooper." The words broke with her whisper, but she didn't give a damn. "I know he doesn't mean anything to you, but Cooper is everything to me. And so much more to Jack. It wasn't until he disappeared that I realized how much."

Kat nodded, then turned quickly away. She leaped to the ground where Nick and Brent waited.

Angeline followed, slower, graceless.

Brent helped Kat fasten the cargo-hold door. "Shouldn't we travel along the river bank? I mean, that's where the smoke came from."

They spread a huge camouflage-imprinted drape over the Cessna, which Angeline thought was pretty clever.

When they were done, Brent hoisted his canvas backpack, then casually passed Nick his doctor's bag.

As if she wouldn't notice.

Angeline huffed a silent breath, but she didn't comment. Why did everyone feel the need to protect her? They would find Cooper, and he would be okay—and that was that.

They loaded their gear, and Kat started toward the dense mangrove trees with purpose in her lengthy strides. "We have to *get* to the river first," she called over her shoulder.

The three siblings hurried after her.

Angeline envisioned them machete-hacking a corridor through dense jungle, but the swamp was a confusing maze of winding channels and skeletal gnarls of elevated tree roots. Cavernous and dark and spooky. She and Jack had lived on Jacqueme Dominique for three and a half years, and they'd never ventured farther than Port Noel's city limits.

She swore under her breath. If the *five* of them made it out of here, she never would again.

An hour into their trek, a series of staccato gunshots echoed through the trees.

Nick whirled and yanked her down, sheltering her body with

his. "Someone's shooting at us!" he yelled.

Chapter Twenty

Angeline sucked in a mouthful of dirt and decaying leaves, then launched into a bout of coughing and spitting.

Kat backtracked and crouched beside them. "Don't be so skittish," she said. "That isn't gunfire."

Brent hunkered down next to her. "Then what the hell is it?"

"Clams." Kat took hold of Angeline's elbow and tugged her up.

"Clams?" Nick sat back on a flat rock and drew a folded white handkerchief from his pocket.

Brent released a tension-laced guffaw. "No shit," he said. "As in chowder?"

"In the mangrove roots," Kat explained. "Island rivers connect to the sea. When the tide ebbs, the clams snap their shells closed in response to the changing conditions. It protects them from drying out as they await high tide again."

"Must be a helluva clam to create that much racket." Brent stood and eased his backpack to the ground. He opened it, then fished out several water bottles. Kat declined the offer, so he passed the second bottle to his brother.

Nick twisted off the cap, poured a generous amount of water on his handkerchief, then handed the bottle to Angeline. She took the cap and shoved it in the flap pocket of her borrowed shirt. The cool liquid dribbled down her chin as she chug-a-lugged, and a dark splotch of dampness spread across the front of her green undershirt.

Kat turned to Brent, hands on her slender hips. "You came to me for a reason, Flyover. You need to trust that I know what I'm doing."

"Absolutely." He raised his near-empty bottle in salute. "No problem."

She shouldered her backpack, picked up her rifle. "Let's get going then. Sunlight will be scarce once this swamp blends into the rainforest. We need to reach the river before nightfall...and you'd better go easy on your water."

Nick stood, his chest heaving. "How far?"

Kat's narrow-eyed appraisal moved from Angeline's cane to her face, then back to the cane. "Half a mile," she said. "Maybe more."

"I'm fine," Angeline ground out, her stare never wavering. She'd considered the argument settled back at the plane. "You lead the way," she added with forced vehemence. "I'll keep up."

Her gut told her if they found the smoldering van, they found Cooper.

No clear boundaries marked the island wilderness. Elevated mangrove roots gradually gave way to mammoth tree trunks, fungus, saplings, and woody vines that climbed to the forest's canopy as if seeking Heaven's liberation. A surprisingly small number of ground plants grew there. Nothing like the choking jungle of vegetation in movies and countless adventure stories she'd read as a girl.

The forest carried its own unique smell: earthy, damp, and musky. The ground was soft, like high-grade mulch. Humidity thickened the air. Temperatures hovered in the eighties. Clothes, hair, and shoes quickly became sticky.

On rare occasions, hazy light filtered through the dense green umbrella a hundred feet above them. But, for the most part, the forest floor remained a deep kind of dark where little wind stirred.

Angeline shuddered. She seldom thought of her phobia these days. But snakes slithered in the dark and coiled in trees to prey upon passersby. Kat got a quick blessing for the borrowed boots, and Cooper a curse for disappearing on her.

Wishing for a flashlight—but not about to ask for one—Angeline tapped her cane on the wide, mottled root of a chataignier and whispered her old mantra. "The only good snake is a dead snake."

"What's that?" Nick slowed his pace and fell in beside her.

"I can walk a quarter mile in six minutes on my treadmill." She lifted her watch into a splinter of light. Her head throbbed, worry tied her stomach in knots, and her hip and lower back ached from continual limping over uneven ground littered with spongy patches of mud and muck. "We've been at it for an hour and a half. Surely the river is close."

Sweat trickled down the side of Nick's face. He blotted the back of his neck, then stuffed his handkerchief in the collar of his shirt. "Tired?"

Angeline studied Kat O'Leary's back. The pilot tromped two yards ahead, the nickel- and hardwood-finished carbine slung over her shoulder as naturally as if it were a third arm. "A little," she whispered. "But don't tell her."

The cries of brown and red howler monkeys, and the call of a lone Macaw drowned out her brother's response. They trudged another half-hour without speaking.

Angeline noted a change in the terrain: the increase in sporadic sunlight and thickening of tree ferns, the reappearance of mangrove trees and the stench of briny swamp water. Birds were everywhere, in every color imaginable.

Nick slapped at his arm, scratched his cheek. He constantly mumbled, "Damn mosquitoes."

Finally, they broke from the trees into full sunlight—or what was left of the sun with dusk settling in.

She caught up to Kat. "I smell smoke."

The pilot nodded once.

Brent broke into a run. "Over there," he shouted. "I see it!"

Wisps of black wafted from the undercarriage of the Chrysler

Grand Voyager. Its hood lay on the ground several yards away, green paint bubbled and blackened. The stench of burning oil and rubber hung in the air like silt. The vehicle had almost burned itself out.

Nick covered his nose and mouth with his folded kerchief. He approached the gaping hole where the driver's door should be.

Angeline noted the Bondo patch on the rear fender. "This is Bernard's van." She kept her distance. The simmering pot of acid in her stomach bubbled over. "Is there anyone inside?"

Nick circled the taxi, peering in broken windows. "Not a soul," he yelled.

Afraid to feel relief, her gaze shot to Kat. "They have to be here."

"Let's spread out and search the immediate area in pairs. There's not much time." Kat slipped the rifle from her shoulder, and in her peripheral vision, Angeline caught the sun's reflection off a small handgun the pilot pitched to Brent.

Kat pointed to her and said, "You're with me."

The water in the pit reached Cooper's knees. He squatted, then helped the boy onto his shoulders.

Tommy wobbled as he slowly stood, hands pressed against the wall's slippery black mud.

Cooper closed his eyes and continued counting to keep the pain and suffocating claustrophobia at bay. "Here we go," he said. "Remember...walk up the wall with your hands, Tom. Grab onto anything you can. Make sure you've got a good grip before you move further up." Pain thunder-bolted in his head as he stepped away from the wall three or four inches to allow the kid room to maneuver. Lifting Tommy was harder than he expected, and the effort had him spent and trembling before he straightened his legs.

Suddenly, the boy started singing. Loud and boisterous verses about, of all things, trash. He all but shouted the words.

Cooper didn't know where he found the strength. "Where'd you learn that song, Tom?"

"Oscar the Grouch teached me it. He lives in a trash can," Tommy said, matter-of-factly. "It's round like our hole. Oscar don't love nothing better'n trash." The boy launched into a louder rendition.

Stopping, Cooper sucked huge breaths but couldn't draw enough air. "I need to rest a minute," he said. "You okay up there?"

Tommy latched onto the first root. "Got it," he yelled.

Cooper squeezed his eyes shut against the blinding pain. Almost there. He slipped forward.

The boy jerked and cried out as he fell. He slid under, then broke the sloshing water sputtering.

Cooper's legs crumpled, and he went down beside him.

"I'm sorry. I'm sorry," Tommy said, choking as he struggled to stand.

Cooper steadied the boy with a hand on his shoulder. "My fault, Tom. I'm weaker than I thought. We'll rest a minute, then we'll try again. Are you hurt?"

"No." Tommy parted wet hair from his forehead so he could see. If he was hurt, he wouldn't say. The kid had guts.

After a few minutes, they tried again. Cooper didn't know how singing his lungs out helped, but the boy reached the edge of the opening. Cooper raised his good arm, placing his hand on Tommy's backside. "I'm going to try to lift you higher. Are the roots big enough to climb on?"

"Uh-huh." The kid's excitement birthed a stutter. "It's l-like the rock-climbing w-wall on my swing set."

Only straight up, no incline. "Good, good," Cooper huffed. "I'll keep my hand on you as long as I can."

Angeline followed Kat along the bank, hesitant to search for bodies among the rocks in the murky river's edge. An eerie ground fog thickened with the setting sun, as if Mother Nature mocked their time constraint. The crescent moon's sliver only stirred the shadows.

Brent and Nick weaved in and out of trees thinning toward the river. They occasionally slapped mosquitoes the size of horseflies feasting on arms, necks, and ear lobes.

Ten minutes passed. They found no one.

A scream broke the cacophony of mating frogs and cicadas.

Everyone froze. Birds fluttered out of trees. Howler monkeys and capuchins joined the deafening racket.

Angeline's grip on her cane tightened. "That scream sounded human."

Kat slid the carbine from her shoulder. She motioned with a sharp wave for Nick and Brent to stay where they were.

Moonlight glinted off the pistol when Brent raised the gun and acknowledged her directive.

She turned her back to Angeline and said, "Flashlight, in my pack. Get it."

Quickly unzipping Kat's bag, Angeline lifted out a fluorescent-green light with a broad lens, and a second semi-automatic pistol the pilot hadn't mentioned bringing. A lightweight AMT .45 Hardballer. Angeline hated guns; she never said she didn't know anything about them...or how to use one. Guns and gun shows were her brother David's passion, and the Hardballer was one of his favorite pistols because of its light handling and potent stopping power.

Kat frowned at Angeline's possession of the weapon, but she didn't address it. "Direct the beam toward your brothers," she snapped.

In the flashlight's milky-white sphere, they saw Nick had a similar light.

She turned to Angeline. "I wish you'd stayed with the plane."

No way that would ever happen. "And I wish we were home, Kat. Nice and safe. But we're not. Cooper's missing, and I intend to find him." Angeline checked the safety on Kat's Hardballer before tucking the pistol in her belt. She redirected the flashlight's beam toward the overgrowth beyond her brothers. "Like you said, it'll be dark soon. Why waste time arguing?"

Nick and Brent joined them. They skirted a thick copse of mangrove trees and entered the swamp.

Brent stuck close to Angeline. He eyed the gun tucked in her belt and whispered, "That's my girl."

As kids, they had spent hours on their grandparents' farm outside Trinity, Texas, shooting cans off barrels and fence-posts with her grandfather's old .22 rifle. She'd been the better shot. Of course, that was more than twenty years ago—before high school graduation and modeling in Paris, before she fell hopelessly in love with Cooper, *died*, and then gave birth to their wonderfully, fabulous Jack.

Before this damn Dutchman.

She grabbed Brent's arm. "Do you think the scream we heard was Cooper?"

He stopped and placed a comforting hand on her shoulder. "If it was, kid, we'll find him."

A wave of nausea rolled through her as they set off again. The scream never repeated.

She jabbed another rock with her cane.

Brent jogged toward Kat.

Nick charged ahead of their group, his flashlight beam like a palsied firefly. High, low. High again. Quaking more with each jerk. Nick was out of his element as much as she was.

Gradually, shrubs and trees gave way to a clearing that appeared man-made. Nothing stirred.

At least, nothing human.

Nick called out in a loud whisper, "What'd you say that mill looked like?"

Kat answered, "Round, like a giant upside-down thimble. Would've been crowned with windmill blades once. Walls of coral block and mortar. Arched doorways. You see something?"

"Got what's left of a building up ahead. Looks like a silo, but shorter, and pretty overgrown. There's a padlock on the doors. The lock looks new." Nick's flashlight beam scanned the turret-like structure rising from the overgrowth of ferns and creepers like an antiquated altar paying homage to the once *King Sugar Cane.*

Kat said, "Stay where you are. I'll check it out."

Angeline and Nick held back while Kat approached the structure, Brent on her heels. The knife from her scabbard made swift work of the ground creepers laying claim to the five stone steps leading to the entrance.

Again, using the knife for leverage, Brent quickly discarded the lock. Hinges creaked as he dragged open the heavy arched doors.

She and Nick moved closer. A waft of smothering warmth and

decay hit them. Their flashlights illuminated brick walls, coiled rope, stacked crates, and a pile of iron gears on one side of the stone floor. Tools, a rough-hewn table and bench crowded the opposite wall. Another set of doors exited the back.

Kat's voice echoed through the cylindrical chamber rising twenty feet or better. She shined her flashlight above their heads. "Those beams and tin roof aren't original to the structure. The lights are modern, and the area's too clean not to have people using it recently. There's got to be a power source."

"Generator's probably out back for ventilation," Brent said. "I'll check."

"Wait," Angeline called out. "I hear...*singing?*"

The others heard it, too. A child's voice.

They left the building, spread out, and trekked deeper into the clearing. Flashlight beams lit the wall-like perimeter of kapok and calabash trees, shrubby tamarinds, and ferns and creepers battling for the clearing's daytime sun.

Angeline stopped and listened again. Images of Jack flooded her head, her boy so small and helpless in a feral place like this.

The oddly familiar lyrics seemed to come from everywhere.

Yet nowhere.

She hobbled to Kat. "I recognize the words. It's Oscar's song, from Sesame Street. Jack knows it by heart. *The missing boy.*" She grasped Kat's arm and shook her. "It's got to be the missing boy!"

Kat issued no-nonsense orders. "Nick, stay with your sister. Brent, look for that generator." She grabbed Angeline's flashlight and pitched it to him. "Take this. There's a smaller one in my pack."

Brent disappeared around the side of the building. Within minutes, the generator chugged a sort of half-life, coughed, then died. A crank similar to a lawnmower's pull-string sounded, and the machine fell into a noisy chainsaw cadence. Barks and screeches rose in surrounding treetops. Light spilled from the structure's interior, making it appear even more of a contradiction to the encroaching wilderness.

Kat raised her hand again, and everyone stood silent. They listened for the boy. Nothing.

Angeline circled the clearing. "I know we heard him." She stirred the air with her cane. "We couldn't have imagined it, not all of us."

The others followed suit. They swept the forest floor with their lights in bridge-like arcs, and cast beams across massive trunks and low-lying vegetation, illuminating red-eyed tree frogs and God knows what.

"Got him!" Brent yelled. His flashlight bounced on the ground as he dropped it and squatted. Three beams swung in his direction, encapsulating a latticework of branches and leaves—and the small hand rising at their edge like a ghoul from a grave.

The boy's weight lifted off him.

"What the—" Cooper lost his footing and waves of water rolled over his head as he slithered to the pit's muddy bottom. He surfaced, thrashing and sputtering, slinging water from his face and eyes.

He looked up as Tommy's feet disappeared through the opening.

Cooper mustered enough strength to yell. "Tom!"

A man's face appeared in the gap created by tossed branches. Cooper blinked and tried to grasp clarity as the face vanished in the wall of black greedily devouring his consciousness.

"Easy, son."

The boy kicked and wriggled. He beat his fists against Brent's chest and connected with his chin several times. Coated in sludge and mud, he was slippery as a bar of soap and stout as any tequila shooter Brent ever had.

"You're safe now," he repeated. "Safe. I heard Cooper yell a name. *Tom.* Is that your name, son? Tom?"

The boy gave what Brent considered a jerky nod, before he launched into another round of flailing fists and kicking.

Angeline stooped at her brother's shoulder. She dropped her cane and flashlight, took the combative boy's face in her hands, and forced him to look at her.

Brent recalled her using the same technique on Jack.

She spoke in slow, clear tones. "Mr. Cooper is our friend, and he needs our help. You have to stop fighting us so we can get to him. Okay?"

The boy's wild eyes reflected fear and vacillation. "The bad man shot him," he whispered as he dissolved against Brent

"Shot?" Angeline yanked up her flashlight and cast its beam inside the pit.

With his hands full, there was no way Brent could stop her from looking. He handed the kid off to Nick.

Kat stood several feet away, gripping the business-end of the sleek carbine.

Nick sat the boy on the ground next to her.

"We need to hurry," Angeline shouted.

Cooper was leaning against the wall, his dark hair wet and matted, skin white as bone. Muddy water reached his chest.

Brent called down to him but got no response. "Damn it, Cooper, open your eyes."

Again nothing.

"Be right back. Keep your flashlight on him," he told Angeline. "Keep talkin' to him. Nick, put a log or a boulder in that trench so the water doesn't rise any higher. I'm going down there." He ran to the building where he'd seen a thick coil of brait rope, similar to the rope he kept in the bed of his truck on the docks back home.

The boy huddled near Kat's booted feet. She'd knelt on one knee next to him but never loosened her grip on the rifle.

The frightened boy's chin quivered and teeth chattered, but his gaze remained glued to the mouth of the hole.

Nick slammed a small boulder in the narrow trench, damming the flow from the river.

Brent felt his sister's palpable fear and his brother's uncharacteristic fury. Hell, his own anger had his damn insides shaking. What kind of monster held human life in such low regard? He shouted over the generator's chug, "We need to loop the rope around a tree, get some leverage. Kat, give Angie your rifle." The pilot opened her mouth to argue, but he quickly added, "She's more than capable, and I need you and Nick at the rope. I'm no lightweight. Neither is Cooper. Holding onto us will be a two-person job."

Kat nodded.

Brent charged the tree-line seven or eight yards away, the coil of rope swinging by his side.

She ran behind him at a diagonal, guiding his footfalls with the flashlight.

He glanced up momentarily, then stopped in his tracks, making Kat stumble and plow into him. Dropping to his knees, he vomited.

She reached for his shirt. "What is it?"

"There." He grabbed her flashlight. Both their hands on the base, he shined its beam toward the trees.

Kat covered her mouth with her hand. "Oh, God."

"God doesn't have anything to do with somethin' this ugly," he whispered.

"The manchioneel," she said.

Brent wiped his mouth with the back of his hand and stood, weaving. "The scream we heard was Bernard's." He folded at his waist, wretched again, and emptied his gut. If Kat hadn't saved him from hanging his hammock on a manchioneel tree the other day, he would've suffered the same unfathomable fate as the cabbie.

"You sure it's him?" she asked.

"Wouldn't swear to it," Brent said. "But he sure looks like Bernard. Same height, build. Race."

Naked but for a pair of soiled briefs, the man was tied spread-eagle to the mammoth tree, his skin so raw, blistered, and bloody he appeared barely human. His sightless eyes stared at them, his twisted mouth frozen in agony.

Brent stepped closer. The man's face was swollen twice its size and features barely discernible. But it had to be Bernard. They'd found his van.

One thing he was damn sure of: Kat's dad was dead to right when he said the devil himself was rooted in the manchioneel.

She grabbed Brent's arm and jerked him back. "Don't touch him."

"We have to see if he's dead."

"He is. But not long. The stench isn't vile enough."

Her voice held a hardness Brent hadn't heard before, and he wondered how much death she'd seen.

Kat turned to him. "We can't let the others see." She pivoted ninety degrees to the right. "Bring the rope," she called out, and pointed. "We'll loop it around that tamarind."

Brent obeyed. She held one end of the rope while he circled the tree with the other. He knotted his end every couple feet to have something to grip while climbing out of the hole, then he fashioned a loop in Kat's end to slip around Cooper.

They rushed back.

"Any response?" he asked Angeline as he tossed both ends of rope in the hole.

She shook her head.

"It'll be all right." At least, he hoped to God it would. "We need to warm Cooper up. See if you can find something in the mill, Angie. Blankets, rain slickers, tarp. Anything. Better leave the rifle here." Brent gripped both ends of rope, braced his tennis shoes against the packed wall, and lowered himself into the hole. The water wasn't as cold as he expected, but neither was there a lick of warmth when he touched the side of Cooper's neck to feel for a pulse.

"Come on, man, open your eyes." He slapped Cooper's cheek. "Talk to me. Tell me what an asshole I am." He slipped the loop over Cooper's head, then around his chest; he eased the rope under Cooper's arms and yelled to his brother. "He's got a gunshot wound to his left arm. Entered front, exited back. As soon as he reaches the mouth, Nick, slide him free and tie off the rope. Use that constrictor knot I showed you. I'll get myself out while you see to his injuries."

Nick's face appeared overhead. "Got it, bro. How're we gonna do this?"

"I'll pull from down here, you and Kat from up there." Brent found a smooth, root-starved track in the wall, and they heaved Cooper up the side.

Angeline's flashlight carved a path of visibility in the lower quadrant of the shaft, illuminating the iron gears. Concrete remained attached to a portion of the components, as if they'd been built into the wall at some time. She brought the light closer and read *Pierpont and Sons, London.* She noted a narrow door to the right of the gears, which didn't appear to lead outside. Storage?

The padlock appeared clean and new. She grabbed a tire iron from a wall hook and banged it against the lock, skinning her knuckles in her hurry. The padlock popped open. Her heart jumped when she shined her light inside and an animal resembling a possum bolted out the door. Dodging the critter, she tripped. As she sprawled atop the stack of empty crates, she grasped at anything tangible to break her fall. The flashlight hit the floor with a dull thud, bounced once, then rolled. A small, blunt-headed snake slithered across its beam. A scream froze in her throat.

Snakes were like rats: you get one, you get a hundred.

To hell with them. Angeline forced herself up. This time Cooper needed her, and she wasn't about to let him down. Clomping across the stone floor in Kat's oversized boots, she snatched up the light and surveyed the small room. No windows. Cooper's claustrophobia would've banished him from such a place.

She crossed to the back wall and banged her cane on the metal sides of a shelving unit. The highest tier stood two-feet taller than the top of her head. A row of sleeping bags hung over the edge. Leaning her cane against it, she snatched two of the bags, staggered out of the room, and slammed the door. Hopefully, trapping the "hisser" and any of his buddies inside.

She reached the pit as Nick and Kat hauled Cooper out. Quickly, she spread one of the bags.

Nick felt for Cooper's pulse and shook his head.

Angeline grabbed her brother's arm. "What are you telling me?"

Chapter Twenty-one

"Cooper's pulse is weak. We've got to work fast." Nick said.

One end of the rope disappeared out of the pit, and out of Brent's view.

After a moment, Nick yelled, "Rope's secure, Brent. Climb out."

Using the knotted rope, Brent climbed up and exited the hole with little effort. But he was soaked through. The temperature had dropped ten degrees with nightfall, and he tightened his jaw to stop his teeth from chattering.

"Let's get Cooper inside the mill," Nick hollered. "I need the light to examine his wounds."

Angeline's gaze moved to Nick, and then fixed on Brent. "There's a table against the side wall."

Nick sprinted to the structure; Brent slogged after him. Wood scraped stone as they dragged the rough-hewn table to the center, directly beneath a long, rectangular light suspended from the ceiling beam with lengths of chains. They ran back, and using the sleeping bag as a gurney, hauled Cooper inside and onto the table.

"I need my—" Nick turned, and Tommy shoved the doctor's bag in his gut. "Thanks, kid." He set the bag between Cooper's legs and opened it.

Kat insisted on keeping watch outside, which didn't thrill Brent, but he'd forgotten the boy. They couldn't let him watch. "Kat," he shouted.

She poked her head inside. "Yes?"

"Don't you have something to show Tom?"

Their gazes connected and held for the briefest moment, her irritation palpable. She frowned but nodded, then crossed the room, grabbed the kid's hand, and disappeared outside.

Cooper moaned. He opened his eyes, then closed them. His raspy whisper sounded as though it filtered through a mouthful of marbles. "Slick?"

"I'm here." Angeline wiped mud from his face with her damp shirttail.

He drew a ragged breath. "The boy?"

"He's scared, but okay. He's worried about you."

Nick poked and prodded making Cooper flinch. "I've got to get this bullet out of his leg." Nick dug through his bag, spilling supplies on the table.

Brent scanned the area and spotted a cut of tree bark. He snatched it up, tore open a gauze pack with his teeth, then spat the wrapper on the floor. He folded the gauze around the bark.

Cooper's eyelids fluttered open. His hand shot out and latched onto Brent's shirtfront with surprising strength. "You're crazy bringing her here," he ground out through clenched teeth.

Brent leaned over the table, his face six inches from Cooper's scowl. "I didn't bring Angie out here, fool. You did. She's in love with you. Although, for the life of me, I don't understand why."

Angeline placed her hands on either side of Cooper's head. Her gaze met Brent's; she gave a consenting nod.

Brent wedged the bark between Cooper's teeth, and pressing his body over his chest, gripped Cooper's uninjured shoulder. He shot a glance to his brother and shouted over the chugging generator. "He's pretty well pissed now. Do it, Nick."

Nick probed the wound in Cooper's thigh, twisted the narrow

forceps, and pulled.

Cooper emitted a feral growl, bucked once, then again, hard enough to lift his shoulders and Brent three inches off the table. The flattened slug left his bloodied flesh; his body went lax.

The bullet struck the bottom of the small, metal bowl Nick placed on the table. He yelled, "Let's clean him up and get the hell out of here."

The generator released the traitorous sputter Brent recalled from countless Gulf Coast hurricanes. It backfired twice, then died. Deafening silence filled the room. An unholy blackness swallowed them.

"I've got it." Kat's flashlight illuminated the table like paint pouring from a bucket.

"Get the hell out of here" turned into fifteen minutes of cleaning and suturing wounds.

Finally, Nick stepped away from the table. Blood muddied his hands.

"Satisfied?" Brent said.

His brother gave a quick nod. "It'll do until we get him to a hospital." Hands raised in front of his chest, he added, "I'm gonna clean myself up at the river's edge. Be right back."

Kat tossed him her flashlight. "Take this."

He caught it and pivoted toward the partially opened door.

Brent called after him. "Night can't get any blacker than this, Nick, and you've got the smell of blood all over you. Watch your step." He turned to the others. "Let's scour the camp and rid it of any traces of us." He chucked the used medical supplies in the smallest backpack, then shoved the bag at Kat. "Better bury these." A rusted shovel leaned against the piled gears and concrete. Brent grasped the handle and carried it outside.

Kat stayed on his heels. "What are you going to do?"

He rolled the boulder from the trench, allowing water to pour into the pit, then hacked a wider gully. *Wasn't it obvious?* "I'm gonna flood this damn hole," he said. "Then I'm gonna bury Bernard."

"I wouldn't advise it." She unzipped the backpack, rolled the boulder inside, refastened the zipper, and dropped the lot in the rapidly filling hole.

Brent muttered under his breath, "And why not?"

"I don't like it any better than you do," she said, getting a firm grip on his arm. "But, if Voorhees comes back, it'll take him longer to realize we came for Cooper if we leave Bernard where he is."

Brent gnawed the inside of his cheek. Kat was right. But he didn't like it, not one damn bit.

Kat suggested they rest in the mill until dawn. She also insisted on first watch because she knew the forest better than the others, and she could hide amongst the wide buttress roots.

Again, Brent agreed with her logic, but he didn't have to like it. Second watch belonged to him.

An hour before sunup they started out from a point behind the millwall, heading in the opposite direction from where they came. Also Kat's idea, in case the Dutchman returned, or sent his henchmen. The crisscrossing tactic was also hers, but it was taking too damn long to reach the Cessna.

Cooper's fever had spiked. Brent rolled the man from his shoulder and eased him to the ground. He slid to the forest floor beside Cooper and leaned against a tree. His body ached like someone had dragged him up an escalator, backwards and buck-naked.

"This isn't working." Kat persisted with the same argument the last two times they'd stopped.

As she bent over Cooper, Angeline jerked her head in Kat's direction. "I won't leave him."

"I wasn't suggesting—"

"No one gets left behind." Brent rubbed his forearms. He rotated his right elbow and shoulder backward; then again, forward. The motion loosened his constricted muscles, but it did nothing to ease the pain arcing in the middle of his back.

Angeline pressed her palm against Cooper's forehead, then his cheek. "He's burning up."

Brent winced. At this rate, he figured Cooper's chance for survival was slim to none.

"That's what I've been getting at." Kat knelt beside Angeline and leaned on the carbine. She pointed to Cooper. "I've seen how rapidly the forest can take a man once he falls ill. Your brother needs more than the few antibiotics he's got in his bag to save Cooper, and Brent can't carry him all the way back to my plane." Shading her eyes, she glanced at the sun. "It's taken three hours to travel this far. We need help, and I know where to get it."

Brent spoke up. "Billy and Mia?"

Kat nodded. "We need their wagon and horses."

He scratched his forearm where a ravenous mosquito left an angry pink welt. "You're right, but you said it would take us a day, maybe two, to reach Billy's place from where we saw the burning van."

"That's if we all go," Kat said. "But you and I can cut that time by half."

Brent twisted left, then right. Irritation laced his raised voice, and he damn well didn't bother weeding it out. "I don't like the idea of splitting up," he said. "We're less vulnerable as a unit."

"Not true," Nick injected, spreading his arms wide. "We're just a larger, noisier target."

Brent dragged himself up using the tree for leverage. "But—"

"What Kat's saying makes sense, Brent. I'm the doctor, and the more logical choice is for me to stay with Cooper." He turned to Angeline as if seeking support for his argument.

"I won't leave Cooper either," she said. "You all know that. And Tommy is only a little boy. He'll tire easily, or need carrying. We should stay. You and Kat go for the wagon and get back here as quick as you can. It's better odds than we have now."

Brent blew out a frustrated breath. Leaving them behind sucked. "Okay. But, for the record, I'm against it."

He watched as Kat, still kneeling, unfastened her rifle's butt trap and produced a straightforward survival kit.

Was there no limit to the woman's surprises?

She tossed a compass to Nick. He caught it one-handed.

"I'd rather you didn't, but if you have to move from this spot," she told him, "keep on a southeasterly track. If we don't come back—" She signaled silence with an abbreviated chop of her hand when he opened his mouth to protest. "*If* we don't come back, a southeasterly path will take you to the river. Follow the river north. You'll eventually run into Billy's place. Tell him Kat sent you, and that he needs to get you to Papa Dan. He'll know what to do."

Papa Dan? Apparently, Brent was the only one who picked up on the dropped name. He stepped forward. He'd only met one Dan since coming to the island, and the man ruled Port Noel's police department with an intolerant hand.

Kat stared as if she read his thoughts. She shook her head. "It's a story for another time," she whispered. She spread snare wire, twine, and a fishing kit on the ground, calling each object by name like a teacher in a class of elementary school children. She passed the final two items to Angeline. "Water-proof matches. Firestarter. Use them sparingly. The last thing you want is to draw attention to yourselves."

Angeline answered with a jerk of her head. She loaded the gear into Nick's backpack.

Still massaging his shoulder, Brent stared from behind his brother. "Damn, Kat. You must've made a helluva Girl Scout."

She studied him a full-blown second before snapping shut the carbine's trap. After draping the rifle over her shoulder, she stood. "I'm a survivor, Flyover. I do whatever it takes to stay alive. Let's hope you can say the same a week from now." She inventoried the group. Her steely gaze settled on Angeline. "Let's hope you all can."

They transferred the remaining water bottle and a generous handful of power bars to Nick's bag. "The water's for cleaning Cooper's wounds," Kat said.

Brent started to shrug his shoulders into the straps of her backpack.

"Hold on." Kat took the bag from him, unzipped it, and withdrew a small hatchet. "Your brother needs to know how to keep everyone hydrated." She removed the leather sheath from the hatchet and called Nick.

Both men followed her to a tangle of hanging vines attached to a mammoth tree higher in the forest's sub-canopy.

Kat removed her outer-shirt and tied the sleeves around her waist. Sweat stained her thin brown tank under the arms and breasts.

Brent flinched when she slammed the hatchet across a vine's lower end. Liquid trailed down her bare arm as she drank, and the want in him stirred. *Lousy timing.*

"Liane chasseur," she said. "Its sap is safe to drink, restorative, and you'll find them growing throughout the forest. Here." She extended her hand to Nick. "You do it."

He took the hatchet, chopped a second vine, and arched a brow.

"Go ahead," she said. "Drink."

Nick lifted the woody cylinder to his mouth. His Adam's apple bobbed as he sucked from the vine. "Amazing," he said, wiping his mouth on his shirtsleeve.

It was Kat who amazed his brother, not some sap-loaded vine. Jealousy manifested in clenched fists as Brent stepped forward. He hated the feeling; there wasn't time for it. "Let me try." He took the hatchet from Nick and swung with exaggerated force, then drank.

Seeming embarrassed as they both stared at her, Kat moved to a low-growing shrub. She plucked several of its purplish-red, plum-like fruit and rubbed them against her shirttail; she pitched one to Tommy and the other to Nick. The fruit rolled.

Laughing, the boy chased after it. He dusted the fruit and took a bite, revealing juicy yellow pulp.

"Camu Camu," Kat explained. "Plentiful like the lianas and filled with nutrients. It's said to contain the largest natural concentration of vitamin C in the world. You'll get sick of eating Camu Camu, but it will keep you strong." She glanced at Cooper and added, "There are some that say it helps with pain."

"Camu Camu." Nick repeated the name. "I'll remember. Thanks, Kat."

She picked another fruit and tossed it to Tommy, followed by a foiled-wrapped granola bar. "The boy must be starving."

The two brothers followed Kat through the overgrowth to a narrow creek cutting through the forest. Brent looked on while she gave Nick a crash course in ways to camouflage himself and the others if it became necessary to hide, and how to use the survival gear she provided. Finally she directed her attention to him. "We need to go."

"Yeah, okay." He wrapped his arms around his brother and squeezed tighter than he meant to.

Nick grunted, then mumbled next to Brent's ear. "Pretty slick thinking back there with the tree bark, bro. Outstanding job."

Embarrassed, Brent shrugged. "Guess it's all those westerns I read to Dad."

When Nick stepped back, his narrow face flushed, their gazes locked, and it occurred to Brent that he might never see his brother and sister again. Chalking his sense of impending doom to an ebb in adrenaline and the unsettling events of the last few hours, he shrugged it off. The state of Bernard's body tied to the manchioneel tree remained a constant inside his head. "Take care of Angie, you hear? And the boy," he told Nick. "Cooper, too. You let that sonofabitch die, and she won't forgive either of us." He tripped on a root when Nick shoved him away.

"Go," his brother said, a noticeable hitch in his voice. "The sooner you get out of here, the sooner you get us out."

Brent jogged behind Kat, skirting wide-trunked gommier exuding milky latex, macaw palms and chataignier, their tapered buttress roots resembling Indian teepees. They'd traveled what seemed hours—and miles.

His calves burned. Fatigue wore on him; the adrenaline rush at finding Cooper and Tommy had long-since waned. Hunger gnawed his insides, and his board-stiff clothes chafed like high-grade sandpaper. He stank of mud and briny river water. But the damn mosquitoes loved him.

Kat stopped abruptly, and Brent slammed into her. Previously, she'd only slowed to check a compass similar to the one she entrusted to Nick. "I'm sorry, Flyover." She bent at the waist, hands braced on her knees, and drew several deep breaths. "You need to stay hydrated same as the others. Sometimes I get so bent on accomplishing a task, I don't think."

Brent licked his dry lips. "I'm okay, Kat. I feel the urgency, too."

"Doesn't matter." She swiped damp hair from her forehead. "You fall out, you're no good to me."

Brent frowned. He wouldn't have put it quite like that, as he had no intention of…"falling out." Hell, the term didn't exist in his vocabulary.

Kat dropped her rucksack, unzipped it, withdrew the hatchet, and passed it to him. "Cut as low as you can on the vine, then drink. But not too fast, and not too much."

Brent drew the hatchet down on a thick liana and drank. The vine's sap tasted as good as any milkshake he'd ever indulged in. After a few seconds, Kat took the liana from him and drank. He gave her a quizzical look.

"Better if we share," she said. "Smarter. Too many cuts, and we leave a trail any guide worth half his salt can follow."

Brent sat on the damp, spongy ground. A green and brown grasshopper with yellow markings landed on a nearby leaf. He thumped its rear. "How far to Billy's place?"

Kat wiped her mouth on her shirtsleeve. "Another couple miles, at least. But another half-mile, and we leave the forest. It'll get hotter than hell." She tucked the liana's cut end into the thick ground vegetation.

Less noticeable, Brent figured.

"You good for it?" Kat said.

"I'm good."

She gave him a rare smile, then fished a yellow baseball cap advertising a hydraulics company from her pack. "I thought as much." She settled the cap on her head, tugging the bill forward, and threaded her braid through the back opening. "Let's do it, Flyover."

He removed his red cap, swiped a hand through his sweat-slicked hair, replaced the cap, bill forward like he'd seen Kat do, then reached over and hoisted her backpack.

"It isn't heavy," she insisted.

"Damn it, woman. Why can't you accept anyone's help?" Brent wiped the hatchet's blade on his shirttail, secured it in the sheath, and then returned it to the backpack. "Hold onto the rifle if it makes you feel better," he told Kat. "But I carry the bag."

She hesitated, like she wanted to add something more, gave a quick nod, and moved forward into the brush.

Brent matched her stride for stride as they easily penetrated the undergrowth of shrubs, herbs, and saplings. He lifted his wrist and grimaced. His watched had stopped, and somewhere along their jaunt he'd smashed the crystal. He unfastened the watch and slid it into his pocket.

A lengthy half mile later, they exited the forest as Kat had predicted. The ground leveled off, but the sun battered them for another hour. Tree ferns, creepers and ground cover thickened, slowing their pace.

According to the sun's position, Brent figured it was near four o'clock. Still they didn't stop. Kat's determination never wavered, and his admiration for her grew, even as his own stamina faltered.

Finally, she raised her hand.

Brent stopped, thinking she sensed his fatigue and was about to offer him a break he'd flat refuse.

She cupped her hand and gazed at the sky. "Vultures."

She said the word so low Brent almost missed it. But he saw them, too, the scavengers circling up ahead.

Kat broke into a run. "Billy's house," she shouted.

Chapter Twenty-two

Angeline watched as Nick and Tommy gathered the Camu Camu fruit for dinner, and she wondered if Kat had made up the name to amuse the boy. She sat on a fallen tree trunk a foot off the ground.

Swathed in a sleeping bag, Cooper slept fitfully. His shoulders rested against her abdomen, his head against her breasts. He'd developed an alarming rattle in his chest, and a chill. Nick claimed the seated position made breathing easier.

She could see it helped.

Some, but not nearly enough.

Kat had left them near a creek. Ten yards upstream, it formed a shallow pool, three feet in the deepest part, and so pristine they could see the bottom. Safe enough for Tommy to splash in and cool off, so long as he remained quiet—and Nick stayed with him.

With one arm wrapped protectively around Cooper, Angeline brushed hair from his feverish forehead. "Rest," she whispered next to his ear. "When Brent and Kat come back with the wagon, we'll take you out of here." She continued talking to him, as she had for the past few hours. About anything and everything—

nothing. Until her throat felt achy and raw.

"Jack would love this place." She waved a hand at the surrounding trees and vegetation, the colorful birds perched high in branches. "And he'd adore Tommy. They're so much alike, Cooper. Funny and fearless. By the way, Tommy's from New Hope, Pennsylvania. *New Hope.* Isn't the name ironic? Nick's been there. He says it's a small town on the Delaware River, not too far from Philadelphia. Quaint. Artsy. Scads of galleries, antique shops, and lovely B and B's. When all of this is...over, we should go there."

Nick squatted next to her. "He hears you, you know." He held up the plump, purplish-red Camu Camu he'd sliced on a flat rock using one of Kat's knives and served on a broad, spineless leaf.

She shook her head. "It looks delicious, Nick, but I can't. My stomach's still tied in knots."

Cooper stirred in her arms. "*Eat.*" His order came out on a gravelly whisper. Worse than hers.

She leaned sideways and studied his face. His complexion held a grayish pallor, his eyes bloodshot and glassy. But they remained open. Her heart thundered in her chest; she steadied her trembling hands. "I will if you will," she challenged.

He ate three slices of fruit and swallowed two of Nick's capsules, washed down with the liana's sap, before his eyelids slid shut.

It was a start, and Angeline's spirits lifted.

She devoured the remaining fruit and half a granola bar, then tucked the rest in her shirt pocket for later. Of course, the bar would turn soggy and crumbled by then. Everything in the forest existed in a perpetual state of sogginess. But, nutrients were nutrients.

So far, thank God, there'd been no sign of Voorhees or his henchmen.

"Where's Tommy?" she asked when Nick returned. He'd pulled off his t-shirt, washed it in the creek pool, and now offered the thick folded cloth for cleaning her sticky hands.

The afternoon brought more of the stifling heat, and a dip in the water sounded heavenly.

Nick checked Cooper's pulse and gave her a thumb's up. "The kid's beat," he said. "I doused his mosquito bites with calamine and left him napping on the other sleeping bag. You should rest, too."

"Maybe later." God willing, she'd also take a dip in the pool while Nick watched over Cooper and the boy.

"Okay then." Her brother unzipped the backpack near her feet. "I'll bunk with Tommy for half an hour. Shout if you need me." He took out the Hardballer, checked the safety, and set the pistol on the log within Angeline's reach. He hesitated, then touched her cheek the way he did when she fell as a child. "Your watch, sis. But no more than a half-hour."

Angeline leaned against the tree trunk behind her log. She stared at the gun, then at Nick's back as he rounded a broad gommier tree and blended into the forest. He looked exhausted.

"Hurry, Brent. *Please*," she whispered.

"If anyone can get us out of here," Cooper mumbled, "it's that hardheaded brother of yours."

She chuckled. Laughter felt good. He was right about Brent, and that truth produced a degree of comfort. "Go to sleep."

Cooper sighed.

Angeline heard the worrisome rattle in his chest again, but she consoled herself knowing Nick hadn't gone far...and he'd given her hope when he checked Cooper's pulse.

New hope.

She began talking again, keeping her voice upbeat and steady. "Tommy's dad thinks the Steelers are awesome," she said. "But Tommy loves the Pirates. Of course, he does. What boy doesn't love pirates? Look at Jack and his mangrove ship. Last season, Tommy's mom won tickets to a Pirate's game in a radio contest. He's hoping she'll get lucky again this year. His mom is always winning stuff." Cooper's shoulders relaxed as he slipped into the rhythm of deep sleep. "Tommy plays T-ball," she continued. "First base. God, I miss Jack..."

Brent huffed to keep up as Kat raced along the river bank, tearing through herb patches and tree fern brakes higher than the top of her head. Her yellow ball cap flapped like a gaping mouth, held only by her braid threaded through the back. Fear for Billy Boudreau and his family electrified the air around her, easy targets with Voorhees running loose.

Finally, they reached the outskirts of the clearing and Billy's homestead. Hairs on Brent's arms bristled. Despite sounds native to the wild, the atmosphere struck him as unnaturally quiet, ominous. He grabbed Kat's elbow, halting her forward motion. "Wait." The wild-eyed look she shot him spoke of terror and panic. "We need to go in slow." He withdrew the pistol from the waist at the back of his jeans. "First me."

She inhaled a quick breath.

"Damn it, Kat," he ground out. "Do it my way this time."

She surrendered with a hesitant nod.

"I need you to stay here and cover me with the rifle in case there's trouble."

Kat slid the carbine from her shoulder and sighted the barrel toward the meticulous encampment.

Brent parted the ferns and stepped into the clearing, his throat so dry he could hardly swallow. He steadied the gun and called out, "Billy." Slightly louder. "Mia."

A flock of sooty-black birds fluttered from the tree where he and Kat had washed up before sitting down to the Boudreau's dinner table. He neared the front of the house, only a yard or two more. His stomach churned.

Bad vibes.

Then he saw what he had feared: Billy's booted feet, barely visible inside the open door. Brent took a step closer.

Billy lay on his back on the stone floor, his legs pointed toward the threshold, arms flung out from his sides—a grotesque crucifixion. Blood soaked his shirt and jeans.

"Stay there," Brent yelled to Kat. "I'm going to check inside the house." He prayed she'd listen.

Heat and humidity thickened the air, and an unsettling mix of sour and sweet veiled the sparsely-furnished room. Signs of a struggle showed in overturned furniture and scattered books.

Billy Boudreau had built his house in shotgun fashion, one room flowing from the doorway of another. Four rooms total. Brent scrubbed a hand over his face and into his hair, sweeping off his ball cap. He left the hat where it dropped on the stone floor. The house's interior lay jarringly still. He ran toward the rear, searching each room, afraid he'd find the bodies of Mia Boudreau and her children.

When he reached the last bedroom and found no other bodies, he doubled over, the gun still gripped in the hand braced on his knee. He drew a steadying breath, then another. Where were they? He returned to the first room. Flies swarmed the area in a buzzing dirge. A spotted beetle scurried across a red and gold cigarette box. Brent swept both aside with his shoe as he knelt, reached out a shaky hand, and touched the side of Billy's throat.

The man's skin was cold as winter concrete. Billy's eyes opened; his bloodied hand shot out and grabbed Brent's wrist. "I didn't know." He struggled to get up

"Don't move." Brent ran, yanked a thick towel from a wall rack in the small kitchen, and rushed back. He slipped in Billy's blood in his haste to stave the flow from his wounds. "What happened?"

"Knife."

Brent kneeled and eased up Billy's shirt. He swallowed hard. Bile coated the back of his tongue. Given the length of the wound, it amazed him the man hadn't already bled out.

"I didn't know," Billy said again.

"Doesn't matter now, man. Whatever it is, it's okay." Brent pressed harder on the compress. Blood seeped through the thick terrycloth and coated his hands. "Who did this to you?"

"Voorhees." Billy choked, and blood trickled from the corner of his mouth. "Tying up loose ends, he said. Where's Kat?"

"I'm here, Billy." The rifle clattered to the stone floor when Kat knelt beside him. Her wide eyes asked Brent the unspoken question.

He shook his head.

Billy drew a determined breath. "Voorhees claimed he needed a spot for research. Insects. A rare species. Took him to the mill to set up base camp." He swallowed, and still grasping Brent's shirt, turned his focus to Kat. "You brought a newspaper. Saw his picture on the front page. Read what he did. I never would've took his money. I swear."

"It okay, Billy." Kat brushed hair from his forehead. "You need to tell us where Mia and the children are. Did Voorhees take them? Did he hurt them?"

Billy's eyes closed. "I sent them away."

Brent leaned close. "But how did you know Voorhees would come back here?"

"Radio transmission cut in. Got on the same channel. He must've stashed a boat in the harbor. I heard him say."

Billy's hand relaxed and slid from Brent's shirt. Brent felt his throat for a pulse. His gaze fixed on Kat.

She slid to a sitting position, and backed away, her movements jerky. Robotic. Color siphoned from her face as she studied his. "No."

Brent stood. He stepped around Billy and wiped his bloody hands on his jeans as best he could, then he reached for Kat and pulled her up. "I'm so sorry."

She collapsed against him, burying her face in his damp shirt. He rubbed her back. He'd never heard a woman cry so quiet, as if grief rose from a place buried so deep inside her she'd abandoned the emotion long ago.

After a few minutes, her shoulders stiffened. She untangled herself from Brent and stepped back. "Voorhees is still out there. We need to find Mia and the children."

He studied her sallow complexion. "Where would Billy send them?"

"To town. Mia would know to go to Papa Dan."

"Daniel Zeller, the police chief?"

Kat nodded. "Billy's dad is Papa Dan's stepbrother. Billy would've sent Mia and the children to him. But the wagon is slow. It'll take them too long getting to town. Voorhees will find them."

"Depends on when Billy sent them away." Brent needed to think. "Hold on a minute. There's a broke-down jeep out back. When we came the other day, you brought packages from the States. Billy ordered parts. Maybe..." He pulled Kat to the door. Outside, they broke into a run toward Billy's shop. Brent noted three vultures had landed in the yard, thirty feet from the front door, biding their time.

The door to Billy's one-room shop hung lopsided on its frame. Pistol raised, Brent peered inside. File drawers stood open, contents scattered. Someone had smashed Billy's radio against the wall.

The Jeep was still parked beside the structure; the faded tarp on the ground next it. He raised the hood. A new distributor cap was in place. "I don't understand." He looked to Kat. "If Billy was afraid Voorhees would come here, why didn't he send Mia to safety in the Jeep?"

"Mia doesn't drive," Kat said. "Never learned. She never needed to. But there's a spare key in one of those tiny magnetic boxes under the rear bumper."

Brent retrieved the key and tossed the box aside. He ran around the Jeep, yanked open the door, and slid behind the wheel. "Get in," he yelled to Kat.

She obeyed without any comment, a sign of her deeper distress.

He turned the key in the ignition. The Jeep emitted a futile whine. He tried again with the same result.

"Maybe Billy didn't fix it yet," Kat said.

"Yes, he did." Brent got out. "Stay here, and I mean it this time. I'll be right back." He turned toward the path. From where he stood, he could see the vultures had moved closer to the house, within ten feet. He twisted back. "Hold on."

"What is it?"

"I'm not well versed in the law, Kat, especially here on the island. But this is a crime scene. We need to preserve it until we can get the police out here." His mind raced. "Do you have a key to the house?"

"Yes." She dug in her pocket and produced three keys on a simple silver ring.

He took the keys. "I'm gonna lock the front door. It's not much, I know. But locking up's all we can do for now, and it'll keep the animals away from Billy. I need you to stay here. I'll be right back."

She didn't move to go with him. Good enough.

Brent ran to the house and bolted inside. He knelt next to Billy, searched in his jeans pockets, and tugged out the rotor. "You're something else, Billy Boudreau," he whispered. "You saw Voorhees coming, and wanted him to think you had a broke-down Jeep. It didn't work out for you, and I'm sorry about that. But it'll work for Kat. I'll see she's safe. Mia and the children, too. You have my word."

"Come on, Slick. Wake up."
Cooper's voice.
Angeline startled awake. Sweat soaked her clothes and stung her eyes. She inhaled deeply, willing her racing heart and pulse to stabilize.

He twisted his shoulders, winced, and stared up at her. "Tell me about your dream?"

"No." She answered too quickly. "I mean, I don't remember it." In the dream, Voorhees had succeeded in killing Cooper, then he came back for her and Jack. She touched Cooper's cheek, then his forehead. Still hot. "How are you feeling?"

He leaned against her. "Like I couldn't wrestle a kitten and come out on top."

"Who's wrestling kittens?" Nick strolled up, a rolled sleeping bag tucked under his arm.

Tommy trailed behind him. The boy's attention was focused on a striking blue and black butterfly.

"Hey there, Tom."

Tommy's head jerked toward Cooper's voice. Seconds passed. His expression showed relief, tinged with concern as he crept close enough to study Cooper. Suddenly, his face lit, and Angeline couldn't imagine a broader grin.

They needed a moment.

She needed a few. "Since you two are here to look after Cooper," she slipped from behind him and eased his back against the log, "do you think it's safe for me to wash off in the creek?"

"Be careful," Nick said. "Because we haven't seen or heard anything doesn't mean Voorhees isn't still in the area. And stay in the pool."

Like she'd go any deeper than three crystal-clear feet. "Ten minutes," Angeline promised. "Long enough to rinse the muck off my clothes and hair." She headed down the half-cleared trail her brothers had forged early in the day using one of Kat's knives and a hatchet. She checked her watch, then left it on the bank in one of her shoes before easing into the cool creek. Five o'clock. Not much time. She waded in with her clothes on. More efficient washing grungy apparel and her body at the same time.

Angeline never imagined a place that grew so dark, so fast. She shivered. A place where you felt as though someone—or some thing—continually watched. She sliced through the water, soaking every grimy inch. Ten minutes was but a sneeze in a place like this. If only Kat had jammed a bar of soap and one of those miniature shampoo samples in her survival kit. Angeline smiled as she hurriedly scrubbed, thinking of Brent's bush pilot.

What a curious mix of tough and tender Kat O'Leary was. A strong-willed, independent woman with enough sass and cunning to, not only survive in a man's world, but flourish there. Their mom would like her, so would Braeden. She hoped her brother was smart enough to latch onto to this one. It was time Brent settled down and fathered himself a houseful of—

A stick cracked in the brush behind her. Angeline eased around. "Nick?"

Nothing.

"Tommy?"

She waded to the bank. While she put her shoes on, minus socks, dusk settled in and shadows loomed where there'd been a hint of sunlight only moments before.

How could she be so stupid?

She shoved the watch in her pocket, snatched up her wrung-out socks, then hurried toward the path, limping in her haste and looking down so she wouldn't stumble. This wasn't a vacation, a week in paradise with valets, trendy boutiques, and room service. Voorhees' threat was real. He'd kill them all without a twinge of conscious.

Angeline increased her pace. Her gaze still on the uneven terrain, she slammed into a solid body. He caught her in his big hands as she went down. Her mouth dropped open. It took a heartbeat to steady herself and gather her senses, another to find her voice. "Bernard?"

Chapter Twenty-three

Angeline peered up at a grinning Bernard as he lifted and steadied her, his big hands grasping her forearms. "Bernard! Thank God. We found your taxi," she rattled on. "Brent remembered the patched bumper, and that's how we knew the van was yours. Then we found Tommy. He's the kidnapped boy Jack told us about. We just didn't know his name then. Voorhees shot Cooper. If we hadn't found both of them when we did, he would've..."

She couldn't go there.

Shock transformed the driver's face. "But Mr. Cooper, he is okay, yes?"

"He will be once we get him to a hospital. I can't believe you found us, Bernard." She rose on her toes and hugged him. "What a stroke of luck. How did you get away from Voorhees? Cooper's been so ill, in and out of consciousness. He hasn't been able to tell us much."

The cabbie threw his head back and laughed. "Bernard is a lucky man, yes?"

"We're the lucky ones," she said. "Cooper and Nick will be relieved to see you're alive and well."

Bernard took hold of her elbow. "Then you must take me to them. Quickly, miss."

The wind kicked up, stirring the humid air. Angeline stopped talking. She drew a calming breath, suddenly aware her clothes were sopping wet and revealed...well, almost everything.

Bernard stood too close. His gaze traveled down her torso and lingered at her breasts.

She eased away, fumbling to fasten three buttons on the long-sleeve shirt, then crossed her arms. Dusk faded quickly to black. Amid the forest's howls and squawks, she heard Nick call her name. "Over here," she answered, suddenly uncomfortable with Bernard's leer. She turned toward camp. "I should've brought a light."

"Bernard has everything you need, miss." He switched on a flashlight, reached around her, and illuminated the path. His other hand went to the middle of her back. He urged her forward.

They walked three or four yards. Bernard had always seemed congenial, but Angeline had never spent time alone with him. Now his closeness increased her discomfort—but then, her nerves were already frazzled.

She stepped up her pace, anxious to get back to the safety of camp. Finally, they reached the clearing's edge.

Nick's flashlight beam swept over her. "Damn it, Angie. No more swims in the creek near dark, okay? It scared the piss out of me when you didn't come back. I thought surely Voorhees had found you."

She rushed into her brother's arms. "I'm sorry, Nick. Time got away from me. But I have good news." She turned and pointed his light toward the path. "Look. Bernard found us."

The beam glinted off a chain around Bernard's neck, and the tiny gold ring it secured. A woman's ring.

"Bernard!" Nick reached beyond her and shook the man's hand. "We saw your burned out cab. Where the hell were you? How did you escape Voorhees?" He ushered the driver into camp.

Angeline ran to Cooper.

"He's slipped under again, sis." Nick left Bernard, crossed their encampment, and squatted beside her. He checked Cooper's pulse. "His pulse has kicked up a notch, nothing alarming. Could even be the sound of your voice. Fever's still spiky. Not unusual given his wounds, and the fact river water—hell, this whole damn forest—is teeming with bacteria. I wish Brent would get back."

Angeline searched over her shoulder and saw Tommy curled on his sleeping bag four yards away, as well as Bernard lingering near the trail. She dismissed the pull of apprehension clenching her stomach. "It's okay, Bernard," she said. "There's been no sign of Voorhees. With any luck, he's left the island."

Nick stood. "Not likely."

Bernard inched closer, a couple feet from where Tommy turned and rubbed his eyes. He studied the boy. His gaze slid to Nick, then hung on Angeline.

Intuition tugged again, refusing to be ignored. Her palms grew clammy. She wiped them on her damp jeans.

Tommy bolted up, his back board-straight. "No," he cried.

Nick turned his flashlight on him. "Tom?"

The boy scrambled up, confusion and panic obvious in his wide-eyed stare. Angeline studied him as his gaze flicked from Cooper to Bernard, then again to Cooper. Chin quivering, Tommy backed toward the overgrowth and pointed a shaky finger at Bernard. The keening deep in his throat intensified.

Angeline stood, her fingers flexing at her sides. Tommy recognized Bernard, but he shouldn't have...

Clearly, he was afraid of the driver.

No. Tommy was terrified.

Nick moved several steps closer. His voice took on a hard edge, as if he'd also picked up on Tommy's fear. "How did you escape Voorhees, Bernard?" He advanced on the cabbie. "You didn't say."

Bernard grabbed for the boy at the same Nick launched himself at the driver. Tommy ducked under Bernard's arm; Nick plowed into the man's chest. They wrestled into the overgrowth, and then back into the clearing. Nick's dropped flashlight rolled, and illuminated their feet.

Angeline ran to Tommy. She grabbed the boy's shirt and dragged him away from the scuffle. "Stay here."

Bernard wrapped his large hands around Nick's throat and lifted him off his feet.

Angeline grabbed a fallen branch. She slammed it across Bernard's shoulders, and the resounding crack vibrated through her arms.

Bernard released Nick.

Her brother dropped, scattering decaying leaves and muck. He didn't move.

She swung the branch again.

Bernard seized the limb and yanked her close.

Tommy ran to her aid, latching onto the man's elbow. "Let her go!"

He flung the boy into the brush.

Tommy somersaulted against a downed tree with a thud.

"Bitch!" Bernard tossed the branch aside. He wrapped Angeline's shirt around his fist and brought her face within inches of his sneer, his breath hot on her cheek. His island persona vanished. "Voorhees is out there somewhere. You should be grateful I found you before he did. I've seen what the Dutchman does to those who anger him. It's a worse horror than you can imagine." The gold ring on the chain bounced against his chest with every breath. "I have waited a long time for you."

She scratched his hands as he lifted her to her toes. "That ring. Where did you get it?"

"Ah, the little Rose," Bernard said. "Pity she had to die."

Angeline struggled to free herself. She tried to claw his face. "Bastard! You killed Rose and let Voorhees take Jack."

Bernard drew back his fist.

She bobbed, and his blow glanced off her temple. Howls and screams in the treetops faded.

When he shook her, the buttons holding her shirt scattered. She slid free of the shirt and staggered back, but she kept her footing.

Bernard cast the shirt aside as he advanced on her. He shoved Angeline with both hands, then dipped and yanked her legs from under her.

Her head smacked against a boulder, then the ground. She lay dazed.

He dropped to his knees, straddled her, and quickly unfastened his belt. The grind of his zipper cut the air.

She bucked. His slap stung her cheek, and the coppery taste of blood filled her mouth.

His big hand pressed against her throat. "All I thought about while Rose fought me," he said, "was fucking you." Using his other hand, he yanked the t-shirt from her jeans. He shoved it up and stared at her nakedness. "There's no one here to save you," he ground out. "I will have you, then I will kill the others while you watch. Cooper last, so he dies knowing you belong to me."

The rush of air chilled her sweat-slicked skin. Angeline bucked again. His weight ground kindling and jagged stones into her back.

He jerked her belt loose and unfastened her jeans.

Cooper's voice dissipated the fog settling thick around her brain. "Get away from her, asshole."

A gun's report sounded. Bernard jerked and twisted, lumbering up off her.

Able to breathe again, she scooted backward, yanking her shirt down. Tommy ran to her; she pulled him in her lap.

A second shot cracked the air, and then another. Like drumbeats, until only the clicking over an empty chamber broke the silence.

Bernard stumbled another step, two. He fell, motionless.

Cooper weaved, legs widespread, one hand latching onto a tree, the other gripping the Hardballer at his side.

Angeline set Tommy on his feet. Using a buttress root for leverage, she got one knee under her; the other knee wouldn't cooperate. She heaved herself up and half-limped, half-stumbled to Cooper.

The pistol dropped, and he slithered to ground.

She caught him and leaned his back against the fallen tree. "Open your eyes, Cooper. Stay with me, you hear? Stay with me."

"Not going anywhere," he huffed.

"Good. Okay. I need to check on Nick."

He grabbed her arm. "Make sure Bernard's dead."

Surely he was.

Angeline turned, but Tommy already assisted Nick.

Her brother rose to his knees, choking and coughing, his back hunched as he sucked wheezy gulps of air.

Tommy helped him to his feet.

Nick staggered to Bernard. He lowered his hand to the man's throat.

Angeline called out. "Is he dead?"

Nick nodded. "Tommy, go help Angie with Mr. Cooper."

The boy obeyed.

They watched as Nick rolled Bernard's body to the far end of camp, his movements jerky and rage palpable. He unzipped Tommy's sleeping bag and spread it. Grunting, he heaved the driver onto the open bag, whipped off Bernard's belt, and then zipped him inside.

Angeline thought dully how odd the bundle appeared with Bernard's calves and booted feet sticking out from the too-short bag.

Nick lifted the cabbie's body, slid the belt under his legs, and cinched it around the bag's opening. He sat back on his heels, kneeling, his chest heaving more for the effort. "When it gets light," he rasped, "I'll move him farther into the brush so the smell of his blood doesn't draw animals to camp."

Brent's hands tensed on the steering wheel as the Jeep bounced along a primitive road Billy had used for his guide business. Ferns raked the vehicle's sides, and vines slapped the windshield. They'd only managed to drive a little more than a mile from the Boudreau house, sticking close to the river, before night cast its shadows along the bank.

Kat touched Brent's shoulder. "We should stop."

His gaze remained fixed on the terrain ahead. "It isn't dark yet."

She gripped the rifle, propped between the seats, its barrel leaning against the dash. "It will be soon. No sense taking a chance on wrecking the Jeep, or Voorhees spotting our headlights."

Brent suppressed his sense of urgency. "Okay. We'll stop, but not here. Voorhees travels the river by boat. We need to get into the forest while there's still enough light." He veered left, through a break in the kapok trees. There were too many hidden roots to travel far, only a couple yards, but enough for the thick trees to provide adequate cover. He figured, with an early start, they'd reach the others by noon tomorrow. If Nick and Angie hadn't moved Cooper and the boy from their spot by the creek.

Big if...

At least, inside Billy's Jeep, he and Kat had shelter. He turned off the ignition and cast a sidelong glance at her. She'd been understandably quiet for most of their journey.

He got out and stretched his legs, then he walked around to the passenger's side and opened the door. "Climb in the back, Kat." He left no room for argument. "Get some rest. I'll keep watch."

She accepted the hand he offered and stepped out. "I am tired."

You're also grieving. Brent didn't say the words; he didn't have to. He took her arm. "Come on. I'll help you up."

She climbed in the back of the Jeep, and shadows ate what little he saw of her pale face. "Don't treat me like I'm made of glass, Flyover. I told you before, I'm a survivor." She punctuated her next few words with pauses in between. "I...don't...shatter."

"Grief isn't a sign of weakness, Kat. It's an entitlement."

She offered no rebuttal.

Brent climbed in, lifted the rifle, and settled it between his knees. "You want to talk about Billy?"

She curled in the back and laid her head on a folded wool blanket. The back was a tight fit, and the old blanket probably scratchy as hell. "The night's not long enough to tell you about Billy Boudreau," she whispered.

"Yeah." Brent laid the rifle across his lap and sank lower in his seat. "I've met a few people like that in my lifetime, too." He chuckled. "And others I could sum up in a belch."

Weariness showed in her audible sigh. "I told you Billy's da is Papa Dan's stepbrother."

"But Billy's not—"

"Black?" Kat snorted. "Nor am I, Flyover. Colorblindness runs in Daniel Zeller's family. You want to hear about Billy or not?"

Well, it was his idea to get her talking. "Go ahead."

"Billy grew up in the States. When he left the army and married Mia, they came here. That's when I met them. I was sixteen. Da died, suddenly, and I got m'self in a pot full of trouble. Papa Dan took me in and sorted me out. He saw I finished my schooling, paid for flying lessons, and invested start-up capital in my business."

"I'm sorry about your dad."

"He was a mean drunk," she said. "He had no business with a child."

"What about your mom?"

Kat shifted positions. The blanket got tossed on the front floorboard. "Don't know her," she said. "Don't care to." She turned her back on Brent, signaling an end to their conversation. Clearly, he'd touched on a raw spot, several raw spots.

Maybe she'd rest a little now. He leaned back and listened, trying to stay alert, though fatigue wore on him as well. Shrieks and howls closed in. The forest existed in a state of perpetual motion. Day or night, it didn't matter.

Brent slapped his neck. Mosquitoes were another constant here.

Humidity thickened the air, and the heat suffocated, even after sundown. His clothes stayed wet. A shudder rippled down his spine. Billy's blood coated his shirtfront and caked beneath his fingernails. Its coppery undercurrent added to the stink of mud and briny river water.

It was the first time he had stopped all day, and his thoughts strayed to Angeline and Nick. He prayed for their safety, Cooper's survival, and that they could return Tommy to his folks. He prayed Mia Boudreau somehow got her children to Daniel Zeller. Then the Chief would know Voorhees was still out here.

Kat slept fitfully. A nightmare. Probably, the first of many.

Brent shook off the image of carnage and a resolute desire for vengeance. He hated that Kat's last memory of Billy Boudreau should evoke unspeakable horror, with the picture of his bloodied body engrained in her soul, forever changing her.

Exhaustion won out, and he drifted off thinking of Kat—and his pledge to Billy. A promise he aimed to keep. Or die trying.

The chug of an engine jolted him awake. Someone shouted. They sounded close, too close. With his watch broken, Brent had no way of knowing the time or how long he slept. *Damn it.* He ought to have his butt kicked for even falling asleep. But, hell, there'd be time for recriminations later. He hoped.

Streaks of sunlight filtered through the forest canopy, although the Jeep remained hidden in the undergrowth's semi-darkness. Kat stirred behind him. Brent twisted in his seat and raised a finger to his lips. Their gazes met. She nodded and eased to a sitting position.

He slid the rifle back to her, then lifted the pistol from the passenger's seat and checked the safety was off. "Stay here," he whispered. "I'll see how many of them there are."

The Jeep's door creaked when he opened it. He raised the pistol and froze. After a few seconds of nothing but bird chatter, he stepped up behind a large palm tree and peered around it. A white cabin cruiser idled in the wide river a good forty feet from where he hid in the trees. He noted two men onboard, neither of them the blond Dutchman.

Brent turned to the Jeep. The rear window framed Kat's face. He signaled two fingers.

She eased out and crept up next to him. "What do we do?"

"Wait." He could tell by her narrowed eyes it wasn't the answer she wanted. "Give me your knife."

She slipped the knife from her scabbard and handed it to him. "What are you going to do?"

Brent brought his attention back to the cruiser. He could feel Kat's chin at his shoulder as she peered over it, her hand on his hip.

One of the men unzipped his pants and peed over the boat's side. The other man laughed, shouted something crude, and drew attention from the cabin below.

A big blond man, dressed in shorts, a green polo shirt, and light jacket, exited the cabin. He tugged a red and gold box from his shirt pocket, tapped out a brown cigarette, and lit up.

Brent thought back to the photograph Angeline had shown him after the spider-bite incident.

"We'll be leaving soon," Voorhees yelled over the boat's idling motor. "You want fresh fruit, you better go get it. And take that." He pointed to a white, five-gallon bucket. "It's starting to stink up the cabin."

The *pisser* zipped his khaki pants, then positioned the gangway.

264 Sharon Cupp Pennington

"Why not dump it in the river, boss?"

The second man laughed. "Too many crocs."

Voorhees turned toward the cabin. He shouted over his shoulder before disappearing below. "Do as you're told."

Brent whispered to Kat, "One of them left the boat. Cover me." Following parallel to the man's path, he waited until he entered the forest beyond the view of those on the cruiser. They now numbered three, including the Dutchman.

His back to Brent, still laughing, the *pisser* dumped the bucket. From where Brent stood, it looked like waste from the galley.

He drew inside himself. He'd never killed a man. The rage at finding a dying Billy Boudreau surfaced. He crept up behind the guy, wrapped his arm around his throat, and plunged the knife in his chest.

The *pisser* jerked. Brent twisted the knife. A gurgling sound rose in the man's throat. Brent eased him to the ground, then dragged the body deeper into the forest, farther away from the Jeep and Kat.

It wouldn't take the others long to miss him.

Brent wiped his hand on his shirtfront, already stained with Billy's blood. He bent over, braced his hands on his knees, and inhaled a deep steadying breath.

How many men could he kill?

He knew the answer as sure as he knew his own name: as many as needed to save Kat. He'd heard what these men did to women. He saw firsthand the fate they adjudicated to Cooper and Tommy. Brent straightened. His hands no longer shook. He slipped back to where Kat still watched the boat, gave a quick nod, and her eyes told him she understood.

"Any movement?" he whispered.

"Two men on deck," she said. "Makes me nervous the way they're talking and pointing to shore."

Brent peered around the palm tree.

One man trudged down the gangway, followed by the other. They reached the bank and separated, apparently to search different areas.

"Otto," they shouted.

Brent didn't like putting a name to the man he had killed. He turned to Kat. "I'll take care of the man on the left first. You watch the other one. Keep your rifle handy." He followed the second man, much the way he'd followed...*Otto*. This one would be wary of his surroundings as he searched for his missing buddy, making him harder to sneak up on.

The man spotted the white bucket. *Damn.* He picked up the bucket, and Brent edged behind a tree when he turned in his direction.

"I am not laughing, Otto," the man shouted. "Show yourself, or we leave you behind." The man turned away. He trekked deeper into the forest.

Brent crept ahead of him. He steadied himself, fisted one hand, readied the knife in the other, and called out. "I'm here." When the man pivoted, Brent punched him in the face.

The man went down on his back, blood spurting from his nose.

Brent dropped to his knees and plunged the knife in his chest.

The man grabbed the hilt with both hands. His eyes grew wide; his mouth opened and closed like a fish out of water. His left hand went lax and slid to the ground, then his right.

Brent's knuckles burned, but there was still another thug in the forest. He needed to get back to Kat. He retraced his steps and had almost reached the palm tree when he heard her swear. He raced to where he'd left her and saw another thug, bigger than the first two, hauling her toward the river.

Kicking, clawing, and swearing, Kat wasn't going quietly.

Brent found her rifle at the base of the palm. He picked it up, aimed for the guy's shoulder, and pulled the trigger. *Jammed.* He swore under his breath. All this time, he'd left Kat with a rifle that didn't work.

His arm around her throat, the guy dragged her through the ferns and saplings to the gangway. Voorhees yanked her aboard. She shoved him. He grabbed her braid, wrapped it around his fist, and pulled her close.

Brent heard him yell. "How many others?"

Kat spat at him. Her head jerked when the Dutchman slapped her.

"Americans," Voorhees shouted. "Show yourselves or Dirk cuts the woman."

The big thug grinned as Voorhees released Kat and shoved her at him. Dirk unsnapped his scabbard, drew his knife, and slid the blade across Kat's forearm.

She cried out as the knife sliced through fabric and skin.

Brent broke from the trees. "Stop," he yelled.

"Don't be a fool," Kat shouted. "They'll kill us both."

Dirk pressed his blade against Kat's throat. A rivulet of blood trickled down her neck to her breasts and tattooed her tan tank top with a small red flower.

Voorhees withdrew a pistol from inside his jacket. "Join us, my friend." He stepped back. "Join us, please."

Brent waded through the overgrowth, slowly, his hands raised. Kat's pistol cooled his skin at the small of his back. He prayed he drew fast enough. It had been months since he accompanied his brother David to a shooting range. His aim was usually dead on. But targets didn't move—and they sure as hell didn't shoot back.

Voorhees shifted toward the boat's stern, allowing Brent room to come aboard. He noted the Dutchman's relaxed gun hand.

Brent stood at the water's edge. He stepped onto the gangway. The boat's motor hummed. His gaze fixed on Kat, and he rubbed his hand across his forehead, his thumb hiked toward the cockpit.

She acknowledged his directive with a wink.

He whipped the pistol out, raised his arm, and fired. The bullet pierced Dirk's forehead.

Brent pivoted and fired again, hitting Voorhees in the shoulder. The big Dutchman's gun clattered across the deck. He stumbled toward the stern.

Dirk dropped like a stone, and Kat ran for the cockpit. Under her control, the cruiser lurched forward.

Voorhees tumbled over the boat's rear and into the muddy water. He surfaced sputtering, and latched onto the cruiser's narrow dive platform.

Kat shifted into reverse.

Voorhees' body slid under, his arms still grasping the narrow dais. He screamed and jerked as the propeller of the stern-mounted inboard cut across his legs. A red cloud tinged the water. "Help me," he cried.

Brent leaped onto the boat. He and Kat ran to the stern.

She stared at Voorhees. Hate mingled with tears in her glassy eyes. "Leave 'im to the crocs."

"We have to be able to tell the others he's dead," Brent said. "We have to be sure. It's the only way."

Voorhees treaded water, and the blood-red cloud grew at the surface. "Help me. Please," he begged. "I'll give you anything. I'll make you rich."

Kat picked up his gun. Brent knew only one outcome would satisfy her. Only one outcome would bring her peace. Both hands on the pistol's grip, she aimed.

He reached his arms around her, steadied the gun in her shaking hands, and placed his finger over hers on the trigger. He squeezed.

Voorhees head jerked back as the bullet penetrated his skull, splattering flesh and brain matter. He floated back in the water. His sightless eyes stared into the brilliant sun.

Birds fluttered from the trees. Howlers and capuchins shrieked. Two yellow-eyed caiman slithered into the river from the opposite bank.

The Dutchman was dead.

Chapter Twenty-four

Voorhees body jerked violently and went under. The yellow-eyed caiman feasted.

A helicopter's *whup-whup* sounded overhead. Brent and Kat shaded their eyes and stared at the insignia on the big whirlybird.

Kat waved. "It's the police!"

Brent swallowed hard at the sight of blood trickling down her arm. "Sit," he ordered.

She sat cross-legged on the deck and frowned, still looking up.

He dashed below to the galley kitchen and retrieved a first aid kit, returned, and sat on the floor in front of her. "You might need stitches," he said as he set aside supplies.

She snorted. "Flesh wound. You've seen too many movies, Flyover."

Brent swabbed the cut with antiseptic. Kat hissed at the stinging, and he blew on her arm. Their gazes locked, and unless he'd been in the wilderness too long, away from civilization and... women, the look she gave him had invitation written all over it. They needed to end this cataclysmic adventure and find a bed.

Zeller's pilot landed in a clearing twenty yards downriver. The Chief climbed out and ran toward the boat, two deputies trotting behind.

Brent assumed Mia Boudreau succeeded in getting her children to safety and crossed them off his mental inventory of persons to get out of this damn forest. He stood.

The police chief ascended the gangway.

Brent grasped his arm and pulled him onboard. "Man, are we glad to see you."

Zeller said nothing, but moved quickly across the deck and crouched in front of Kat. A smile lit her face. He unfastened the tape, lifted the edge of gauze, and peered under.

He shook his head. "You take too many chances, Katrien."

She nodded. "Yes, sir."

Katrien? Brent moved behind the Chief and watched him gently redress Kat's wound. "Voorhees is dead," he told Zeller. "I shot him. And then there's Dirk over there."

Zeller stood. He stared at Brent an extended moment before speaking. "I saw the shootings from above. Both were clearly self-defense. But we need to retrieve the bodies for identification purposes." He turned to the deputy nearest him and said, "Shut off the motor and secure the scene." Addressing the second deputy, he pointed to a fishing net on a pole ten or twelve feet long. "Use that rod to get Voorhees close enough to the boat, then pull him onboard. Stow both bodies in the cabin."

The second deputy's complexion blanched as white as the 23-foot cruiser's paint job. He grabbed the pole and sulked to the stern.

Brent peered around Zeller. He saw part of Voorhees' body had surfaced. Apparently, what was left of him didn't appeal to the crocs.

Zeller started toward the stern, but Brent caught his arm. "Make that four bodies, Chief. There are two more thugs in the forest. If one of your men will follow me back to the Jeep, I'll show him where they are. Then I need to get out of here. We found Charlie Cooper and the missing boy. Cooper's hurt. Angie and Nick stayed with him."

Kat got to her feet. "I'm coming, too."

Brent and Zeller turned in unison. "No."

"You stay here," the Chief added. "We will bring them back, and then transport Mr. Cooper and the boy in the heli—"

"My sister and brother, too."

Zeller turned to Brent. "Of course." The Chief went to the stern, spoke briefly with his men, then followed Brent toward the gangway.

Kat intercepted them. "Hold on a minute," she said. "Neither of you is thinking straight. I know this forest better than anyone. I can get you to the others faster. This..." She raised her arm. "This is nothing. Papa Dan...*the Chief* can send his helicopter to the old mill to meet us. There's adequate space to land. They'll fly Cooper out from there."

Zeller listened from behind her. "She is right. I will meet you with the helicopter at the old mill, while my men drive Voorhees' boat downriver so the bodies can be processed. You and Katrien can fly back in her plane. It is the best plan."

Hands fisted on her hips, Kat agreed with a quick jerk of her head.

Brent turned full circle. He stopped in front of her. "I want you out of here, damn it. Now."

"Then stop wasting time," she argued. "Get the Jeep. I'll make certain the helicopter pilot knows how to find the mill."

Brent trudged down the gangway, muttering obscenities as Zeller's deputy walked silently beside him. They passed the palm tree. Brent snatched up Kat's useless rifle and tossed it in the back of the Jeep. He scrubbed his hands over his face and shuddered. She could've been killed. He spoke to the deputy. "The bodies are over there, behind that cluster of trees. You're gonna need help moving them."

The deputy disappeared into the brush.

Brent got behind the wheel of the Jeep, slammed the door with exaggerated force, cranked the ignition, and drove through the break in the kapok trees. The Jeep lurched to a rocking halt next to the copter.

Reality hit him like a wet towel to the face: he'd fallen for the feisty pilot. Hard. An itch of need crawled down his spine and settled in his aching groin. What in the hell was he going to

272 <i>Sharon Cupp Pennington</i>

do about it? She loved this island. He loved his life back in the States. It kept him close to family and a job most regular Joe's would kill for; no boss breathing down his neck, no time-clock to punch, and pay that placed a worthwhile-dollar on hours spent in the merciless Texas heat.

Kat waved to Zeller on the boat, then climbed into the Jeep. "Let's go get your sister," she said.

"How long do you think it'll take us to reach them?"

"Three hours, maybe four. Definitely faster in the Jeep than when we left them on foot."

They traveled Billy's rutted path as far as they could, then Brent steered the Jeep into the forest where the floor remained relatively clear. Adrenaline replaced the fatigue that wore on him earlier. The prospect of getting everyone to safety loomed like a bright light at the end of a dark and treacherous tunnel.

Kat manned the compass, although Brent suspected she could find anything in this damn rainforest barefoot and blindfolded. Both of them remained on edge. He felt every bone-jarring rut in the trail and knew she did, too.

Neither spoke.

Finally, they reached the creek. Brent traveled along its bank honking the horn. He hoped the others would distinguish its sound from the chronic squawks, yowls, and screeches indigenous to the forest.

Tommy broke from the trees first, followed by Nick.

Brent stopped the Jeep and jumped out. He ran toward them, lifted the boy to one hip, and wrapped an arm around his brother. Then he handed Tommy to Kat. "How's Cooper?"

Relief poured out of Nick, his smooth surgeon's demeanor obviously shaken. "No better, but no worse. We need to get him out of here. By the way, Bernard is dead. He was working for Voorhees all along. Can you believe it? Where'd you get the Jeep?"

"Whoa, one question at a time." Brent thought back to the body tied to the manchioneel tree. He and Kat were careful not to let the others see it. "How did you know Bernard's dead?"

"The jerk came into camp last night intent on murdering us all. Well, accept Angie." Nick cast a glance to Kat and Tommy. "I'll fill you in later." He stopped. "Whose blood is on your shirt?"

Whose blood wasn't on his shirt? "Another long story," Brent said. How did he tell his brother, a doctor who saved lives and limbs on a daily basis, that in the course of a morning he'd witnessed one man die—and killed four others. "Zeller's got a helicopter coming for you. They'll meet us at the old mill."

"I need to check on Cooper," Nick said.

Kat and Tommy walked ahead of them on the narrow trail. The boy's hands in constant motion, he never stopped talking. Once they returned him to his family, he'd have one hell of an adventure to tell.

Angeline ran toward them. "Brent! Kat!"

The two women hugged.

Brent staggered when his sister threw herself in his arms. He stepped back and studied her face. Her lower lip was busted, and her cheek appeared bruised and swollen like it housed a bad tooth. Her face appeared as pale as he'd ever seen it.

They needed to get her home.

She needed to hug Jack.

Nick crouched next to Cooper and stared up at Brent. "How're we going to do this? That old Jeep'll only hold so many."

Brent squatted. He draped his arm across his brother's shoulders. "So it'll be a little crowded," he said. "Hell, Nick, we all stink like the damn river. Including you. It won't be so bad." Angeline's indignant look told him he'd better not press the stinky river point. "How soon can we load everyone?"

Chapter Twenty-five

Soon was but a heartbeat. Angeline hovered as Brent lifted Cooper over his shoulder and hauled him to the Jeep. Her face throbbed from Bernard's slap, and her back ached from when he'd shoved her to the ground.

They settled Cooper on the passenger's seat, then Nick helped Brent remove the Jeep's cover. Angeline and Kat sat in the rear, facing backwards. After Nick placed Tommy on Angeline's lap, he wedged himself in next to Kat.

When they reached the abandoned sugar mill, in the insufferable heat and over bumpy terrain, the helicopter waited.

Chief Zeller, shirtsleeves rolled to his elbows, paced the clearing's perimeter. He motioned Brent over, and Angeline studied their faces as they launched into a brief hand-gesturing conversation.

Brent sprinted back.

"Careful," she said, as they removed Cooper from the Jeep and placed him on a stretcher. Finally they would get him to a hospital for proper care.

Her brothers, Zeller, and Kat hoisted the stretcher and carried it to the helicopter. Angeline grabbed Tommy's hand and followed. She had turned many times since Bernard's demise and found the boy underfoot, which was more than okay. She missed Jack something awful.

"Were your men able to pull Voorhees' body from the river?" Brent asked Zeller.

Cooper's hand shot out and grabbed her brother's arm. His voice remained a raspy whisper. "Voorhees is dead? You sure?"

Angeline caught Brent's glance to Kat on the opposite corner of the stretcher. "I'm sure," he said.

She knew Cooper would have to see the Dutchman's body for himself, and as horrible as it sounded, she needed that same proof.

"The bodies are on their way to the hospital," Zeller added. "We should have official identification of Voorhees within a week, but the evidence retrieved from his boat points to that conclusion."

It wasn't enough. "What kind of evidence," she asked, as she fell in beside the Chief.

They reached the helicopter. Brent helped Zeller stabilize the stretcher. Angeline's spirit soared. Cooper remained the most alert she'd seen him since they pulled him from that dreadful pit.

"We retrieved a few items, Miss St. Cyr," Zeller said. "A briefcase and laptop, passports, some correspondence and papers pertaining to the boat's ownership. I can say with ninety-nine percent certainty the body on its way to our morgue is that of Willem Voorhees."

She'd demand the other one percent—for her own peace of mind. For Jack and Tommy, and all the other loved ones the Dutchman had stolen and murdered.

Brent hoisted her into the helicopter, and then Tommy. The boy clung to *Dr. Nick's* dusty black bag. It seemed the two had become jungle conspirators.

Tears threatened as she watched her brothers assess each other, neither speaking. They did this quick bumping-hug she'd witnessed a hundred times at sporting events, each patting the other's back. Then Nick climbed in and slid the door closed. Zeller ran around the front of the copter and climbed in, filling the copilot's seat.

The *whup-whup* of rotors sounded, and within seconds, they lifted high above the thick canopy of endless green. Cooper reached up; Angeline grasped his hand and silently vowed she'd never set foot in this God-forsaken swampland again.

Two hours later, the Cessna rolled to an easy stop in front of the open hangar doors at Jacqueme Dominique's small airport.

Brent's rented Ford Escape sat where he'd parked it on... He couldn't think what day it was. Exhaustion swam through his system, filtered by frustration. He squeezed his eyes shut. After the encounters with Voorhees men this morning, he wasn't sure he even recognized himself.

"You didn't have a choice, Flyover."

He opened his eyes.

Kat stared at him, those tiny flecks of gold in her eyes mesmerizing.

"The reasonable part of me knows that," he said. "But it doesn't make those men any less dead."

"Then listen to what that reasonable part is telling you." Kat released her seatbelt. She removed a small clipboard from the pocket beside her seat and scribbled a few notes on the papers attached. "You're a good man, Flyover. You did what any good man would do to save the people he holds dear. Remember when I said I do whatever it takes to stay alive and that by week's end, I hoped you'd be able to say the same? Well, you can, Saint Brent, and I'd trust you with my life. Any time, any day, any situation. I don't hold many in such regard."

Brent swallowed his surprise. Their flight from the rainforest had been stiff, an unsettling flip-flop of awkward silence followed by almost-frenzied conversation. "Are you okay?" he said.

"I will be," she assured him. "Right now, I'm so tired my brain's gone numb."

Emotional overload. He related, big time. "I almost forgot to tell you," he said. "Back there, when the helicopter waited for the others at the mill, Chief Zeller told me he found the body tied to the manchioneel tree. I told him we'd seen it, too. That I thought it was Bernard. But, according to Nick, Cooper shot Bernard last night. So Bernard's dead, too, and we have no idea who the poor bastard is Voorhees tortured. Zeller is sending the copter back for both bodies."

Kat sighed. "We experienced one murder on our island last year. Voorhees arrives, and we've more than quadrupled that count in a single day. It's sickening. Go ahead and get out," she added. "I'll pull the Cessna into the hangar."

Brent got out and walked what seemed a gazillion steps to the rented Escape. Stars twinkled in the black sky like a blanket of tranquility—yet he felt upheaval. A shift in his world.

Kat called to him. "Flyover?"

He turned, his hand on the open car door.

"There's a shower in the apartment upstairs. If you want to clean up, I'll throw your clothes in the washer. I might even be able to rustle us up something to eat."

He nodded. The idea of being alone didn't sit well with him either. "Okay if I park my rental inside the hangar?" He noted the tension roll off Kat's shoulders when he accepted her hospitality.

She moved a few feet inside the building. "I'll wait for you here."

Flying insects swarmed the runway lights. Grit crunched under the radial tires as he drove the Escape inside the hangar. He exited and shoved the keys in his pocket. "You sure about this?"

"As sure as I can be about anything right now."

He helped Kat secure the hangar doors, then followed her up the wooden stairs. Her loft-like apartment was neat and functional. Organized, but not overly so. The furnishings a mix of new and antique, its eclectic nature suited her.

She pointed left. "Bathroom's through the bedroom over there. Set your clothes outside the door. I'll see what I've got in the fridge."

If she was anything like his sister, Kat O'Leary knew the contents of her refrigerator down to the half-empty jar of Spanish manzanilla olives. She was offering him space.

Space equaled thinking time. Brent wasn't sure he wanted it.

He turned the shower on full throttle. While steam filtered into the room, he stripped and piled his clothes by the door. The simple act of separating his skin from the blood on his shirt was cathartic. He left the door ajar and climbed in the shower. Both hands braced against the tile, he threw his head back, letting the water pelt his face and run over his shoulders and back, washing away the remnants of death that seemed so enduring.

The glass door opened. Kat stood there, naked, her hair fastened with a rubber band in a loopy bun, her narrowed eyes questioning. His gaze slid over her, appreciating every curve and gentle nuance as desire ate greedily from inside him like a ravenous beast. He reached for Kat's hand and felt the beast awaken in her, clawing and scrambling over unmitigated pain and grief.

Brent held himself in check. He pulled her inside the stall and under the warm spray. He reached for the soap, lathered her body, and then his. She leaned against the wall, her sigh audible despite the water raining down.

Her back pressed against the tile, he lifted her. She wrapped her legs around his waist. He was already hard. Their gazes locked, and he plunged inside her. While one arm held her in place, Brent nudged Kat's head down with his other hand and smothered her cries with his mouth, as he drove deeper, his tongue seeking the solace she generously offered.

They came up for air.

"More," she whispered.

Brent pulled out of Kat and turned her around, straining to hold the beast's savagery at bay. He bent her over, hands on her shoulders, and drove in again. Harder and deeper, releasing the urgency.

At some point, they reluctantly separated. He tugged the band from her hair and tossed it aside. Raven strands clung to her skin, and a resurgence of need enveloped him. Brent reached for the bottle of shampoo, squeezed a glob in his palm, and worked the pink liquid through her hair. The lather smelled flowery, girlie.

He turned her toward the spray and said, "Rinse." Then he grabbled the bar of soap and gave his hair a quick wash.

Kat opened the shower door and fumbled for one of the towels she'd placed on a nearby stool. Brent reached around her, took the thick towel, and tossed it aside.

She angled a look over her shoulder. He turned and lifted her. Her long legs again went to his waist. His mouth nuzzled her breasts, plucked at her nipples. He carried her across the room and laid her on her bed, noting the gothic headboard of forged iron. Invincible, like her.

The mattress waffled as he straddled Kat, then he rolled so she ended on top. His hands shot to her waist. He lifted her. She eased him inside, grasped the iron headboard, and lowered herself achingly slowly. Brent tensed as she greedily took all of him. Again and again, until they were both drenched with sweat and sated.

With Brent still inside her, Kat collapsed on top of him, her damp hair like a veil of black concealing her emotions. There was something undeniably carnal about her lying on his chest, the two of them still connected. He rubbed his hands along her back and felt her smile against his skin, as desire burned through him on another scorching wave.

"Stay with me 'til morning?" she whispered.

Morning came with sunlight bursting through the mini-blinds on the hospital windows, but the dark clouds threatened afternoon showers. Angeline eased onto the bed next to Cooper.

"You're killing me," he whispered.

She kissed his cheek, then rested her head on his uninjured shoulder and placed her hand on his chest. "This is the appetizer. Wait until I get you home."

His fever broke during the night, but true comfort still came in the blips and bleeps of the machines monitoring Cooper's vitals. And the fact Nick remained within shouting distance.

"When will that be?" Even a raging fever hadn't stopped Cooper from letting anyone who'd listen know how much he hated hospitals.

She gave him the same answer the last time he asked, and the time before. "Nick's working on it."

An hour ago, under her brother's disapproving stare, she'd had an orderly wheel Cooper down to the morgue. "You've got to let go of your anger," she told him as they stared at Voorhees' sheet-draped corpse.

Cooper braced his hands on the wheelchair's arms and struggled to stand. The orderly rushed forward, but Angeline held up her hand and the young man stopped a yard from where they stood.

His face void of color, Cooper slumped back in the chair and squeezed his eyes shut. "It was supposed to be me that killed him, Slick." The IV swayed on its portable stand when he tapped a fist to his chest. "I earned the right."

A wooden chair scraped the tile floor as she dragged it over and sat next to him. She reached for his free hand. "Sometimes fate has a way of intervening." It seemed surreal sitting a foot from what remained of Voorhees' body, this monster who had caused harm to so many. He hardly looked evil now. "If you hadn't been with me the night Bernard came into camp, Cooper, he would've...you were meant to save me."

He thought about it for a second. "Yeah, I was. And don't you ever believe I haven't thanked God I was where I needed to be."

"We don't always get what we want the way that we want it," she added. "But, this time, we did get justice. I mean, look at him. Willem Voorhees won't hurt another soul. We have Brent and Kat O'Leary to thank for that. Make peace with it, Cooper. At least try. For yourself, and for Jack and me. So we can move forward as a family."

"Give me a minute, okay?"

"Take as long as you need." She took the orderly's elbow and steered him toward the exit. "We'll wait by the door."

Cooper leaned forward and yanked the sheet off Voorhees' body. The eerie fluorescent lighting bounced off his mutilated torso. The Dutchman's legs remained jagged stumps, one arm severed below his elbow.

Angeline smothered a gasp behind her hand, then turned quickly away.

The orderly's face paled.

"It's all right," she whispered. "However grotesque this is, he needs to see it."

The young man mumbled something unintelligible.

Cooper spent the next few minutes talking to Voorhees. Angeline couldn't hear what he said, and she wouldn't ask. She would never ask.

He'd work it out, and that was all that mattered.

When they had returned to his room, Nick reconnected the

monitors and logged in Cooper's vitals. He gave Angeline his customary thumbs up, and she read understanding in her brother's eyes.

Now Chief Zeller spoke with Nick in the hall, and she wondered about the topic that kept them there twenty minutes.

Nick entered, and the door closed behind him with a whisper-soft hiss. "Those beds aren't built for two, you know."

Angeline laughed. "Give us a break," she said. "We've earned it. Besides, you can't tell me *Dr. Nick* never slipped away with a pretty nurse to an empty hospital room when he interned in Chicago."

Cooper snorted. "Perks."

Nick checked the monitors. "Thought you guys would like to know Tommy's parents are on their way here."

Angeline slid off the bed.

Cooper caught her hand before she put a breath of distance between them. His eyes remained closed, but the strength of his grip sent a wave of thanksgiving through her.

"That's wonderful news." She asked the questions for him. "How, where...when did Zeller find them?"

Nick scanned Cooper's chart. She could tell by his raised brow and quirky half-smile, her brother was pleased with what he read. "The Beck's were on vacation, a six night cruise out of Fort Lauderdale, their ship anchored off the Jamaican coast. Officials uncovered no foul play when Tommy disappeared and assumed he accidentally fell overboard. They prayed his body would wash ashore on one of the islands. Like there was a chance in hell of that happening. Zeller got the bulletin day before yesterday and reported what little he knew of the kidnapped boy. With Jack's description and Tommy filling in the blanks, his parents got the best news they'll ever receive." Nick raised his hands. "I intend to be there for the reunion."

"I promised Tom a new shirt," Cooper whispered.

Angeline laughed.

Nick removed the stethoscope from around his neck and listened to Cooper's chest, in spite of the bleeping monitors. "Angie's got your back, pal. Thanks to inventory from her shop, Tommy looks brand new head to toe. He's outside with Zeller, still worried about you. Feel up to a visit?"

Cooper smiled. "You bet."

Perfect timing, thought Angeline. She helped him scoot to a sitting position.

Nick replaced Cooper's chart and crossed to the door. "There's one other bit of news," he said. "Zeller and his deputy found some poor sap tied to a tree near the old mill. He's pretty sure the guy is one of Voorhees' goons. Maybe he wanted the million-dollar bounty, and the Dutchman used him as an example of what happens to those who betray him. According to the passports found on the boat, all thugs were accounted for but one. Some fellow named Erik Geis. The body's bloated and grossly disfigured, but the Chief's still hoping for a positive ID."

Nick pulled open the door and poked his head out.

A second later, Tommy burst in, leaving Daniel Zeller lingering in the doorway.

Once the chattering boy was seated on Cooper's bed, the three of them left his room.

In the hall, Angeline turned to Nick. "When can I take him home?"

"By home, are we talking about your house on the island, or Cooper's place outside New Orleans?"

Angeline caught Zeller's arched brow. "You already know my answer." While Cooper slept, the three of them had held a lengthy discussion about her selling the island property. She expressed her wish to sign the sprawling beachfront house over to Mia Boudreau, no strings attached, and fully furnished—whenever Mia was ready. No way would those children go back to a house where their father had so brutally died.

Zeller arranged a realtor friend to handle the details.

If Mia agreed, Angeline also hoped to leave management of the souvenir shop, Pearls, in her hands.

"Okay," Nick said. "The beachfront house tomorrow afternoon, if Cooper's doing as well as today and his lungs remain clear. New Orleans in two or three days."

Brent woke with the sun blazing through Kat's window. He fumbled for the clock on her bedside table and squinted at the numbers in digital red. Noon.

The sheets on her side of the bed felt cool. He smelled bacon and onions, something spicy. Naked, he rose from the bed and found his clean clothes folded at the foot. He chuckled under his breath. After last night's shower, why bother?

Bare as the day he was born, he swaggered into Kat's kitchen, eager for another round of love-making, his lust evident in the fact his penis was hard as a steel rod. "Mmmm," he ground out. "Something smells as good as..."

Well, hell. He yanked Kat's note off the refrigerator.

She had scribbled a few lines about a morning meeting with an important client at the Hotel LeNoir—and then she thanked him for the sex. Thanked him!

Disappointment sliced Brent's good mood. No gratitude for being there, or offering a supportive shoulder, or even a "catch you later." Kat had thanked him for sex. And she used *the word*, like he was a stud she ordered over the telephone or some guy she'd picked up in a bar last night. A casual one-nighter.

Well, there was nothing casual about the sickening feeling that crawled through his gut when Dirk had held a knife to her throat on Voorhees' boat. And there wasn't one causal iota lodged in the way Brent felt now.

Kat ended her note by telling him there was an omelet in the microwave.

"Payment for services rendered?" He wadded her note and threw it across the room. "You got off light, O'Leary."

He opened the microwave door. Slammed it shut. What was the matter with him? He paced the room, stopped at the window, raised a slat on the mini-blind, and peered out at the bustling airport. All the while his insides churned. Where'd all this anger come from? He was as much about good sex as the next guy, and sex with Kat O'Leary sizzled. The idea of commitment usually sent him running. He should feel exalted.

He returned to the bedroom and yanked on his clothes. Barefooted, he jogged down the steps and trudged to his rented Ford.

It took him half an hour to reach the hospital, and another five minutes to find Cooper's room. Brent knocked and simultaneously opened the door. He drew back. Heat rose in his face as he stared at Kat perched on the edge of Cooper's bed, one leg folded beneath her, the picture of intimacy.

Her gaze locked on him, and her laughter died. "Cooper and I left a conversation unfinished," she explained. "I needed to square things. Now I should be going." Kat stood and straightened the snug skirt of her little black dress. Tan legs, silky-smooth in nylons, poured from the hem as she slipped her feet into black stilettos. She gave Cooper a quick hug, retrieved her envelope-sized black purse from a tray table littered with the remnants of a bland hospital lunch, crossed the compact space, and eased past Brent in the doorway. A whiff of subtle perfume lingered in her wake.

He raised a hand toward Cooper before the man could say anything. "Be right back." He charged out the room. In the outrageous heels, Kat had only made it a few yards down the hall when he grabbed her arm. "After last night, all I get from you is a damn note?"

"I had business to see about," she said.

"But I thought we'd—"

She jerked her arm from his grasp. "And what did you think? That we'd be a..." She air-hooked two fingers on each hand in that annoying gesture teenagers used these days for emphasis. "... *couple?*" Her brogue thickened. "Life doesn't come tied in a neat little ribbon like a bloody fairy tale, you know. We've known each other what, a week? We don't have a relationship, Flyover. We had sex. You needed it, I needed it, we did it. End of story." She started down the corridor, then turned back. "Don't get me wrong. I am fond of you. Obviously. But you have a life in the States, *a good life*, and I have to earn a living. This job offer pays too well to pass it up."

He counted the days inside his head. A week sounded astoundingly right. "Where are you going? What job?"

She backed toward the elevators. "I'm goin' home to pack. Like I told you in my note, I had an appointment this morning with John Emmanuel Argos. He offered me a job. I accepted."

Argos...Argos. Kat hadn't said who she was meeting, but the name rang a familiar bell. Brent's brain slid into cruise mode.

Manny Argos. He scratched the back of his neck. *Shipping, yeah. That was it.*

Argos ships sailed in and out of the Houston Ship Channel all the time. The Argos Calido, the Argos Stefania...

He'd tied up and sailed more than his share.

"You're going to Greece?"

"Argos needs a pilot, and—"

"For how long?" The handsome Greek magnate flashed old money on television and in news rags every other day, usually at some posh opening or charity event, always with voluptuous eye-candy draped over both arms.

"For as long as I want, Flyover. It's really not your business."

"So, you're blowing me off?" Brent St. Cyr had never begged a woman for anything. "You're not even giving us a chance to get to know each other better?"

Kat turned away from him. A bell dinged. The elevator doors hissed open on a stir of disinfected air. She stepped inside and jammed her fist against the button.

Brent braced one hand on the closing door. The other hand shot to the back of Kat's neck. He pulled her forward, his mouth smothering her protest. He shifted directions and drove his point home with a deeper kiss, giving his tongue free reign. "This isn't over between us," he whispered against her trembling lips. "No day, no way." He released her and stepped back into the corridor.

The elevator doors hissed shut.

Chapter Twenty-six

New Orleans, four months later...

Angeline shaded her eyes from the brilliant October sun peeking over Raison-Belle Amandine's high-hipped roof and belvedere. She watched from the yard below as Cooper swayed in a hammock tied between columns on the third floor gallery. His *good leg* hung over the edge, the toes of his bare foot dictating the hammock's lazy cadence.

Earlier, when she'd peered out the tall, narrow window from their bedroom, he read James Rollins' *Map of Bones* while listening to "Hoodoo Man Blues" by the legendary vocalist and harmonica player Junior Wells, circa 1965.

Funkified blues, Cooper called it.

Now the book lay facedown on his chest. At this rate, he'd never get past Chapter Two—and she'd hidden three more novels in a drawer upstairs.

Reading and music seemed the only ways to get him to stay still for any length of time.

An oversized Panama hat with a gaudy tropical band obscured

his face, a welcome home gift from Montgomery. "If you're going to play the roll of wealthy plantation owner," the detective had told him, "you may as well look it."

Angeline smiled. In the spring, his body well recuperated, Cooper's hiatus from teaching would end, and they'd settle into this mundane life. She couldn't wait.

The hammock stilled. He called out. "Got enough room in this oversized sling for one more, Slick."

Angeline laughed and looked around for Jack before answering. She spotted their boy a few yards away throwing a stick for the new puppy Cooper insisted they buy. A black lab, all paws and tongue.

"You say that now, Cooper. Then I climb all those stairs, and we end up in bed. *Again*."

The hammock's gentle sway resumed. "Doc says I need the rest."

"Nick's visit was a month ago."

He lifted the edge of the Panama hat and peered down at her. "Suffered a relapse. Must've been the...shower we took last night. You ought to be the cleanest woman in the parish."

Her brother's visits had gone from once every other week to once a month, a sign of Cooper's progressive healing.

"I've been working in the yard all morning," she said. "Someone's got to. I'm hot and sweaty and gross—"

"Stop, you're turning me on."

Cooper's laughter apparently gained Jack's attention, because he ran toward the house, the puppy yapping at his heels.

Angeline often caught him watching them. He'd only asked a few questions when they told him Cooper was his dad, and the two immediately slipped into a comfortable relationship. Father and son were more alike than Cooper would ever admit: stubborn, outspoken, inquisitive jokesters, and loyal to an admirable fault.

And this fixation the two of them had with numbers?

Scary.

She walked past beds of purple asters, blue Bachelor's Buttons, golden calendulas, and the silvery-leafed Dusty Miller, flourishing in autumn. The stately oaks arcing over the flagstone carriage drive were ablaze with red, orange, and gold.

Torches of autumn, she mused, lighting the way into winter. For once, she wouldn't mind the cold.

Deeding the beachfront house to Mia Boudreau was the right decision. Angeline heard from Daniel Zeller only yesterday that she and the children had finally settled in.

No one had heard from Kat O'Leary, including Brent. Not even so much as a solitary postcard from Greece. But the lack of communication didn't worry the Chief. Kat would surface when it suited her. She always did, he told Angeline.

Meanwhile, Brent had transformed into a brooding workaholic since insisting Mathieu Fournier give the million-dollar bounty for killing Voorhees to the pretty pilot. He told Angeline in confidence that if Kat controlled her own fortune, she wouldn't need one from Manny Vargos.

But, according to Zeller, Kat had placed fifty percent of her bounty in trust for the Boudreau family.

Angeline wondered if Brent knew. She suspected not.

A maverick breeze chased crackling leaves across the yard. She lifted a fat pumpkin and hauled it to the nearest tree, two windows down from where Cooper rested in his hammock. Everywhere she stepped was like walking in autumn snow. They'd given up raking two weeks ago, much to Jack's delight.

"I take your silence to mean you're considering my offer?"

Cooper again.

Angeline smiled. Did she include diehard optimist in her description of father and son? She placed the pumpkin at the base of the tree's mammoth trunk, where ten others waited in their hay-filled, makeshift pumpkin patch. Jack's idea. "I'm considering lunch. You hungry?"

"I'm always hungry."

Well, that much was true...in one way or another.

Meteorologists predicted a cold front for tonight's Halloween festivities. Cooper and Jack had already done the *real* Pumpkin Patch in Olde Towne Slidell, and "Boo at the Zoo" where they'd ridden the Mombassa Ghost Train. The Mortuary, a fourteen-thousand square foot haunted house on Canal Street, complete with costumed actors and animated effects extraordinaire, stood next on Cooper's ghoulish itinerary.

Regret tugged at Angeline. He wore himself out making up time he'd lost with Jack.

According to Cooper, no other city in the world celebrated All Hallows' Eve like New Orleans. They'd already attended numerous parades and parties. But tonight's was a private affair.

She stepped back to survey her amassed pumpkins. *Perfect.* "What time are you picking up Braeden and Montgomery at the airport?"

Cooper stood. The Rollins' novel landed in the swaying hammock, pages bent at an angle. Junior Wells' less bluesy "Good Morning Schoolgirl" drifted down from the open window of their bedroom and the turntable inside. Cooper had picked up the vintage record player at a yard sale three days ago, along with the stack of vinyl albums.

How could she help but love the man?

"Their flight arrives at six," he said. "But, what with security these days, I need to get there early. Think I'll take Jack along so he can watch the planes come and go."

"He'll love that." She turned at the lab's incessant barking, waved, and signaled Jack to come in. "Lunch in five, sweetie." He waved back and threw another stick. "Now, Jack."

Cooper said she needed to relax and give Jack breathing room. They were safe here. Voorhees was dead. They'd seen his body in the morgue, or what was left of it.

And Angeline would lighten up, someday, when suffocating dreams of dead children and bubbling pits no longer haunted her nights.

Jack followed her up the exterior stairs. Actual living space in the plantation house started on the second level. When she opened the front door, Jack ducked under her arm and raced down the wide central hall. His dingy sneakers slapped the hardwood floor, and the sound echoed to the high ceilings. He turned at the last minute and darted toward the grand staircase. The gangly black puppy put on his brakes, slid across the polished floor, and skidded into a door facing.

She called out. "Don't forget lunch, Jack, and don't forget to feed Fred."

"It's already forgotten." Cooper laughed behind her. "Besides, it's almost three. You lost track of time again, Slick. Jack and I ate sandwiches two hours ago. Fred devoured another shoe. Looks like one of yours this time."

Angeline leaned into him as Cooper's arms snaked around her waist. His hands eased beneath her damp t-shirt. He splayed his fingers across her rib cage, and his thumb grazed her nipple, sending an achy draw to her belly.

"Later, cowboy," she whispered. "You need to change and head to the airport. You know what Saturday evening traffic is like in the city. And I've got a scrumptious dinner planned. Lots of Halloween goodies for the kids." She turned and caught their reflection in a gilt-framed mirror. Cooper looked good, a touch thin maybe, a little pale. She loved the longer hair.

He nuzzled her neck, nipped an ear lobe—sniffed noisily. "You're not so gross."

She laughed and untangled herself from his arms. "Have I told you how much I love it here?" she whispered. *How much I love you?*

He pulled her back. His mouth feasted on the other side her neck. "At least a thousand times." He released her and gave her derriere a little pat. "I'll be down in a few minutes. Is Jack okay with what he's wearing?"

"He should change his shirt and put on his new sneakers. Oh, and those shorts have mud on them. Looks like he sat in it. He should also brush his teeth...and his hair. See if you can tame that cowlick."

Cooper chuckled on his way up the stairs. "Is that all?"

Angeline turned from the mirror, then glanced back over her shoulder. Nick initiated talk of the facial scar during his last visit and recommended several plastic surgeons.

Cooper said once that her scars were as much a part of their future as Jack. But she promised Nick she'd think about having the procedure done. She studied her watch as another ten seconds ticked off and smiled. Okay. Now she could tell her brother, in all honesty, she gave her scar the thought it deserved.

Fifteen minutes later, Cooper and Jack clambered down the stairs.

She sighed. "Look at the two of you," she said. "My handsome

292 *Sharon Cupp Pennington*

men."

Jack wore denim shorts and a red shirt with some sort of plane on it, a white t-shirt underneath. Cooper's New Orleans Zephyrs cap rested on his head, an ingenious fix for the unruly cowlick.

Cooper kissed her cheek. "The house looks great, Slick. Real festive," he said. "We'll be back about seven."

Angeline closed the door behind them and locked it. The house did look festive with its orange and black streamers, and dangling skeletons and bats.

Cool for ghouls, Jack would say.

But Halloween decorations weren't the only changes to Raison-Belle Amandine. Cooper had given her free reign with the house's formal interior. Gone were the cumbersome velvet drapes that reminded her of the island press conference. Milk-glass figurines and knick-knacks found restful homes in boxes in the attic. Faded Aubusson rungs were rolled and stored. English water color prints and portraits of deceased relatives leaned against attic walls, including the first portrait she'd ever seen of his grandfather, Etienne Raison. She'd given Belle an eclectic facelift, and balanced old with new. Shutters were thrown open on the second and third levels, and sunlight flooded spaces once cloistered with bad memories of Cooper's childhood. No wonder the man was claustrophobic.

These days were all about new beginnings and rekindling old friendships. Montgomery visited often because he was a native, his mother lived in New Orleans, and there was still her February wedding to Bull Scully in the offing.

Angeline's stomach did a mini-somersault. This would be Braeden's first visit to New Orleans since the accident. The mood needed to be right, upbeat and comfortable.

It wasn't that Braeden didn't want to come. Platypus Pearl's latest adventure hit the bestsellers list its first week out and set off a whirlwind tour of interviews, book-signings, and television appearances. Next to Maggie and little Tulip, Jack was Pearl's biggest fan.

Angeline added a little more prep to dinner, then headed upstairs, stripping off her t-shirt as she went. She dropped the shirt in the wicker hamper inside the bathroom, and turned the shower on full blast. By the time she sat on the bed, tugged off her tennis shoes and socks, and scooted out of her khaki Capri pants, steam bellowed through the bathroom door.

The hot shower invigorated her, but Angeline knew better than to linger. Cooper was right in that time easily escaped her these days. Six months ago, she never imagined such bliss.

Wrapped in a thick towel, she retrieved two shirts from the closet and laid them on the bed. Cooper liked the long-sleeve tunic in deep claret with the shirred neck and cuffs; she preferred the pale green "big shirt" with the three-quarter length sleeves, button cuffs, and overstitched pin-tuck detail down the back. Both shirts complimented jeans.

She shimmied into her jeans and slid the tunic over her head. Her short-cropped hair had almost dried, but she passed a blow dryer over it anyway. She fished tiny gold hoop earrings from the jewelry box atop the antique tallboy, then stepped out onto the gallery.

For once, the local weatherman had nailed it. Long sleeves were perfect for the chill in the air.

Croaky toads and acoustically talented cicadas celebrated the onset of night. Angeline fastened the earrings. Soon the single light in the belvedere Cooper had set to a timer would cast an ominous glow over the landscape. She recalled the one-eyed Cyclops analogy from her first visit here. Perfect for Halloween.

Her head jerked at the sound of footsteps on the hardwood floor. Too early for Cooper to have returned with their guests.

She picked up the small gardening trowel next to a large pot of crystal-white zinnias, moved toward their bedroom, and stopped cold as the intruder stepped from the shadows. "What are you doing here? How did you get in?"

His slicked-back sandalwood hair and chunky black-framed glasses didn't fit the familiarity of the man's voice. "I've been watching you, doll."

"I know you," Angeline said dully.

"You should." He laughed and stepped through the open French doors into the gallery's waning sunlight. "I was around for two of the most important headlines in your life. Death and resurrection."

She studied his obsidian eyes, so dark there appeared almost no iris. "Walter Wallace?"

He grinned his Cheshire cat facsimile. "One and the same, doll."

"You look different."

"This is the way I looked before your accident. I changed my appearance for a while. Now I'm back."

Angeline backed against the iron balustrade as the reporter advance on her.

He produced a Canon EOS, seemingly from nowhere, and snapped a photo.

She flinched, raising her hands in front of her face as he snapped another. She swung at him, her knuckles stinging when she clipped his camera. The trowel clattered across the gallery's wide-planked floor. "Get away from me."

"We got unfinished business."

Anger and indignation bubbled to the surface. "You little worm, how dare you come into my home. I'm calling the police."

"Go ahead," Wallace challenged.

Her cell phone was charging downstairs in Cooper's study, and no way could she get past him to make it to the phone beside the bed.

Wallace clicked his tongue. "Oh, great emotion. Anger, I like it. Hold that pose." A series of flashes set off again.

Angeline blinked the starbursts from in front of her eyes as a kaleidoscope of images flooded her brain: shopping in the French Quarter with Braeden, laughing as they feasted on pralines, stepping into the street at the corner of Renaud and Saint Severin, and then looking up to catch the sun's glint off the gun pointed in their direction.

In her mind's eyes, her gaze darted to the shooter's face. Walter Wallace's face.

She swallowed, her throat dust dry. "Those photos won't do you any good," she said, struggling for composure. "There's no market for them. With all the celebrity antics going on, I'm already yesterday's news."

"Wrong." The reporter laughed like a jackal. "There's always demand for photos of dead celebrities, doll. Especially if one takes a dive off a third floor balcony. And I'll be right here to capture the moment like before."

"Before?"

Wallace snapped shot after shot; the jet-bursts of light dizzied Angeline. The wind kicked up. It whipped her hair and battered the tunic.

"I only meant for the bullet to graze you," Wallace said. "Then I'd happen to be there, and get the exclusive." He laughed again.

She backed away. "You're the cause of all of our—"

"How'd I know you'd stop in front of a moving car? What was I supposed to do when opportunity presented itself, walk away? Grainy as it was, I pulled in six hundred grand for the photos of the Lincoln hitting you. But that was more than five years ago, and money don't last squat. I'm smarter now. I'll sit on these pictures for a while, then get triple what I made on the others."

"You're crazy. My husband will be back any minute now." The flashes continued, like a strobe on the darkened gallery as night set in. Angeline's hip connected with the iron railing and threw her balance off. Wallace's hand shot to the middle of her chest...

Cooper turned his Blazer onto Raison-Belle Amandine's long carriage drive. The light in the belvedere came on, and the car's headlights illuminated Angeline going over the third floor railing.

Braeden gasped; Montgomery swore. Cooper's heart hung in his throat.

Motion around them slowed as her freefall appeared almost choreographed. A light rain pebbled the windshield, and for a few torturous seconds, the rhythmic pluff-cuff of windshield wipers seemed the only sound.

"Oh, God." Braeden sat in the front seat between Montgomery and Cooper. The three children slept in the back.

Cooper floored the gas pedal. The Blazer lurched forward, its tires spitting rainwater and gravel.

"Who's the son of bitch with her?" Montgomery said.

Flashes repeated, like some weird kind of lightning speak, as the man leaned over the balcony and continued photographing Angeline. Thunder growled its discontentment when the man disappeared inside.

Cooper reached across Montgomery and Braeden to the glove box. The Blazer fish-tailed as he punched in the button, and the box fell open. He yelled at Montgomery, "Get the gun."

"Tarnation, Coop, what are you doin' with a frigging—"

"It isn't mine." He hadn't touched one since... "Just get the damn gun!"

The car skidded to a stop. Braeden snatched the Hardballer from the glove box and shoved the pistol in Montgomery's hand.

Cooper bolted from the car and ran toward Angeline, slipping and sliding on the wet flagstone.

Her assailant bounded down the exterior stairs and took off running.

Montgomery gave chase, shouting over his shoulder to Braeden, "Keep the kids in the car. Lock the doors."

Cooper knelt beside Angeline. His hands shook as he lifted her head. Ooze coated his palms. "Come on, baby. Open your eyes."

Her eyes shot open; her hand went to the back of her head. "Ouch, damn it."

Cooper yelled to Braeden, "Call 911."

"Wait." Angeline sat. She tried to stand, but she couldn't get enough traction in the thickening gunk. "That Walter Wallace is an idiot." She lifted one hand, and then the other. "A degenerate little worm." Rain washed chunks of stringy orange and dime-sized seeds to the pavement.

Cooper blinked. Pumpkin?

She batted his hands away. "I'm all right. I think." Hysterical laughter poured out of her.

"What?" Cooper said, dumbfounded. "What is it? You're scaring me, Slick."

Angeline snorted, then hiccupped. "Remember when you first brought me here, and I tripped on a flagstone rut and ended up in that puddle?"

He was at a loss what to do. She didn't appear hurt. There was no blood. "Yes?"

"This is worse, Cooper." She launched into another bout of uncontrollable laughter, and could hardly get her words out. "I just obliterated Jack's pumpkin patch."

Their heads jerked at the sound of Wallace's whiny voice. "Hey, let go of me. I didn't do nothing. I wanted a few photos, is all. No harm in that. She fell, I tried to grab her."

Cooper helped Angeline to her feet, both of them unsteady in the gooey glump.

"He's the creep who shot at Braeden and me in New Orleans." Angeline swiped her hands on her jeans. Bits of hay sprouted from her hair. Clumps of pasty yellowish-orange splattered against the flagstone as she charged the reporter. Rain increased, creating a stew of pumpkin innards and muddy water.

Wallace shrank from her grasp, straining against the relentless hold Montgomery had on his jacket.

The wail of sirens grew louder, then diminished to a blip-blip as two cruisers rolled to a stop. Three small faces joined Braeden's behind the Blazer's windshield.

"Let's get everyone inside." Montgomery shoved his cell phone back in his pocket. "We'll let the cops sort this one out."

Angeline pointed her finger at the drenched reporter. "He's not setting foot inside my house."

Cooper liked the way she said *my house*. Hell, he liked everything about her—sans the orange slime.

Montgomery relinquished Wallace to one of the uniformed officers, then walked over to speak with the other. He finished up, returned to Cooper's Blazer, and helped Braeden cart kids inside.

Handcuffed, the reporter dodged the thunderstorm's worst in the back seat of a cruiser.

Under the cover of Belle's eaves, Cooper listened while Angeline gave a brief statement and promised an appearance tomorrow morning at the stationhouse.

The police hauled Wallace downtown. Ironically, he'd be tomorrow's headline.

The next few hours passed in a flicker of Halloween fun and spooky mayhem, eats and treats. Eleven o'clock, with kids tucked in bed, Cooper sat in a rattan chair on Belle's second floor gallery.

Montgomery sat across from him, a cup of strong chicory coffee cooling on the table. His booted feet rested atop the intricate iron rail.

The rain had ceased, and croaking toads and cicadas enjoyed the refreshing aftermath. Fireflies flickered in the distance, adding a bit of magic to the night. The predicted front left enough chill in the air for comfort and a reminder the holidays were around the corner.

Hay and pumpkin still littered the flagstone below, but that was tomorrow's chore. Jack and the klutzy pup should love it.

The green shutters stood open, as they usually did these days, and through the narrow floor-to-ceiling window, Cooper watched the animated conversation between Angeline and Braeden.

Montgomery linked his fingers behind his head and sank deeper in the floral chair cushion. "Nice out here, huh?"

"Yeah," Cooper said. "If we can make it through another month without a catastrophic hurricane. What do you think they'll do with Walter Wallace?"

Montgomery angled a long, searching look across the table and reached for his coffee. "Hard to say. The cops took his camera in as evidence. Plenty of photos there to show intent."

Cooper leaned forward and rested his elbows on the table. "But there's no law against taking pictures."

"Guess it depends on what's in the photos," Montgomery said. "Wallace told Angeline he's been watchin' her for a while. In my book, that makes him a stalker. She claims he was in the house when she showered and changed, so now he's a peeper." He took a long draw of coffee. "All kinds of possibilities there. We also have a jimmied door on the ground floor that constitutes breaking and entering."

Cooper tamped the anger rising from his gut. He knew what he'd like to do to Wallace.

Yep. All kinds of possibilities there, too.

Montgomery seemed to study him over the rim of his cup. "I still have enough connections in New Orleans to keep him thick in trouble for a while, and I'll see he gets plenty of the kind of press he dishes out. If he gets off…and that's a mighty big if, Coop, I don't think he'll hang around. Guys like Wallace always have bigger fish to fry." He laughed then. "Let's face it, you guys are boring. The highlight of your day is choosin' what kind of soup to use in making dinner."

Cooper decided he'd take boring in a heartbeat. He turned his attention back to the window and the laughing women sitting in front of the fireplace, candles lit on the carved cedar mantle-piece.

Braeden had brought photograph albums. She and Angeline sat side by side on the contemporary sofa, flipping pages. Repair to their relationship had come a long way since June.

He settled deeper in his chair and lifted his sneakered feet to the iron balustrade, a yard or so down from Montgomery's. Yep, he thought, wounds heal in stages. Sometimes taking eons, sometimes only a few months…with the help of love, a bit of luck, and enduring friendships.

And, at long last, he'd found plenty enough of each to last him a lifetime.

Other books by Sharon Cupp Pennington

Hoodoo Money